Alex Barclay studied journalism at university, and worked for a period in fashion and beauty journalism as a copywriter in the RTÉ Guide. In 2003 she left the fashion industry to write *Darkhouse*, the first of two novels featuring NYPD detective Joe Lucchesi. She won the Ireland AM Crime Fiction Award at the Irish Book Awards for her novel *Blood Runs Cold*. Alex lives in County Cork, Ireland.

You can discovermore about the author at www.alexbarclay.co.uk

HARM'S REACH

When Special Agent Ren Bryce discovers the body of a young woman in an abandoned car, solving the case becomes personal. But the more she uncovers about the victim's last movements, the more questions are raised. Why was Laura Flynn driving towards a ranch for troubled teens in the middle of Colorado when her employers thought she was hundreds of miles away? And what did she know about a case from fifty years ago, which her death dramatically reopens? As Ren and cold case investigator Janine Hooks slowly weave the threads together, a picture emerges of a privileged family determined to hide some very dark secrets — whatever the cost.

ALEX BARCLAY

HARM'S REACH

Complete and Unabridged

CHARNWOOD
Leicester

First published in Great Britain in 2014 by
HarperCollins*Publishers*
London

First Charnwood Edition
published 2016
by arrangement with
HarperCollins*Publishers*
London

*A catalogue record for this book is available
from the British Library.*

ISBN 978–1–4448–3028–6

Published by
F. A. Thorpe (Publishing)
Anstey, Leicestershire

Set by Words & Graphics Ltd.
Anstey, Leicestershire
Printed and bound in Great Britain by
T. J. International Ltd., Padstow, Cornwall

This book is printed on acid-free paper

To Ger McDonnell
for finding lost plots, unravelling twists,
and being an unflawed heroine

Prologue

Ingrid Prince realized that the white walls in every Prince family home created a diorama effect. People watched from the outside, studying, deducing, then leaving, even after brief encounters, with lasting judgements. Ingrid Prince, the beautiful, radiant wife! Robert Prince, the handsome, wealthy husband, a man of fine stock!

Oh, what they see . . . and don't see.

Ingrid closed her eyes.

I am safe. I am safe. I am safe.

'Close those beautiful cat eyes, Ingrid, and say it three times. 'It' is wherever you want to take us. I am Tahiti. I am Tahiti. I am Tahiti. Then — bam! — eyes open — bam! — I shoot!'

She could hear Sandro Cera's voice in her head as he stalked around her all those years ago. Handsome, talented, orphan, immigrant Sandro Cera, the rags-to-riches-and-back fashion photographer; Ingrid Prince, at his feet, blonde, tanned, extended on the white floor of a freezing studio in Brooklyn, shivering by a faulty space heater.

Camera in hand, Sandro would rise up onto the balls of his feet, crouch down, close in, create distance, his body twisting and turning as if he was the one to be captured.

Ingrid did as he asked, closed her eyes, used his three-times trick.

'No lips moving!' Sandro said. *No leeps.* 'These are thoughts I'm talking about. Three times, sweets, three times: I am silent, I am silent, I am silent!'

'My teeth are chattering is why my lips are moving!' said brave, bold, new-girl Ingrid, just turned seventeen. 'I'm fucking hypothermic . . . times three.'

Click flash click flash click flash. And the photo that made them both famous was the one that was taken just afterwards, as Ingrid laughed, her head thrown back, then forward, the lens capturing a warm and beautiful smile with no Brooklyn ice, just St Tropez, St Tropez, St Tropez.

It was a different world. It was New York in the Nineties — when they partied below ground and cauterized their hearts' wounds with the fire of quick fucks. Sandro Cera had been dead years — a gradual, then sudden junkie demise. In the live art installation of Ingrid's life, Sandro Cera was the lightbulb in the corner, flickering ominously, bound to blow.

Yet his was the advice she was now hearing.

Three times.

I am safe. I am safe. I am safe.

Ingrid looked around the Colorado rental. Even the temporary homes she sought refuge in were white-walled, sparsely furnished, neutral. When their SoHo loft was shot for an interiors magazine, the stylist pared it back even more, took pieces away. Pieces: furniture, paintings, sculptures, reality. How suddenly the landscape can change when its elements are plucked away.

Ingrid heard a noise at the front door. Light on her feet, she walked out into the long polished hallway. Her suitcases were at the end by the door: a set of five, olive green, edged in brown leather with accents of gold.

Now, there was banging at the door, hammering. Ingrid froze. The door burst open. She felt a rush of adrenaline.

This is not how it ends. This is not how it ends. This is not how it ends.

She backed into the kitchen, then turned, set to run for the French doors, but she could make out two dark figures standing there. Ingrid was briefly blindsided by her reflection in the glass.

She knew what she looked like to others. She knew what her husband looked like.

A Swedish proverb came to mind: *Alla känner apan, men apan känner ingen.*

Everyone knows the monkey, but the monkey knows no one.

1

Five weeks earlier...
Denver, Colorado

Special Agent Ren Bryce was sitting in an aisle seat of a three-star hotel conference room, primed to run. She was dressed in blue jeans, a white tank and gold strappy heels. Her dark hair was in a shiny ponytail, her makeup was for going out. Since she'd sat down, she had been twisting the silver-and-gold cuff on her narrow wrist, opening it and closing it. It was shaped like a lightning bolt.

I wonder does it work? Will it make me fly? Or zap people.

She looked around.

Men, women, no children, gathered in a beige room on a sticky Sunday night. Everyone so, so miserable.

There was a lectern in front with an A4 printout stuck to it that read: 'Bipolar Support'.

Annnd so explains the misery.

Up ahead, a large lady moved awkwardly to the stage. She was wild-haired and makeup-free, except for the crazy shade of cherry on her lips. She looked as if she had dressed under pressure; grabbed a blouse and skirt from a peg in the hallway on her way out the door and slipped her feet into a pair of sandals she'd left in the garden.

'Partying . . . ' she began.

Oh, dear God, do not laugh at this poor woman whose only parties may have been Twilight-themed.

The speaker continued: 'Sorry,' she said. 'Before I start, I should say that tonight I am going to talk about mania.'

This will be good . . .

Ren checked her watch. She was here only because her boss had told her to come.

There's a first time for everything, Gary Dettling, and a last time. In this particular instance, they are one and the same.

Gary Dettling had been her boss in the Undercover Program and also her case agent on the deep cover investigation that nearly destroyed her. She had done a dazzling job, though. Her investigation was the exemplary one, the one still used in UC training. Ren's own boyfriend, Ben Rader, had studied her case. But the official story didn't include the part where, within months of finishing the investigation, the exemplary agent was diagnosed bipolar. Ren had yet to talk him through that bonus feature.

She looked around the room at the ordinariness of everyone.

What could any of you know about what it's like to be me?

The woman at the lectern continued: 'Imagine telling someone who has been at a spectacular week-long party that the next night, they have to be in bed by ten p.m. As they are dancing on a table, laughing, swigging from a vodka bottle, surrounded by friends, new and old, you tell them that, really, they should stop. This feeling,

5

this amazing feeling is not good.

'As you reach out to prise the bottle from their hand, they will see you as reaching inside their soul to switch off a light. And they will claw at your hand to stop you, and as they do, they will look into your eyes with one of two things: an anger so intense that it could take your breath away, or a hurt so deep that it could break your heart. Who are you to take away their high? You are supposed to love them, you are supposed to value their happiness above all else.

'And the following will happen: they will attack, and it will hurt. It will hurt.' She looked up at the crowd. 'Face the manic, face the consequences. Poop the party, prepare to be pooped on.'

I need to get out of here. This is wildly accurate.

Ren bent down to grab her purse from the floor. She caught sight of the little orange bottle of mood stabilizers inside.

Five months. Yay . . . great to have you on the show . . .

'And as your loved one attacks,' the speaker was saying, 'and as the pain rips through you, they will further your pain by turning to someone else instead. Who can they find to party with when you won't? Who can they spend all their money with? Maybe all *your* money. Who can they have all that sex with? Not you. You are pathetic. You are a nag. You want them to be miserable. You just want to control them. That's all you want. You don't really love them. You are now the enemy.'

6

There are people crying in here. I can hear people crying.

'Hey, nice tits,' said the guy three seats away from Ren.

What the? Ren turned to him. *And Happy Manic Descent to you!*

The guy shifted one seat closer.

Ren held up a finger to him. 'OK, you have to be shitting me.'

'I'm not!' he said, beaming. 'You are really beautiful.'

May the scales of mania fall from your eyes.

'This is not happening,' said Ren, her voice low. 'Go back to your seat. And . . . ' She pointed at the lectern.

This is for you, buddy.

He did as she asked.

'Dayum, though . . . ' she heard him say.

The woman on the other side of him slipped her hand under his, squeezed it, gently. His wedding band shone.

Another lost victim, searching for the husband who is right there, but gone on his travels, not a care in the world.

'Your loved one will retreat,' said the speaker, 'or run . . . or hide from you. Or at least will attempt to. They don't yet know that what they are running from is pain. Overwhelming pain: loss, rejection, grief, fear. They don't know yet, because they're having too much fun. Secret fun. They can't admit that while you're sick with worry, they're having a blast. They may see your tears, but they don't feel them. They're waiting for a text or a drink or a party or a pay check or

7

new friends who don't know who they are or who loves them or what really lies in their heart or what needs to be protected. Your loved one may endure your interventions, your attempts at reasoning with them, but really? They're in their own world. It takes different things to get through to different people; it won't always be obvious. And what worked once before may not work the next time.

'Until you find a way, they will dig their heels into the bright green grass of their dazzling universe of plenty. They will tune into whoever is emitting the same Day-Glo frequency. Imagine a fluorescent pink jagged line running through the city just above head height, visible only to the manic or the drunk, or the drugged, or all of the above. And they are each holding a magical hook and they can just reach up and ride around on that line all night long. And they will do that until, eventually . . . days, weeks, or months later, they will lose their grip.'

Ren closed her eyes. *And that, ladies and gentlemen, is the beautiful, damaging world I miss.*

She walked to the back of the room and quietly made her way out.

The name is Mania . . . Mrs Mania.

I-80, Nebraska

Laura Flynn changed radio stations until she heard what she needed: words that would find her in the dark; a song that would fill this little car with the right message, a song that would back up her journey. This wasn't her first life-changing decision. There had been others; some born of tragedy, others born of happiness or kindness or love. This was different — this was the consequence of an extraordinary misjudgment. She was halfway across Nebraska, halfway into a cross-country expedition and, if she stopped too long to consider it all, she should have been searching for a song with madness in the title.

Here I am, twenty-six years old, a girl from a small coastal village, yet it is in the Midwest I find myself at sea.

She changed station again. She heard an evangelist; deep, male tones of crazy. *This is what I'm talking about.*

'*Right here, right now,*' came the voice, '*in the terrible darkness of our world, sins — like rats — are crawling out of every gutter, creeping into our homes, burrowing under their foundations, the foundations of righteousness and virtue. A virus of sin is finding the weakest chambers of our sinful bodies, where it will fester, from whence it will spread. I'm talking about diseases of the mind, the soul, the heart, the loins.*'

Laura Flynn laughed out loud.

The presenter's voice cut through. '*Those were the words of Howard Coombes, who will be speaking at Monday night's service to honor the victims of the Aurora Theater shooting.*'

'Oh, Lord, have mercy, we are both headed in the same direction,' said Laura. *It might just be hell.* She laughed again.

I can laugh. At least, I can still laugh. Even at my 'seriously, is this really my life?' moment, the 'how did it all come to this?' Janey Mac!

'Janey Mac' was a polite alternative to Jesus Christ. It was years since her sister had told her about a guy called Janey Mac who used to drink in the dive bar where she had worked in Yonkers. Janey Mac got his nickname long before then. It was a three-story nickname. His last name was McMullen. Mac. He thought he was God. Jesus Christ. And he was a supplier of guns. Janie's Got a Gun. The result was: *Janey Mac.* When he fled to Chicago to get away from a warrant, he became Janey Mach 3. Laura liked that. And as a story, it always raised a laugh.

Laura's sister had once mixed with the wrong kind of people. But sometimes the wrong kind of people ended up being exactly the kind of people you needed.

The car filled with flashing lights; headlights from behind. They flashed again. It wasn't a police car. She drove on. The lights flashed again.

Maybe I have a broken taillight. Maybe the trunk is open.

This was her first time driving the car, maybe she was missing something. She checked the panel in front of her; no warning lights. She pulled in. Her heart was pounding. The car behind pulled in too. *Should I be nervous?* She could see someone, a man in black, pulling a mask up over his face, running toward her. *Oh my God.* Her heart rate shot up. Then he was in her side mirror. Right there.

10

No, no, no. She began to scramble for the door handle. Her fingers were numb. *Move. Move. Move.* But he was there, he was opening the door. It was open. He was holding a gun. Laura stared up at him, willing herself to speak, willing herself to tell him no, don't do this, why are you doing this. Nothing came out. *Speak! Scream! Shout!* She managed to turn her body toward him. His eyes, vaguely familiar, stark in the rectangular cut-out from his black mask, flickered.

Confusion? Fear? Does it matter?

Laura closed her eyes, squeezed them shut. The blast deafened her. There was a second one. She felt a searing pain in her ear. She could smell earth, the grass, the night. She felt a breeze. Through the ringing in her ears, she heard footsteps. When she opened her eyes, he was gone. Her ears still ringing, she could make out the sound of his car door open, then slam shut, the engine starting, the car skidding, turning, leaving her behind.

Her whole body started to convulse.

What was that? What the hell was that? How could he miss? He was right there. He must have more than two bullets.

Minutes passed. She sat with her hands clamped onto the steering wheel, her forehead pressed against it.

She thanked the same God she had once cursed for taking away her mother and her sister before their time. Her father was a different story, he had danced with death from the moment he brought a bottle of whiskey to his

11

lips. He was no match for even the slowest of the Devil's quick steps.

I am one of those people from those blighted families, my life's journey a series of join-the-dots tragedies.

She put her foot on the gas.

But I'm alive. Thank you, God. Thank you. This is not my time.

New York

Robert Prince's vast TriBeCa office was lit only by the antique desk lamp on his custom four-thousand-dollar desk. There was one framed photo on top — his wife, Ingrid. He sometimes Googled her, just for fun. He had been reading a gossip piece on them from two weekends previously, their 'rumored baby news!', and was now looking at a Tumblr page dedicated to her early modeling work, created by someone who was probably in junior high at the time. Robert wondered if it was easier for a man like that to idolize an image from the past; was the extra remove a small way of justifying why he couldn't have her? Not because a woman like that would always be untouchable to a man like him, but simply because she no longer existed in that form. This man had described her as *a woman of exceptional beauty*. Robert felt a small stab of envy that it was not he who had formulated this perfect description of his wife, that he had not presented it to her himself, maybe on a hand-written card on a tray at

12

breakfast time. He loved her like no other woman. Not that there had been many. He had never been a ladies' man. He respected them too much. He was Ingrid's man.

His cell phone rang and the face of exceptional beauty flashed on the screen. He picked up. 'Hey, sweetheart.'

'It's me!' said Ingrid at the same time.

Robert loved how she announced herself on the phone. Of course it was her. But she spoke every time as if it would be a surprise to him. Maybe it was something about her bouncy Nordic twang.

'I just got a PDF of our magazine spread,' she said. 'The *official* announcement. Oh my goodness, listen to this: 'The Baby Prince'! How pregnancy suits me. They call you my 'besotted husband'; I have 'tamed Robert Prince'!'

'I *am* your besotted husband,' said Robert. 'But can you tame a mouse?'

'Mouse!' said Ingrid. 'Tiger.'

Robert laughed. 'With you, I'm a mouse.'

'Well, journalists see you in a different way . . . ' she said.

'As they see you . . . ' said Robert.

There was a short silence.

'The photos are great,' said Ingrid.

'Good, good,' said Robert.

'I have to warn you, though, they've used that old shot of you with the Lotus — '

'Well, you can get them to remove it — I presume the purpose of the PDF was for pre-approval.' Robert had a collection of eleven historic racing cars. The Lotus Series 2 Super

Seven had been his favorite. And it had been totaled on New Year's Day, through no fault of his.

'I'll see what I can do,' said Ingrid. 'But I love it. It just captures you so well. You look so happy.'

'Well, now I feel a little sadder,' said Robert.

'It's only a car, everyone's alive,' she said.

'I know that,' said Robert. 'I know. Speaking of precious lives, is Laura back?'

'No,' said Ingrid, 'but I was expecting her about an hour ago.'

'You didn't go to the airport?' said Robert.

Ingrid laughed. 'No, Robert. You're very sweet, though. She was getting a cab. She insisted.'

'And you haven't heard from her?' said Robert. 'And she's late?'

'No, but I'm sure she's fine.'

'I tried her phone; it was diverted to voicemail.'

'She was probably in the air,' said Ingrid.

'I worry,' said Robert.

'I know. But there's no need.' Ingrid paused. 'I miss you.'

'No — you miss New York.'

'What?' said Ingrid. 'That's not true. What are you talking about? Are you OK?'

'I am,' said Robert. 'Of course I am. I love you, sweetheart. Sleep tight. I'm going to finish up here shortly. Text me when Laura gets in.'

'OK — sleep well,' said Ingrid. 'Talk tomorrow. Love you.'

Robert ended the call and stared out into the night. He looked down at the letter on his desk.

14

It was dated August 1st, 1919, written by his great-grandfather, the source of much of his wealth, copper-mining star, Patrick Prince.

Dear Fr Dan,
   I hope this finds you in good health. Thank you most sincerely for accepting Walter into your community for the coming months. Though now just sixteen years old, he is already showing signs of acuity and I have no doubt that, in business, his efforts will bear fruit. Please do not let that blind you. I want you to put him to work on the ranch, in the barns, and tending to those less fortunate. I want him to rise with the sun, and to brighten with it.
   Please help me, Dan, please help my son. As you know, I made my fortune mining the depths, drawing forth from the earth to provide for my family and to allow others to provide for theirs. However, my keen sense of what lies hidden has failed me in matters personal. From the shadows, my reasoning would be that the reach of good men is often hindered. In contrast, I fear that harm's reach has no bounds, and — far worse — invisible fingers.
   All the best,
   Pat

Family was important to Robert Prince. Life was important. He considered birth, death and after-life carefully. He slid open his drawer, took out his Bible and set it on top of the letter. He let his hands rest on the black leather cover, his fingertips on the debossed golden letters. All over the world, people were reading this same text and finding different messages.

Different messages.

Robert opened the Bible on a random page. He wanted to find the right words. Wasn't that all anyone wanted? To know . . . to *feel* . . . the right words.

2

Special Agent Ren Bryce leaned over the map that was spread out on a table in Wells Fargo in Conifer, Jefferson County. It was two thirty p.m., she was tired, her sleep had been haunted by the braless support-group lady with the insightful mind. She was haunted now by lunch smells — tuna sandwiches and broccoli soup. There was also a hint of gasoline in the air.

'I am on a losing streak,' said Ren. 'I've never felt less deserving of the title special . . . or agent. Today I have been an agent of zero. We could have our own true crime show — *The After-The-Fact Files*.'

'Harsh,' said Cliff. 'We're fifty miles from base camp . . . we're not *The Avengers*.'

Ren made a face. 'I like to think of us that way . . . '

'Well, I will always assemble wherever you are,' said Cliff.

For twenty-five years, Cliff had been with the JeffCo Sheriff's Office, but, along with Ren and eight others, now worked for the multi-agency Rocky Mountain Safe Streets Task Force in Denver. Cliff had a gift for making witnesses and suspects believe he was one of them: weary, disgruntled, disappointed with life, put-upon by authority figures. He once told her that sometimes he felt they revealed their secrets to him because they believed he would bury the

17

information out of solidarity. He managed to convince even the brightest felons that he operated under duress, and really, if he could just catch a break, he'd be running free, happy and lawless. Cliff James — warm, huggable, big-bear, chuckling, family-man Cliff, who cared about justice more than most — could have missed a vocation as a Hollywood star.

'We need to assemble where the bandits are,' said Ren. The bandits had first drawn Safe Streets upon themselves one month earlier. This was their fourth strike; always the same M.O.: they entered the bank wearing beanies pulled down to their eyebrows and snowboarding masks pulled up to their noses — the ones with graphic prints that gave them the lower jaws of sharks. Funny for snowboarding with your buddies, not so much for bank customers confronted with a blur of sharp teeth, wild eyes and gunfire. Safe Streets could have called them the Jawsome Bandits, but that was too complimentary. They were, instead, the Shark Bait Bandits.

The first robber would spray the ceiling with bullets from a semi-automatic, then jump onto a counter or a table. He roared and growled and, as customers dropped to the floor, the second guy moved to the counter. He would show the cashier a note requesting cash, as if the gunfire was too subtle a message. The note also offered a bullet to the head in exchange for a dye pack or a tracking device.

Cliff rested his elbow on Ren's shoulder.

'Look,' he said, pointing to a small little enclave of houses on the map, 'Iroquois Heights.'

Ren had Iroquois heritage; it gave an exotic twist to looks whose ethnic origins were a mystery to many.

She smiled. 'It's a sign! Hey — you are too big to lean on me,' she said, turning to look up at him.

'I was going easy,' said Cliff, standing up.

'Unlike . . . ' said Ren. She nodded toward the corner where Gary Dettling stood with his hands on his hips, staring over at them. He was the only man she knew who could put his hands on his hips and not look ridiculous.

'He is not a happy man today,' said Cliff.

'And when you say 'today', you mean 'for quite some time' . . . ' said Ren.

'He's coming our way,' said Cliff. 'Eyes on the map.'

Jefferson County stretched westward from the city of Denver up into the mountains bordering Gilpin County, Clear Creek and Park. It was seven hundred and seventy square miles of every crime and mentality that came from spanning big cities and boondocks.

The Conifer locals unlucky enough to have been present when their Wells Fargo was hit were feeling a little plagued. It was not long ago they had been hit by a wildfire that moved as if it had plans to rescale the town and bring it back to its roots. Over the years, Conifer had been expanding slowly, adding grocery stores, gas stations and charmed out-of-towners who settled in the foothills until the snow startled them out of their mountain fantasy and into Kendall Auto Sales looking for tire chains.

19

But the unpredictable snowfall was nothing compared to the onslaught of the wildfire. It roared and spat at them for two weeks, darkening their skies, driving them from their beds or keeping them lying awake in them, fearing for everything. And then, it was gone. The fire died before it took away a single home. The firefighters had not performed a miracle as some people saw it. The firefighters had carefully strategized, and won a war; only the charred landscape bore the scars.

Detective Denis Kohler from the Sheriff's Office walked over to Ren, Cliff and Gary. Kohler was tall and flat-bodied, with a lean to one side and a slight bow to his legs. His brown hair flopped across the right side of his forehead and he often ran his fingers through it, even though it was too short to get in his eyes.

'OK, our guys followed your bandits ten miles,' he said. 'Looked like they were headed for Bailey, but they lost them. The car was found on a service road, torched. They made off on foot.'

'That's new for them . . .' said Ren.

'Well, they had the full weight of the JeffCo Sheriff's Office bearing down on them this time,' said Kohler, smiling.

Ren laughed. She liked Kohler. 'Did they find anything in the car?' she said.

'It's destroyed,' said Kohler. 'Looks like they crashed first. We're waiting for it to be towed.'

'And it was taken from the parking lot at the spa outside the business center . . . ' said Gary.

'Yup, a lady customer came out — car was gone,' said Kohler.

Ren shook her head. 'I don't know why women feel the need to go to spas, said no woman ever.'

'What about cameras?' said Gary.

'We don't have a lot to go on with this route,' said Kohler. 'We've spoken with CDOT, we'll see what they've got.'

'Gary,' said Cliff, 'I have that appointment, so, if you're all OK here?'

'Sure,' said Gary, 'go ahead.'

Cliff hugged Ren.

'Bye, big guy,' she said. 'We shall avenge another day.'

'Take care, Cliff,' said Kohler.

Ren stared down at the map. 'Is this the service road?'

Kohler looked at where she was pointing. 'Yes.'

'Would you mind if Gary and I swung by?' said Ren. 'That's right by Pine Gulch Cemetery. They could have gone through there, come out the other side and grabbed a car from that garage.' She pointed again. 'If they did that, they could have driven right down Pine Valley Road. They may not have been heading for Bailey after all. Or at the very least, Pine Valley Road was a panic move . . .'

'Sure, go ahead,' said Kohler.

'Gary?' said Ren. *Earth to Gary.*

He nodded. 'Sure. Great.'

★ ★ ★

No car had been stolen from the garage by Pine Gulch Cemetery. Gary swung back around and they drove down Pine Valley Road, past where the Sheriff's Office detectives and crime scene investigators were waiting for a tow truck to take the charred shell of the getaway car back to the lab.

'That's the spa lady's . . . ' said Ren. 'She probably came out of there with her little disposable flip-flops . . . or flaming red upper lip . . . mascara under her eyes, desperate to get home before she met someone.'

Gary tuned Ren out a lot. But today, the radio wasn't even on. She stared out the window. The road was quiet, dusty, and bordered by pines, but if you looked through them, you could see where the wildfire had taken many of them away. They drove for fifteen minutes in silence; the type that only Gary could create — a very specific and dense one.

Breathe.

They rounded a bend onto Stoney Pass Road and drove a little further.

'Hey,' said Ren.

Gary had no reaction.

You are a very distracted man, lately. 'Slow down,' said Ren.

Up ahead, a white Hyundai Accent was parked at the side of the road. The passenger door was closed, the driver's door, half open.

'We could be in luck,' said Ren, sitting forward.

Gary slowed.

'Rental plates,' said Ren. 'Whoa, whoa, whoa . . . what the hell? That's a body . . . '

Gary cut the engine. They jumped out of the

SUV and drew their weapons. Slowly, they walked toward the car.

'It's a woman,' said Ren.

She had been shot in the head at close range; there was little left of her face. She had also been shot in the chest, her ruined torso half out of the car; one arm dangling down, the ends of her pale brown hair trailing in the dirt.

'She hasn't been here long,' said Ren. She checked her watch. It was 15.48.

'One to the head, one to the chest,' said Gary.

'Looks like whoever shot her was standing in the open passenger door. Look at the spatter.'

Gary nodded.

'The glove box is open,' said Ren, 'maybe she was trying to get something out of there . . . a weapon . . . a purse . . . Or maybe the shooter was.'

'They tried to wipe it down,' said Gary. 'Carjacking?' he said. 'Could be connected to the robbery. The bandits ditched their car, flagged her down, maybe . . . didn't take the car because they were disturbed? Or panicked?'

'Would a woman pull over if she was alone?'

'Unless she wasn't alone . . . '

'Hey,' said Ren, pointing to the ground. 'Cell phone.'

She put on gloves and picked it up. When she stood up, she looked into the car again. All at once, she could feel her heart lurch, her legs weaken, her stomach turn.

Oh, no. No. No. No.

She stared up at Gary. 'Jesus,' she said. 'She's pregnant.'

3

Janine Hooks, Jefferson County Cold Case detective, walked into her office for the last time. On her desk was a potted plant, wrapped in tissue, a burst of pink in the dimness of a Seventies-style office in shades of brown, with half-closed vertical blinds that, even if open, would reveal nothing more scenic than the parking lot of the JeffCo government complex.

Janine often sat in the visitor's chair at her small desk with her back to the door . . . and from behind, got mistaken for a man. Or worse still, a boy. 'Son, I'm looking for . . . '

But it didn't make her move. She didn't want to watch the passing parade, she didn't want to be watched. And now she would be; her boss had told her she had to move down the hallway to an open-plan, fluorescent-bright office with three other investigators. It felt like a step backwards and she was experiencing unpleasant cubicle memory. She wondered was he trying to force her into the world; a world to which she had been an adjunct since 2005, when she'd solved her first cold case in between her regular workload. When the sergeant who appointed her retired, he took her aside a few minutes before his speech.

'I'm going to tell you something,' he had said, 'and I don't want you to take it the wrong way. Years ago, I walked into that tidy little cubicle of

24

yours, and I see all these photos of dogs. I mean, we'd been working together a while at this stage, but it was just this particular day, I walked in and I really looked at everything you had around you, all the things that were dear to you. And there's this one photo of a dog with a bone. And the light in his eyes was a spectacular thing. He was fierce. He was gripping this bone, no one would take it away from him, and he was so goddamn happy. And I swear to God, I thought — that is Janine Hooks.'

Janine smiled at the memory. Later that night, he had mentioned her again — in front of the entire office, as part of his leaving speech. 'I came in one day and Janine had her arm stuck right in to the back of the refrigerator,' he said, 'and she was pulling something out . . . I don't know what the hell it was, but it was slimy, it was green, and it stank. And it was nothing to do with her. It wasn't her mess to clean up. But she did it. Sure, that innocent little face of hers was looking a little screwed up, but that was it: no bitching, no whining. That is why Janine Hooks gets to wear the cold case crown. And she wears it so well.'

'That and the fact there were no other suitors,' Janine had said.

'You had me at 'skeletal remains'.'

They all laughed, and over the laughter, he shouted for everyone's attention again . . .

'Seriously, everyone,' he said. 'I am going to miss you all, I am going to be back in here bugging the crap out of you, you all know that. No one should have favorites, but I'm retiring, I can say what the hell I like, and Janny Hooks, I will miss you most. If you asked me the main quality I think a cold case detective needs, I would say 'tenacity'. You have it, more than anyone I know. If I had to throw in a few more, I'd say passion, loyalty, thoroughness, persuasiveness. Janine Hooks will make use of every resource she can, she will find resources hiding in the back pockets of politicians or down the sides of sofas, or up people's fat lazy asses. She will find things. Janine Hooks will find things.' He raised his glass to her. 'Cold cases, warm heart.'

Like the magnanimous man he was, he had set her up to succeed. And she would never forget it. And she knew that, toward the end of his speech, he wasn't looking at her. He was looking at his successor, he was telling him 'Don't you cut this unit, don't you let Janine Hooks go'. Because in the three years she'd been stuck with his successor, she had to fight for everything she got. So the tenacity, the resource-finding, the doggedness, was seared into her and to not do what she was doing was unimaginable. And fortunately, her current sergeant — the third since her first boss left — was third time lucky. He got it. Maybe he didn't quite get her, but he got her job, and maybe that was all Janine Hooks needed him to get.

They got on well, she knew he liked her. But she suspected he worried about her. He had already made his decision about moving her to the main office when Special Agent Ren Bryce appeared one day. Janine could see what he was thinking: Janine Hooks has a friend! A hot, sociable friend who seems heterosexual! Or maybe not, these confusing days! Janine knew that with her short, side-parted dark hair and her small bones and her tucked-in shirts and tidy pants and no makeup that she sent out a message. But, didn't everyone?

Anyway, by then it was too late for the sergeant to change his mind about her move. She was capable of making friends, it appeared. In the general population, out in the investigators' bullpen, she could make even more.

Janine lingered in the office doorway. She gave one last glance around. She went to her desk, and pulled out the first of the cards that were spiked into the soil around the plant.

Be careful. This could be a plant. Love, Ren XX

There was a second card beside it.

Hope you're not feeling too uprooted. Love, Ren XX

There was a third.

Stay strong, man. Love, Ren XX

There was a fourth. Janine laughed. Seriously?

Is this a moving experience for you? Love, Ren XX

Janine laughed again. She could always rely on Ren. They were friends just a year, but she knew she was closer to Ren than she had ever been to anyone. She went to pick up the plant. It was only then she noticed the flashing light on her desk phone. She pushed the button.

The message had come in the day before while

27

she was out with the sergeant — he had treated her to pizza across the street at Woody's. She didn't know who felt more guilty — him for uprooting the homebird on a Sunday or her for ordering just a salad.

She pressed the phone to her ear. The line was crackling from a loose connection. At least she'd have a new phone now. Ren told her to find the positives.

'Hello . . . Detective Hooks?' The accent was Irish, with a hint of American. 'I found your name online and I wanted to talk to you about one of your cases. Could you please call me back? My name . . . ' She paused. 'My number is 555-134-2235.'

Janine scribbled the number on the back of one of Ren's cards.

In all forty-seven of her open cold cases, Janine knew of no specific Irish connection. She decided to let this young, nameless girl be the first call she made as soon as she laid her comfort plant on the desk of her new office. She wondered if the guys would laugh at her.

'Nice plant,' said Logan. Their desks faced each other. 'My mom's a florist,' he said. 'I had one of those in my college dorm. I looked after it well until lightweights started pouring drinks into it.'

'You should see this one on tequila . . . ' said Janine.

Logan laughed. She laughed back.

'Here,' he said, 'take one of these.' He reached across the desk and handed her a giant chocolate chip cookie wrapped in paper.

28

A cookie and horticultural bonding. 'Thank you,' she said.

She started to unwrap the cookie but instead of eating it, she picked up the phone and called the Irish girl's number. It rang for several seconds. She was about to hang up. Then someone answered.

'Hello,' said Janine. 'My name is Janine Hooks, I'm calling from Jefferson County Cold Case —'

'Janine?' came the voice.

Janine paused. 'Ren?'

4

'This can't be good,' said Janine.

'It's not good,' said Ren. 'Who were you calling?'

'I got a voicemail on my office phone yesterday — I just heard it now — a young woman, didn't leave her name, wanted to talk to me about one of my cases. She didn't say which one.'

'Did you make any appeals recently?' said Ren.

'No,' said Janine. 'I mean, the website is always there, anyone can read it any time, but . . . ' She shrugged.

'Gary's with me,' said Ren. 'I'm putting you on speaker.'

'Hey, Janine,' said Gary, 'we got patchy coverage here. Can you call this in? Your guys are not far, we drove past them at the junction with Pine Valley Road . . . we're on Stoney Pass Road now.'

'Sure,' said Janine. 'What's happened?'

'Well, your poor caller was pregnant,' said Ren, 'and now she's laying dead by the side of the road . . . GSW to the head and chest.'

'Oh my God,' said Janine. 'Where exactly?'

'About half a mile from the junction with Highline Road . . . I can see a sign for Evergreen Abbey to the left and The Darned Heart Ranch to the right.' She paused. 'Darned Heart?

30

Seriously? Craft and brimstone . . . '

'This is weird, guys,' said Janine. 'That's a ranch for troubled teens — '

'The tautologous troubled teen . . . ' said Ren.

'The Darned Heart already has some scar tissue,' said Janine. 'It used to be The Flying G Ranch, a Girl Scout camp. A Girl Scout aide was sexually assaulted and strangled there back in '63. August 18th. It's one of mine . . . '

'No way,' said Ren. 'That *is* weird. What happened?'

'Victim's name was Margaret 'Peggy' Beck,' said Janine. 'Sixteen years old. She was alone in her tent overnight, because the friend she was sharing with was in the infirmary. The next morning, little Peggy was found dead, zipped up in her sleeping bag. At first, the folks at the camp thought it was natural causes, so they didn't call the authorities right away. They just packed up her things to hand over to her parents. It was the last day of camp, the other girls were being collected by their families. Eight hours went by before the authorities were finally called. It turns out that not one of those Girl Scouts heard a thing during the night. Even though Peggy fought back, the poor thing — they found skin under her fingernails. Three hundred people were interviewed during the investigation and nothing. It breaks my heart, that one.'

'Did you process the skin?' said Ren.

'Yup. No match,' said Janine.

'When you say 'troubled teens',' said Ren, 'how troubled?'

'Zero to hero: addiction issues, attitude

31

problems, problems with the law, eating disorders. I checked out their website when they opened to see what we were letting ourselves in for. And it costs an absolute fortune to stay there. They pull in a lot of spoilt little rich kids.'

'Have you had any problems with them?' said Ren.

'Our guys have definitely brought a couple of runaways back,' said Janine.

'Runaways?' said Ren. 'Kids can run away from this place? Isn't security tighter than that?'

'I'm speculating here,' said Janine, 'and this is not official, but I think it's all part of the treatment. The ranch's policy is to trust the kids, because they know these kids' parents have given up trusting them. So, management believes that because they have faith in these kids, they won't disrespect them . . . '

Ren laughed.

'I know,' said Janine.

'Is it privately owned?' said Ren.

'Very privately,' said Janine. 'By Kenneth and Kristen Faule. He's ex-NFL . . . Broncos. They never had kids of their own, so this was their way of . . . you know 'giving back'.'

'Hate that expression,' they both said at the same time.

'They take in teens from all over,' said Janine. 'If their parents are flashing enough cash . . . '

'They're not going to give us access too easily,' said Ren.

'No,' said Janine. 'And I've met Kristen Faule. Do not be fooled by her Disney ways . . . she's one of those cornered mama-bear types.'

32

'Disney ways,' said Ren. 'Hmm. So, what was the nature of your meeting?'

'Well, she came to pick up one of the kids that Kohler had brought in,' said Janine. 'Of course, she was pissed, like it was our fault.'

'I'm rolling my eyes.'

'She totally rubbed me the wrong way,' said Janine. 'Since the ranch opened, it's like we've become unwitting participants in her treatment plan. She lets the kids roam free, we pick them up.'

'Seriously, how many times has this happened?' said Ren.

'Fewer than my annoyance indicates,' said Janine.

'And what about the abbey?' said Ren.

'It used to be a religious abbey,' said Janine, 'but now it's a 'community of women'. As far as I can tell, it's like a hippy commune, women's shelter and self-sufficiency thing rolled into one. Really, though, I don't see how they're any different than the nuns; a bunch of women living together, saying prayers, doing charity work. They have basically no possessions — any money they do get is handed over to the director and distributed to whatever charities they all decide on. Three years ago, when I first took on The Flying G case, I spoke to the director . . . '

'Slash head of the cult?' said Ren.

'Oh, they're definitely not a cult,' said Janine. 'They're missing the undercurrent of crazy . . . '

'How big is the property?' said Gary.

'About one hundred and fifty acres,' said Janine. 'You know something — if this girl is pregnant, this could have nothing to do with my case or The Darned Heart — she could have been headed to the abbey, if she was trying to get away from a bad situation.'

'True,' said Ren.

Gary had gloves on and was walking around the side of the Hyundai. He was opening the back door.

Grr. This is Janine's scene.

'I hope that's *your* car door I hear opening,' said Janine.

You're a brave woman.

'Please tell me you are wearing gloves,' said Janine.

You're a very brave woman. Gary will not dignify that with a response.

'We got her purse,' said Gary, standing up, swatting away the flies that had begun to gather. 'And passport ... Irish.' He opened it. He looked at the photo, then at the victim.

'Her name is Laura Flynn.'

5

Ren walked over to Gary. He handed her the passport. She looked down at the photo. Laura Flynn was a sweet-looking girl with light brown hair, kind blue eyes, a heart-shaped face. She was the type of girl a man would be happy to bring home to his mother.

I haven't spoken to my mother in weeks. I hope she isn't worrying about me. Does this girl have a mother somewhere worrying about her? Is some mother over in Ireland going to have to take the worst possible call to take as a parent?

Laura Flynn was just twenty-six years old.

The same age I was when I was diagnosed. She looked down at Laura Flynn's body.

Twenty-six years old. And I thought I got a death sentence.

Perspective, Ren. Perspective.

'The lining is torn,' said Gary, looking into the victim's purse. He swiped his hand through the tear, found nothing.

'That's weird for a very new-looking purse,' said Ren. 'Maybe she was stashing something in there.'

'Guys, how do you think an Irish girl like that could know anything about The Flying G case?' said Janine. She paused. 'To be open-minded, I will say 'any of my cases'.'

'And it's an Avis rental, Janine, by the way,'

35

said Gary. 'If you can work some magic.'

'OK,' said Janine.

'No SatNav,' said Gary.

They could hear Janine typing. 'Hold on, guys, news just in: someone reported a burning vehicle at The Darned Heart at twelve thirty today.'

'What?' said Ren. 'First a burning vehicle, half an hour later, a bank robbery, and two hours after that, a woman's body is found . . . '

'Sounds about right,' said Janine.

'Well isn't this a darned part of Jefferson County,' said Ren. She took Janine off speaker. 'Come our way.'

'Sure,' said Janine. 'I shouldn't be more than an hour. And thank you so much for my plant — it's beautiful. And your notes. You're nuts.'

Oh, you have no idea. Or maybe you do.

★   ★   ★

Ren and Gary walked toward his SUV. They looked up when they heard the sound of an engine coming from the same direction they had driven in.

'What, pray tell, is this?' said Ren.

A minibus appeared up ahead.

'We need to screen this off,' said Gary. He took a crime scene screen from the trunk of his SUV and went back to the victim's car. Ren approached the minibus, holding up her badge. The driver leaned out the window.

'Where are you coming from?' said Ren.

'Boulder,' said the driver, a warm-faced woman with a frosted nest of honey-colored hair.

'Just taking m'ladies back to Evergreen Abbey.' She smiled.

Ren looked in and saw twenty or so women. The ones who weren't sleeping were craning their necks toward her and out the front of the bus.

Ren leaned into the driver. 'We've got a crime scene up ahead . . . Is there another way you can reach the abbey?'

'There sure is,' said the driver.

'If you wouldn't mind,' said Ren. 'Thank you.' She nodded.

You are dying to ask me what's going on.

'Can I take your name and the name of the director of the abbey?' said Ren.

'Sure,' said the driver. 'She's Eleanor Jensen, and I'm Betty Locke, chaffeuse, locksmith, carpenter . . . ' She smiled.

'OK, Betty, thank you,' said Ren. 'We'll be in touch.'

Ren went back over to Gary.

'Ladies of the abbey,' said Ren. 'Someone better go talk to them before this gets legs.'

This is beyond screwed up. There is a pregnant woman behind that screen in front of me.

Wrong. Wrong. Wrong.

Why, on this beautiful, seventy-degree, clear-blue-sky Monday is a pregnant woman lying dead on the side of the road?

Where were you going? What were you hoping to do? Had you named your baby, had you picked out clothes, painted a nursery?

Stop.

Ren stared up at the sky, but the clouds were moving too quickly, morphing into strange shapes, drawing her eyes left and right, making her head spin. She lowered her head and let out a deep breath.

She looked into the car. There was an iPod on the floor, some candy wrappers. She looked into the back. There was a pair of women's shoes behind the passenger seat. Ren glanced down at the victim — she was wearing silver and blue sneakers, but she had nice black pants on, ones she could have dressed up with different shoes.

'She either had a passenger or was about to have one,' said Ren to Gary. 'A lady driver would keep her change of shoes in the passenger well, unless she didn't want them in the way of a passenger. Where was the purse?'

'Behind the passenger seat,' said Gary.

'Someone was about to join her very soon,' said Ren. 'Driving alone, she would have that beside her otherwise.'

Ren looked around the car, the trees, the road. She walked out into the middle of the road and did it all over again.

'So,' she said, 'the car was parked. If this woman had arranged to meet someone . . . she could have chosen this spot, where the trees are diseased . . . there's just one short stretch of reddish brown along this part.'

They turned as a Jeep came toward them.

'It's Dr T,' said Ren.

Barry Tolman was the Medical Examiner for Jefferson County. He was quiet and unassuming,

38

a dignified pacifist of a man who got to see the results of the violent happenings of Jefferson County and sixteen other counties. They met him by the victim's car.

'Hello, there, Ren, Gary.'

'Hi, Dr Tolman,' said Ren.

'You're going to have to start calling me Barry.'

'Sorry,' said Ren. 'I know. My parents drilled respect for doctors into me.'

'You can say 'elders',' said Tolman.

Ren laughed.

'This is what I'm talking about . . . ' said Tolman, looking down at the body.

'Yes,' said Ren. 'I read your interview in the *Post*.'

'I am a tired old man,' he said. 'No one is listening. 'People kill people, not guns', 'Take the guns out of the hands of the mentally ill'. It's always the crazy activists with the catchphrases. Like the mere act of repeating their mantras legitimizes them. Hell, a sane guy buying a gun is not necessarily going to be sane ten months later when he walks in on his wife sleeping with his best friend . . . or when he's up to his eyeballs in debt and his employer throws him out on the street . . . Do we hand this person a weapon that can kill sixty people? The voices inside are the loudest.'

'New World Order,' said Ren. 'I'm really looking forward to it.'

He smiled. 'What is the sorry tale here?'

More cars began to pull up: Sheriff's Office investigators, and Kohler.

Gary waited until they had all gathered before he filled them in.

Crime scene investigators arrived and began processing the scene.

'We'll leave you guys to this,' said Gary. 'Ren and I will pay a visit to the abbey . . . '

'Would eight a.m. tomorrow morning work for you?' said Tolman.

'An autopsy,' said Ren, 'always a bright start to the day.'

★ ★ ★

The temperature was rising and the sun beating down as they arrived at the abbey, deepening the rich brown of the clay roof tiles, making the white stucco walls glow. Evergreen Abbey was Spanish Colonial Revival; a protruding porch, curved gables and parapets, and a vast arcaded entrance under an arched window of similar size. The rest of the building was set back, spreading out on both sides, with perfect rows of arched windows. The building was simple, elegant, welcoming, but austere.

'Wow,' said Ren.

'Everyone should work in a building with a little history,' said Gary.

'I thank you for that every day,' said Ren. Though the main FBI building in Denver was a dazzling new office on 36th Avenue, the Safe Streets team, at Gary's insistence, worked out of a building that was only ten minutes, but a world away in The Livestock Exchange Building, built in 1886.

They walked up the abbey steps to the huge wooden door. Ren rang the intercom bell and they were buzzed in to a cool, dark foyer, tiled in an ornate pattern of rich blue, yellow and white. There was no office, just two battered leather sofas and a door with pin code access.

'I think we're in some kind of delousing chamber,' said Ren. 'They know where I've been.'

The internal door opened and a woman in her late fifties walked through. She looked more bohemian gallery owner than head of a retreat for women. She had short, springy black hair with a narrow, off-center band of gray curving through it.

'Eleanor Jensen,' she said, shaking Ren's hand first. 'You're very welcome.'

'SSA Gary Dettling,' said Gary. Gary's tone had fallen on the right side of confident, the side that didn't make him sound like an arrogant asshole, which he wasn't. Ren had seen how some people reacted to him if his tone was off.

With Eleanor Jensen, she saw a flash of something different across her face. Ren sometimes forgot how Gary fit so well with how women imagined an FBI agent to be: tall, fit, serious, in control. He was the handsome hero who made them feel safe. And made them want to sleep with him.

He had never made Ren feel she wanted to sleep with him. *Sleep with? No. Fuck hard all night? Yes.*

But he was her boss. And he was a loyal husband, with a teenage daughter. And he had no interest in her. And he gave nothing sexual away.

Which makes you sexier. Which annoys me when it occurs to me.

She and Gary had been alone together many late nights — in the office or in some strange bar in a strange town during a boring investigation ... and she sometimes felt that, after the tip-you-over final beers, they almost bounded off to their separate beds in relief.

Disaster averted ...

I. Am. In. An. Abbey. Jesus.

I haven't had sex in nine days. Nine!

Ben Rader, come back.

Give my roaming filth a destination.

6

Eleanor Jensen led them through a beautiful carved wooden door into a white marble hallway.

'We'll go up to the library,' she said.

'Well, that's an offer we can't refuse,' said Ren.

'It is rather beautiful,' said Eleanor. 'The first abbess here was a well-known author. She wrote many books on the Benedictine life. We pretty much live by those principles.'

You are babbling for comfort. You came to this remote place for a reason, to shelter from the cruel outside world, and now it has crept in after you.

Ren's cell phone rang, startling her, a violation in the quiet hallways. It was Janine.

'I'm sorry, I'll have to take this,' said Ren. She stopped.

'Ren? Apparently, there was a second call from The Darned Heart saying that they had the burning vehicle under control, that there was no need to involve the fire department or the Sheriff's Office. I just called them there to tell them, under the circumstances, that we would be sending investigators.'

'And whose vehicle was it?' said Ren.

'A car belonging to Burt Kendall — from Kendall's Auto Sales and Auto Parts. He also provides machine operators for his vehicles. They're digging foundations for building work at the ranch. They don't work Mondays. They had left some vehicles and machines there over the weekend.'

'OK,' said Ren. 'See you in a little while.'

Eleanor Jensen was guiding Gary through the door of the library, a spectacular room with a line of floor-to-ceiling arched windows overlooking the grounds. The remaining walls were lined with mahogany bookshelves.

'Wow,' said Ren, as she followed behind. 'This is beautiful.'

'Please take a seat,' said Eleanor. 'I believe you are the bearers of bad news.'

'Yes,' said Gary, waiting for the women to sit down before he did. 'I'm afraid we found the body of a young woman on Stoney Pass Road. We're trying to piece together what happened, and we'd like to ask you a few questions.'

'Oh my goodness,' said Eleanor. 'That's terrible . . . what happened? Can you say?'

'It was a shooting,' said Ren. 'We found her in her car.'

'I can't believe it,' said Eleanor. 'It's so safe here. I've never questioned that for a second.'

'We'd like to talk to everyone who was here today,' said Gary. 'How many people live here?'

'Thirty-four,' said Eleanor. 'At least I can make your workload a little lighter; the bus you met . . . there were twenty-two women on that who have been in Boulder for the past two days. We lend our support to different causes in different places, depending. Eight more women are in Denver at a seminar. So, including me, there were just four of us here.'

'If we could get a list of all the residents before

we go, that would be great,' said Gary. 'Just mark in the four who were here. Investigators from the JeffCo Sheriff's Office will be arriving to take care of interviews.'

'OK,' said Eleanor.

'Can you give us a sense of what you do here at the abbey?' said Ren. 'What kind of women come here, how does it work?'

'Well, a lot of women have come here from very different lives,' said Eleanor. 'They're looking for freedom of all kinds. Usually they've been controlled by something else — addiction, a violent partner, sex, money . . . They don't want to feel controlled by anything else, by what they may see as the restrictive nature of being, for example, in a religious order. It's psychological. So the abbey suits them, in that it's a spiritual community.'

Gary's cell phone rang. 'Excuse me,' he said. He stepped outside.

'I'm sorry,' said Eleanor. 'I'm talking too much, I'm babbling . . . please stop me. I know you're busy people . . . '

'You're being very helpful,' said Ren. 'Don't worry. I was wondering, could you tell me a little about The Darned Heart?'

'Well, they're a private organization — some of those kids are from important families. And they're vulnerable. The owners are very protective.'

Ren nodded. 'Your property adjoins the ranch — do you see much of the kids?'

'A little,' said Eleanor. 'They've got stables, so we often see the kids trekking. And we take care

45

of the ranch's laundry. Sometimes Kristen sends kids over here to work — she wants to show them a different life to what they're used to. These are often privileged kids, they have everything done for them, they have that sense of entitlement — you can't really blame them. It's all they know. They have no respect for anything. It's really sad that their parents have allowed that to happen. And in a few hours here, there's little we can do to change that. All I could wish for is that they see something that inspires them to change, but I'm probably being a little naïve. They probably laugh at us over there, I've heard them call us Dyke National Forest . . . you know, the ranch borders Pike National Forest . . . but some of them, some of them are nice, polite, respectful kids. Some of them talk more than others, tell us a little bit about their lives. Others come in, do their duty like it's the worst penalty they've ever been given.

'We told Kristen and Ken that if they want to send a child here, the condition is that they help prepare, serve and eat a meal with us. Whether they're here to wash one of the pick-ups, build a wall, clean out a barn, they need to get a feel for what it is like to be more than just a republic of one. They're alone a lot at home, they have parents who work, they communicate with people through technology. They're disassociated. And when they're together with their friends, it's not exactly a time for spiritual growth.'

Ren nodded.

Eleanor's gaze drifted. 'I'm sorry. I'm just

. . . shocked by all this.'

Ren nodded. 'I understand.' She stood up and walked over to the window.

'Do you think this was a random shooting?' said Eleanor.

'We don't know yet,' said Ren. At the edge of the property, she noticed a small timber cabin.

'What's that cabin over there?' said Ren.

'In there is the closest thing you'll find to a nun at Evergreen Abbey,' said Eleanor, joining her. 'We kind of inherited her. Delores Ward. She's in her seventies, she's been here forever. She might be moving into the abbey, though . . . there's an ongoing boundary dispute with the ranch. Technically, the land Delores' cabin is on belongs to the ranch. None of us knew until the Faules had a survey carried out when they decided to build the theater. When they realized, the land — it's about four acres — was incorporated into the building plans by the Faules' architect, without consulting us. They all just assumed that we'd go along with it, because it was the law. Obviously, it's not as simple as that. Delores has been there for over fifty years. She wants to live there until she dies.'

'Well, I guess it's her home,' said Ren.

'Of course,' said Eleanor, 'but it got water-damaged. One of the excavators struck a pipe. The cabin's damp now, it smells. Delores could have a beautiful room here overlooking the grounds, we'd do it just the way she wanted it, but she won't hear of it.'

'What's the current state of play?' said Ren.

'Well, it had reached a stalemate,' said

Eleanor. 'Realistically — who is going to sue a little old lady and an abbey devoted to charitable works without bringing down a load of bad publicity on top of them? The abbey's been here over a hundred years. The ranch, in this incarnation, only four. The Faules can't rock the boat around here. They need the local community.'

Ren nodded.

'They're being very understanding, actually,' said Eleanor.

As they try to flood, then burn a little old lady out of her home. What next?

'Really?' said Ren.

'They drained the land, repaired the pipe and agreed to halt construction works for six months to see if Delores would reconsider. They even offered to buy her a new cabin and install it wherever she wanted on the grounds of the abbey.'

'Well, that's very generous,' said Ren. 'I'm surprised she didn't take them up on that. Does it really matter *exactly* where the cabin is? Is it a matter of principle?'

'Principle, sentimentality, fear of change . . . I don't know. I tried to reassure her about helping her with the transition, but she was steadfast. She's a tough cookie for such a lady.'

'It can't be the warmest place in the winter,' said Ren.

'It isn't,' said Eleanor. 'I just have to keep reminding myself it's her home.'

'Were you here earlier today?' said Ren.

'In the library, no,' said Eleanor.

'Did you see smoke over at the ranch around lunch time?' said Ren.

Eleanor nodded. 'Yes — actually Kristen called us to let us know that a car had caught fire by the cabin, but that it wasn't at risk, that we weren't to be alarmed. And I knew Delores was in the chapel, anyway.'

'Can you please check with the other women if they saw anything?' said Ren.

'Yes, I can do that.'

'Eleanor, has a woman called Laura Flynn ever been in touch with you?' said Ren.

'I couldn't say off the top of my head, but I can check my emails and talk to the others, see if they heard from her. I don't handle the website — there may have been some contact that way.'

'Do you think we could get a hold of any inquiries people made about the abbey in the past six months?' said Ren.

'Absolutely,' said Eleanor. 'I can have that emailed through to you by tonight.'

Ren handed her a business card. 'Thank you. And could we also get a list of anyone who carries out work here at the abbey . . . landscapers, carpenters, etc.'

'Yes,' said Eleanor. 'But we're pretty self-sufficient, we take care of most of the work . . . '

'Good for you,' said Ren.

Gary came back into the room, but stood just inside the door.

'Ms Jensen, thank you for your time,' he said.

'That's my cue,' said Ren. 'Thank you again.'

* * *

Ren and Gary walked down the steps of the abbey. She talked him through the rest of her conversation with Eleanor.

'I'd like to find out if anyone saw the car before it went on fire, though. It's a little too coincidental . . .'

'Because of the robbery?' said Gary.

'Yes,' said Ren, 'but also I'm wondering about how close it was to Delores Ward's cabin.'

Gary nodded. 'That call I got? It was Eli Baer in New York.'

Eli Baer was Safe Streets' favorite contact in the New York office. He was a short, perfectly-groomed nerd who threw himself into all tasks with an intensity and efficiency that had clearly been with him from birth. It was easy to imagine him in kindergarten with a pristine shirt buttoned up to his neck, slim pants that were maybe an inch too short and shiny, shiny shoes.

'This is going to be a big one,' said Gary. 'The victim's employer reported her missing this morning. These are big shots. Let's just say we'll be 'assisting' JeffCo more. His name is Robert Prince — he's a multi-millionaire, married to an ex-model. Laura Flynn was their housekeeper. She was six months pregnant. They live in New York, but have been going back and forth to Golden since January.'

'OK,' said Ren. 'Why Golden?'

'You can ask Mrs Prince,' said Gary. 'She's there now — at their rental. I've mailed you the address. You and Janine can take care of the notification.'

'And what about the victim's actual family?' said Ren.

'We've got nothing on that yet,' said Gary. 'All I know is that Mr Prince was very concerned when he called this in, so whether this housekeeper is family or not, they seem to really care . . . According to the Princes, the victim was going to stay with a friend in Chicago, but we've no confirmation on that yet. No one could get hold of the friend.'

7

Janine Hooks had arrived at the scene by the time Ren and Gary got back from the abbey.

'Hey, girl,' said Janine. She gestured to the body. 'Well, this is terrible.'

'Ugh.'

'Anything from the abbey?' said Janine.

'Not yet,' said Ren. 'We're waiting on the director to get back to us on a few things. There's certainly a nice view of the area close to the vehicle fire. I'm wondering did anyone see anything . . . I'd like to be armed with something concrete before I talk to the owners.'

Janine nodded. 'Oh, yes.' She took out her notebook. 'OK . . . as I was driving here, Logan Teale — who I now sit opposite, nice guy — got more lowdown on our victim: Laura Flynn from Waterford, Ireland, been living in New York for the past five years — just got her citizenship this year. She flew from Denver to Chicago last Thursday on a return ticket, due back last night, but obviously didn't take the flight. She rented the Hyundai at nine thirty p.m. Thursday at O'Hare. She filled out the form saying the drop-off would be there too. So she was either lying on the form or she made a last-minute decision to come here.'

'So,' said Gary, 'she drives from Chicago to here, that's what — a fourteen-hour drive?'

'I guess so,' said Janine.

'When was the flight due in?' said Ren.

'Last night,' said Janine.

'So, when did she set out?' said Ren. 'Did she stop anywhere along the way? Did she stay somewhere overnight? She couldn't have slept in the car with that bump . . . '

'No,' said Janine.

'So — any idea which case she had information for you on?' said Ren.

'No,' said Janine. 'I have a few with New York links, but I just can't see how a young Irish woman in New York five years could know a thing about them. Or about a 1963 homicide in a Colorado Girl Scout camp. Like I said, hundreds of people were interviewed — who knows how far and wide they scattered? A lot of the people were young and could still be alive. Too many for now to narrow it down. But obviously, anyone can show up from anywhere at any time about any case . . . even still, though, why would she come all the way to Colorado?'

'Oh, we got more info on that,' said Ren. She filled her in on the Princes.

'Ah,' said Janine. 'So she wasn't staying too far away.'

'Maybe she had some old relative 'fess up on his deathbed,' said Ren. 'An old Irish drunken uncle comes clean.'

'Not to be racist . . . ' said Janine.

'Noo,' said Ren. 'So, was our victim a pregnant runaway heading for shelter in the abbey, or was she doing some poking around at The Darned Heart Ranch, or none of the above?'

'Did she get here yesterday, do some poking

around, come to a conclusion, then call me?' said Janine. 'If she was coming to me because of information she had on a case, and the wrong person knew about it . . . ' She shrugged. 'But what I don't understand is how long she's had this information . . . like, why would she decide only now to bring it to my attention . . . when she's six months pregnant?'

'I know,' said Ren, 'it doesn't make sense.'

'It had to have been something that was, if not *more* important, certainly *as* important as her baby. It's not like my cases are time-sensitive . . . '

'Unless she suspects someone who hasn't got long to live . . . '

'Or she thinks someone is about to destroy evidence . . . '

'It's all so strange,' said Ren.

'There could have been another reason why she was here.'

'Sex, love, money, drugs . . . '

'Well, we can safely say that sex has taken place,' said Janine.

'Unsafely . . . ' said Ren. 'So, is this a screwed-up love story? Was she running toward a man she loved? Was it the same man as the father of her baby?'

Kohler came up to them. 'The Sheriff's been in touch,' he said. 'The news is already filtering out. We need to notify the victim's employers ASAP.'

'Janine and Ren are going to take care of it, if that works for you,' said Gary.

'Sure,' said Kohler. 'We're going to take away

54

the burnt-out car from the ranch.'

Gary nodded.

'So, you're all done?' said Kohler.

'Yes,' said Janine.

'Nothing more to see here,' said Ren.

'Well, be on your way,' said Kohler. 'Do you know where you're going?'

'I do,' said Ren.

'See you back at the office,' said Gary.

Ren got into Janine's SUV. 'I have been chauffeured all day,' she said. 'I'm getting to know what it's like to have a revoked license.'

'It suits you,' said Janine.

'It doesn't,' said Ren. 'You have no idea how much stress I release while driving.'

As Janine drove, Ren kept checking her phone for coverage.

'Finally,' she said, as they hit Highway 285. 'Let me see what I can get on the Princes.' She did a Google search. 'OK — Robert Prince is fifty-five years old and has made rich lists at various times under the 'Inherited Wealth' category. He has also publicly dismissed this categorization, because he has also had many business ventures of his own in all kinds of areas . . . some more successful than others.'

'What kinds of business?' said Janine.

'You name it, really,' said Ren. 'On the personal and political front, Robert Prince is a devout Catholic, attended Harmon's, a small private Catholic school, is a serious pro-lifer, has made several cash donations to pro-life politicians. In 2005 and 2010, he was up for election as head of the highly influential Order of

55

Catholic Business Leaders of America, but failed in his bid both times. In 2006, Robert Prince, then forty-eight, married former model, Ingrid Frank, Swedish, then twenty-seven, and they moved to a sixteen-million-dollar apartment in SoHo.'

'His first marriage?' said Janine.

'Yes.'

'Any shenanigans?'

'Nothing that's gone public.'

'Yet . . . ' said Janine. 'Any other heirs to the Prince fortune?'

'No,' said Ren. She paused. 'Unless he's got some children of love tucked away somewhere . . . which, let's face it, they always do.' She paused. 'Could Laura Flynn have been pregnant with her master's baby?'

'And he reported her missing to deflect . . . ' said Janine.

'Wouldn't anyone assume that an autopsy would include DNA testing of the fetus?' said Ren.

'You're assuming that anyone thought that the body would ever be found,' said Janine.

'You are correct, I was,' said Ren, 'which is a rookie assumption. So whoever killed her was interrupted before they could remove the body and dump it? What are we leaning toward . . . ?'

'I don't like leaning,' said Janine. 'Obvious one first: failed carjacking, which we can't rule out, but is definitely at the bottom of the list, because of the call to me. Alternatives: random shooting. She's driving along for a pre-arranged meeting with Person A. She pulls into the side of the road. Person B, the shooter, comes up, fires, drives away. Or the victim's driving along for a pre-arranged meeting with the shooter . . . '

'Or,' said Ren, 'she's got no plans to meet anyone, the killer flags her down pretending he needs help, she stops, he pulls open the passenger door, she reaches for a gun in the glove box or he reaches for the glove box where maybe she has money . . . '

They went quiet.

'What if,' said Ren, 'our bandits are driving by and they just shoot, they just want to cause a distraction . . . they just kill the first person they see . . . '

'Or they killed her before the robbery,' said Janine. 'They had chosen their getaway route; having a body there would stop whoever may have been pursuing them.'

'What if someone else knew about a pre-arranged meeting and killed her?' said Ren. 'Someone she knew or someone the other person knew. Was the other person there? Were they shot? Did they witness something?'

'Our guys will be checking local hospitals . . . '

'There's also the possibility that our bandits are witnesses . . . ' said Ren. 'And they're not exactly going to be lining up to help.'

'Maybe she was one of them,' said Janine. 'Maybe she was to take the cash and go one way, they were to go the other, so if they were pulled over they'd have nothing . . . she's home and dry with the money.'

'Maybe,' said Ren, 'the word *maybe* is making my head spin.'

'What if,' said Janine, 'she was with someone who turned on her and killed her . . . someone she knew?'

' 'What if' is just another maybe,' said Ren.

'You should write country songs,' said Janine.

'I write them in my head all the time,' said Ren.

'Sorry . . . back to Robert Prince . . . inherited wealth . . . inherited from where?' said Janine.

'Robert Prince is heir to the Prince family millions . . . hundreds of millions. He is the son of Acora Prince and Desmond Lamb. His great-grandfather was Patrick 'Prince' O'Sullivan, son of Irish emigrants who settled in Butte, Montana, when they fled the potato famine. They had three sons, the most successful of which was Patrick. Patrick got involved in copper mining, met and married his wife in Butte, made lots of money, made even more when he sold the mine. The last name Prince is because . . . do we need to know this?'

'Yes,' said Janine. 'For curiosity's sake.'

'We both know that curiosity has a record . . . ' said Ren.

'That's appalling,' said Janine.

'OK,' said Ren, 'the Prince last name is because the O'Sullivan family looked after the grounds of a castle back in Ireland and the locals used to joke that the O'Sullivan father had ideas above his station and that he thought he was the prince himself. So Patrick, who by all accounts was a great joker, changed his name to Prince when he became a big shot. Patrick's son, Walter Prince, is Robert's grandfather.'

'Well, Acora Prince certainly liked the name, seeing as she didn't change it to her husband's and didn't allow her son to either,' said Janine. 'Unusual for those times.'

'Rich families are weird,' said Ren.

'So, there's an Irish connection,' said Janine. 'The Princes. The Flynns. Where in Ireland are they from?'

'The Princes? West Cork.'

'And Laura Flynn's from?'

'Waterford,' said Ren. She Googled a map of Ireland. 'Well, they weren't neighbors,' she said, 'they're over one hundred and fifty miles apart.'

8

Robert and Ingrid Prince's holiday rental was eight miles south of Golden and designed to make the most of the spectacular view out over the front range.

'It's like a hotel,' said Janine. She drove up to the gates.

'It's like a glass box,' said Ren.

Janine pressed the intercom button. A woman answered.

'Hello,' said Janine, 'I'm looking for Mrs Ingrid Prince?'

'Yes, speaking.'

'My name is Detective Janine Hooks, I'm from the Jefferson County Sheriff's Office, I'm here with SA Ren Bryce from the Rocky Mountain Safe Streets Task Force in Denver. We'd like to speak with you about Laura Flynn.'

'Laura?' said Ingrid. 'Why? What is it? What's happened?'

'Could we please come through?' said Janine.

'Yes, I'm sorry, of course,' said Ingrid.

The gates swung open. Janine drove in and parked beside a gold Range Rover.

'Do they own this place?' said Janine.

'No, but they could — that's the main thing,' said Ren.

'Yes,' said Janine. 'OK, now let's go hang with a Swedish former model, just in case we were feeling too good about ourselves.'

★ ★ ★

Everything about Ingrid Prince's face said model
— everything about her posture, her aura, the
movement of her long limbs. She even managed
to open the door with grace. She was wearing a
floor-length gray strapless jersey dress with an
oversized beige cotton cardigan. Her blonde hair
was tied up and she had on a gray cotton
headband. Her skin was flawless, unlined,
glowing.

'Come in, please,' she said. 'Take a seat.'

She gestured to an open-plan living area.
There was a magnificent curved stone fireplace
with a thick oak beam running the length of the
chimney breast and an alcove beside it stacked
with logs. On the floor in front lay a pristine rich
cream rug. Three brown leather sofas were
arranged in the center of the room around a
solid, blocky coffee table in the style of a vintage
suitcase.

After a moment's seating panic, Ren and
Janine sat side by side, and Ingrid Prince sat
perpendicular.

'Please,' said Ingrid. 'Just tell me.'

Janine leaned forward. 'I'm afraid we found
Laura Flynn's body this afternoon close to Pike
National Forest — '

'Body?' said Ingrid. 'Pike National Forest? I'm
sorry, I'm not following . . . '

Ren shifted forward in her seat. 'Mrs — '

'And where's Pike National Forest?' said
Ingrid.

'I'm sorry to tell you that we found Laura

61

about sixty miles south of here,' said Ren.

Relief flooded Ingrid Prince's face. 'No, that's not Laura. Laura's in Chicago. She just didn't make it back. She must have missed her flight. My husband was just concerned that — '

'Mrs Prince, I'm afraid we have been able to identify her body,' said Ren. 'She was the victim of a shooting. Her car was found — '

'No,' said Ingrid. 'She wasn't driving! She was flying, then she was getting a cab, then . . . a shooting? No. I don't understand . . . No.' She started crying hysterically. 'No,' she said. 'No, please. Please don't tell me this happened to Laura. Please. Her baby. Her baby. She was pregnant. The baby. Did . . . did they save the baby?'

'I'm sorry,' said Ren. 'I'm afraid that was not possible.'

Ingrid broke down. She clutched her stomach.

It was only then that Ren realized that Ingrid Prince had a tiny bump of her own.

9

Ingrid Prince followed Ren's gaze down to her belly. She looked up at her.

'I know . . . can you believe it?' she said. 'Laura finds out she's pregnant and, two months later, I do.'

'So, you're four months along?' said Ren.

Ingrid nodded. She welled up. 'This is not right. Poor Laura . . . the baby . . . and . . . I get to . . . ' She shook her head. 'I'm still here. My baby's here. It's too much.'

'I'm going to make a call to our victim advocate,' said Janine. 'She can come stay with you until . . . are you expecting your husband back tonight?'

Ingrid nodded. 'He'll come back now.'

'OK,' said Janine. 'We'll have someone wait with you, if you think that's something you'd like?'

'Thank you,' said Ingrid. 'Yes.'

Ren waited until Janine had made the call.

'Was this a robbery?' said Ingrid. 'Was anything taken from the car?'

'Her purse was there, her suitcase . . . ' said Ren. 'We don't know what else she may have had with her.'

'And she was just found, alone, in her car . . . ' said Ingrid.

'Yes,' said Ren.

'What a horrible way to . . . I just didn't think

this was going to be . . . the news I would hear. I was worried about her when she didn't return, but I was worried because she was pregnant, you know, that she might have taken ill. I thought maybe she had been admitted into hospital. Apart from that, I thought maybe she had met up with the father of her baby . . . I know the relationship didn't end well.'

'Do you know his name?' said Ren.

'I'm sorry, I don't,' said Ingrid. 'Laura mentioned an old boyfriend called Johnny once or twice, but she never gave the name of the baby's father. She said that she didn't want anything to do with him. She just said that he was bad news. And, sorry — he's Irish . . . that's the only other thing I know.'

'Did she say where he lived?' said Ren.

'No,' said Ingrid.

'But you thought she had met up with him in Chicago?' said Janine.

'No, no — I thought that maybe he could have known her friend, or followed Laura . . . or waited with the friend if he had heard Laura was going to visit. I've had all day to think these things . . . but nothing came close to the reality.'

'Does the father of the baby know that she's pregnant?' said Janine.

'I don't know,' said Ingrid.

'When did Laura tell you she was pregnant?' said Ren.

'About six weeks ago,' said Ingrid.

'And did she plan to continue to work for you?' said Janine.

'Absolutely,' said Ingrid. 'Obviously she would

be taking some time off, but . . . ' Her voice cracked and she began to cry again. 'I'm so sorry,' she said. 'I just can't believe this is happening. The baby, everything, it's just so sad. Laura's had a tough time, she was a strong person to come through that, and this is what happens? It's so wrong.'

'I know,' said Ren. 'So, Laura's baby was due in September . . . '

'Yes,' said Ingrid.

'And what was the plan in terms of work?' said Ren.

'Well — we summer in the Hamptons,' said Ingrid.

Summer is not a verb.

'We were happy to hire staff there,' said Ingrid, 'and Laura would be back to work when she was ready. This might not sound orthodox, but, as I said, we're like family.'

'And, speaking of family,' said Janine, 'do you have details of Laura's?'

'That's another tragic story,' said Ingrid. 'Her parents both passed away in Ireland within a few years of each other. Laura was still in college at the time. Laura's sister, Saoirse, had already moved to New York and Laura followed her over. Within months of Laura arriving, her sister died.'

'How?' said Ren.

'She was out . . . partying,' said Ingrid. 'It was Laura's twenty-first. Saoirse fell down some stairs at a bar. She'd been drinking. It was just a freak thing.'

'That's a lot for Laura to have gone through for such a young woman,' said Ren. 'What kind of support did she have?'

'Well, me,' said Ingrid. 'And some friends, but not many. She was a sweet, shy kind of girl.'

'And where did she hang out in New York?' said Ren.

'Different Irish bars,' said Ingrid. 'I don't know which ones. You might find out more on Facebook . . . I presume you'll be checking that? But she really hadn't gone out much in the past few months. She said she just didn't feel like it. We'd stay in and watch TV, watch movies — if Robert was working late or traveling or out at a function that I wasn't attending.'

'Can you think of anyone who might have wanted to harm Laura?'

'No . . . but do you not think this was random?' said Ingrid.

'We don't know yet,' said Ren.

'Mrs Prince,' said Janine, 'Laura had a return ticket from Denver to Chicago, but she chose to drive a rental car back.'

'What?' said Ingrid. 'I have no idea why she would do that. That's a long drive . . . especially if you're pregnant.'

'Did you speak with her over the weekend?' said Janine.

'She just called me on Thursday night from Chicago to say that she had arrived safely,' said Ingrid. 'And she said she'd see me Sunday. Last night . . . '

'Were you to pick her up at the airport?' said Ren.

'No,' said Ingrid. 'She was going to get a cab home.'

'What time was she due back?' said Ren.

'I was expecting her around ten,' said Ingrid. 'But I had gone to bed. I was exhausted. I didn't notice she hadn't returned until this morning.'

'And where was your husband?' said Ren.

'Robert's been in New York for the past five days,' said Ingrid. 'He travels back and forth. I spoke with him last night, he asked about Laura. I said . . . she was late, but I was sure she was fine . . . ' Her eyes filled with tears. 'I'm sorry.'

'No need to apologize,' said Janine. 'Mrs Prince, can you tell us how long you've been staying in Golden?'

'Since November,' said Ingrid. 'We were kind of using it as a base for ski season. Loveland is the closest resort to Denver, Golden's halfway between the two . . . '

'And now it's May,' said Ren. 'You decided to stay on . . . '

Ingrid nodded. 'I love it here, so does Laura . . . did Laura. Robert is getting busier and busier . . . '

'Mrs Prince, was there anything unusual in Laura's behavior recently?' said Ren.

Ingrid took a while to answer. 'No . . . I'm trying really hard to think. No. She was a little upset about her friend's mother . . . '

'What friend?'

'The friend she went to visit in Chicago. Nessa Lally. She was from the same town in Waterford. You might find her on Laura's Facebook . . . The trip was last minute. Nessa's mother died back in

67

Ireland, but Nessa's illegal, so she couldn't risk flying back for the funeral. Laura said she was devastated. Oh God, you're not going to report the girl to immigration or anything, are you?'

'No,' said Ren. 'We just need to speak with her, find out some more about their trip and why Laura didn't fly back to Denver. Were there any problems at work, Mrs Prince anything you can think of that might have made Laura reluctant to come back?'

'To us? No, not at all,' said Ingrid, 'like I said, we were like family. We were very close, and Robert was like a father to her.'

'The trip and the shooting might not be connected,' said Janine. 'We just need to get a sense of Laura, what might have been going on in her life.'

'So on the day before she left,' said Ren, 'did anything happen out of the ordinary?'

'No,' said Ingrid. 'Not that I can think of. She was quiet, but she had just heard about Nessa's mother that morning — Wednesday. We were just watching TV that night, hanging out . . . and now . . . now she's gone.'

Ren sat forward. 'Mrs Prince, have you ever heard Laura mention a place called Evergreen Abbey?'

'No,' said Ingrid. 'Abbey? Like, nuns?'

'There used to be nuns,' said Ren. 'Now, it's a community of women who do a lot of work for charity. But it's also, effectively, a shelter for women . . .'

'Shelter?' said Ingrid. 'But Laura would have

68

no reason to go to a shelter.' She paused. 'We . . . we were her shelter . . . Robert and I.'

The hurt in her voice was heart-wrenching. 'I understand,' said Ren. 'Do you think Laura might have had a friend who went there? Did she mention anyone who was in trouble or worried about something or trying to get away from a bad situation? Could she have been going there to visit someone?'

'Not that I know of,' said Ingrid. 'She talked a little about her friends, but she was quite private. I knew about the Chicago girl only recently. It was like Laura mentioned friends when it was a big event, an engagement, a wedding, a baby, a funeral. But, you know, if a friend was in trouble and was running away from something, I don't think Laura was the type to betray a confidence. I can't see her telling me that.'

'Mrs Prince,' said Janine, 'it looks like Laura may have had some information on a cold case from here in Jefferson County. Bearing in mind she is from Ireland, she lives in New York, she is young, she has a small circle of friends, it is quite extraordinary that she could have information. Is this something she was interested in? Cold cases? Web sleuthing?'

'Not that I'm aware of,' said Ingrid. 'She read crime novels, but so do I. Web sleuthing — she had access to our computer — I'm sure you can find that out.'

'Can we take a look at the computer?' said Ren.

'Of course,' said Ingrid. 'You can take that away with you.' She reached over to a side table and handed a laptop to Ren.

'Did Laura ever mention a place called The Flying G Ranch?' said Janine.

'No,' said Ingrid. 'Where is that?'

'It adjoins Evergreen Abbey,' said Janine. 'Although The Flying G is now The Darned Heart Ranch for troubled teens.'

Ingrid shook her head.

'Has Laura ever mentioned the name Margaret or Peggy Beck?' said Janine.

'No. Who are they?' said Ingrid.

'She's a young girl who was murdered there in the early Sixties. Peggy was her nickname.'

'What has that got to do with Laura?' said Ingrid.

'We're just trying to connect some dots,' said Ren.

As opposed to showing our hand.

'Well, she hasn't mentioned either of those places to me.'

'OK,' said Ren. She stood up. 'Well that's all for now, Mrs Prince. We are so sorry for your loss. If there's anything else you can think of, please call either myself or Detective Hooks.'

They handed her their cards.

'The more information we have the better, obviously,' said Janine.

'Of course,' said Ingrid.

'How can we reach your husband?' said Ren.

'I know he has meetings in New York all day today,' said Ingrid. 'I'm sure he'll fly here as soon as I can get hold of him. I'll get him to call you right away.'

Janine's cell phone buzzed, and the doorbell

rang within seconds. 'That's the victim advocate,' she said, 'let me go get her.'

Ingrid started weeping. 'Victim advocate . . . ' she said. 'I can't believe I need a victim advocate . . . '

10

Janine and Ren drove toward Denver.

'Thank you for ferrying me home,' said Ren.

'Pleasure.'

'That woman is a wreck.'

'I know,' said Janine. 'Poor thing. They were definitely close.'

'She's pregnant *and* her housekeeper's pregnant, though . . . ' said Ren.

'Just a little bit coincidental,' said Janine.

'Hmm,' said Ren.

'We need to meet this Robert Prince guy,' said Janine.

'See if he impregnates us . . . just with a stare,' said Ren.

'I'll say one thing,' said Janine, 'that Flynn family . . . '

'Just a tiiiny bit jinxed,' said Ren.

'I mean, it's been one death after another,' said Janine.

'Maybe they're like The Incredibles, a big spy family . . . that has to be taken down . . . ' said Ren.

'You're terrible, Muriel . . . Oh my God, why are we laughing?'

'Because we have to,' said Ren. 'Because it's what we do. Because, why oh why oh why does a pregnant lady get to die today?'

'I know,' said Janine. 'Now, explain this to me: the Princes rent a house in November in

72

Golden. They want to ski, I get that. But why are they still here? They've rented it all the way through to the end of May. Wouldn't you cancel that if you found out you were pregnant, so you weren't going to be skiing, plus you have the option of a second home in the Hamptons if it's a change of scenery you're looking for . . . '

'I know,' said Ren. 'It doesn't make a lot of sense. But, then, it's not like I'm thinking we've just walked away from a murderer . . . a liar, maybe.'

'I was just about to say the same thing,' said Janine. 'Something was a little off.' She paused. 'Hey — it's nine o'clock — news.'

'Already?' said Ren. 'This day has flown.'

The report of Laura Flynn's death was the top story.

'The pressure is on,' said Ren. 'On you.'

'Thanks for that,' said Janine.

'But we will do everything we can . . . ' said Ren.

They talked over the next story, until they were drawn into the mad ramblings of an evangelist.

'Is this still the news?' said Ren.

'We might learn something . . . ' said Janine.

'*And in so doing, the devil visited upon the Earth a faithful following of fornicators, a plague of pornographers, a harem of homosexuals —* '

'A harem?' said Ren. 'Seriously? Who's this dickhead?'

The report continued. '*That was the voice of evangelist Howard Coombes, who was assaulted earlier today at Centennial Airport.*'

73

'Woo-hoo!' said Ren. 'I cannot stand that man.'

'Coombes, who is here to attend a memorial for the victims of the Aurora Theater shooting, was being interviewed outside the building by one of our own presenters . . . Here's the audio . . .

"I'm just here as a show of support to the people of Aurora who were so affected by — "

Another man's voice broke into the interview: *"What about supporting the rights of citizens to marry the person they love? What about the rights of a man to marry a man or a woman to marry a woman?"*

There was the sound of scuffling and it went back to the studio.

'The angry protester threw a milkshake at Mr Coombes, later describing it as an impulse attack, but making a point that the sentiment behind it still stands.'

'High five to the milkshake man,' said Ren. 'Howard Coombes — the voice of reasonlessness . . . High five also to the producer for running the sermon from *before* Coombes was caught fornicating with a 'homo-sekshil' — '

'Did I miss that?' said Janine. 'Isn't he married with mini-me-vangelists?'

'Oh, yes he is,' said Ren. 'His son, Jesse, was the child evangelist — he was touring at five, being interviewed on television — it was insane. The family were building up their empire for years. Then the father got caught with a man-of-the-night in a motel. Busted! But he got all repentant, so the family stuck by him and he

74

blamed it all on the other guy. He gave one of the most odious speeches I've ever heard, saying the guy was a 'homo-sekshil of the worst kind', the kind who takes money from a married, God-fearing man going through a crisis, a man questioning his life and his ways, a vulnerable man, who did not seek answers from this stranger, but found only more questions. I mean, it didn't even make sense.'

'He said that? 'Of the worst kind'? What an asshole,' said Janine.

'Well, hopefully, he's an asshole on a flight back to California.'

'What's he doing getting all up in our business anyway?' said Janine.

'I know,' said Ren. 'He is out there directing his wrath at people whose sin is to love? He should be pointing his daggers at the kind of people who would take a pregnant lady's life. OK . . . deep breaths. Deep breaths.'

'Yup,' said Janine, 'take your rantin' pants off.'

'I like that — rantin' pants,' said Ren. 'I'll get home, swap them for my fornicatin' pants.'

'Is yo' man paying you a visit?' said Janine.

'No,' said Ren. 'Sadly. Realistically? We're talking pajama pants tonight. Ah, the challenges of the long-distance relationship.'

★ ★ ★

Ren arrived home at nine thirty to an exceptional welcome from Misty, her black-and-white border collie and beloved friend. For a little over a year, Ren and Misty had been

75

house-sitting a beautiful Gold-Rush-era home in historic Denver. It was owned by Annie Lowell, a Bryce family friend who had been a widow as long as Ren had known her. She was eighty-two now and busy traveling across Europe. She had been due back two months earlier, but had fallen in love with so many places on her trip, she kept extending it. Ren loved Annie . . . and loved that she was having such a good time.

Ren had recently auditioned dog walkers to look after Misty when she was working. She had settled on Devin, a sweet student from across the street, who loved Misty like she was her own. Ren had recently told Devin that Misty was a cadaver dog in her spare time, but it hadn't broken Devin's dog-walking stride.

When Ren walked into the hall, there was a box of Mike and Ike Berry Blast on top of the newel post with a pink Post-it stuck to it. Devin always left little things for Ren inside the door: notes or candy or something totally random.

Aw. Always something sweet to come home to.

She read the note.

Sugar rrrrrrush! Hope you cleaned up the streets today! Misty ran a marathon! Still no dead bodies, tho! ☹☹☹Devin ☺ ☺ ☺

Ren laughed as she walked upstairs. She lay on her bed and called Ben.

'Ben Rader, this is a time for hugs.'

'What's up?' said Ben.

'What's up is we found a pregnant girl dead

76

on the side of a road.'

He listened quietly as she told him everything.

'Well, I wish I was there to give you those hugs,' said Ben. 'I'm sending you some down the phone. And there'll be real ones at the weekend.'

'Thank you, man.'

'Make yourself some hot chocolate. Crank up the comfort. I need you to be there this weekend. I can't have you running away to a lady commune . . .'

'No chance,' said Ren. 'And don't worry — here is always cozy. It just feels like home.'

'Well, I can't wait to be home with you,' said Ben.

Ooh . . . home. Sounds a liittle too committed.

11

The following morning, Ren was in the office by seven. She sat at her desk in the small space where, over the years, the team-within-a-team had been cemented: Ren Bryce, Robbie Truax and Cliff James. There had been a fourth — Colin Grabien, IT and financial expert, and nemesis to Ren. He had resigned from Safe Streets five months earlier, not long after Ren had punched him in the face and told him she knew he had gotten his position by shafting the other candidate. She had kept it quiet; she didn't want to ruin his career. She hoped he saw the error of his ways. He requested a transfer, and attributed it to the changing career of his soon-to-be-wife. Since then, Gary had drafted in different financial and IT experts from 36th Avenue, but he hadn't made a decision on his permanent replacement.

Ren could see Robbie Truax's computer was fired up. He was the only one in. Robbie was ex-Aurora PD, a solid member of Safe Streets. If honesty, earnestness and goodness could take a physical form, it would take Robbie Truax. He walked into the bullpen and gave her a weary hello.

'You know what I can't help?' said Ren. 'When anyone else sits in Grabien's chair, I'm kind of thinking that I'll come in some day and they will have morphed into him . . . morphed into an asshole. Like the chair itself changes people.' She started up her computer. 'I think the chair has taken on an ominous vibe,' she said. 'Stephen-King style.'

'So no matter who sits there, we're in trouble,' said Robbie.

'Maybe,' said Ren.

'There's a lot of darkness in there,' said Robbie, pointing to her head.

'Caused by the absence of lightbulbs.'

'Oh, I don't know about that,' said Robbie. He never let her beat herself up too much, even when she was joking.

Cliff arrived into the office, looking shattered. He mustered up enough energy to give Ren one of his gorgeous smiles and a wink.

'Hey, big guy,' said Ren. 'Were you two pulling an all-nighter or something?'

'Are you saying I'm fat?' said Cliff. He stretched back on his chair. 'Why is it that women can say to men they look like crap, but men can't say it to women?'

'Who said anything about looking like crap?' said Ren. 'Maybe I meant you smell like you slept in your clothes.'

'I slept in the nudie, as always,' said Cliff.

'There is no greater gift than those intimate mental snapshots,' said Ren.

'Mental?' said Cliff. 'They can't be better than the photo books . . . '

'The pages are getting tattered,' said Ren. 'They're worn through.' She paused. 'Now, speaking of pages, I am about to enter the Facebook world of Laura Flynn.'

'Facebook . . . ' said Cliff. And his tone expressed exactly how he felt about it.

'This is bizarre,' said Ren after a few minutes' trawling. 'There is no mention of her pregnancy anywhere. She's not a major poster of photos, but the ones she has put up are all head-and-shoulders shots.' She scrolled down through the images. 'Looks like this was a secret pregnancy . . . but from who? The father? The Princes knew . . . but they're not Facebook Friends. So maybe the father is connected to one of these twenty-two Friends she does have. And this is also weird: there's no Nessa Lally, the girl she was to have stayed with in Chicago. But then, I guess, not everyone is on Facebook.' She paused. 'Could this be a surrogacy situation? Could Laura Flynn have been acting as a surrogate for the Princes? Ingrid Prince could well have a Moonbump and a prescription for Prednisone.'

'And I am going to ask you what the heck both of those things are,' said Cliff.

'Prednisone is an anti-arthritis drug,' said Ren, 'but it causes weight gain that mimics pregnancy weight gain — like water retention in the face and neck. And a Moonbump is a faux pregnancy belly — they're used in movies or by women who are adopting or using a surrogate and would rather people not know for whatever reason.'

'Gee whizz,' said Robbie.

'Let me Google Ingrid Prince and see whether there are any suspect baby bump photos . . . ' said Ren, 'the kind that fold and the like.' Ren typed, then paused. 'Four months is probably a little too early for that . . . I was thinking six months.'

'So there's a two-month difference in their due dates,' said Cliff.

'That way the baby comes before the paparazzi start sniffing around,' said Ren.

She went back to scanning Laura Flynn's Facebook posts.

'Laura Flynn's friends are almost entirely non-slutty,' said Ren. 'Low levels of selfies and duck face. And Laura — she looks like such a regular girl. Just a nice person. Like, she dressed as Little Red Riding Hood last Hallowe'en. A regular one, not an 'adult' one. She volunteers at a soup kitchen . . . '

Ren did another search. 'Hold on . . . more weirdness. I just ran her 'illegal' friend, Nessa Lally, through our databases and she is, in fact, one hundred percent legal. If her mother is dead, which I'm now thinking she is not, Nessa is free to go back to Ireland all she wants.'

She sat back. 'So, Laura Flynn. Almost-entirely-secret pregnancy, trip to Chicago with secret drive down to Colorado, phone call to Janine Hooks . . . there was lots of secret shiz going on.'

'Let's see what the autopsy tells us,' said Robbie.

'You know we're also going to take in the ranch and abbey afterwards,' said Ren. 'We need to talk to a little old nun-like lady, who may or may not have seen a car being torched.' She gathered up her things.

'I can't help feeling I'm drafted in for religious

organizations and old ladies,' said Robbie.

Ren paused as she walked by him and held a hand to his cheek. 'But look at that face . . . '

He shook his head away from her.

'You have a way about you,' said Ren.

People told Robbie things because he made them feel that whatever information they gave him, it was a blessing, he would cherish it, and he would use it to successfully fight the forces of evil. No matter where he'd been and what he'd seen, he truly trusted and he inspired trust. His bright blue eyes told them 'We are going to solve this. I will take care of this.'

Robbie Truax: Action Boy.

Ren glanced at him.

Tired-looking Action Boy.

The little old ladies saw him as the ideal grandson. He was single, Mormon and virginal, because he never wanted to do what so many of his friends had done: marry so he could have sex. Robbie was waiting for the right woman to come along. He had long believed it was Ren. He had once broken his no-alcohol vow for one night only to be a little more like the kind of man he thought Ren would want. He had tried to kiss her and he had told her how he felt. And she let him kindly know that, though she adored him, she thought of him in a different way; the worst way possible for him: as a brother.

Even if she had been physically attracted to him, even if he didn't believe in no sex before marriage, Robbie wouldn't do sex. Robbie did love.

Bless you, innocent, pure, breakable Robbie.

The autopsy lasted two hours and was a difficult one for everyone. Ren, Janine, Robbie and Kohler were now standing in a corner, as Tolman talked through the findings. Tolman was a smart, thorough medical examiner, who explained everything clearly.

He glanced at Janine and Ren.

'You know, Janine, I remember a time when you told me not to speak to Agent Ren Bryce . . . now look at you guys.'

'It was a dark moment in our history,' said Ren.

'Darker for her than me,' said Janine.

Shame. Shaaame.

During a previous investigation, Ren had gotten her confidential informant to steal a file from Janine's office, but he had put it back in the wrong place, and Janine had made the connection to Ren. By the end of the mercifully successful investigation, Janine had also solved a cold case and the two women had ultimately bonded over bad things and good intentions.

'Aw, the lesser-spotted blushing of Ren Bryce,' said Janine. 'Let's just say that at the time of said incident, Agent Bryce was using her superpowers for good . . . '

'Some day you will tell me,' said Tolman. 'OK — down to business: we've got a twenty-six-year-old woman, pregnant, sustained multiple gunshot wounds, while sitting in a parked car. Cause of death was a severe head injury caused by a gunshot wound at close range. I recovered one projectile from behind the left scapula. Also noted was a gunshot wound to the chest, causing severe injuries. I recovered a second projectile just beneath the scalp behind the left ear. Both appear to me to be from a large caliber weapon. Manner of death: homicide. Time of death — anywhere from ten a.m. to when you found her at 15.48.

'The pregnancy was approximately six months gestational age,' said Tolman. 'The fetus was viable. If it were born today, it would have been capable of living on its own. There were no signs of deformity. The death of the fetus is associated with maternal death, caused by the gunshot wounds.' He paused. 'Do you know who the father is? Is there a question of paternity? I'll retain tissue here — I can get testing through the university lab, if you need it.'

'Great,' said Ren. 'We don't know yet. We also have to consider it as a possible surrogacy situation.'

'Well, keep me posted,' said Tolman.

'Oh,' said Ren. 'Is it a boy or a girl?'

'It's a girl,' said Tolman.

Those words were not meant for this room.

12

Robbie sat with his laptop at a spare desk beside Janine's. Ren was sitting on the edge of Janine's desk, her office phone up to her ear.

'Well, it's ringing,' said Ren. 'And it's an overseas ringtone. Nessa Lally may just be in Ireland after all.'

Her eyes were on Janine's piano fingers as she waited.

'You are such a fast typist,' said Ren. 'It's insane.'

'You know it, girl,' said Janine.

'Hello,' said Ren, sitting up. 'Is this Nessa Lally?'

'Yes.'

'My name is Special Agent Ren Bryce. I'm with the FBI in Denver. The Rocky Mountain Safe Streets Task Force. Is this a good time?'

'The FBI?' said Nessa. 'Seriously?'

'Yes, ma'am,' said Ren. *That ma'am will convince her.*

'Is everything OK?' said Nessa.

'I'm afraid not,' said Ren. 'I've got some bad news about your friend, Laura Flynn.'

'Laura Flynn?' said Nessa.

'Yes,' said Ren, 'I'm sorry to tell you that she was the victim of a homicide.'

'Oh my God,' said Nessa. 'No way. Laura? No way. In Denver? What was she doing in Denver? I knew she'd moved to New York, but . . .'

What? 'You knew she'd moved to New York?' said Ren.

'It's just . . . I haven't seen her in years,' said Nessa. 'How did you even get my number?'

'Aren't you friends with Laura?' said Ren.

'Not now, no,' said Nessa. 'I used to be, there was a big gang of us used to hang around together, but we haven't seen each other in, easily, six or seven years.'

'Laura told her employers last week that your mother died and that because you were illegal you couldn't fly back to Ireland for the funeral, so she was going to spend the weekend with you for support,' said Ren. 'We obviously now know that you're legal . . . '

'Thank God I am,' said Nessa. 'My mam did die last week, but yeah, I came back from Chicago for the funeral. But, Laura . . . that's so weird. I haven't spoken to her in years. Someone else must have told her about mam.' She gave a grim laugh. 'In fairness, she always used to use me as an alibi in college when she was lying to her mother about where she was staying.'

I wonder what she was lying about this time.

'What did Laura study in college?' said Ren.

'Psychology,' said Nessa. 'She's got a degree. But it's impossible to get a job in it. And she would have needed a PhD in the States to do more with it. I don't know anyone who can afford to do that.'

'Was there anyone else she might have known in Chicago?' said Ren. 'Anyone else from your hometown?'

86

'I don't know,' said Nessa. 'But I can ask around for you.'

'Did any of her friends end up in New York?' said Ren.

'Yes,' said Nessa. 'I can get their names for you if that would help?'

'Yes,' said Ren. 'Thank you. Nessa, what kind of girl was Laura? Was she the type to get involved with the wrong crowd?' *What a shit expression*. 'Was she a risk-taker?'

'No, not at all,' said Nessa. 'Her father and her sister were big drinkers . . . and that definitely turned Laura off it, like she was very conscious that addiction runs in families. So I doubt she'd ever get into anything serious, like drugs or anything like that, if that's what you mean. She dated a few losers, but not, like, psychos or anything.' She paused. 'Jesus, though, Laura really did have a shitty childhood with her father being such an alco around town and her mother always taking him back or showing up and they'd have huge rows in front of everyone. Laura always kind of rose above it. She was like one of those little flowers you see growing in a weird place. Like on the side of some shitty road in the middle of nowhere.'

★ ★ ★

Ren slid off Janine's desk and grabbed a chair to sit on.

'If you lead a tragic life, don't you deserve to have a beautiful death?' said Ren. 'Garlands of white flowers, unicorns, dancing sprites, lyres, lutes . . . not sure if they're the same thing . . . '

'Me neither,' said Janine.

Ren filled her in on the other side of the conversation with Nessa Lally.

'What I'm kind of confused about,' said Ren, 'is the surrogacy thing . . . if this *is* a surrogacy. Aren't the Catholic Church anti-surrogacy, anti-IVF . . . '

'They are,' said Janine.

'How would that sit with Robert Prince?' said Ren. 'Wouldn't this look bad if it came out? That this prominent Catholic was, in fact, using a surrogate? I mean, that's a massive conflict right there.'

'Wouldn't he have just not gone along with it in the first place if he had such a problem with it?' said Janine.

'Who knows?' said Ren. 'Change of heart? Or is he one of those men that messes with women's heads?' She paused. 'Maybe it's the Order of Catholic businessy thing.' She Googled it. 'OK — OCBLA. The Order of Catholic Business Leaders of America. Let me go back over this. So he failed in his bid to be elected chairman in 2005, and in 2010.'

Five-year term.

Next election: 2015.

Ren Googled the former chairmen.

'All the former chairmen were multi-millionaires, all male, all married with kids. Robert Prince was unmarried when he first ran. He was married when he ran a second time in 2010, but he had no children. He didn't get elected. So, if this surrogacy had been successful, he would have

88

had a child by 2015 . . . albeit in a manner that would go against the beliefs of all the members of the organization.'

'Cynical,' said Janine.

'Yes,' said Ren. She searched to see if he was running for the following year. There was no mention of it.

'Let me call Eli Baer in New York.' She dialed his number. 'Instant response, I love it. Eli, it's Ren Bryce. What do you know about the Order of Catholic Business Leaders of America?'

'Apart from it takes a long time to say it, it's an exclusive new-but-old boys' club . . . ' said Eli.

'Secret handshakes . . . ' said Ren.

'Yes.'

'Do you know of Robert Prince's involvement with it?' said Ren.

'I do not,' said Eli, 'but I know who to ask.'

'Also, has anything else come up on Robert Prince . . . like issues with women?'

'Nothing serious,' said Eli. 'I know a cop who worked private security for him a few times. He said he was a real control freak. That was it. Really cared about his image. He made his date change that night. They went to pick her up, she came down in a really short dress and he got out of the car, went back into her apartment with her and when they came back down, she was wearing something a lot more conservative . . . '

'No black eye or split lip . . . ' said Ren.

'Nope,' said Eli. 'Really, Prince just came across to him as a rich jerk. But I guess he does have an image to protect . . . and this lady wasn't quite tying into it.'

'No escort or hooker tales?' said Ren.

'No,' said Eli, 'but you know he can afford to be a very careful man if that's what he's into.'

'I know . . . ' said Ren. 'OK, thanks for that.'

'Any time,' said Eli.

Ren put down the phone. 'Prince is a control freak,' said Ren. 'That's all we've got. And Eli will look into the Order of Secret Handshakes.'

'Another thought,' said Janine. 'A less conspiratorial one — if Laura Flynn had a psychology degree, could she have been going for a job at the ranch?'

'That's going to be part of my angle when we go and talk to the private folks of The Darned Heart Ranch. Firstly, I'm all about the employees, not the 'guests'. Then — bam! — burning car.'

Detective Kohler stuck his head into the office. 'Briefing here at six p.m. Ren, Robbie — can you make it?'

'We sure can,' said Ren. 'In the meantime, we're going to speak with the Faules, see if anyone saw anything, if they know anything more about the car, and if they're harboring murderous, pyromaniac teens.'

'OK,' said Kohler, 'we'll see you later.'

Ren turned to Janine. 'Do you think the parents of the teens know about the Faules' trusting approach?'

'Lord, no,' said Janine. 'It's not like they would say that out loud. But, in the Faules' defense, look at the adjoining property: an abbey. And it's only the abbey boundary that is really crossable, unless you're Bear Grylls. The Faules aren't stupid. If the kids wander into the abbey, they'll be seen, they'll be pretty safe, and more than likely, they'll be treated compassionately if they're discovered. Obviously, a couple of the kids have strayed further, which is where we came in. What they do is prey on some kindly visitor to the abbey to drop them into town. Or they hide in the back of a truck. Or they reach out to one of the teen volunteers that come in and out of the abbey.'

'So Kristen Faule thinks she's got some kind of magic wand that will transform these kids,' said Ren. 'When it's highly likely that most of them have been blackmailed into going there in the first place and are just biding their time. 'You won't get a car for your sixteenth birthday if you don't get a handle on your behavior/ you are forbidden to see your boyfriend or girlfriend/we'll take away your iPad, trauma of traumas' . . . '

'We were simple children, really . . . ' said Janine.

'We were,' said Ren. 'It's shitty that some of these parents are sending their kids off just to get them out from under their feet, to get a break from all their drama, or worse, that they want to protect their own reputation. I think the minority are the ones who want their child to be happy and healthy and . . . fixed. It's a great thing what the Faules do. I'm sure they've helped a lot of kids . . . I just suspect some of these kids are beyond help.'

13

The sign for The Darned Heart Ranch arced over the iron entry gates, the words rendered in oxblood metal. Ren had parked outside the metal art shop in Conifer the day before; all metal signs had been jumping out at her ever since. She drove up the dusty driveway. Robbie had opened a map of the ranch on his iPad.

'The ranch is laid out like an actual diagram of the heart,' said Robbie. 'We are currently driving up the inferior vena cava.'

'And what does that do?' said Ren.

'It carries de-oxygenated blood from the lower half of the body to the right atrium.'

Ren looked at him. 'Wow. I wasn't actually expecting an answer.'

They pulled into the parking lot. Ren looked at the map. The main office of the ranch was a three-thousand-square-foot log cabin tucked into the right ventricle; there were recreational areas in the left atrium, troubled teen residences in the superior vena cava. There were stables, a tack room, a hayloft and maintenance units tucked into the cardiac muscle. Beside that was a school with several classrooms, beside that an indoor basketball court and a separate shower house and toilet block. There was a separate two-story building close by that housed staff. And a three-bed ranch-style home where the Faules lived.

'It's kind of a mix of old and new,' said Ren. 'OK — let's go. See if we can make a cardiac arrest . . . '

Robbie was staring out the window.

You don't laugh at my jokes any more.

'Are you OK, Robbie?' said Ren. 'I mean, am I OK? Have I done something?'

He shook his head. 'No.'

'Because if you don't change that attitude, young man, I'm going to leave you here, let them beat the trouble out of you . . . '

Robbie smiled.

That's better . . . a little better . . .

They got out of the Jeep. Ren looked around.

'Can you take some photos of the vehicles parked here?' she said.

Robbie used his iPad to quickly take a few dozen shots from different angles.

'Some very nice cars,' said Ren. 'Look at this fleet of four . . . ' Black, sleek, top-of-the-range executive vans. 'Ferriers of children to rehab. What a strange world we live in.'

They walked through the parking lot.

'Looks like someone jizzed up the side of that one,' said Ren, pointing to another black car.

'How do you just come out with things like that?' said Robbie.

'It's shameful,' said Ren. 'I apologize. But it's a ranch for teens . . . hormones are rampant.'

'That doesn't mean — '

'Robbie, I'm kidding. Jesus. I don't think a kid's been out here jacking off. It doesn't even look like jizz. Relax.'

They went into the reception of the main building, showed their badges and asked to speak with Kristen Faule.

'Sure,' said the girl at the desk, 'please, take a seat.'

Kristen Faule arrived within ten minutes. She looked to be in her mid-forties, her snowy blonde hair tied back into a plait that reached halfway down her back. The only makeup she wore was to define her eyebrows and darken her lashes.

'I'm Special Agent Ren Bryce,' said Ren, 'and this is Detective Robbie Truax. We're from the Rocky Mountain Safe Streets Task Force in Denver. Thank you for seeing us.'

'My pleasure,' she said. 'Come on through to my office. My husband is on his way, he'll join us there.'

'Thank you,' said Ren.

But why are you talking like you're auditioning for a Disney movie and/or musical? Disney ways. I get it. Janine, I love you.

★   ★   ★

Ren and Robbie followed Kristen Faule into a large room that was like a combination living space, office and bookstore. It had a beautiful stone fireplace with a yellow ceramic jug of flowers in the hearth. There was a smell of freshly cut wood and oil. Everything looked rugged, rustic, but new.

'This is a beautiful room,' said Ren.

'Thank you,' said Kristen. 'We've just had it

remodeled. I only moved back into it a month ago.'

'It will age real well,' said Ren. 'I love the shelves.'

'Hand-crafted,' said Kristen. 'They're my favorite feature.'

'And they must be custom file cabinets,' said Ren.

She nodded. 'They are. I hate the metal look. I wanted everything to have as natural a finish as it could.'

Instead of sitting at her desk, she guided them over to two facing sofas. They were all halted by the mountains of cushions on top.

'Just move them out of your way,' said Kristen.

How many times a day do you have to say that to people?

Ren rolled her eyes at Robbie as they both plucked up cushions and set them on an empty console table.

The room overlooked a flagstone courtyard bordered by blue spruce.

'I know you had detectives from the Sheriff's Office here yesterday to let you know about the homicide,' said Ren.

'Yes — how terribly sad,' said Kristen.

Ren nodded. 'She was only twenty-six years old.'

Robbie leaned forward and took a brochure for the ranch from a stack on the table. 'Do you mind?' he said.

'Not at all,' said Kristen.

'The Darned Heart . . . ' said Robbie.

'It's a play on words,' said Kristen.

No way!

There was no doubt she had explained this a thousand times, but there was clearly no loss of enthusiasm. 'These kids — or their parents — often feel like they are damned,' said Kristen, 'which is a terrible thing when they're still in their teens. The kids have the strangest type of independence; it's independence without the emotional maturity to handle it. And without the respect for authority that allows them to accept guidance from people who do. They want to do everything themselves and don't want to listen to anyone. And then something happens in their lives and they break.

'It doesn't matter what their financial circumstances are, they are all, in some way, broken. Their hearts are broken. And we like to think we can help mend that. Darn it.' She smiled. 'It's in honor of my grandmother, who always said you could 'knit a problem away'.'

Do not laugh. Do not laugh.

That voice, though.

Kenneth Faule strode into the room, fresh from the shower, broad-shouldered, gray-templed, wide-smiled. They made their introductions.

'Yesterday's victim,' said Ren, 'her name was Laura Flynn. Does that name sound familiar to either of you?'

Kristen and Kenneth looked at each other. 'No.'

'She was a psychology graduate,' said Ren. 'Could she have perhaps been in touch about a position here at the ranch?'

'Well, obviously, we do hire psychologists,' said

96

Kristen, 'but we're not hiring right now, so she couldn't have been responding to an ad or anything like that.'

'She may have been coming here speculatively,' said Kenneth. 'That's happened before. People become aware of the ranch for whatever reason and they drop in their résumé, but it's unusual.'

'Obviously, we get emails . . . ' said Kristen.

'Would you mind checking your inbox, just to confirm that?' said Ren.

'I can do that right now,' said Kristen, going to her desk. She called up her email. 'OK, I've typed in her name — nothing here.'

She sat back down beside her husband.

'How many staff do you have working here?' said Ren.

'Twenty-eight, not obviously all on at the same time,' said Kristen. 'That includes canteen staff, cleaners, myself and Kenneth. In terms of the residents, we're obliged to have a ratio of one staff member to every four.'

'We provided the Sheriff's Office with a full list in the last half hour,' said Kenneth.

'We appreciate that,' said Robbie.

'We'd also like to talk to you about the burning vehicle,' said Ren.

'Oh,' said Kristen.

'What happened?' said Ren.

'It was a disaster,' said Kenneth. 'We have a fire pit that the kids sit around certain nights, you know, sing songs, tell stories, that kind of thing. Whatever happened, I guess the fire was still smoldering after last night, Kendall's car was too close, it went up.' He shrugged. 'It was an accident, and we're going to compensate Mr Kendall.'

'Well, we'll see what the lab comes back with,' said Ren.

'With respect, I think that's probably a waste of resources at a time like this,' said Kenneth.

Hello?

'A car was found burnt out after the robbery at Conifer,' said Ren. 'That's only a few miles from here. And with the shooting of the young woman . . . '

Kenneth glanced at his wife. 'OK . . . I'm sorry. I guess so.'

'So, are you having construction work carried out at the ranch?' said Ren.

'Yes,' said Kenneth.

'We're building a theater,' said Kristen, her eyes bright. 'We're going to expand our drama program. And we'd like to invite traveling theater companies or bands or singers to come here and perform for the kids.'

'That's wonderful,' said Ren. 'Could you email us the names of all those who are working on the site?'

Sorry to burst your bubble, Disney girl, but I'm not here to chat about Glee club.

14

Ren reached forward and took a second brochure. 'Do you mind?' she said. The center folded out into a map. 'Can you show me on this exactly where the car was found?'

Kenneth paused, then pointed to the north-ernmost part of the property. *The aorta.*

'OK, thank you,' said Ren. 'That area borders Pike National Forest, is that correct?'

'Yes,' said Kenneth.

'And to the east — at the other side of this treeline is Evergreen Abbey?' said Robbie.

'Yes,' said Kristen.

'Are you sure that the fire was accidental?' said Ren.

'Yes,' said the Faules at the same time.

'How can you be so sure?' said Ren.

'The kids are supervised the entire time,' said Kenneth. 'There is no way they could have gotten out to that part of the property without someone noticing.'

And you believe that?

'It happened very close to Delores Ward's cabin on the abbey grounds,' said Ren.

'Yes,' said Kenneth. 'We let the abbey know as soon as we realized. Delores wasn't there at the time. She wasn't in any danger.'

'You were lucky the flames didn't travel any further,' said Ren. 'Would I be right in saying that there's a boundary dispute between you?'

Kenneth raised his eyebrows. 'Dispute?' He turned to Kristen. 'I wouldn't call it that, sweetheart, would you?'

'No,' said Kristen. 'We've come to an agreement with the abbey, with Eleanor. Relations are very pleasant between us still.'

So no subtle threats . . .

Ren nodded. 'It would be very helpful to our investigation if, along with the staff list, we could get a full list of the residents staying here too.'

'I'm sure it would be,' said Kenneth, 'but you know that's not something we can do. For confidentiality reasons.'

'You can understand,' said Ren, 'that with the issues that some of your residents may have . . . ' She paused. 'I mean, these are troubled kids.'

'They may be troubled,' said Kristen, 'but they're not killers or vandals . . . or bank robbers, for that matter.'

'I'm not saying they were responsible for the bank robbery,' said Ren, 'but arson is often linked to anger, particularly in teens, and I would venture you have your fair share of angry teens at The Darned Heart.'

'They're in therapy,' said Kristen. 'They have no need to act out.'

Are you for real? 'Really?' said Ren. 'And what about the kids who have run away from the ranch?'

Kristen looked away. She let out a breath. 'That's different. That's a freedom thing, it's not about destruction. Lord knows, we all climbed out our bedroom windows at some point in our teens. Didn't mean we were going to go on a rampage.'

'You're very trusting,' said Ren.

Kristen eyeballed her. 'And I'm proud to be.'

Ren reached down into her purse and took out a pack of cigarettes that had been there for three weeks, and still had fifteen left.

The real/trick cigarettes.

'Excuse me,' said Ren, 'is there somewhere I can smoke?' *Euphemism for explore . . .*

A flash of irritation crossed Kristen Faule's face.

'Of course,' she said.

'Do you mind, Robbie?' said Ren.

He couldn't help smiling wide. 'I'll be right here when you get back.'

Kristen led Ren down a bright hallway and pushed open a back door into a small seated smoking area. She hesitated when she saw a teenage boy sitting hunched at the end of the bench, smoking a cigarette, his head bowed. He was wearing Beats headphones and hadn't heard them come out. He had very straight, too-dark dyed-black hair that fell to the nape of his neck. He was thin, dressed in blue jeans, a pale blue check shirt, navy-blue Converse. He looked like he was trying to appear casual, but failing. The jeans looked fresh from the factory.

Kristen Faule seemed torn between sitting with Ren and leaving her there.

'Everything at the ranch is confidential,' she said as she turned and walked away.

'Of course,' said Ren. *I won't tell anyone about your knitted ways.*

The boy's cigarette was coming to an end. He turned toward the trash can. He stopped when he saw Ren. He pulled his headphones off.

Words, not music.

He turned off his iPod and put it down beside him.

'Ma'am,' he said. Simple, polite, slight drawl.

'Hello,' said Ren. *What are you in for?* She lit her cigarette.

'This is a beautiful place,' he said.

'It is,' said Ren. *What are you in for?*

'It's peaceful,' he said. 'It's right for these kids. It's what they need.'

'Oh,' said Ren. 'You're one of the counselors?'

He nodded. 'Yes,' he said. 'Just — for the summer.'

'You look so young,' said Ren.

His mouth smiled, his eyes didn't. He could have been cute, except for the starkness of his hair, the advanced age in his eyes, the air of defeat.

Looks more troubled teen than counselor.

He finished his cigarette, stubbed it several times on the side of the trash can, and put it in. He pulled out a small bottle of hand sanitizer from his jeans pocket and rubbed some into his hands.

'Well, I've got a lot of experience,' he said.

He reached up to tuck a strand of hair behind his ear. Ren saw the beginning or end of at least five raised white scars under his left shirt-sleeve.

'I know where these kids are coming from,' he said.

Ren nodded. 'It's great that they have this

facility, that there's help out there.'

'Yes, ma'am. Are you here for work?'

'In a manner of speaking,' said Ren. 'I'm part of the team investigating the shooting down on Stoney Pass Road.'

He nodded solemnly. 'That was a terrible tragedy,' he said. 'Hard to believe it could happen somewhere like this.'

'Did you speak with anyone from the Sheriff's Office?' said Ren.

He shook his head. 'No, but I guess Kristen has me on their list and they'll be coming my way. A lot of my colleagues have spoken to them already.'

He bowed, looked like he was going to tip an invisible hat, and walked away.

Strange young man. And strangely familiar.

★ ★ ★

Ren arrived back into the Kristen Faule's office. 'Sorry about that,' she said. 'I've tried so many times to quit . . . '

Kristen gave a tight smile.

Ren turned to Robbie. 'Well, I think we're about done here, Detective?'

He nodded. 'Yes.'

'If you need anything else, do let us know,' said Kenneth.

'Oh, we will,' said Ren. 'How many kids are staying here? Can I ask that at least?'

Kenneth and Kristen glanced at each other.

'Forty-three,' said Kenneth. It looked like Kristen had no plans to answer the question.

'Well, thank you both for your time,' said Ren.
Ren and Robbie walked out to the Jeep.

'My eyes,' said Ren. 'Everything in that room was knitted. It's like the yarn version of Willy Wonka's factory.'

'Chain smoker, Ren . . . '

'Yes, I know. I met one of the — very young — counselors out there,' she said. 'Definitely a cutter. Scars up his arms . . . he looked so sad.'

'Well, they're probably the best ones to help,' said Robbie. They got into the Jeep.

'Or keep you mired in your issues,' said Ren. 'I'd like to see hope beaming out from every pore of my counselor. One thing I know is that the Faules are a defensive pair. I am seeing headlines: *Faule from Grace*.' She started the engine and drove slowly down the drive.

'You just want these people to be corrupt,' said Robbie. 'You can't deal with the wholesomeness.'

'What?' said Ren. 'Wholesomeness is a huge part of my life. It is what I aspire and fail to live up to daily.'

Robbie snorted.

What is with sweet Robbie suddenly thinking I'm a cynic?

'OK, are you ready to put your lil-ole-lady charms to work?' said Ren.

'Charms . . . ' said Robbie.

'Stop that,' said Ren. 'I guess the best thing to do is drive through the abbey grounds as far as we can to the cabin of this nun-in-everything-but-name. Actually, here — take my notebook — look to the last few pages. I wrote her name down.'

He flipped through the pages. 'Delores Ward?' he said. 'Cabin Lady?'

'That's her,' said Ren. 'Best-case scenario for the Faules: a spark from dying embers set off a vehicle fire. Worst-case scenario: a kid took the car for a great escape, needed an alternative ride to get any further, tried to carjack Laura Flynn, failed, killed her, returned to the ranch and destroyed the evidence.'

15

Robbie knocked on Delores Ward's door.

'Solid,' he said.

'Important to note . . . ' said Ren. 'Door of faux-nun: solid. Check.'

Robbie gave her a patient look.

They could hear the shuffle of feet from inside.

'Slippers: cozy,' said Ren.

Delores Ward looked out the small window and they raised their badges. She let them in. The room was all autumn shades of timber, upholstery, fabric, and ornaments. It was neat and tidy. One miniature white fan in the corner was struggling to cool hot air that smelled of damp and wintergreen.

It was hard to know: were the cabin's dimensions a form of self-denial, or like the drawing tight of a comfort blanket — the world was vast, the abbey imposing; the cabin, just right?

Ren was drawn to the wall covered with dozens of old postcards.

'How can I help you?' said Delores.

Let me tear the postcards from your wall! Let me know who wrote to you, Delores Ward. Who did you mean something to, who helped to brighten your little home with four-by-six windows onto the world?

'We're here to ask you a few questions about

yesterday,' said Ren. She and Robbie had moved to the long window that overlooked the boundary between the abbey and the ranch.

'Please take a seat,' said Delores. 'I'll make us some coffee.'

Ren and Robbie sat on the brown sofa underneath the window.

Delores went to the sink and began taking down cups, setting them on a tray. Her movements were slow and almost soundless. She was a woman blessed with good genes. Her skin had barely slackened and any lines she had were concentrated around her eyes. She had short hair in shades of gray, cut as if it were just the practical thing to do, no different to clipping her fingernails.

She poured coffee into two mugs and was about to carry the tray to the table, when Robbie jumped up and did it for her.

'Thank you,' she said. She smiled. Robbie drew smiles from people in the same way babies did.

Delores pulled up a stool in front of them.

'Please, sit here,' said Ren, standing up.

'No, no,' said Delores. 'I'm fine right here.'

Ren picked up her coffee.

No cookies. And I'm starving. Focus.

'Now, what can I help you with?' said Delores.

'That's ranch property right through there — at the other side of those trees,' said Ren.

'Yes,' said Delores. 'There would have been more trees if not for the Hayman fire, ten years back. It thinned out a lot of them.' She paused. 'It turns out, this is ranch property too.'

'I know,' said Ren, 'we're not here about that.'

'Good!' said Delores. 'I'm tired of the whole thing.'

'Boundary issues are no fun,' said Ren. 'But I heard the Faules have been quite understanding.'

Delores raised her eyebrows. 'They're playing the long game.' She paused. 'They've probably put my details into a death clock.'

'How do you even know what a death clock is?' said Ren, laughing.

'Oh, one of the kids from the ranch told me one time,' said Delores. 'Sometimes they come to dinner. You never know what they'll come out with.'

'We were wondering if you saw anyone hanging around the vehicles over there yesterday around midday?' said Ren.

'My eyesight is not what it used to be,' said Delores, 'but I know that I *heard* some voices . . . male, hard to say what age, though.'

'Would you have any idea what time that was at?' said Ren.

'That could have been anywhere between ten and noon . . . I went to the chapel then.'

'Is there anything you could think of that might narrow that timeframe down?' said Ren. 'Were you listening to a particular show on the radio, was it before or after you ate your breakfast?'

'Oh, I have my breakfast at six a.m., sweetheart,' said Delores.

'Good for you,' said Ren.

'I can't think of anything in particular that would narrow the time down, no,' said Delores.

'Did you take a coffee break?' said Ren. *From what, I don't know . . .*

'No,' said Delores. 'I'm sorry I can't be more helpful.'

'That's OK,' said Ren. 'Do you see much of the kids from the ranch, apart from when they stop by the abbey?'

'From time to time,' said Delores. 'They're the type of kids who are drawn to boundaries . . . '

'And do they ever cross them?' said Robbie.

'Not that I'm aware of,' said Delores. 'But, of course, that means nothing. I sleep with the blinds down, the door locked, my eye mask on and my earplugs in. I'm guessing were these kids to make a move, it would be under cover of darkness.'

'Well, not necessarily,' said Ren. 'Did you notice anything yesterday? Were there any kids around?'

'No,' said Delores, 'not that I saw.' She paused. 'I heard about that poor lady. How cruel life is.'

'You believe that life is cruel . . . ' said Robbie. *Boldly go, Robbie.*

'Oh, no,' said Delores. 'I should have said how cruel life *can be*. I do believe that life can be cruel. I'm sure you see evidence of that every day. I pray for the world every single day.'

'Yes, it can be dark out there,' said Ren. She took out her card and placed it on the table. Robbie did the same.

'If anything occurs to you,' said Robbie, 'please call either of us.'

'Thank you so much for the coffee,' said Ren.

Delores picked up the cards. 'Good luck with your investigation.'

* * *

Ren and Robbie made their way to the Jeep.

'She is very sad about the eyes,' said Ren. 'I wonder what 'cruel life' she ran away from.'

'Maybe it was more about the life she ran away to,' said Robbie. 'Don't you ever want to get away from everything? It's all in-your-face, technology, being bombarded with images, scrolling bars, banner ads, commercials that start playing when you're trying to watch the news and it's just this . . . assault.'

'Oh, I agree,' said Ren. 'And our job is *helped* by technology. The only thing I will say is that at least we're of the generation that might scrape through without the utter obsession with it that teenagers have now.'

Robbie shrugged.

'It's the reach that technology has,' said Ren. 'If it was a horror movie, it would be like an octopus that has millions of tentacles — a megapus? — a creature that goes into every single home on the planet and sits down right in the middle of the hallway. Then, its tentacles begin to slide out and crawl into every room, up onto the sofa, right between people, into their hands, up onto the dinner table, into their beds, sometimes right up their asses. And then, it sucks and sucks and sucks the lifeblood out of them. And then it does a big shit right there in the hallway, but no one can get near it to clean it

110

up. And no one can eliminate the stink. Or the hideous creature. And then they realize that they can't imagine a time without him. And then they realize, 'Hold on a second, I don't even have a life any more. I don't have a life to save — he's got us all. So if the creature goes, well, we're all gone too.' And so he stays and feeds and shits.'

Robbie stopped walking. 'I think that might just be the most depressing thing you have ever said to me.'

'So to answer your question,' said Ren, 'yes, I could totally see myself moving into a remote cabin and cutting myself off from the world. I have one million reasons. I might go back, see does her sofa fold out . . . '

Robbie smiled. 'Me too.'

'See, you get it,' said Ren.

You are a sweet, innocent soul.

★ ★ ★

Ren and Robbie arrived back at Janine's office just after lunch.

'Well, speaking to the Faules and Delores Ward has thrown the investigation wide open . . . ' said Ren.

'Really?' said Janine. Then she looked up at Ren. 'Ah . . . you got nothing.'

'*Yet*, fine lady, *yet!*' said Ren. 'Can I grab a desk?'

'Sure — go ahead,' said Janine.

Ren took her laptop from her bag. 'Now . . . ' She did a search on Kenneth and Kristen Faule. Robbie sat beside her.

'OK,' she said, 'I have not found a trail of slaughtered children . . . goddammit.'

He smiled.

'The closest the Faules have been to badness was back in 2002 when Kenneth Faule's ex-Broncos teammate and best bud, Derrick Charles, allegedly went off the rails, beat the crap out of his wife, strangled her, and shot their two children . . . '

'Ooh, I read about that,' said Janine.

'Well, he's in Stateville,' said Ren, 'but is adamant he's innocent and that he was framed. Kenneth Faule still visits him twice a year, good Christian that he is.'

'Bet you're thinking that Faule framed him, aren't you?' said Robbie.

'Well, I was,' said Ren, 'until I read the next bit . . . Faule says he mounted a campaign to raise finances for Derrick Charles' appeal. Apparently, Charles is one of those broke playas; the prosecution used his financial troubles against him at trial . . . suggested his wife confronted him about his gambling and he lost it.'

Ren's cell phone rang.

'Gary,' she said.

'Ren,' said Gary, 'are you alone?'

'I can be,' she said, standing up.

She turned back to Robbie and Janine. 'Talk among yourselves . . . '

She walked into the hallway.

'Are you on your way back?' said Gary.

'No, I'm in Golden . . . Kohler's having a briefing at six o'clock.'

'You know you have an appointment with Dr

Lone after work,' said Gary.

My eyes are now alight. I can feel them. They would burn through you if you were here. Hold your tongue. Hold it.

'Sometimes I get the feeling you might be looking for cases to take you away from your appointments,' said Gary.

'OK, it was me,' said Ren. 'I robbed the bank and murdered the girl . . . ' *Stop now. Gary does not joke about your mental health.*

'Ren, I shouldn't have to tell you — '

'You're right, Gary.' *You shouldn't fucking have to tell me.* Her heart was suddenly pounding. 'I'm sorry,' said Ren, 'but would it be OK if you left my treatment in my hands? Can you just trust that I'm doing this?'

There was a lengthy pause. 'OK, Ren. I will.'

Ren was bound by Gary to attend a psychiatrist and to take medication. Gary had taken away her fast pass for the rollercoaster ride. And he monitored with a height restriction sign — she couldn't be too high or too low. She had to bang her head on it.

Over and over.

16

Kohler stood outside the doorway of the conference room, herding the crowd.

'Can you give me one second?' said Ren, pointing to her phone.

'Sure,' he said, 'go ahead.'

Ren moved down the hallway and dialed Dr Lone's office. She leaned into the wall.

'Dr Lone?' she said. 'I didn't expect you to answer . . . '

Fuckity fuck. Grow up, Ren.

'It's Ren Bryce here — I'm so sorry I can't make it today. Can we reschedule? I've gotten caught up in an important case.'

And I don't feel like talking today. And I want to stay in Golden. And I want to have pizza later with Robbie and Janine in Woody's. And, let's face it, I'm on mood stabilizers, so there's only so much therapy-worthy shit going on in my life right now.

'That's not a problem,' said Dr Lone, 'can you do six thirty a.m. tomorrow?'

Eh, no. Way . . .

'Perfect!' said Ren. 'See you then.'

She dashed into the conference room where Kohler was just starting.

'Ladies and gentlemen,' he said. 'Thank you all for coming. And thank you to our friends at Safe Streets for being here.'

'Pleasure,' said Ren.

'OK,' said Kohler. 'I'm going to start with the preliminary autopsy report we just got from Dr Tolman. No major surprises; cause of death: GSW to the head at close range, second wound to the chest. Bullets indicate a large caliber weapon was used. Ballistics are on that. Judging by the angle, the shooter was likely in a standing position outside the passenger door. No trace of the weapon.

'As you know, we've launched an appeal for information from the public. We're following up on various leads, but nothing of major significance. Nothing has come through on the roadblocks near Stoney Pass Road. But we did get a call about a car on the road to Bailey going out of control, smoke coming out the back ... sounds like it was the getaway car in the Conifer robbery.'

'So, the car let them down — they weren't planning on stopping, the driver lost control?' said Ren. 'Was accelerant used on either vehicle?'

'We'll know tomorrow,' said Kohler. 'But that's about all we're going to know on any of the vehicles until next week ... three vehicles in the impound lot in one day is a big ask.

'OK,' he continued, 'the victim had printed out a Google Map of JeffCo. Just so you all have your heads wrapped around the geography ... ' He pointed to a map on the wall behind him. 'You can see here, the ranch property and the abbey are adjoining. The ranch has an entrance/exit at six o'clock, a lesser-used exit at eleven o'clock. The abbey has one entrance/exit at three o'clock. Where the body was found, if you drive up ahead to the fork in the road, take a left onto Highline Road and you're heading for Colorado Springs, passing the entrance to the ranch. Take a right and Stoney Pass Road continues west toward Breckenridge, passing the entrance to the abbey. Obviously, this is not the main road to Breckenridge, so anyone going that way would be favoring the scenic route, have business at the abbey or any other properties further along that road; there are not a lot. We're on that. Same goes for the road to Colorado Springs . . . We're also looking at visitors to Pike National Forest. To our victim — she paid in cash for the rental car at O'Hare, used her Irish driver's license for ID. The Avis gal who rented the car to her said she remembered her, because she was alone and pregnant and she felt bad for her. She said the victim seemed a little edgy, but said it was late and she just put it down to 'tiredness and hormones'.'

'Been there!' said one of the female detectives.

Kohler laughed, then continued. 'Our friends in Bolingbrook PD have confirmed that Laura Flynn stayed in the Ramada Bolingbrook on I-53 while she was in Chicago. Victim's employers have solid alibis . . . Ingrid Prince was in their rental in Golden on Monday, there was a cleaner there who confirmed that. Robert Prince was in New York at meetings all day Monday.'

'Some of Agent Bryce's FBI buddies in New York have searched the victim's bedroom in the Princes' apartment in SoHo,' said Kohler. 'Victim had no laptop of her own — she used

Mrs Prince's. We took that away on the day. We're going through a list of people in JeffCo with priors for violent assault, carjacking, firearms offenses, robbery . . . etc.' He nodded toward Ren.

She stood up. 'We're investigating the Shark Bait Bandits,' said Ren. 'We can't rule them out of involvement in this. Nor can we rule out anyone at The Darned Heart Ranch. Detective Truax and I just got back from there and we're a little concerned that they're trying to get us off the trail of the burnt-out car. Apparently, they're protective of their teens — and their business — so unless we have something warrant-worthy, we can't touch them. So what I'm hoping for is something that can gain us more access. The ranch is obviously the closest property to the scene.'

'How many kids stay there?' said one of the detectives.

'At the moment, forty-three,' said Ren.

'And the women at the abbey?' said someone.

'There were just four residents there that morning — the rest were away on trips,' said Ren. 'They're looking into any correspondence from people making inquiries at the ranch — it's a possibility that that's where the victim could have been headed.'

'Yes,' said Kohler, 'I don't know if you all know that the victim had left a voicemail for Janine about having information on one of her cases . . . she didn't specify.'

'It could be The Flying G Ranch case from 1963,' said Janine, 'which is now part of The

117

Darned Heart Ranch. Or that could have been coincidence.'

The room went quiet.

'Anyone got any more questions?' said Kohler. No one piped up.

'OK,' he said, 'well thank you all for your hard work. Long may it continue . . . '

They laughed.

Ren caught up with Janine as she walked down the hallway. She was about to head into her old office.

'Damn, I have to stop doing that,' said Janine.

'Aw,' said Ren.

'It's still so weird . . . '

'Are your files still in there?' said Ren.

'Not even,' said Janine.

'I was thinking maybe we could look at what case Laura Flynn may have had information on and see if that can shed some light . . . ' She smiled. 'Let's go plunder your case files . . . '

'But . . . ' said Janine ' . . . it's broad daylight . . . '

'What do you mean?' said Ren.

'Shouldn't you be stealing them under cover of darkness?' said Janine.

Ren gasped.

Janine laughed. 'Do you want some ice for that burn?'

They walked to her new open-plan office and went to her desk.

'OK, if we're going broad strokes, we're looking at forty-seven cases,' said Janine, 'and what we *can* do, instead of taking away the big files, is take the comprehensive one-page résumés that I've written on each of them.'

'Janine Hooks, you are as anal as the day is long. I love it.'

'And so are you,' said Janine, 'in your own special anal-when-it-suits-you kind of way.'

'So, what's the deal?' said Ren.

'They're all in one document; I'll print them out. We'll work away here, grab some dinner later, maybe we can take these back to my place after, do it in comfort.'

'My cozy queen,' said Ren.

★ ★ ★

Two hours later, Janine, Robbie and Ren were sitting at a round high table in Woody's, beers in front of them, plates cleared away, except for Janine's half-eaten salad. A short silence had descended.

'So, tell me, how is Mr Rader?' said Janine, turning to Ren.

'He is very good,' said Ren.

'Excuse me,' said Robbie. 'I need to use the men's room.'

Internal eye-roll.

'Ben Rader is totally adorable,' said Ren. 'You know him. When he smiles — it's like a flash goes off, as if he holds you there, then it's like you walk away with a Polaroid of that moment. This bright, shiny rendering of Ben Rader. But it's thin, and it's 2D, and it's not his fault.'

'Whoa, whoa, whoa — what?' said Janine. '2D? What are you talking about?'

'I don't know,' said Ren. *I really don't,*

119

actually. 'What I'm saying is . . . I'm having trouble finding his depth . . . but I know it's there. Like, I know there are real feelings behind those dazzling Polaroids.'

'Of course there are,' said Janine.

'Maybe I'm not explaining myself well,' said Ren. 'It's like . . . each of his emotions is like a rubber duck in the bath that he's holding under the surface. Then, suddenly, the duck breaks free, but where it pops up is nowhere near where the surface had been looking disturbed earlier. Does that make sense? The water might be choppy up by the faucets, but the duck will explode through the surface at the other end.'

'Most of the time, the duck just floats,' said Janine.

Ren laughed. 'I love you.'

'Can you accept that a person can be untroubled?' said Janine.

'Not so much.'

'Well, what a shame.'

'Come on — are you telling me you are one hundred percent untroubled?' said Ren.

'Oh, this isn't about me . . . '

Because if it was, we wouldn't be having this conversation. We have never had that conversation where I tell you that I worry about you. I could barely look at your plate.

Robbie came back.

'Did I miss anything?' he said. 'Janine — did you order some actual food?'

No. No. No. Stop. Stop.

'I was here for lunch, Robbie, eating a pizza that was twice the size of your girl-pizza.'

He smiled. 'Well, I don't know where you put it,' he said.

'It's right here,' she said, patting her stomach, 'providing an absorbent landing spot for my beer. Would y'all like to come back to my place?'

'I'd like that, but I've got to get going,' said Robbie. 'I hope you don't mind.'

'Um, we came in my Jeep,' said Ren. *And I do not want to leave for some clean-liver.*

'Stay over,' said Janine. 'I'll drop you in to the city tomorrow.'

Ugh. Six thirty! To evil arch-enemy, Batman!

'I shall get a cab in the morning,' said Ren. She handed her keys to Robbie. 'And you, go, enjoy whatever poor substitute of a night awaits you.'

'Thanks, Ren,' said Robbie, 'you're sure this is OK?'

'Yes,' said Ren. 'Allow me to walk you to your vehicle . . . '

She gave Janine a meaningful look.

17

Ren put her hand on the door of the Jeep before Robbie had a chance to open it. He turned around to her.

'OK,' said Ren. 'This may not be quite the right time, but you have got to tell me what the hell is going on. I am freaking out. It's like, 'Where is my Robbie gone?' You're like — '

'My parents split up,' said Robbie.

'What?' said Ren. 'Your parents? When?'

'Over the holidays . . . '

'The Christmas holidays? It's frickin' *May*! Why didn't you tell me?' *What kind of friend am I?*

'I was embarrassed,' said Robbie. 'You know how I talk about them. And I hoped they might get back together.'

'What happened?' said Ren. She held up a finger. 'You don't have to answer that. But how are you? How are they?'

'My mom is devastated. My father is . . . well, I think he's had some extra-marital . . . ' He shrugged.

'I'm so sorry to hear that,' said Ren.

'They hadn't been . . . intimate . . . for years,' said Robbie. 'My mother felt the need to tell me that, which didn't help . . . '

Intimate . . . creepiest word on the planet.

'I thought he was so in love with her,' said Robbie. 'And, really, he was just . . . well, I don't know. I feel like they sold me a lie. I bought into this idea of true love. I mean, you know me.'

'But true love exists,' said Ren. 'It does. If your parents are anything like you've said they are, they did love each other. It was love. It *is* love.'

'Can you love someone and lie to them every day of your life?' said Robbie.

'I . . . I don't know,' said Ren, 'but . . . yes, I do believe that there are all kinds of love.'

'But my mother thought it was real, romantic love . . . all kinds of love. She was tricked. And my dad had the outward appearance of the perfect family with the choirboy son.'

'I'm so sorry,' said Ren. They hugged for a long time.

'Thanks,' he said.

'Why didn't you tell me sooner?' said Ren.

'We were busy, then you met Ben . . . '

'There's Ben and me,' said Ren, 'but way before that, there's always been you and me.'

And I will kill you if you make Ben stand in the way of that.

'I know,' said Robbie. 'I know.'

Sad face.

★ ★ ★

Janine was waiting in the doorway when Ren got back.

'What was that all about?' she said.

'Nothing — just Robbie's been a little weird and I wanted to see had I done anything to offend him . . . '

'And . . . ?' said Janine.

'No, he's got family stuff going on,' said Ren. 'And that, Detective Hooks, is about the only thing I got to the bottom of today.'

'Tell me about it,' said Janine. 'So . . . want to, look at those résumés?'

'Oh, yeaaah,' said Ren. 'Check it out, people — we *know* how to party.'

★   ★   ★

Janine rented a cute two-bedroom apartment off Main Street in Golden.

'It's like walking into a hug,' said Ren.

'Aw, thank you,' said Janine.

'But it is,' said Ren. 'It's just warm and cozy and old-school. I hate that bachelor minimalism crap. Unless it's a hotel . . . ' *For having sex in all night.*

'Wine or beer?' said Janine.

'Red, please,' said Ren.

Janine came out with a glass of red wine and a beer and put them on the table. She pulled the pile of case notes out of her bag.

'OK — twenty-three for you, twenty-four for me.'

'No,' said Ren, 'give me an even number — twenty-six, twenty-four, twenty-two . . . '

'You're such a weirdo,' said Janine. 'Take twenty-two. I'm an expert in these . . . '

'Never make anything sound even remotely competitive,' said Ren.

Janine laughed. 'It would be no different if they were your files. Except more of yours would be solved.'

'Dead witnesses, obsolete phone numbers, undocumented people, vagrants, women listed only under their husbands' names, perished evidence, botched autopsies, and on and on . . . the odds, Miss Hooks, are ever in my favor.'

'Aw,' said Janine.

'Now, go, go, GO . . . ' Ren slapped her palm down on her pile of résumés. 'Wait!' she said. 'How tenuous are we going, here?'

'It's a blunt instrument,' said Janine, 'but . . . let's see . . . we have Laura Flynn: Irish, from Waterford, lives in New York, was staying recently in Golden, Colorado. If New York/ Waterford/Ireland/Conifer is mentioned — or hinted at — anywhere on that one page, it's in.'

'Do not forget that the Princes 'summer' in the Hamptons . . . '

'We'll throw it all into the mix,' said Janine.

They began to read through the pages and the details that Janine had extracted for the résumé: name, age, occupation, status of the case (missing person/homicide), last-known address, last confirmed sighting, last unconfirmed sighting . . .

'We forgot to include Chicago,' said Ren. 'If Laura Flynn was on a mission to Chicago, then returned here with more information to call you . . . '

'Our net is being cast wide . . . ' said Janine.

They began again.

'These ones make me sad,' said Ren, holding up a page that was mostly blank.

'I know,' said Janine. 'Needs-a-miracle.com.'

★ ★ ★

Ren and Janine kept reading, drinking and stopping for chats. Two hours passed and there were two piles: of thirty-two and fifteen.

'Thirty-two possibilities,' said Janine. 'Hmm.'

'I was kind of expecting a major cull,' said Ren. 'Like, a slaughter.'

'And we haven't even reached stage two yet,' said Janine. 'The actual reading of thirty-two case files.'

'I have marked stars on some of mine, though,' said Ren. 'Those with that something extra that made my ears prick up.'

'Why didn't you tell me that? I could have done stars.'

'Well, go back over yours tomorrow,' said Ren. 'The Girl Scout murder at The Flying G . . . that's a hard one to ignore.'

'I did mention that three hundred people were interviewed for that . . . ' said Janine.

'You did,' said Ren. 'I'm interested in the staff, and the girls in the tents close to where Peggy Beck's body was found. And 'drifters'. I love a drifter.'

'There is no way you can get away with talking to anyone about this right now,' said Janine.

'Ah, but I'm on excellent terms with the cold case detective,' said Ren.

'For what that's worth . . . ' said Janine.

'What the heck is that supposed to mean?' said Ren.

'Nothing,' said Janine.

'Hmm,' said Ren.

'Hmm yourself.'

Ren looked at the clock. 'OK, it's one a.m.,

I'm going to bow out gracelessly.'

'Everything is there for you on the bed,' said Janine.

'I know who I'm dealing with,' said Ren.

* * *

Two hours later, Ren woke up. For a moment, she didn't know where she was. She heard the creak of a chair. She heard it again. She got out of bed and walked the short hallway to the archway that led out of the living room.

Janine was sitting at the table with a one-thousand-piece jigsaw puzzle in front of her. She was in the early stages, but her tiny fingers were swiftly locking pieces into place.

Ren felt this sudden pang.

Oh my God . . . what if anything ever happened to you, Janine Hooks?

'Hey,' said Ren.

Janine jumped. 'My heart!'

'I'm sorry,' said Ren.

'Please tell me I did not wake you,' said Janine.

'No, I just had that 'It's the middle of the night, do you know where you are?' wake up thing.'

'You must think I'm crazy,' said Janine.

'I do not,' said Ren.

'I'm sorry I have to do this now,' she said.

'Why would you be sorry?' said Ren. 'Do you mind if I stay?'

'Of course not,' said Janine.

Ren sat into the corner of the yellow sofa

opposite her, and pulled a giant cushion close.

'All the pieces are blue,' she said, gesturing toward the jigsaw. 'I can't even look at it.'

'It's a seascape,' said Janine.

'It's stressful to look at.'

'It's calming.'

'You are calm already,' said Ren. 'You are my . . . thing that calms me.'

'You wouldn't have said that if you saw me this morning.'

'What? Tell me more.'

'I've just been given extra shifts on call,' said Janine. 'Like, twenty percent more than usual.'

'And . . . you don't want to do the extra hours,' said Ren.

'I do . . . it's not that. I'm nervous. I know the sergeant likes me, but first he moves me out of my office, now he's increasing my hours on call. I'm just worried that he's trying to integrate me more because they're going to pull the cold case unit. Like is he doing me a favor setting me up as an integral part of the team, so I have a fallback or I feel needed . . . I don't know.'

'They are not going to cut you,' said Ren, sitting up. 'No way. You're getting results for them. And they all love you.'

'No they don't.'

'Of course they do. Are you nuts?'

'There's a lot of political stuff going on,' said Janine. 'And why would I be safe when so many other places aren't? Look at Denver — there was a cold case unit for a while when they had the grant. They had twelve investigators, then they cut it. Aurora had two — they pulled at least one of them, maybe both. Lakewood assigned an investigator and a part-time retired guy. Last I know, they pulled both of them.'

'Why don't you talk to your sergeant?' said Ren. 'Do you think he knows something?'

'No,' said Janine. 'I mean, I don't know.' She shrugged.

'Well, it's worth a shot. He might be able to reassure you. There's no point in worrying about this unnecessarily.'

'I know . . . '

'So back to you not being calm earlier today . . . ' said Ren. 'What did you do?'

'A few drive-bys.'

She pushed up her pajama sleeves, then added another tiny blue piece to the big blue sea.

★ ★ ★

Ren arrived into Safe Streets at nine the following morning. Something was clawing at her. Something was amiss. Something was wrong. She went over to her desk and sat down.

Gary arrived in to the bullpen immediately and came straight for her.

Her heart started to pound.

This is bad.

There was a Post-it in his hand.

Ominous.

'Ren,' said Gary, 'the pressure of the important case is off.'

What the what? 'What?' said Ren.

Gary ignored the question. 'Someone from the squad has to attend a two-day seminar on

129

multi-agency critical response put on by the Colorado Department of public safety.' He looked at his watch. 'Starting at nine thirty.'

Ren was motionless.

'You'll represent Safe Streets,' said Gary. 'Take good notes.'

He slapped the Post-it down on her desk.

It said: **Dr Lone, Monday, 1 p.m. Important.**

Oh. Fuck.

Fuckity fuck.

And fuck you, Gary.

18

Matt Bryce's laughter was crystal clear through the phone's speaker, filling Ren's Jeep. Her brother, older by a year, was her first port in storms of all kind.

'I forbid you to laugh!' said Ren. 'No merriment!'

'You *call* me for merriment,' said Matt.

'That's true,' said Ren. 'And, in my defense, I did wait. If I had called you at any point before now, your ears would have bled.'

Matt laughed again. 'Gary is great.'

'Gary is an asshole. I mean, he *promised*. Is this his idea of leaving my treatment in my hands?'

'Eh, no,' said Matt. 'This is the *fallout* from him leaving your treatment in your hands.'

Silence. 'He's still an asshole.'

'A clever one, though,' said Matt. 'So, how was the punishment seminar?'

'Punishing,' said Ren.

'And you're on your way to your appointment now?' said Matt.

'I am.'

'Then, job done. Gary Dettling one, Ren Bryce zero.'

'I don't like that kind of score.'

'It's why we don't play board games.'

'But I always win.'

'Get some help today with your competition issues,' said Matt.

'Everyone knows it's the winning, not the taking part.'

'Well, there's the spirit that bit you in the ass,' said Matt. 'Seeing that you've had to 'take part' in both a seminar and a therapy session ... while believing yourself to be 'winning'.'

'I rang you why?'

★ ★ ★

Dr Leonard Lone was dressed in all black, as if he was joining Ren in the superhero fantasy; she had discovered early in their relationship that he was a billionaire philanthropist. He was slight, graying, bearded and wore sandals.

But he could be Batman.

For Ren's first month with him, she rocked up to her appointments on a high . . . and just as she was beginning to plummet, Lone prescribed her mood stabilizers before the low took her under.

Leonard Lone had surprised her. She hadn't known if he were fierce enough to help. He was leaning toward her now, waiting for her to finish the point she was regretting having started.

'I guess, what it is . . . is that . . . sometimes, other people's emotions toward me feel like weakness,' she said. She looked toward the window. 'Like, positive emotions. I cannot believe I'm going to say this out loud, but if a man loves me, I believe that the man is weak. All I want is his love, I love love, but I can't help seeing it as a weakness. And I worry that I will never truly, truly love someone because I don't want to feel that fear.'

'What fear?' said Dr Lone.

'I don't know,' said Ren, 'but I often see fear flitting around the corners of men's eyes if they love you. And I never know if that's always the way — how could I — or is it just me? Does loving me instill fear in people? Is loving me an uncomfortable thing to do? Or do they know, is the instinct there, that as soon as they love me, I will be gone? Not right away, but I will be gone.'

'Because they love you?' said Lone.

Ren shrugged. 'Maybe I just don't want to belong to a club that would have me as a member . . . '

'That's a harsh judgment to make about yourself,' said Lone.

'Well, I can only tell you the truth.'

'You talk a lot about the man,' said Dr Lone. 'What about *you*, Ren? What about what *you* want, what about who *you* love?'

Ren paused. 'I don't know if I can love, like, really love. Can you really love if you're, like . . . armored?'

'What are you armored against?' said Lone. 'What's the worst that can happen?'

'Have you ever seen someone utterly fall apart because they've lost someone?' said Ren.

'Yes, I have,' said Dr Lone.

'Don't you think it's horrific?' said Ren. 'I never want to do that. I never want to be in that position.'

'Why?' said Dr Lone.

'Because . . . ' *The loss of control is the most terrifying thing I could imagine.*

'No one can go through life escaping loss,' said Dr Lone.

'I know that,' said Ren. 'But you can minimize it.'

'By not loving?' said Dr Lone.

Ren shrugged.

'By not loving, while admittedly wanting to love . . . ' said Dr Lone.

'Exactly,' said Ren.

Dr Lone smiled. He waited. 'Have you ever fallen apart because you've lost someone you loved?' he said.

La la la la la.

Ren stared up at the ceiling. She tried to shake her head.

Awkward angle.

As she lowered her head, she could feel a single tear make a trail down her cheek, then her neck, stopping when it met her collar.

Ugh.

Dr Lone waited.

'There might be someone now,' said Ren. 'I mean, this might be in anticipation . . . '

'You're talking about Ben.'

Ren nodded.

'And you've said there are no problems in your relationship.'

Ren laughed and cried. 'I know.'

'Yet you fear you might lose him.'

'I fear I might get rid of him before that can happen,' said Ren. 'I'll be the loser before I end up being the looz-ee.'

'Can you trust in Ben, can you trust in the relationship?' said Dr Lone.

'I think I can trust him,' said Ren. 'He's a good man. He kind of hints that he loves me. It's really sweet. And he knows that I like him a lot. But . . . '

'Is there something else?' said Dr Lone. 'Is there something that's bringing all this to the forefront?'

One day, you will fly through the sky, land in front of me, deem me sane, and fly away. But we will always find a way to stay in touch . . .

'Ren?'

'I have to tell him I'm bipolar,' said Ren. 'I know him — I suspect he'll be fine with that because he's a good guy . . . and he hasn't seen the dark side. Yes, I love him. But I also know — and he won't — despite that, at some time in the future, I will think that I love other men too. At the same time. Like, I will really believe that I love someone else. Or that I want to be with someone else. And I won't know that I didn't really mean that until it's too late. I'm like a cheater who doesn't cheat. Even though I did cheat on him . . . before we were officially going out, but still . . . '

'Ben has told you that that was OK,' said Dr Lone. 'He understood why that happened. So try to let that go. And after that, it's about what you do with the feelings you have toward other men.'

'I haven't mastered that yet,' said Ren.

'Your alternative is to stay single,' said Dr Lone.

Noooooo! 'That's not what I want.' *Hey, I could try an open relationship. Ewww. Though . . . maybe that would make my life easier. Or I could try multiple marriages . . . Oh my God, if I married Ben, I would be Ren Rader . . . total Avengers name.*

135

I could take on Batman . . .
This is exhausting.

★ ★ ★

Ren turned on her cell phone as she got into her Jeep. There was a message from Janine to call.

'Hey, lady,' said Ren.

'Preliminary results from the lab on the cars,' said Janine. 'The one from the ranch? An accelerant was used: there are pour patterns all over it. The one from the robbery — there were just traces of accelerant in the trunk. Looks like there was a short on the wiring in the trunk.'

'Hmm,' said Ren. 'So . . . someone torched the car at the ranch . . . '

'Put the remaining accelerant in the trunk of their car . . . '

'And didn't a witness say they saw smoke coming out of the trunk of the getaway car before it crashed?'

'They did,' said Janine.

'But that car was stolen — they must have had to transfer the accelerant into whatever car they left the ranch with.'

'Yup.'

'So, maybe not a random act of arson by a troubled teen . . . ' said Ren.

'I mean, we have no idea who's staying at the ranch,' said Janine. 'And 'troubled' is different things to different people. Think you could work that up into a country song?'

'I'll give it a shot,' said Ren. She paused. Janine waited. 'OK, I got it: 'Troubled is the word I say before I say your name, and troubled's got these tiny hooks that always catch the blame.''

Janine laughed.

'Hooks!' said Ren. 'I didn't even do that on purpose!'

'So . . . are you saying — in your profound lyrics — that if we're throwing blame around, it's too easy for it to land on the troubled teens?'

'Yes,' said Ren. 'But I'm not saying that that's not the reality. Sometimes, easy is the way it is.'

'There's also a song in that . . . ' said Janine.

'Please do not encourage me,' said Ren. 'Here goes: 'Easy is the way it is, and easy's good for me. If you want it hard, and want it bad, then take my friend, Janine . . . ''

Janine laughed loud.

'OK, stop with the lyrics,' said Janine.

''I've lost my words, I've lost my soul — ''

'Stop!' said Janine.

'You're missing out . . . '

'Maybe it was an insurance job by Burt Kendall?' said Janine. 'He's the only one who benefited from that car being burnt out.'

'Yup, the choice of location is very convenient,' said Ren. 'Clever man. Dozens of suspects protected by confidentiality, owners keen to protect their image. And he wouldn't have to explain away the accelerant if he wanted the insurance company to think it was some kid acting out.'

'We need to check into the finances of Mr Burt Kendall,' said Janine.

19

Ren arrived into Safe Streets and threw down her purse. 'Afternoon, Clifford.'

'Afternoon, Renard,' said Cliff. 'Nice lunch?'

'Delicious.' *I ate several helpings of discomfort. And went back for more.*

Ren sat down at her desk and went to the *Denver Post* website, scanning the main stories. A week had passed since the murder. In the side bar, there was one small piece on the lack of progress in the investigation.

Great.

Underneath, another piece caught her eye.

'Well, looky here,' said Ren, 'someone has posted a link to a YouTube clip of eeee-vangelist Howard Coombes' milkshake bringing all the boys to the yard. Is it cruel to watch this? I hate watching videos of people being humiliated.'

'But you can't stand the guy,' said Cliff.

'Even still, though . . . it makes me feel dirty.'

'But we love you when you're dirty.'

'Don't you love me all the time?' said Ren.

He raised his eyebrows.

'I invited that,' said Ren. She pressed play. 'I have my answer — it's very cruel.'

'Get back to work, young lady.'

'Hold up,' said Ren a few minutes later. 'I've just spotted a little piece about wifey Coombes, who has been seen without her wedding band. Seriously? If your husband sleeping with another man wasn't enough to make you take your wedding band off . . . '

Get back to work.

As she sat back, she realized there was a mug of coffee on Colin Grabien's desk.

'Who's here?' said Ren.

'The panic, the panic,' said Cliff.

Gary walked in as she was asking. 'Roger Cornett is here for a few days,' he said.

What? 'Seriously?' said Ren. 'Is that chair doomed to be filled by an asshole?'

'All chairs are,' said Cliff.

'I'd be seeing a doctor if my asshole were *filling* it . . . ' said Gary.

Gary has made a joke. The world has gone mad.

'Sorry, Gary — you know Cornett is a total dick,' said Ren. 'There's definitely a diagnosis there . . . '

'Roger!' said Cliff, looking past Ren, standing up, reaching out his hand. 'Welcome back.'

Ren's heart plunged. *Oh. Dear. God.*

She turned around to see no one behind her.

'That was so mean,' she said. She turned to Gary. 'Aw, Gary, please. Please don't consider Cornett as a permanent. He is a hater of humanity.'

'And a lover of numbers,' said Gary. 'This is business, Ren.'

Do not smile at me, handsome boss.

Gary smiled more. 'You handled Grabien.' He paused and grabbed the mug of coffee from the desk. He took a drink. 'Roger Cornett is not

139

here, Ren. You can relax.' He walked out the door, laughing.

Ren turned to Cliff. 'That was two jokes in a row — what the hell? And this is not business, by the way. It's home. It's home!'

'You young people,' said Cliff. 'You have no lives.'

'I know, I know,' said Ren. 'One minute, I'm prom queen, the next my office is my home. That and bars.'

'You were never prom queen,' said Cliff.

'You are not wrong,' said Ren. 'I did, however, make out with her. Even though I had not voted for her . . . which made me feel a little guilty.'

'How is the Vatican on that kind of guilt?' said Cliff.

'They're big fans of me feeling guilty,' said Ren. 'For themselves? Not so much. Robbie gets repression of sexual urges, I get guilt.'

'Ren, can you please quit talking about all that?' said Robbie.

'I am sorry,' said Ren. 'And you are right. I think I am a little fascinated by the whole thing.'

'Robbie has been afflicted with the curse of having happily married parents,' said Cliff. 'It has been proven that that can actually mess people up, that you won't settle for less.'

Oh my God, Robbie, you have told no one.

'I don't know,' said Ren. 'Ben's parents are happily married. And he has totally settled.'

Her phone rang. It was Barry Tolman.

'Ren, sorry, I was out of town for a couple of days. I wanted to let you know that one of my staff here at the lab got a call directly from

140

Robert Prince last Wednesday.'

'Robert Prince?' said Ren. 'What did he want?'

'Well, he was asking about the release of the body. He thought it would be coming directly from the morgue. They put him in touch with the funeral home.'

'OK . . . '

'He asked about the fetus,' said Tolman. 'About whether it could be . . . transported in a separate coffin.'

Oh my God. 'Well, I think that's the surrogacy question answered,' said Ren. 'Jesus. That's heart-breaking. We'll try to get some buccal swabs from the Princes so we can confirm everything. Thanks for letting me know.'

Ren put down the phone, struck by the realization that Laura Flynn was buried by now.

How quickly you can be gone, how quickly you can be in the ground or ashes in the wind.

Ren called Eli Baer. 'Hey, Eli — did you get anything from Laura Flynn's memorial service?'

'She was cremated at Rooks Funeral Home in Southampton on Saturday,' said Eli. 'There was a short service, and they scattered her ashes at sea. It was a small affair, as you can imagine. The Princes were there, both very upset, some of their friends, some of Laura's friends from New York — mostly Irish.'

'Was there a guy called Johnny there?' said Ren.

'No,' said Eli. 'And, by the way, it seemed none of her friends knew she was pregnant.'

'That's just so strange,' said Ren. 'I'm thinking surrogacy. Or the father is a married man . . . '

141

'You're still thinking Robert Prince . . . ' said Eli.

'Well . . . '

'I don't know if this is going to make things better or worse for you,' said Eli. 'But I got some more on the OCBLA. Robert Prince was not *supposed* to be running in 2015, but one of the candidates — there are only two — dropped out at the beginning of the year; he was diagnosed with brain cancer. Robert agreed to take his place. This is a position he really wants. My source told me that when he wasn't elected in 2005, he went all out to curry favor with the other members for 2010. Rumor has it he donated millions to a diocesan fund to pay off victims of child sexual abuse by the Catholic Church in Denver.'

'And that's a good thing?' said Ren. 'Jesus Christ. I wonder was he looking for anything in return, like land? I don't get how these lay people are willing to pay for these priests' actions.'

'Unless that's their thing too,' said Eli.

'I'm not getting that vibe from him.'

' 'He seemed like such a nice scout leader/clown/ elementary school teacher/swim coach' . . . ' said Eli.

Ren laughed. 'My radar is usually good for that kind of thing . . . '

'If I find out any more, I'll let you know . . . '

She put down the phone and filled the others in.

'So, the pregnancy was secret,' said Cliff. 'And he wants to be head of an organization where he

142

needs to be a model Catholic. That's a worrying combination.'

'Maybe Laura Flynn wasn't the target at all,' said Ren. 'Maybe the baby was . . . '

20

Ren slid her keyboard toward her.

'There's another option . . . it could also be that there's another heir to the Prince throne out there that this new baby was going to usurp . . . Maybe it's in someone else's interest to make sure this little girl was not born.'

Ren Googled Robert Prince and his former relationships. He had clearly been careful. There was very little information; scattered over the previous three decades were no more than ten photos of the same five or six beautiful girlfriends on his arm at major events. Ren followed their trails through the internet; there were four marriages, three divorces and seven children between them. There was no suggestion of Robert Prince as a babydaddy, but, then, if he was, it was likely his offspring and their mamas would have been paid lots of money to remain invisible.

She came across an article from February about the restoration of the Prince family mansion outside Butte. It was to be opened to the public in time for Christmas. Robert Prince and his wife, Ingrid, were expected to attend a gala charity opening night . . .

Seven months from now. They had probably chosen that night to introduce the new baby to the world.

Ren found the phone number of the public

relations officer for the project — a woman called Barbara Hynes.

'Hello,' said Ren, 'I'm Special Agent Ren Bryce, I'm calling from Safe Streets in Denver. I'm investigating the death of Laura Flynn; she was the housekeeper for Robert Prince and his family.'

'Yes,' said Barbara. 'How can I help you? I read about the case. It's very sad.'

'Had you ever spoken with Laura Flynn for any reason?' said Ren.

'No,' said Barbara. 'I deal directly with Robert Prince.'

'How long have you been working with the Prince family?'

'We have a connection that goes back over a century,' said Barbara. 'My great-grandparents worked for the family, as did my grandparents. I've worked for twenty years as a local historian out of the library in Butte, so when it came to handling the PR for the renovation, I put myself forward . . .'

'Have you had many dealings with Robert Prince?' said Ren.

'Yes, I've met him a few times while working on this.'

'And what's he like?' said Ren.

'Well, to set aside my PR hat,' said Barbara, 'he's businesslike, brusque . . .'

'Really?' said Ren.

'He's a take-charge kind of guy,' said Barbara. 'I get it, he's a successful man, he's used to doing things his way.'

'Had you met him before the renovation

project?' said Ren. 'Do you know much about him?'

'Just what I get from the media or anecdotal stuff from my relatives. Why do you ask?'

'I'm just trying to get a sense of the family,' said Ren. 'The Princes are the closest to family that Laura Flynn had.'

'Well, I know that family is very important to Robert Prince. During the renovation — it would have been late November — we found some things belonging to his ancestors. There were papers and letters from Patrick Prince, his great-grandfather, correspondence from one of the old law firms in town, Redmond O'Loughlin. The letters were sealed, we didn't open them, obviously . . . but there were other letters connected to Robert's grandfather, Walter.'

Letters that you mention with no small amount of distaste.

'What kind of letters?' said Ren.

'It's not a very pleasant story and, to be honest, it would be embarrassing for the Princes if it got out,' said Barbara. 'This goes way back. A lot of the Irish who emigrated to Butte weren't very literate. But Patrick Prince was taught to read by the local priest, and went on to become a very well-educated man, as did his children. When his son, Walter, was in his early teens, he helped the Irish immigrants to write letters home . . . I think his father was encouraging him to be . . . kind. Anyway, he obviously never mailed any of them . . . they were all still there.'

'That's a terrible thing to do,' said Ren.

'And I can't think of any other reason to do it

146

apart from spite,' said Barbara. 'It's not like these people were revealing any great secrets when they were dictating these letters. It was just to let their families know how they were doing.' She paused. 'I don't think Walter Prince was a very nice man.'

'Really?' said Ren.

'I know my grandmother certainly didn't think so,' said Barbara.

'Why not?' said Ren.

'He was . . . just unpleasant, by all accounts.' She paused. 'We had a young journalist come here last year who was working on a piece about the renovation of the mansion. The project got a federal grant and this young man's nose was out of joint because the family is so wealthy. But, there you go, wealthy people take advantage of these kinds of opportunities — I guess that's why they're wealthy. This kid uncovered a story about Walter Prince. There was a terrible case from 1919 — the Orchard Girls . . . Three young girls disappeared in Butte, mostly from disadvantaged families, broken homes . . . One, she was a young girl from an Irish family, she was only ten years old, was found raped and murdered in a culvert on the outskirts of town. The second girl, she was Irish too, was last seen in the same area, but never found. And the third one was a young Mexican girl whose father worked at the orchard. He was the last to see her alive. Rumors went around about him and he became the prime suspect. But he had a lot of supporters, people who said he doted on his daughter, he was good to all the kids in the area, he didn't have a bad bone in his body. Anyway, he was found beaten to death shortly afterwards: a group of vigilantes caught him on the way home one night, tortured him to try to get him to confess, then killed him. Apparently, the ring leader was Walter Prince. He would have only been about sixteen at the time.'

'And . . . this young journalist was going to have this article published?' said Ren.

'None of the newspapers here would touch it,' said Barbara. 'He was going to publish it online . . . until he got a Cease and Desist from the Princes' lawyers as soon as they got wind of it.'

'Do you know the journalist's name?' said Ren.

'Yes, but he passed away a few months back,' said Barbara.

Curiouser and curiouser.

'Drugs,' said Barbara. 'His name was Jonathan Black.'

Ren Googled him and read a small piece on his death — it had happened in January and was classified as an accidental overdose. One of his friends was interviewed, said she was in shock because she knew that Jonathan wasn't a user. She had met him two days before he died, said he was in high spirits, that he was working on a big story, that he didn't have any history of depression . . .

Death by rattling the bones of the Prince family skeletons?

'What did you do with the Prince items you found?' said Ren.

'I packaged everything up and mailed it to

Robert Prince in New York with a note asking him to call me when he received it,' said Barbara. 'He did, and he thanked me. I suggested we try to get the immigrants' letters mailed to their descendants in Ireland, but he wouldn't hear of it, because it would have shown his grandfather, Walter, in a very bad light. He said that he wasn't even going to open them, that he would shred them and he asked me to treat the whole matter as confidential, which of course I did. You're the law, so I can obviously say it to you.'

'And were there other items in the box?' said Ren.

'Yes — family photographs, things like that. I took a look at the photos, thinking I could maybe use them in our little history room — we've set one of the rooms aside and there is an audio-visual presentation and people can get a sense of what it was like in the house, things like that. But when I mentioned this to Robert Prince, he said absolutely not.'

'Was there anything strange or inappropriate in the photos?' said Ren.

'No,' said Barbara. 'Not in my opinion. They're just of the Prince family, some of their neighbors at a picnic on the lawn. No illegitimate children or ladies half-undressed — '

Ren laughed.

'But what really got to me was that he had a few photos of the Prince Christmas Ball . . . his grandfather and grandmother hosted a ball at the mansion every Christmas Eve and it was a huge event — I think there was only one year, two at most, where it was hosted elsewhere.

Anyway, the invitations were like gold dust. They're the kinds of photos people want to see when they come to visit a historic house like this.'

What was Robert Prince's issue?

'How are you with the preparations on the house?' said Ren.

'It's all on track,' said Barbara. 'It will be beautiful. We're using the launch to revive the Christmas Eve ball.'

'Well, good for you,' said Ren.

'I love this old place,' said Barbara. 'I'll be glad to see it fully restored.'

'When did you last speak with Robert Prince?'

'That time when he called to thank me for the package.'

'And how was he?' said Ren.

'He was thankful, polite, but I sensed a certain tension,' said Barbara. 'I'm sure that realizing that you have a family member who carried out such a callous act as Walter Prince . . . well, it can't have been easy. He did say that he was looking forward to the house being restored, being back for the opening, but I wasn't sure he meant it. And he hasn't been in contact since.' She paused. 'Come to think of it, I sent a second package and he didn't call to thank me for that.'

'What was in that?' said Ren.

'An army badge, 1st Special Forces. We found it in a garden shed after the first package had already gone. I didn't know who it belonged to. I wrote a letter to him to say to let me know what he found out, but he never did. A few weeks passed and I did my own bit of research and, would you believe it, it was his father's, Desmond Lamb's. Everyone saw Desmond Lamb as kind of a nobody, which is terrible. You know . . . just the gardener who married the rich employer's daughter. It certainly didn't seem like some great passion brought them together. I don't know why his military history was kept hidden. Apparently, these 1st Special Forces guys had been deployed to Japan, then sent on a secret mission to South Vietnam in 1957, well before the war. Desmond Lamb had been brave, but I get the feeling Robert had always thought him weak. Though I suppose beside a man like Walter Prince, anyone would seem reduced.'

Did you discover any darker secrets than a military history, Robert Prince?

And could Laura Flynn have stumbled across them?

★   ★   ★

Ren got off the phone and filled the others in on her conversation with Barbara Hynes.

'I can get in touch with the ME in Butte about the journalist OD,' said Cliff.

'Thanks,' said Ren.

'Anything on the secret baby front?' said Cliff.

'Not so far,' said Ren. 'Let me look into the surrogacy more. I'm not really sure how it all works.' She began Googling. 'OK — it seems the average surrogate gets paid about fifty thousand dollars and their medical expenses are covered. Everyone seems to have a different kind of relationship with their surrogate. Some parents keep a kind of distance, others are right there in the delivery room. Couples can go through an agency or they can choose their own private surrogate, which is obviously what the Princes did. I'll call Janine — I think we need to pay them a visit. I guess we can wait until Mr Prince gets back to Golden . . .'

21

It was Friday before Robert Prince came back to Golden. He welcomed Ren and Janine into the living room and stood awkwardly by the fireplace. He was dressed in navy pleat-front pants and a green short-sleeved golf shirt that was tight on his muscular arms, and clung to his small, incongruous stomach. He looked like a man who was more comfortable in a suit, who felt in some way vulnerable dressed down. He seemed lost in the vast showhouse rental. Ingrid came in from the kitchen and gestured for him to sit down. He nodded. Ingrid sat beside him, taking his hand.

Ren didn't wait to get to the point.

'Mr and Mrs Prince, I have to ask you, was Laura Flynn acting as your surrogate?'

The Princes looked at each other. Robert gave a small nod to his wife.

'Yes,' said Ingrid. 'She was. How did you know?'

Ren glanced at Robert Prince, but decided to say nothing about her conversation with Tolman.

'I . . . I'm sorry I lied,' said Ingrid. 'It was such a personal thing. We had tried for a baby for a long time and nothing had happened. It was not an easy decision, but we desperately wanted to have children. When we decided on surrogacy, we wanted the mother to be someone meaningful in our lives, not a stranger. We approached Laura. She agreed and . . . ' Her eyes filled with

153

tears. 'We could never have imagined it would end like this. None of this is something you ever think could happen. I . . . just . . . didn't know what to say when you called to the door. I was shocked. Robert wasn't here to talk to. I didn't want any public scrutiny. It's selfish, I know. It's so horribly selfish. But I was devastated. We lost our baby, we lost Laura. It was all so terrible. Then I was imagining headlines about us, about being fakes and trying to fool everyone. We've just had to put an article on hold that was going to formally announce the pregnancy.'

Robert Prince put his arm around his wife and pulled her close. 'It's OK, sweetheart. It's OK.'

It is not OK to lie to us, though. It's not.

'And when the baby was born, you would say that it had arrived prematurely,' said Ren.

'Yes,' said Ingrid. 'That way, it's before any media attention around the due date, so the paparazzi aren't hanging around, waiting. It gives us breathing space.'

'So,' said Janine, 'can you tell us about your arrangement with Laura?'

Ingrid straightened herself. 'She was our gestational surrogate . . . ' She paused. 'It was my egg and Robert's sperm.'

Ren nodded. 'I'd like to get a DNA sample from both of you, if that's OK.'

'Why would you need that?' said Robert.

'Just for confirmation,' said Ren.

'We're confirming it now,' said Robert. 'We were trying to keep the surrogacy private for no reason other than we're private people and it was a private decision. We didn't want our children

154

knowing that they were born to a surrogate. Ingrid didn't want to be constantly fielding questions about surrogacy every time she was interviewed and nor did I. We would have been included in every pregnancy, surrogacy, adoption, older-fathers article in every newspaper and magazine . . . '

'And it's not what defines us,' said Ingrid. 'I want to be known for my charity work, we both do, and Robert for his business interests . . . '

'I'd rather not be known at all,' said Robert.

'I understand where you're coming from,' said Ren, 'but we still need to run the DNA tests. Laura Flynn and the baby she was carrying — your baby — were murdered. We need to know why. I'm sure you do too.'

'But that doesn't have anything to do with Ingrid or me,' said Robert.

'We don't know that yet,' said Ren. 'We have to look at every possibility.'

'What do you need us to do?' said Ingrid.

'It's just a buccal swab — a swab of the inside of your cheek,' said Ren. 'I have everything here. I can do it before I go.'

Ingrid glanced toward Robert. He nodded.

'In terms of payment for the surrogacy . . . ' said Ren.

'We cover her medical expenses,' said Robert, 'obviously, we cover her accommodation and living expenses, as we always have. And she was to receive a hundred thousand dollars when the baby was born. I insisted on giving her twenty-five thousand beforehand to reassure her. She was not happy about that — she trusted us, of course — but I just felt it was the right thing to do.'

I don't remember hearing about her bank account having twenty-five thousand dollars in it.

'Mrs Prince, you spoke to us about Laura having an ex-boyfriend,' said Janine.

'Yes,' said Ingrid.

'How long ago did they break up?'

Ingrid shrugged. 'Last year, I think.'

'So, if he saw his ex-girlfriend was pregnant shortly after they broke up, and he still had feelings for her, his first assumption is not going to be that she is acting as a surrogate, is it?'

Ingrid nodded. 'No. I understand.'

'It is important for us to know as much as we can,' said Ren. 'There are angles you may not have considered — anything could be relevant.'

'We'll do everything we can to help,' said Robert.

'Will you be staying in the area?' said Ren.

'Yes,' said Robert. 'I've taken some time out of work.'

'Is there anything else you can think of that might impact on the investigation?' said Janine.

'No,' said Robert.

Ingrid shook her head. 'Not that I can think of right now.'

'Well, thank you for your time,' said Ren. 'And I'm so sorry for your loss.'

She couldn't help glancing at Ingrid's belly, hidden behind a loose-fitting top. She realized then that Ingrid Prince would be forced to announce a miscarriage in the coming weeks.

22

The evidence vault at the Sheriff's Office was a giant gray windowless warehouse with cinderblock walls. Ren and Janine went down to hand over the Princes' swabs to be processed by the JeffCo criminalist at the CBI lab. Janine made the most of a Colorado Bureau of Investigation grant, which allowed overtime to be paid to criminalists to test any evidence likely to have DNA. If Janine pitched a case to her sergeant, and it was approved for, testing, and DNA evidence was discovered, she could have thirty hours' overtime for investigative work on the case. Janine's first sergeant had been right — she ferreted resources out of everywhere she could.

'I get it, I really do get the privacy thing,' said Ren, as they walked back up the stairs, 'but, Jesus, this is their babymama's murder we're talking about. Their *baby's* murder.'

'I don't think Ingrid Prince knows what to think,' said Janine.

'And he's . . . cold.'

'He has not grown up in the real world,' said Janine.

'He does seem very protective of his wife,' said Ren. 'But in a controlling way . . . she looks at him a lot before she answers questions.'

'He clearly loves her, though,' said Janine. 'But there's some strange energy, I don't know.'

'I never quite understand those kind of

relationships,' said Ren. 'I like being looked after, but controlled? I wonder are the cans all facing the same way in the kitchen cabinets . . . ?'

'I wonder has he ever been inside his kitchen?' said Janine.

'We do get a strange little window into people's lives,' said Ren.

'And make swift and damning judgments.'

'I wonder what people would think about me and Ben,' said Ren.

'That you rhyme and that you'd have cute babies,' said Janine.

'Babies . . . ' said Ren.

Janine waited. 'Are you going to finish that sentence?'

'I do think *he'd* make very cute babies,' said Ren. 'Weirdly, I don't see myself as being part of the deal.'

'Like, he's self-pollinating?' said Janine.

'Stop,' said Ren. 'I mean . . . it's babies. Ooh — we could have two, call one of them Jerry and the other one Stimpy!'

Janine laughed.

'But babies . . . ' said Ren. 'Routine. Car pool . . . soccer . . . baking . . . jeans that don't fit.'

'Yes. And what would happen to all the thoughts that you have carefully lined up in your brain . . . facing the same way?'

Ren laughed. 'My thinking patterns are quite depressing.'

Is it the meds? Is it Dr Lone's favorite, 'catastrophic thinking'? Is it just how I feel? How the hell am I supposed to know?

'They are,' said Janine.

158

'What are?' said Ren.

'Your thinking patterns are depressing,' said Janine. 'It's more over-thinking.' She laid a hand on Ren's forearm. 'Your life is going to work out, Ren. It already has. Relax. When is Ben back . . . to continue this spiral of misery?'

Ren laughed loud. She looked at her watch. 'Two hours.' She paused. 'And thank you.'

★ ★ ★

There was a newspaper in the reception of the Sheriff's Office with a front-page photo of a sheriff from the neighboring county, speaking at a protest against the changes in Colorado gun law.

'Look,' said Ren. 'Look who's standing behind him.'

'Howard Coombes!' said Janine. 'Didn't we just get rid of him? Is he touring now?'

'He's quoted,' said Ren. 'Blah, blah, blah *This new ban on magazines that hold over fifteen rounds will not stop criminals. As American citizens, we have Second Amendment Rights and . . . you know, my father was born not far from here — Jefferson County, Colorado, and if he were alive today, frankly, he would be horrified by what the Democratic party is doing to this state. People have the right to defend themselves . . . '*

'Against milkshakes . . . ' said Janine.

'You have to check out the video,' said Ren. 'I feel bad, but I did. And then, strangely, I see a link that his wife is no longer wearing her

159

wedding band. Dramz. If she forgave him for his previous sinning . . . what is this new development . . . ?'

'OK, you need to stop following links . . . ' said Janine.

'I get paid to follow links,' said Ren.

'Not to celebrity gossip,' said Janine.

'It stimulates the investigative mind . . . ' said Ren.

They walked past the conference room.

'Let's see if there's anything new here,' said Janine.

The room was empty, but there were traces of earlier activity all around it.

'Kohler will pitch a fit,' said Janine. She started to walk around, gathering mugs, throwing food wrappers in the garbage. 'This is disgusting.'

'It is,' said Ren, helping her. 'What is wrong with people?'

'What is wrong with them is that their mothers always picked up after them, and their wives were dumb enough to carry on the tradition.'

'We would make baaad wives,' said Ren. 'I could manage the whore in the bedroom part, though.'

'Ladies,' said Kohler, walking in.

They jumped.

Please do not have heard that last part.

Kohler watched Ren throw some candy wrappers in the garbage.

'And here we have yet another example of the FBI thinking they can clean up every mess the Sheriff's Office makes.'

160

'You said it,' said Ren.

'An interesting development from the lab,' said Kohler. 'They found two shell casings in Laura Flynn's rental car . . . from a .22.'

'What?' said Ren. 'Not the murder weapon?'

Kohler shook his head. 'Nope.'

'That's nuts,' said Janine. 'I'm presuming the rental company cleans their cars out thoroughly each time . . .'

'Two shooters?' said Ren. 'Which is total overkill.'

'Two attempts on her life?' said Kohler.

'Jesus,' said Ren, 'are we sure she's not some drug queenpin?'

'Did they run the casings through NIBIN?' said Janine. The National Integrated Ballistic Information Network was an interstate database of ballistics information. Digital images of shell casings could be automatically matched.

'Yup — nothing,' said Kohler.

But Janine had an extra trick up her sleeve. 'I'll send them to Consolite for processing,' she said. Consolite was a lab in the UK that had developed the technology to lift fingerprints from shell casings.

'OK,' said Kohler. 'It's a long shot . . .'

'How long will it take?' said Ren.

'A couple of weeks,' said Janine.

Ren pointed to a large photocopy pinned to the wall. 'Is this a map of Evergreen Abbey?'

'Kind of,' said Kohler. 'It's a copy of the original plans — not all of the buildings were built. We got them from Eleanor Jensen when we were searching the grounds.'

Ren squinted. 'Dated 1906? I hope you searched in costume, hired re-enactors . . . '

She studied the plans. One side was a map of the interior of the main abbey, the other side featured the rest of the buildings in the grounds. They were all marked with a different letter of the alphabet and there was a key at the bottom of the page.

Ren scanned it: chapel, school, schoolmaster's lodgings, theater, guest house for visitors. Only the abbey, the chapel and the stables had been built.

'What happened to these great plans?' said Ren.

'Funding dried up, according to Eleanor Jensen,' said Kohler. 'There were plans to build the school — a boarding school, but it never happened . . . '

'Where did the original money come from?' said Ren.

'There were a lot of rich Catholics in Denver at the time,' said Kohler. 'A lot of them had more money than they knew what to do with.'

'That's number one on my list of problems I'd like to have,' said Ren. 'It's a shame they couldn't finish the work.'

'There's a rumor that they might do more in the future,' said Kohler. He stabbed a finger at the map. 'OK, Ren, you'd like to hear something creepy, wouldn't you?'

'Always,' said Ren.

'And we know Janine would,' said Kohler. 'Now, see this . . . ' His finger was on a small square of land to the northeast of the abbey. Ren leaned in, then glanced down at the key of the map.

'The cemetery,' she said.

'Yes,' said Kohler. 'I asked about it when we were there. Eleanor Jensen said not to worry too much about it, it was totally overgrown, barred up, the entrance gates were rusted, it was a ruin . . . '

'Ghosts!' said Ren. *Please let there be ghosts.*

'Well . . . ' said Kohler. 'Could be. When we got there, yes, it was exactly as she said, it looked impossible to even access. But when we finally found a little clearing to look through, the entire cemetery had been cleaned up. I'm talking weeding had been done, the graves were tended. It was pristine.'

'How did anyone even get in there?' said Ren.

'Two of the fence posts were gone,' said Kohler. 'I'm guessing someone squeezed through there . . . that's the only place I could think of.'

'If it wasn't so inaccessible, I'd say this has Delores Ward written all over it,' said Ren. 'She has the look of a grave-tidier about her.'

'A grave-tidier,' said Kohler. He turned to Janine. 'Where do you get these people from?'

'I drug her up,' said Janine.

'To the eyeballs,' said Ren. She looked at the plans again. 'How big is this cemetery?'

'Not big,' said Kohler. 'It's got about twenty plots. It was more a private resting place for the staff at the abbey — well, the nuns, I guess. But apparently, they were kind enough to take in some of the ladies of the night from the surrounding towns too . . . the types that no one wanted poisoning their good Christian earth.'

'Well, thank you, Kohler, that was suitably creepy,' said Ren.

'And thank you for the litter drive,' said Kohler. 'Heads will roll.'

'Oh,' said Ren, 'did you find twenty-five thousand dollars in Laura Flynn's checking account?'

'Twenty-seven,' said Kohler. 'And five in a savings account. The twenty-five in the checking account was a lump sum that came from Robert Prince's personal account.'

'That was the first surrogacy payment,' said Ren.

Ren and Janine walked down the hallway. 'OK, I shall take my leave,' said Ren. 'Mr Rader is back. I need to get the hell out of the office at five.'

★ ★ ★

Ben Rader didn't look like an FBI agent. He looked like he trashed stages with a guitar, that beneath his clothes he was tattooed and pierced. As an undercover agent, he had been the perfect chameleon, because his looks could be dirtied up and his charm was never far from the surface.

He walked in the door of Annie's house when Ren opened it, dropped his bag, slid his arm around her back, and kissed her as he pushed her to the end of the hall and against the wall.

You are the sexiest man alive.

'Hi,' he said. He stared into her eyes.

He does this in real life.

'Hello, there,' said Ren.

'I like this,' he said, touching the small black bows on her shoulder strap, running his hand down the black corset. 'Oh,' he said, 'it unhooks here . . . at the front.' He started at the bottom and popped the clasps achingly slowly, without dropping his gaze until it had fallen to the floor.

'Hello to you too,' he said. 'I have missed you.'

'They've missed you too,' said Ren.

'Well, they're getting an extra three days with me,' he said. 'I did a switcheroo.'

'Get nekkid.'

23

Ren drove into Safe Streets Monday morning.

It's nice to have Ben Rader back.

Very nice.

Too nice.

It will end.

Stop.

He is incredible.

I will make the most of the incredible sex.

Before it all ends.

Because it will end.

That's the credible part.

Shut . . . . Up.

Ren released a breath she was unaware she'd been holding.

Discontentment is a scourge.

She started to think about Laura Flynn and whether she had ever had a sense of contentment in her life. Her family life was tough, her parents died, her sister died, then she was left alone in a strange city. Ren wondered if the Princes had put Laura under any pressure to be their surrogate. Did they feel she owed them because they had taken her in? Did she feel she owed them? Or was it as simple as they chose her because she was a young, healthy employee who they trusted and who trusted them?

Could a couple entrust the most precious of life to someone . . . and something change so drastically they would later have her killed?

What if something had shown up in the baby scans? The baby was healthy according to Dr Tolman. But what if for some reason the Princes thought there was a problem?

Ren called Dr Tolman.

'Barry, it's Ren. I know you said the fetus was viable, so I was wondering is there a possibility that a fetal abnormality might have shown up erroneously on a scan of the Flynn baby? Like, could a scan be misinterpreted easily? When would the last scan have happened?'

'Probably at twenty weeks,' said Tolman.

'And what's the twenty-week scan?' said Ren.

'Well, it checks fluid levels, organ and bone development. They take a lot of measurements, give the gender if they can and if the parents want to know.'

'So it would show up any problems with the baby . . . ' said Ren. 'And is there a chance that an error could be made?'

'I would imagine this couple and their surrogate were getting the highest level of treatment with the most advanced technology and experienced staff. I don't think a mistake was likely. I couldn't say for definite, obviously.'

'OK,' said Ren.

'There is the possibility that your surrogate saw a 3D image of the very healthy baby inside her and wanted to keep it for herself . . . '

Maybe with no one left in her family, and a succession of crappy boyfriends, she found a different way to create a family . . .

★ ★ ★

167

Safe Streets was slowly coming to life when Ren arrived in. As she sat at her desk, the phone started to ring. She picked up.

'Hello, is this Special Agent Ren Bryce?' It was a woman's voice, an English accent.

'Yes,' said Ren.

'Are you dealing with the Laura Flynn murder investigation?'

'Yes,' said Ren.

'I . . . might have some information. I don't know if it means anything, but I thought I'd let you know. My name is Simone Spencer, I'm friends with the Princes. Laura's sister, Saoirse, used to be our nanny.'

'Oh,' said Ren. 'OK. What can I help you with?'

'I wanted to let you know that I found some strange internet searches on my computer,' said Simone. 'Sometimes, Laura called by to use it. I came across a search from back in February . . . about second-trimester abortions.'

WTF? 'And are you sure it was Laura who searched for that?'

'Well, I'm not sure, no . . . I just know that Laura used the computer and . . . she's the only person I know who's pregnant. The searches were deleted, but my husband discovered by accident that the computer automatically captures page views and stores them. He was looking for something else and he found a record of these searches.'

'Were there others?' said Ren.

'Just about what states carry them out,' said Simone. 'It's illegal here in New York, but not in

Colorado. Where Laura was found . . . there's a clinic within about fifty miles of there. It's called The Stoneford Clinic. She had looked through their site.'

'Thank you for this information,' said Ren. 'Simone, were you friends with Laura?'

'I would like to think so, yes,' said Simone. 'I was very fond of her, as I was of Saoirse.'

'Did she mention anything to you about a termination?' said Ren.

'No,' said Simone. 'Obviously, she may have been looking it up for a different reason or . . . I'm not sure. I know that she was having this baby for Ingrid and Robert . . . to help them. That was the kind of girl she was.'

'Did Laura use your computer a lot?' said Ren.

'Now and then,' said Simone. 'But usually just if she was up to something sweet, like buying a surprise birthday gift or printing off a special recipe. I mean, Ingrid would do the same for Robert's birthday or whatever.'

'Did Robert monitor their internet searches?' said Ren. 'Could they not have just deleted the history on Ingrid's laptop?'

'I guess so,' said Simone. 'I can't imagine Robert trawling through the computer to check up on them. He's not that kind of guy.'

Conflicting reports . . .

'Maybe it all just added to the excitement, sneaking down to our apartment,' said Simone.

'We'd like to take a look at your computer, if that's OK?' said Ren.

'Of course.'

'We'll send someone from the FBI office in New York,' said Ren. 'Please keep this confidential. And thank you for your call.'

Ren sat in stunned silence. She called Janine to fill her in.

'And I have something for you,' said Janine.

'I can hear the edge of excitement in your voice . . .'

'Are you sitting down? The lab picked up a partial print from Laura Flynn's rental car. We got a match. Kohler arrested a young man in the Ace-Hi Tavern in Golden January 8th; he had gotten into a bar fight. His name is Conor Gorman. Do you want to know who he lives with?'

'I do . . .'

'A Mr and Mrs Robert Prince.'

'What?'

'He was one of the Faules' trusted runaways,' said Janine. 'And his aunt is Laura Flynn.'

24

Ren could feel her blood pressure soar. 'What the fuck is wrong with the Princes?'

'We're going to hear it all,' said Janine. 'They're protecting him, he's grieving . . . '

'Oh, he knows something and they know he knows it — he's sixteen, he could say anything to us. Has he been at the ranch since January? Was he sent there to get him away from whatever was going on in the house?'

'If Laura was thinking of having a termination,' said Janine, 'she might have gone to him for help.'

'And someone stopped her before she got there . . . ' said Ren. 'But would you confide in a teenage boy about something like that?'

'It's a harrowing decision to make . . . if that's what happened,' said Janine. 'And he's the only family she's got.'

'It's a dangerous decision to make, more to the point,' said Ren. 'This is not her baby to abort. Plus we know Robert Prince has to be anti-abortion if he's a staunch Catholic.'

'Surely that would make him protective of all life,' said Janine. 'Killing a woman and her unborn child, because she was planning to kill her unborn child . . . '

'I know . . . it doesn't add up,' said Ren. 'The question is — why would she have wanted to have an abortion?'

'The only thing that makes sense is that she discovered there was something wrong with the baby . . . ' said Janine.

'Or if the Princes made up the surrogacy story after she went missing,' said Ren. 'What if the twenty-five thousand they paid into her account was the first of a payment to keep quiet about an affair with Robert Prince?'

'Innneresting,' said Janine. 'I can imagine Ingrid Prince going along with that to protect their image.'

'It's him,' said Ren, 'Robert Prince. There's something about him. He's concerned that I'm treating them like bad guys, but then they're lying? If they have nothing to hide, then why are they lying?'

'It might be motivated by something else,' said Janine. 'It's not necessarily because they have something to do with Laura Flynn's death.'

'We'll see what our next little chat reveals,' said Ren.

'I'm not going to the fancy rental this time,' said Janine. 'I'm hauling their asses in here.'

★ ★ ★

Ingrid Prince sat alone in the interview room of the Sheriff's Office. She was dressed in jeans, a loose orange T-shirt and an oversized beige cardigan. She was fidgeting with one of the buttons. Fear flickered in her eyes.

Janine and Ren sat in silence for some time.

'You're sure you're happy to talk without your lawyer present?' said Janine.

'Yes,' said Ingrid. 'I've nothing to hide.' She paused, wide-eyed. 'Not that Robert does, but . . . lawyers are part of his world . . . it's just how it is.'

Hmm. Lawyers aren't part of yours? As a former celebrity model with an agent and endorsements?

'Mrs Prince, why didn't you tell us about Conor Gorman?' said Ren.

'Please . . . call me Ingrid.'

Yes . . . now's a good time for that shiz.

Ingrid shifted forward in her seat. She took a deep breath. 'We were trying to protect him.'

'Protect him?' said Ren.

'Conor is a troubled young man,' said Ingrid. 'He has a tough family history, as you know. His father died when he was a baby. Then his mother died when he was just eleven years old. He had no one else. Laura wanted to adopt him, but we figured that would be a big ordeal. It was all very difficult. Laura blamed herself for Saoirse's death — because it happened at her twenty-first birthday party. Of course, it was not her fault at all. When it happened, Robert and I talked and we decided that we would take Conor in.'

'There were no other relatives . . . ' said Ren.

'No,' said Ingrid.

'It was very kind of you to do that,' said Ren.

'You would have done the same,' said Ingrid. 'We had the means. We were already very fond of Laura. Saoirse Flynn had been working as our friends' nanny, so that was how the connection was made.'

'Which friends?' *She asked innocently . . .*

'Simone and Alistair Spencer. They live on the second floor of our building.'

'So . . . you took Conor in,' said Ren. 'How did that work out?'

'Well, he was already showing signs of trouble, even though he was so young. Obviously we allowed for the fact that he had just lost his mother. But . . . even as time passed, we could see that he had issues. His mother was young when she had him, his father was an alcoholic, and never really on the scene . . . apparently he died before Conor's first birthday. No one spoke about him. I don't think he was a great loss. To be honest, I think Saoirse had a drink problem too — a weekend problem, you could call it. But she was a wonderful nanny. She was amazing with the Spencers' kids. But . . . Conor . . . there's no denying he had issues.'

'How long has he been at the ranch?' said Ren.

'Since January.'

'He was arrested in Golden the same month — is that right?' said Ren.

Ingrid nodded. 'Yes — he got into a bar fight. I was staying in Golden at the time, Robert was away on business, so I went to pick Conor up. I brought him back to the ranch. I told him . . . there's a Swedish proverb, like, if you lash out, you're going to get hurt. Angry cats get scratched skin. I told him that. I feel for him. I really do, but he needs to get a handle on his anger. That's what we're hoping for. I care about Conor.'

'How did he end up at The Darned Heart in

174

the first place?' said Ren.

'The first time was November,' said Ingrid. 'His behavior had gone out of control. He began drinking heavily, smoking dope, staying out late, not telling us where he was. He wouldn't listen to any of us. He and Robert butted heads a lot. We really wanted to support him, but Robert was at the end of his tether . . . '

'And how did that manifest itself?' said Ren.

'Robert told him he'd throw him out — but only to shock him. I can promise you that. Conor is such a bright young man, we couldn't bear the idea of him wasting that, of flunking out of high school . . . we wanted to save him.'

'So, what happened?' said Ren. 'How did he end up agreeing to go halfway across the country to a ranch for troubled teens? It seems like quite a leap.'

'Well, we decided to go to Golden, so we wouldn't be too far away,' said Ingrid. 'But when we were all back in our house in the country for New Year. Conor got drunk, caused a scene, which was embarrassing enough. Then he stole the keys to one of Robert's cars and crashed it. He was lucky to make it out alive. He just left the car where it was and disappeared for three days. We were out of our minds with worry. Laura was distraught. When he came back, finally, she pleaded with him to get help.'

'How did he react to that?' said Ren.

'Well, I think our reaction scared him,' said Ingrid. 'Or maybe it proved that we all cared. It was a combination of things.' She shrugged. 'Whatever the reason, he saw the light.

Obviously, Robert was particularly furious with him . . . he'd destroyed one of his prized possessions . . . '

All this recklessness, all this crashing and burning . . .

'But still he was happy to pay for him to go to The Darned Heart,' said Ren.

Ingrid shrugged. 'Well, it meant Conor wouldn't be under our feet . . . and, if we were staying in the country, Robert's collection was no longer in danger . . . '

'So, you don't believe your husband did this for Conor's benefit?' said Ren.

'No, no — of course he did,' said Ingrid. 'I'm sorry. But, probably, it was more for Laura's benefit. Robert is . . . was . . . very fond of Laura.'

'And how does he feel about Conor?' said Ren.

'Robert has gone to great lengths for him,' said Ingrid.

'Has Conor ever been diagnosed with anything?' said Ren.

'Not as such,' said Ingrid, 'but over the years he's been treated for anger issues and addiction issues. He was attending an off-site rehab facility, Wellness Partners, while he was at the ranch. It's not far from there — it's at the Denver Tech Center.'

'And did you have to pay separately for that treatment?' said Ren.

'It was included in the cost, but I guess the Faules pay that to the facility.'

'Where is Conor now?' said Ren.

176

'He's still at the ranch,' said Ingrid. 'We thought it best for him to be there with professionals.'

'You know we'll need to speak with him as soon as possible,' said Ren.

'Of course,' said Ingrid.

'Do we have your permission to do that?' said Ren.

'You'll need to discuss that with my husband.'

Ingrid slid forward in her seat as if she was about to stand up and walk them to the door.

'Mrs Prince, the next matter we have to talk to you about is a very delicate one,' said Janine.

Ingrid frowned; a flash across her smooth brow. 'OK . . .'

'We discovered that Laura carried out some online searches about abortion clinics,' said Janine.

The color drained from Ingrid Prince's face. She tried to repeat the words, she tried to say 'abortion', but she couldn't. 'I'm sorry . . . what?'

Janine and Ren both nodded.

'She did a search for clinics that carry out second-trimester terminations,' said Ren. 'There was one in Jefferson County — The Stoneford Clinic. Does that name sound familiar to you?'

'Oh my God,' said Ingrid. 'No. She wouldn't have dreamed of doing something like that. Not in a thousand years. That wasn't Laura. That was a huge part of why we chose her. She would have no reason in the world to abort our healthy baby. She loved our baby. She did everything right. Everything.'

'Is there anything you can think of,' said Janine, 'that might have changed her mind about going through with this?'

'No,' said Ingrid. 'Absolutely nothing. Nothing had changed between when we agreed to this and now.'

'Is everything in your marriage OK?' said Ren.

'My marriage?' said Ingrid. 'Yes, of course it is. Sometimes I think people like to think of couples like Robert and I as being miserable. It all looks so perfect on the outside so something must be wrong. People assume so much about the wealthy.'

Miaow.

'I'm sorry,' said Ingrid. 'That's an embarrassing thing to say. But, I'm just . . . I'm confused. Everything I believed in is falling apart.'

25

Robert Prince arrived at the Sheriff's Office with his lawyer, a slight, curly-haired man with gold-rimmed glasses and a brown suit that was too long in the jacket, sleeves and pants.

Unusual for a wealthy man to have such an unkempt lawyer.

'Hello again, Agent Bryce, Detective Hooks,' said Robert, 'this is my lawyer, Christopher Bergin.'

'Pleased to meet you.' They shook hands.

'Can I see my wife, please?' said Robert.

'Absolutely,' said Ren. 'After we talk.'

They went into the interview room and sat down.

'Mr Prince,' said Ren, 'there are several things we'd like to talk to you about. Firstly, what is your relationship with Conor Gorman like?'

He raised his eyebrows. 'We were trying to protect him. To answer your question, I don't quite know how I would classify my relationship with him. It would be great if I could sit here and say that I'm like a father to him, but that's not the case. I'd say uncle if it was an affectionate relationship, but it isn't really. I'd say mentor if it wasn't for the fact that Conor wouldn't do anything I suggested, in fact he would be more likely to do the opposite.'

'Do you like Conor?' said Ren.

'I do,' said Robert. 'He's a messed-up kid, but

I can't hold that against him. He's had a difficult life. I've always just wanted to help him. That's why we didn't want to bring him into all this at this time. We didn't want to upset him any further. He was very close to Laura. He has no family left — that can't be easy.'

'Do you think the ranch is the best place for him right now?' said Ren.

'Personally?' said Robert. 'No. But Ingrid is insisting.'

'Why?' said Ren.

'She told me she needs space. We've found ourselves in a strange situation. Laura was the glue that bound us all together. Ingrid was concerned that Conor might have looked to her to replace Laura's role in his life and she didn't want that to happen. She has her own grief to deal with.'

'Mr Prince,' said Janine, 'this is difficult for us to tell you, we've just told your wife, but we've found evidence that Laura had been researching second-trimester terminations online.'

Robert Prince paled.

'I know that's not easy news to hear,' said Ren.

'I don't believe that she was doing that,' said Robert. Firm, authoritative, final.

'What makes you so sure?' said Janine. Her tone was kind.

'We've known Laura for five years,' said Robert. 'She was a kind-hearted, caring Irish Catholic who agreed to be a surrogate to two people who love each other very much and cared about her very much. Whoever your source is, they're mistaken. Can you please note in writing somewhere how vehemently I am disagreeing with this? It's simply not plausible.'

Ren did as he asked. 'Mr Prince, when was the last time you saw Laura?'

He paused. 'Two nights before she left for Chicago.'

'And how did she seem?' said Ren.

'As always,' said Robert, 'relaxed, happy, sweet. She was just an infectiously nice person, the type who cheers up the room, without it being all about her or without her wanting any attention, if that makes sense. That's Laura. Nothing deeper or darker.'

Ren nodded. 'She sounds like a lovely person.'

'She was,' said Robert. His voice caught. He shifted in his seat, recalibrated, returned to his default composure. 'Is there anything else I can help you with?'

'Do we have your permission to talk with Conor at the ranch?' said Janine.

'Of course, but please, go easy on him,' said Robert. 'And I'd like Mr Bergin here to be present for the meeting.'

Shit. 'That's not a problem,' said Ren.

Robert nodded. 'I worry that someone like Conor could be misunderstood. He can be a little sullen and . . . well, he can rub people the wrong way.'

'We'll bear that in mind,' said Ren. 'One more thing — will you still have Conor live with you when he finishes up at the ranch?'

'Honestly, we don't know,' said Robert. 'Ingrid and I are not really in a place to discuss that right now. And it depends on what Conor wants.

181

He's no longer a minor. Either way, I'd like to continue to support him . . . for Laura's sake too.'

★ ★ ★

Ren and Janine went for coffee in the kitchen of the Sheriff's Office.

'What do you make of Robert Prince?' said Ren.

'I'm not sure,' said Janine. 'Am I getting a 'guarded because he's guilty of something' vibe, or 'guarded because he's a wealthy man living in the public eye'?'

'I don't get why he's supporting Conor's treatment,' said Ren. 'Why would he do that?'

'Because he's a good Catholic?' said Janine. 'Or he doesn't want to look bad to other people by kicking Conor out.'

Ren nodded. 'Well, the ranch is a good way of getting Conor out of the way, but not quite abandoning him. All under the guise of support.'

'The lawyer seemed OK; he didn't butt in, he wasn't getting all defensive,' said Janine.

'Strategy, strategy . . . '

They walked down the hallway to Janine's office.

'Can I take home some of those files?' said Ren. 'The ones that match the résumés?'

'Sure,' said Janine. 'I can give you my duplicates.'

'That would be great.'

Ren followed her to the open-plan office and to a battered five-drawer file cabinet.

'You'd think they'd get you a new one . . . ' said Ren.

Janine laughed. 'So, which ones do you want?'

'There's one I want to look at first,' said Ren. She took a list from her bag. 'OK, let's see if you know which one it is: clue number one: 1957 . . . '

Janine turned to her. 'Missing Person: Viggi Leinster, starlet, socialite, New York, dahling.'

'Ooh . . . ' said Ren. 'You're good.'

'I've only one 1957,' said Janine.

'Can you remember the deets?' said Ren.

'Vaguely . . . Viggi Leinster, briefly big on the social scene in New York. Only nineteen years old when she disappeared.'

Ren read from the one-page résumé. 'She was last seen on October 28, 1957 at Vescovi's, a restaurant in New York city. She had been attending the after-show premiere of *Nights of Cabiria*.'

'Yup — that's the last *confirmed* sighting,' said Janine.

Ren scanned down the page. 'The last *unconfirmed* sighting was . . . '

'Denver,' they both said at the same time.

'But . . . 1957?' said Janine. 'New information now? From an Irish girl? Is that likely?'

'I know,' said Ren.

'I have a theory on Viggi Leinster,' said Janine. 'I believe that she disappeared on purpose. The man she was suspected of having an affair with, a gangster called Angelo Marianelli, also disappeared . . . six weeks later, I found out. I'm thinking Viggi Leinster may have been threatened because of something he was doing, he got her out of the way, and followed her a little while later when it was safe.'

'Where did the gangster love story come from?' said Ren.

'His name is mentioned in the file,' said Janine. 'One of the busboys in Vescovi's caught them in the coat check one night . . . '

Ren read it again. 'And Viggi Leinster's neighbor was the one who reported her missing.'

'Yes,' said Janine. 'She's dead now. They're all dead.'

'They're. Allll. Deaaaad.'

Janine laughed.

'Maybe one of the cops on the case was Irish,' said Ren, 'maybe he was heading to the grave with some serious information, his granddaughter/ grand-niece Laura Flynn comes to New York, he gets a little drunk, opens up to her and tells her what really happened.'

'All without one cliché taking place,' said Janine.

'Hey — what about the missing gangster — he could have been in Chicago . . . maybe that's why Laura went there . . . ' She paused. 'I'm going full-blown cliché on this.'

'I can see that,' said Janine.

'Who's got the gangster case?' said Ren.

'A cop in New York,' said Janine. 'We've spoken, we've shared notes. But that was, like, four years ago. I can call him in the morning, if you like.'

She slid open one of the drawers to the file cabinet and handed the folder to Ren. 'It's not exactly bursting at the seams. Do you want to take any others?'

'I'm thinking these four too,' said Ren. She pointed to her list.

'You're taking five?' said Janine. 'I thought you didn't like uneven numbers.'

'I don't,' said Ren, 'it depends. And please, for your own sake, do not expect consistency from me. Ever.'

26

That night, Ren and Ben sat on the sofa in Annie's house after dinner. She told him about the investigation, and the Princes' surrogacy.

'I wonder what it would be like to fake a pregnancy,' said Ren. 'Like, it must be weird to have to keep up a whole nine-month lie, ten-month lie, whatever length pregnancy is supposed to be now. I mean, it must take a special kind of . . . I don't know . . . '

Ben laughed. 'You'd know all about lying, undercover agent Remy Torres.'

Pause. 'Hey, that's different,' said Ren. 'I'm not lying to the people I love.'

'So, where exactly did you tell your family you were for that whole year you were living with a crime queen in a drug compound?' said Ben.

'Living with a crime queen . . . Jesus. And where do you tell your family you are?' said Ren.

Ooh, this wine is performing well tonight.

'Now, I tell them I'm under covers . . . with a hot bitch.'

'Ha, ha,' said Ren.

She grabbed the bottle of wine and poured the last of it between them.

'Anyway, this isn't about me,' said Ben. 'I don't think it *takes* a special kind of anything. It's just . . . it is what it is. I don't know what you expected me to say.'

'I don't come to conversations with expectations,' said Ren.

'Okaay.'

'Do you?' said Ren.

'No, but . . . where are we going with this conversation?'

'I don't know,' said Ren. 'Do we need a destination?'

Ben made a face.

Don't look at me like I'm nuts.

'I just resent you tying me and work into this,' said Ren. 'I mean . . . what's your point?' *That I have the capacity to lie to people I love? Which I actually do. Which I hate.*

'I don't have a point,' said Ben.

'That's ridiculous,' said Ren. 'Of course you have a point.'

'I don't,' said Ben. 'Relax.'

Relax?!?!?!?!?

'Relax?' said Ren. 'Seriously?'

'Yeah, seriously. What the hell?'

'I'm talking about a woman faking a pregnancy and you're talking about — '

'OK, correct me if I'm wrong,' said Ben, 'but didn't you infiltrate that gang by pretending to Domenica Val Pando that you had lost a baby? I mean, that's what we were taught . . . use anything to make an entrance . . . '

Oh my God. I had completely forgotten that. How could I have forgotten that? 'I . . . I . . . cannot believe you're bringing that into this. It's completely different.' *How can you not see that?*

'How can you possibly think that that's

completely different?' said Ben.

'It's work!' said Ren.

'But, say you're a celebrity and you're faking it because your body is your fortune and you don't want to ruin it and you're going on tour, so you don't want to be pregnant or whatever . . . that's work too.'

'That's bullshit!' said Ren. 'And why are we even having this conversation?'

'You tell me,' said Ben.

'What the fuck is that supposed to mean?' said Ren.

'Nothing! You started talking about people lying . . . '

Fuck this. 'I don't think it's very fair you bringing up UC stuff. It just gives me the creeps that you learned about me or had that kind of access to me before we met. I guess I've only just realized that.'

'Oh, no, you don't,' said Ben. 'I had access to a case study of an agent called Remy Torres, of her undercover process. Two very different things.'

'Don't bet on it,' said Ren. 'You can honestly separate what you know about me profession-ally?'

'Yes.'

'You can honestly look at me and not think 'my girlfriend lay with a gun to her head, while a woman was raped right in front of her' and not think 'my girlfriend must be very fucked up after that' or 'my girlfriend got close to a beautiful little brown-eyed boy, took the place of his psycho mother for a year, then abandoned him' and not think 'my girlfriend is one heartless bitch'?'

'What are you doing to yourself?' said Ben. 'What is with the torture? I don't think any of those things. I'm not fucking around here, Ren. We're together six months. I know all this about your past. I have known all along. If you want to push me away, give one big push, OK? Don't do lots of little ones, so I don't realize I'm at the edge of the cliff until I'm at the bottom.'

Whoa.

'Is that a little too honest for you?' said Ben. 'Is that scaring you?'

Shut up. Shut up. Shut up.

'I separate you and your work,' said Ben. 'Just as I'd like to think you do with me.'

'The difference is I don't know anything about your UC work,' said Ren.

'Well, I'd be happy to tell you.'

'You honestly think I want to know what tramps you've fucked and what titty bars you've hung out in and what nasty shit you talked and — '

Stop. Listen to yourself. Stop.

'Stop,' said Ben. 'Let's just end this right now.' He stood up.

End what? Panic. Panic.

'This is going nowhere,' said Ben. 'It feels to me like you just want to argue for the sake of it. And I'm not interested.'

He got up, grabbed his jacket and left.

Ren ran to the window. She watched Ben get into his rental car, slam the door and drive off.

Breathe. Breathe.

She sat down on the sofa.

What an asshole.

I can't believe I said all that to him.

Tramps and titty bars . . . what the hell? He is a kind man. What am I saying to him? He is honest, and sweet and problem-free. Maybe he's not honest. Maybe he is a liar. Maybe he has been lying to me all along.

Stop. Stop. Stop.

I am a psycho. I am one of those psycho girlfriends. But I'm not. I'm really not. Hey, aren't the meds supposed to stop this kind of shit? Oh my God, is this my real personality? Am I a psycho?

27

Ren grabbed her phone. She called Matt.

He answered. 'Ren Bryce Tailored Trauma Services . . . how may I direct your call?'

'I need to speak with your manager.'

'Ooh . . . management level,' said Matt. 'I'm afraid you're stuck with the lowly, unpaid intern. What's up?'

'I had a fight with Ben.'

'About?'

'Stupid things. I was questioning someone lying, Ben was saying I was a liar too . . . because of my undercover work.'

'Well . . . um . . . that's a fact,' said Matt. 'You both lie as part of your jobs . . . '

'I know . . . ' *I know. I know.* 'But he was being a total asshole.'

'Pause and reflect,' said Matt. 'Was he . . . really being an asshole? I am not saying you are to blame for all arguments. I am simply prompting you to ponder this.'

Grrr. 'I may have gotten a little . . . fired up.'

'Was there liquor on your breath?' said Matt.

Grrr. 'Maybe.'

'And what happened?' said Matt.

'He grabbed his jacket and walked out,' said Ren.

Matt laughed. 'Did he fling it over his shoulder, catalog-style?'

'OK, why are you laughing?'

'You don't want to know.'

'I definitely want to know now,' said Ren.

'Well, he walked out on a fight with you while you are . . . you know . . . on medication. What would he have done if he was in a fight with the unmedicated you? Ha . . .'

'Thanks,' said Ren. 'Thanks for that.'

'Pleasure.'

'And how can you be so sure I am taking my meds?' said Ren.

'Ah, yes,' said Matt. 'Some day you will acknowledge the flaming red flags of your lunacy. And the gentle ripple of the white flags of sanity.'

'Ah, yes,' said Ren, 'lunacy is in the eye of the beholder.'

'You say beholder, I say 'endlessly tolerant brother'.'

Ren laughed.

'Don't let this derail you — seriously,' said Matt. 'You've been doing great. Ben will be back. This is nothing.'

'Well . . . I hope so,' said Ren.

'Of course he will,' said Matt. 'Sounds to me like you guys are great together. You don't need drama. Call him. You deserve calm.'

'Oh my God — you're saying I deserve boredom . . .'

'Stop,' said Matt. 'Don't freak me out.'

'I'm kidding, relax.' *Except, I'm not really.*

'So,' said Matt, 'have you had any further thoughts on actually telling Ben . . . ?'

'That I'm nuts?' said Ren. 'Ben took his seat just in time for *The Sane Show*. He doesn't need to see the coming attractions . . .'

Ren was about to walk up the stairs to bed. The files from Janine's office were on the floor in the hallway. She paused. Then she bent down, picked them up and took them into the dining room. She went into the kitchen and made a pot of coffee, grabbed a bottle of water and set them both on Annie's giant mahogany table.

Screw you, Ben Rader. Coming all this way to fight with me. Dickhead.

Ren went back into the kitchen, got a box of cookies and the Mike and Ike that Devin had left her. She sat down and opened the Viggi Leinster file.

OK, let's see what you've got.

There were fifty witness statements, from the staff and guests at the movie premiere and at Vescovi's, where the after-party was held. The Vescovis themselves were not among them.

Assuming that was the name of the owner.

She opened her laptop and Googled Vescovi's. It was featured on some obscure New York City nostalgia-style photography websites. She clicked on one and was brought to a page that told her it was owned by Marco and Elisabetta Vescovi. The restaurant was opened in 1954, soon became hugely popular with the glamorous elite of the city, but its popularity waned and by 1959 Marco Vescovi had gambled away his fortune and was unable to maintain the business. But he was still able to open a new restaurant the following year, on a different site, which remained open until his death in 1992.

Elisabetta Vescovi was still alive and living in Bensonhurst, New York.

Ren searched some more, but found nothing else.

She grabbed her phone and texted Janine.

R u up?
y

Ren called her. 'Hey, I'm in the Viggi Leinster file. Do you have any idea why the Vescovis weren't interviewed . . . the restaurant owners? There are no witness statements here from them.'

'I do not know that,' said Janine. 'It was possibly because they weren't there that night.'

'On the night of a movie premiere party?' said Ren.

'They could have been on vacation, they could have been in hospital, jail, anywhere,' said Janine. 'I'll check that out. Have you gone through the whole file?'

'Almost,' said Ren.

'And?' said Janine.

'My main issue is the dearth of witness statements for a night like that,' said Ren.

'I know,' said Janine, 'but . . . that's not what we're here for. The exercise is not to solve one of my cases, it's to find a possible link to Laura Flynn . . . '

Ooh. 'I know,' said Ren. 'I'm not trying to do your job or anything, I'm just . . . curious. There should be more guests on that list. This was a high society event and there seem to be lots of statements from busboys and ticket-takers and waitresses. It's light on party guests.'

'I know,' said Janine, 'but . . . honestly, hours of your valuable time could go by in a sea of these statements.'

Grrr.

'And aren't you supposed to be having a romantic evening with Mr Rader?'

'That's a story for another time,' said Ren.

'Please tell me you have not had a fight . . . Can you only take him by the weekend?' She laughed.

'No . . . ' *No.*

'What is wrong with you?' said Janine.

'I do not know,' said Ren. 'I was tired . . . '

'Is he there?' said Janine.

'He stormed out.'

'Well, I'm sure he'll be back when he's cooled off. And Ren? Make up with him. Don't be afraid.'

'Stop that,' said Ren. 'You're assuming this was an insignificant argument.'

'Mm, OK . . . Was this a significant argument?'

'No,' said Ren.

'Were some of the things he said to you correct?' said Janine.

'Yes.'

'And did you throw in a few nasty comments?'

'I did.'

'Right, my judgment stands,' said Janine. 'In the matter of Ren Bryce v Ben Rader, I order Ren Bryce to get a grip.'

'Thank you, Your Honor.'

'In the meantime,' said Janine, 'do not drive

yourself nuts with all these. Skim them, if that's possible.'

Don't be ridiculous.

'I called Kristen Faule, by the way,' said Ren. 'I've set up a meeting with Conor Gorman at two p.m. tomorrow.'

★   ★   ★

Ren went back to the file and Janine's cross-referenced notes with the Angelo Marianelli disappearance. It was in December 1957; six weeks after Viggi Leinster. One witness, a busboy in Vescovi's, had said that he was aware of an affair between Angelo Marianelli and Viggi Leinster.

Ren went back to the statement of Viggi Leinster's neighbor. It was strange that there was no mention of a man ever calling to Viggi Leinster's apartment. Wouldn't this man she was having an affair with be visiting her apartment? Or was he wealthy enough that they met in hotels? Starlets were like lightbulbs to moths. She was beautiful. She would have had all kinds swarming around her . . .

There was a print-out of Angelo Marianelli's mugshot clipped to the page. He was a pinch-faced, birdy, mean-looking man. There was nothing of the charming rogue about him.

What were you thinking, Viggi Leinster?

The doorbell rang.

Shit. Ben.

What were you thinking, Ren Bryce?

28

Ren went to the front door, checked it was Ben, and let him in.

'Hey,' he said.

'Hey,' said Ren.

He walked into the living room.

'You've been working . . . '

'Yup,' said Ren. 'What have you been doing?'

'Thinking,' he said. 'I just drove around . . . then I called into Gary.'

Jesus Christ. I forget you are colleagues/ friends. Please tell me that Gary Dettling assumes I have not told you I'm bipolar. Please tell me you did not say we had a fight.

'Don't worry, I didn't say anything about us,' said Ben.

'Thank God,' said Ren.

'I'd never cross that line. Neither would Gary.'

I feel horrible now. 'Ben, I'm sorry about earlier. I . . . really am.'

'I'm sorry too.'

'But I don't think you have any reason to be,' said Ren. 'I didn't like that you walked out, though . . . but I can see why.'

He held his arms open. 'Come here.'

'Are you sure?' said Ren.

He laughed and hugged her. 'We have no reason to fight,' he said.

He held her against his chest. 'I know,' she

said. *Tell that to the psycho inside me.*

'I'm so sorry,' said Ren. 'I really am.'

'Hey,' said Ben, pulling back. 'I know you are. Me too.' He held her face and kissed her gently on the lips. 'Let's go to bed.'

★ ★ ★

Ren woke up in the middle of the night, agitated, disoriented, stiff. Her first thoughts were all about Laura Flynn and second-trimester terminations. She remembered Ingrid Prince's words about the surrogacy:

'Nothing had changed between when we agreed to this and now.'

Was that true?

Ren grabbed her phone and typed in a reminder to go through the Princes and Laura Flynn's lives over the previous six months.

Why am I so agitated?

She looked at the clock.

It's five a.m. — that's why. The biggest piece of shit of a time on the clock.

She switched off the phone, and turned around to Ben. He was fast asleep, smiling at something. He was a handsome, handsome man. She buried her head against his chest and he wrapped his arms around her.

Warm and safe, warm and safe.

★ ★ ★

The office felt empty the following morning. There was an eerie silence in the hallway.

198

The entire building is frowning upon my lateness.

And walking slowly will not in any way salvage time or halt its passage.

She went into the bullpen. It was only when she got to her desk that she realized someone was sitting opposite it. In Colin Grabien's chair.

Cur-sed chair.

'Whoa,' she said. 'You scared the . . . '

Broad-shouldered, smartly-dressed, stars-in-a-cop-show good-looking. Dark, non-nerdy side-parted hair, blue eyes. Non-sexy-to-me-but-possibly-to-most-other-women-what-is-wrong-with-me.

He half-stood. 'Hello,' he said, reaching out his arm. Ren walked over and shook his hand.

Smells of Pasha de Cartier.

The scent of hotness. And a permanently fired-up boyfriend from my youth.

'My youth' . . . grim.

'You must be Ren.'

'Despite all efforts to the contrary, unfortunately, yes, I must be Ren.'

'I'm Cujo Chastain.'

What. The?

He smiled.

Very nice smile.

'The guys told me to say that. My name isn't Cujo Chastain . . . '

'Stephen King,' said Ren. 'They're so mean.'

'I believe you think the chair is cursed.'

'No, because only a crazy lady would think that, and I am sane . . . unless you will be working here for a period longer than a few hours, which is about as long as I can ever keep up that charade . . . '

He smiled. 'I'm Everett.'

'Oh, you were here while I was TDY'd to Glenwood Springs a few years back.' *Exiled on Temporary Duty after Gary worked out I was sleeping with a confidential informant, even though neither of us said it out loud . . . release breath.*

'Yes,' said Everett. 'I enjoyed my time here. You were missed, though.'

Aw. 'So, where is everybody?'

'Your Shark Bait Bandits have struck again. In Littleton — FirstBank, Chatfield and Wadsworth.'

'Shit — did I miss that?' said Ren. 'Shit — did I forget to turn my phone on this morning?' She had discovered the lateness of the hour from Annie's wall clock.

'D'oh.'

'I have never done that before,' said Ren. *Not . . . accidentally.* She took out her phone. *Shit.* She turned it on.

'Well, anyway,' said Everett, 'I'm just here working on some horrible trail of financial irregularities that I am one hundred percent addicted to unraveling.'

'You're one of those,' said Ren.

'I am,' said Everett. 'I used to be a trader.'

'Yet you passed a drug test . . . '

'When you say passed . . . ' He smiled, then gave one of the best laughs.

Excellent power laugh. Four bursts, done. Superb. I like you, Everett Whateverett.

'What's your last name?' said Ren.

'King.'

'Son of Stephen?' said Ren.

'Unless my mother has been hiding something for the past forty-one years . . . then I'm going to say no.'

'It's your real name,' said Ren.

'It is. I. Am. King.'

'I'll be yo' queen if you know what I mean and . . . ' *Please stop before you finish with 'let's do the wild thing'.*

Everett looked at her.

'Ooh,' said Ren. 'Tone-Lōc fan?'

'Isn't everyone?'

'I didn't mean that in that sense, by the way,' said Ren.

'Sexual harassment, day one . . . this is not looking good for you, Agent Bryce . . . '

'I'm going to take a seat now. And try not to be myself for the next little while. But I need coffee first. Can I get you one?'

'Yes, please. If you don't mind.'

'I do not mind.'

He's a keeper, Gary Dettling.

Her phone beeped with seven missed calls; two from Gary, three from Robbie, two from Cliff. There were some 'Where r u?' texts thrown in too.

Shit.

She brought coffee back and set it on Everett's desk. 'Can I be so bold as to ask a favor?' she said.

'Sure,' said Everett, 'go ahead.'

'I'm working on the Laura Flynn case — the shooting of the pregnant woman outside

Conifer. Her employer is a multi-millionaire called Robert Prince. Investigators at the Sheriff's Office are on this, I know, but . . . if you got through Gary Dettling's net, I know you have to be good.' She paused. 'I was an anomaly.'

'I'm listening . . . '

'Could you look into Prince's financials for me, see if there's anything that might be amiss? He and his wife have been lie-telling and . . . I'm just not quite sure why.'

'But you think it might be financial?' said Everett.

'Not exactly,' said Ren. 'It's just, you know the way with a lot of wealthy people, the financial and personal are so tightly intertwined that an issue with one can completely unravel the other?'

'I have certainly seen that,' said Everett. 'I'll look into it . . . '

'On the down low,' said Ren.

'Yes, Tone.'

She smiled. 'I really appreciate it.'

When she got through her coffee, she was ready to call Gary.

'Hi, Gary, it's Ren — I'm sorry I missed your call earlier — '

'Not good enough,' said Gary.

'Sorry,' said Ren.

'What the hell were you doing?' said Gary.

'I completely forgot. I couldn't sleep in the middle of the night. I turned my phone off. I never do that.'

'That's not acceptable,' said Gary.

'I know. I'm sorry. It won't happen again. So

. . . Bandits: Welton Street first, Glendale, Englewood, Conifer, *then* Littleton?'

'Well, there's nothing to say they're working in a strict east/west order . . . ' said Gary.

'Anyone injured?' said Ren.

'One customer with a broken nose, smashed with the butt of the gun.'

'OK,' said Ren. 'Are you sure you don't need me there?'

'Yes,' said Gary. 'We've got it covered.'

'OK,' said Ren, 'well, I'll see you back at the ranch.' She put the phone down.

Everett looked up from his computer.

'You have not made your boss happy today . . . ' he said.

'I have not,' said Ren. *Boyfriend last night, boss today.*

'And I can't say I was too impressed with my coffee,' said Everett.

Ren smiled. 'OK . . . I really need to find something to redeem myself with this morning.'

★ ★ ★

Ren went into Gary's office when he got back.

'Just so you know, Janine and I will be going to The Darned Heart later to speak with Conor Gorman.'

Gary nodded.

'And I'm working my butt off on the bandits . . . ' *says Ren as an invisible tumbleweed rolls through the silence* . . . 'I'm just sorry about earlier.'

Gary nodded. He looked down at his desk.

'Ren,' he said, 'you might want to take a look at your shirt.'

She glanced down. Two buttons were gone from her gray shirt, showing most of her pink bra and the cleavage it was enthusiastically supporting.

Oh. Dear. God. 'Shit.'

So much for redeeming myself.

She closed the door behind her and ran to the ladies' room.

Please let there be another shirt here. Please.

She pulled open the door of her locker. There was a white shirt hanging in plastic.

Please let there be a nude bra here. Please.

She found one in a pile of other clothes.

Thank God, thank God.

★　★　★

She changed, then sat back down at her desk and texted Ben:

Stop ripping off my shirts . . .

Ben replied right away. It's my ™ move.

Glad to be one of the lucky ladies.

He texted back. The only lady.

Hmm.

Hide this jealous weirdness.

She texted back XX

29

Kristen Faule kept Ren and Janine waiting for over twenty minutes in the lobby of The Darned Heart. Eventually, a short, smiling blonde with legs like a wrestler appeared from behind the front desk and led them to the office. The introductions were awkward. Kristen sat at her desk with Ren and Janine on stiff wooden chairs facing her.

Pass to the comfortable sofas: revoked.

'I'll call Conor to the small meeting room when you're ready to speak with him,' said Kristen.

'Thank you,' said Ren.

Kristen clasped her hands and leaned toward them. 'You have to understand, we were under strict orders to keep Conor's presence here confidential. Our aim is very simply to help the teens who stay here. You know we're bound by confidentiality, and it's unfortunate under these circumstances, but I'm protecting the residents — not because they've committed a crime, but because they are in treatment. That's why they're here. They need time away from disruption and dysfunction.'

'It's not as straightforward as 'resident X didn't commit a crime',' said Ren. 'Resident X may have seen something that will help find the killer of a pregnant young woman. There are all kinds of possibilities. Conor got in a bar fight

— who knows what could have happened as a result of that? They could have found out where he was, decided to get their own back on him . . . This is our job, Mrs Faule. This is what we do best. We cast our net wide. And we need your help.'

'I want to help,' said Kristen. 'But you know my hands are tied . . . unless you have something more concrete.'

'Has Conor spoken to you about the death of his aunt?' said Janine.

'No,' said Kristen. 'He may have spoken to one of the counselors, but obviously, those conversations are strictly confidential.'

'Does Conor have any particular friends here at the ranch?' said Janine.

'We don't really encourage the kids to break away like that,' said Kristen. 'We like them to be supported in a group fashion. If they're branching off in ones or twos — '

'Mrs Faule, I get what you're saying,' said Ren, 'but I think we both know that it doesn't always go the way the grown-ups plan. These kids don't exactly have a good track record with rules. It would help if you could point us in the direction of someone who knew Conor a little better than the rest of you.'

'Excuse me,' said Kristen. 'I did nothing wrong. You know that the children who stay here are entitled to privacy. Unless you have a warrant, I can't do anything. I'm not trying to be difficult here. Please understand that — '

'I'm sorry, but I can't,' said Ren. 'I'm at a loss as to how, when something like this happens, you don't throw every single bit of information at me that you possibly can, just to help. You're a helper, Mrs Faule. That's why you chose to do something like this, right? That's why I chose to be an FBI agent. I love helping. So does Detective Hooks here. I'm having a hard time with all this . . . ' She shrugged. 'With your attitude . . . not to sound like a camp counselor about it. I'm repeating myself when I say how important your co-operation in this investigation is . . . '

'I really do understand that,' said Kristen.

'There's a killer who is still out there,' said Janine. She paused. 'Or in here.'

'Come on,' said Kristen. 'There is hardly — '

'You don't know that,' said Janine.

'And I am co-operating,' said Kristen. 'Like I said — it's down to confidentiality.' She let out a breath.

'Can I talk to you about your approach to rehab here?' said Ren. 'You use an outside facility, Wellness Partners, based at the Denver Tech Center?'

Kenneth Faule burst into the room, his arm outstretched. He paused mid-stride.

'Oh,' he said, looking at Janine and Ren. 'Welcome.'

'Thank you,' said Ren. *Welcome?*

Kenneth went to Kristen's desk and set a cell phone down on it. Kristen shook her head, weary. She took a sticker from a box in her letter tray and stuck it to the back of the phone. Kenneth wrote something on it, handed it back to her and she put it in a drawer.

'Cell phones are forbidden here for the teens,' said Kristen, 'but someone always gives it a try. They get it back on their way out the door. And it's not always the kids doing it. Sometimes it's the parents sneaking a phone to them, giving in to their demands. I wonder sometimes do the parents actually miss the disruption in their home? Is the silence too much for them . . . ?'

Or the lack of dramz.

'Sorry for interrupting,' said Kenneth. 'I'll let you get on with it.' He left.

'We were talking about rehab,' said Ren.

Kristen nodded. 'Yes, when we started out, running a rehab facility was not part of our plan. I didn't want to go down that route, I saw it as a very dark world that I knew nothing about. I hope that doesn't sound terrible. I saw the ranch as . . . I was naïve, I admit it . . . I saw the ranch as kind of a go-back-to-your-roots type of place, an innocent place. Of course, a lot of these kids have no such roots. And so many of them have addiction problems — illegal and prescription drugs. I never would have believed it was that bad. So, we outsourced the rehabilitation elements on a day basis. Kids who need that kind of care are brought there for a few hours every morning, then return here for the rest of their treatment.'

'What time are these sessions at?' said Ren.

'They leave at nine and usually get back between eleven thirty and twelve,' said Kristen. 'I spoke with Detective Kohler, so did our bus driver. They didn't see anything that day.'

'Do you have plans to introduce rehab

facilities here?' said Ren.

Kristen frowned. 'Well . . . yes,' she said.

Ren waited.

'Is that an issue?' said Kristen.

'No,' said Ren. *But I'm venturing you could do with the withdrawal of the long arm of the law.* She stood up and shook Kristen's hand. 'Thank you for your time.'

You strange, competitive, faux-serene oddball. What are you hiding?

'Let me take you to Conor,' said Kristen.

30

The meeting room smelled of fresh shower gel and toothpaste. Conor Gorman, his messy dark hair still wet, was sitting at the edge of the sofa, his knees wide, his forearms balanced on his thighs, his head bowed. He was dressed in black jeans, a gray T-shirt and scuffed black biker boots. He had the look of a wanderer, like someone who didn't belong, not just on a sofa covered with bright fleeces in the forced cheer of The Darned Heart Ranch, but on any sofa anywhere — because that's what ordinary people did. They sat on sofas and were ordinary. The only difference was that not many ordinary people had the small, quiet might of suited lawyer Christopher Bergin beside them. He stood up and shook hands with Ren and Janine.

It was only then that Conor looked up. He fixed first Ren, then Janine, with the palest blue eyes, stark under the thick lines of his eyebrows.

This is that dark Irish thing that women love.

He had just turned seventeen, but there was something magnetic about him that went beyond his years, something sorrowful that came from his core.

'I'm so sorry about your aunt,' said Ren.

He raised an eyebrow. He looked around as if he would find a punchline or a set of handcuffs.

'Thank you,' he said.

He stared down at the floor. The chain around

his neck hovered, drawing attention to its ugliness. The rest of his jewelry looked more his style: two twisted red ropes on one wrist, a black G-Shock watch on the other, a black and silver band on his right thumb. Ren could see how strange a fixture Conor Gorman would be in the Princes' lives, how he wouldn't blend in. He would be like a rubber mark on a marble floor.

'How are you holding up?' said Ren.

He shrugged.

'Is being here helpful?' said Ren.

He hesitated before he answered a tentative, 'No.'

'Then why are you here?' said Ren.

'To make the Princes happy . . . ' said Conor. 'They paid a lot of money for this, it's what Aunt Laura wanted . . . ' He shrugged again. 'I know I have issues . . . but . . . '

'Conor, can you tell me what happened the day that your Aunt Laura was murdered?' said Ren.

'I left the ranch — '

'Let's start with how your aunt came to be close by,' said Ren.

'She was coming to meet me,' said Conor. 'I had spoken with her on Saturday night.'

'How did she get a hold of you?' said Janine. 'Cell phones are forbidden at the ranch, right?'

'She called the front desk, pretended she was Ingrid Prince . . . she did a good Americany Swedish accent . . . ' He tried to smile, but the words had caught in his throat and he ended up fighting back tears.

'And why wouldn't Laura have just said who she was?' said Ren.

If she wasn't hiding something . . .

'I don't know,' said Conor. 'I asked her, but she just said she didn't want to get into it. She told me I was to meet her at twelve on Monday.'

'Did she say why?' said Ren.

'No,' said Conor, 'I said 'But I'm not allowed out of here — just come to the ranch.' She was like 'I won't make it by tomorrow, and then I'll have to wait until formal visits next Sunday. And I have to see you this week.' She said to meet by the little stand of dead trees on Stoney Pass Road . . . She'd seen them on Google Maps.'

I knew it!

'How did she sound to you on the phone?' said Ren.

Conor shrugged. 'Just . . . normal.'

'Anything else?' said Ren.

'No,' said Conor.

'Was Laura the type to hide her emotions?' said Ren. 'If she thought, for example, that telling you something might worry you.'

'Laura always looked out for people,' said Conor. He wiped away tears. 'This is so messed up . . . '

'Did she express any concerns about her pregnancy to you on the night she called?' said Ren.

'No — I had no idea she was pregnant.'

'Do you know the circumstances of the pregnancy?' said Ren.

'What do you mean?' said Conor.

'Did you know that Laura was acting as a

surrogate for the Princes?' said Ren.

His eyes went wide. 'No.'

'How do you feel about that?' said Ren.

He shrugged. 'Weird. I mean . . . in general. I guess I don't understand going through all that for someone else. Aunt Laura was a good person. She and Ingrid were close. And Robert . . . '

'And Robert what?' said Ren.

'Well . . . just I guess he gets people to do what he wants . . . '

'What do you mean by that?' said Ren.

'Just he's that kind of guy,' said Conor. 'He's a nice man, I guess, but he likes to be in control.'

Hmm.

'Do you like Robert?' said Ren.

A flicker of something crossed Conor's face. 'Yes.'

'You can be honest, here,' said Ren. 'You have to be honest . . . by law.'

He nodded. 'I did like him. I do like him. He can be intimidating, that's all. He's a rich guy . . . he's just different to regular people . . . '

'Different how?' said Ren.

'I don't know . . . '

'And how do you get along with Ingrid?' said Ren.

His face softened. 'Good. I like Ingrid.'

'And did you have a problem with her insisting you stay on at the ranch after your aunt's death?' said Ren.

'That was Robert,' he said.

'No — it was Ingrid,' said Ren.

Conor frowned. 'Who told you that? Robert?'

Ooh — you do not like that man.

'How did Robert get along with Laura?' said Ren.

'Good,' said Conor. 'They liked each other a lot. Aunt Laura's very smart; they had lots to talk about.'

'Did you ever get the sense there was anything more between them?' said Ren.

'No. No . . . no way.' He paused. 'But then, I've been away a lot . . . '

Ren nodded. 'OK, back to when you were meeting Laura.'

'I was coming from rehab that day,' said Conor. 'I forged a note from the Faules saying that I had chores at the abbey, so that the driver would let me out there. When he was gone, I walked to where I was to meet Aunt Laura . . . ' He stared at the ground, preparing for the next part. 'She was already dead.'

'I'm so sorry that you had to find your Aunt Laura — that you had to see her that way,' said Ren.

'That's . . . that's when I found out she was pregnant . . . '

Oh, dear God.

'That must have been a terrible shock,' said Ren. 'I'm so sorry.'

'What time was that at?' said Janine.

'It was about — I don't know — twelve thirty by the time I made it there?' said Conor. He was clenching his jaw. His knee started bouncing up and down. 'It was terrible.'

'What did you do?' said Janine.

'I freaked,' said Conor. 'As I was walking

214

toward the car, I could see this darkness on the windscreen. I thought it was shadows from the trees or something. It was . . . blood. I pulled open the driver's door. She was dead. I knew she was. But I pulled her back to just . . . to just make sure she was . . . to check that she definitely wasn't still breathing . . . but I knew, I knew . . . ' He welled up.

'It's OK,' said Ren. 'Take your time.'

'Then . . . I couldn't really move her back. And I was afraid I'd, you know, destroy evidence. I panicked. I ran back to the ranch.'

'And did you have blood on your clothes?' said Ren.

'Yes,' said Conor. 'I did.'

'What did you do with them?' said Ren.

'Put them in the garbage,' said Conor.

'Did anyone see you?' said Ren.

'I guess not,' said Conor.

'Did you sit inside the car?' said Ren.

'No,' said Conor.

'Are you sure about that?' said Ren.

He nodded. 'Yes.'

'Conor, we found your fingerprints on the dash on the passenger side of the car . . . '

He started to cry. 'I don't know,' he said. 'It's all a blur. I guess I sat inside. I don't want to think I did. The car was horrible.' He shook his head. 'I remember now. I . . . I wanted to get something to clean my hands. I was . . . covered in blood. I . . . thought there might be something in there . . . a cloth, whatever.'

'Did you find anything?' said Ren.

'No,' said Conor. 'No.' He rubbed his face.

215

'Conor, why didn't you tell the Faules about what happened?' said Ren. 'Or why didn't you call the authorities?'

He looked up at her, fear flickering in his eyes.

Ren thought of the ranch, the burnt-out car, the Faules' rehab facility plans, the murder of Laura Flynn, the terrible collision of circumstances that could destroy a business like The Darned Heart overnight.

Oh my God. Did you tell the Faules and they silenced you?

31

Conor Gorman shifted in his seat. 'I don't know why I didn't do anything,' he said. 'I was freaking out. I . . . she was dead. There was nothing anyone could do . . . I mean . . . I was covered in blood. What if someone thought I did it? I was . . . getting treatment for anger issues . . . I didn't think any of that would look good.'

They waited for him to continue. He didn't.

'You said earlier that you were aware of the possibility of destroying evidence,' said Ren, 'so you must know that as time passes, evidence is also compromised.'

'Yes,' said Conor. 'I wasn't thinking straight. I . . . just . . . I can't believe it now, even.'

'Do you know anything about the car that was burnt out at the ranch that morning?' said Ren. 'Someone made a call about it at twelve thirty p.m.'

'No,' said Conor. 'I heard afterwards, but just that it was an accident.'

'Conor, did you steal the car from the ranch to get to where you were meeting your aunt?' said Ren.

'No,' said Conor. 'I didn't. I told you. I got dropped off by the bus. You can ask the driver.'

'OK,' said Ren. 'Conor, can you talk to us about why you were sent to The Darned Heart in the first place? I'd like to hear your side of things.'

'I was causing trouble,' he said. 'The atmosphere had gotten really bad at home. I was convinced they were all, like, planning something or trying to get rid of me. I found out at rehab that that was probably because of all the dope I was smoking. It makes you think stuff like that. And I'd been doing a lot of it, and a lot more drinking, sneaking out, staying out late. I totally believed that Aunt Laura had regretted taking me in after my mom died and that I was embarrassing her, so by the time Robert was sending me here, I was kind of OK with it. Until I got here. I didn't like it. I tried to run, but Kenneth caught me before I even left the building. It didn't matter . . . I didn't want to be there, everyone knew it and, luckily, the Princes said I could come back and spend New Year with them and Laura in the Hamptons.'

'And when did you go back to the ranch again?' said Ren.

'A couple days after that . . . after I crashed Robert's car. It was bad. I knew I could have died. Aunt Laura begged me to sort myself out, told me she couldn't provide for us without her job, and that we were lucky to have the Princes and that I wasn't to do anything to rock the boat. Obviously, now I know she was pregnant by then too, so . . . it was probably even worse for her. I didn't want to mess things up . . . it was my mom's anniversary and it just hit me hard — she wouldn't have wanted this for me. There was no way that she did everything she did, worked so hard, to have a son who was a loser. Like, she

218

was doing all this for me, and then I grow up and be a druggie or a drunk? That was it for me. So I agreed to go to the ranch and to do my last semester there and stay through the summer.'

'Who chose The Darned Heart?' said Ren.

He shrugged. 'Robert, I guess. I mean, he was paying for it. They were able to get me a place quickly . . . I know there's a waiting list because it's so out of the way — it's not one of the famous ones that the paparazzi stalk. And the staff doesn't leak information. There are some seriously famous kids here.'

Ooh. Like who?

'Conor, if you were happy and ready to go back to the ranch right after New Year, why did you leave only a few days later?'

His eyes darted left and right. Short, sharp, didn't see the question coming.

'Uh . . . I just . . . wanted a drink,' said Conor. 'One more drink. It was dumb.'

'How did you get to Golden?' said Ren.

'I went through the abbey grounds, got a lift with some guy that was volunteering . . . '

'Do you have his name?' said Ren.

'No,' said Conor. 'I've no idea who he was.'

'That night, you got into a fight,' said Ren. 'What happened?'

'Just, I got really drunk, there were a bunch of students in there from the college, one of them was being an asshole and I lashed out, punched him in the face. It was just drunken stuff . . . The Sheriff's Office came, took me away. Then they called Ingrid, she came and picked me up. She brought me back to the ranch. She made me see

219

that that was the right thing to do.'

'The students you got in a fight with . . . were they local?' said Ren.

'Well, they were from the School of Mines,' said Conor, 'so I guess so.'

'Did they know where you were from?' said Ren.

'They guessed I was from New York,' said Conor, 'but they didn't know I was staying at the ranch.'

'And have you seen any of them since then?' said Ren.

'No,' said Conor. His eyes were fixed, again, on the floor. 'I know I've let myself down,' he said. 'I've let everyone down.'

'You made some mistakes,' said Ren. 'You know better now.'

He looked up. 'Thank you.'

Ren stood up. 'And thank you for your time. Mr Bergin, could I speak with you alone outside?'

'Sure, of course,' he said. He closed the door behind him.

'I'd like to ask you about a Cease and Desist you sent to a journalist in Butte, Montana, called Jonathan Black,' said Ren.

Bergin processed the information. 'Yes, he was about to write a defamatory article about the Prince family. I was instructed by my client to put a stop to that.'

'Were you aware that Jonathan Black died shortly after that?' said Ren.

'I was not,' said Bergin. 'What happened to him?'

'Officially, an accidental overdose.'

Bergin tilted his head. 'And do you have an unofficial theory?'

No, but I have a stare . . . a long meaningful one. 'No,' said Ren. She shook his hand. 'Thank you again.'

★   ★   ★

Janine and Ren walked to Ren's Jeep.

'Did you see what Kenneth Faule wrote on that sticker?' said Janine. 'I saw you writing.'

'I thought I was being subtle,' said Ren.

'To them, you were. You didn't write it until halfway through the conversation, and you wrote it up the side of the page.'

'How did you know that's what it was?' said Ren.

'Because it was a number that neither of them had just said. I knew that much.'

'It was 96226.'

'Are the kids inmates now?' said Janine. 'They just have numbers?'

'Well that kind of conflicts with the Faules' trusting ethos, doesn't it?' said Ren. 'Though it does tie in with the whole confidentiality thing.'

★   ★   ★

That night, Ren lay on Annie's sofa, curled into Ben Rader's arms, her back pushed up against his chest. The room was dark, except for the glow of dying candles on the stone hearth.

I don't want you to go.

He kissed the top of her head. 'Your hair smells like cloves.'

'Interestingly . . . so does my shampoo.'

He took her arm and held it up to his nose. 'Your arms smell like ginger.'

'I'm aiming to be fit for human consumption at all times.'

'You've hit your target.'

She laughed. She turned around to him. They kissed.

'I wish I didn't have to go,' he said.

Me too. 'At least we have tonight.'

He kissed her again. 'So, what are we going to do?'

'What do you mean?' said Ren.

'I mean, you and me, traveling between D.C. and here . . . '

Nothing? 'Traveling doesn't bother me,' said Ren. 'Does it bother you?'

'No, but . . . it's getting harder to leave you.'

Oh, God. 'Aw . . . '

'It's more than 'aw',' said Ben. 'I miss you when we're not together.'

I don't deserve you missing me like that.

'I miss you too,' said Ren.

'I hate going to bed without you.'

'Me too.'

I don't deserve any of this. Because I am lying to this man. I am lying and he is wonderful.

'Ben, I'm just going to come out and say this,' said Ren. 'I'm . . . I've got . . . well, it's like . . . '

I can't do it. I cannot bear saying this out loud. It hurts. It hurts. It hurts. Make it stop. Make it go away.

222

'You've got what?' said Ben. She could feel him feel the tears on her cheeks. He sat up. 'What is it?' He pulled her up to sit beside him. He had taken her hands in his before she even realized it and was drawing her into his arms.

'Ren, what is it, baby?' He held her head to his chest. He stroked her hair.

This man is a saint.

'Don't cry, honey. Please, what is it? Are you OK?'

No. I never was, and I never will be. Ben took his seat for The Sane Show. He doesn't need to see the coming attractions. It wasn't funny the first time. I laughed, but it wasn't funny. And this is not funny. This is real life. This man is a good man and I am a piece of shit. I can't do this to him. I can't not.

She looked up at him. 'I'm . . . bipolar.'

Dun. Dun. DUN.

32

Ren could feel Ben gripping her tighter.

Ugh.

As she blinked through her tears, she could see the corner of the Bryce family photo that Annie Lowell had so sweetly hung on the living room wall; Ren's mom, her dad, her brothers — Jay, Beau and Matt. And Ren, laughing, looking off to one side.

Let's rewind. I will turn out sane. Beau won't kill himself. Jay will be . . . not so 'Jay'. And Matt will carry on as he was always meant to be.

Ren realized Ben was talking. 'Baby, it's OK,' he was saying, as if she had just told him dinner was running late. 'It's OK,' he was saying again. 'Don't cry.'

This man is nuts.

Ren pulled away from him and stared at him. He was smiling.

That smile has no place in this conversation.

'But . . . it's really not OK,' said Ren.

'Honestly,' said Ben. 'I never would have guessed.'

No trace of sarcasm.

'You are the first person who has ever said that to me,' said Ren. 'Usually, I get 'I kind of figured there was something there . . . ''

Ben shrugged. 'Nope.'

'I feel bad,' said Ren, 'because I told Matt I didn't want to tell you because you had taken your seat for *The Sane Show*.'

'What — and you didn't want to ruin my entertainment?' said Ben.

'Worse,' said Ren. 'I was glad you weren't aware of the coming attractions.'

Ben laughed. 'That's funny, Ren. Don't feel bad. Are you feeling guilty about that?'

'Thanks,' said Ren. 'But you shouldn't be cool with this. I mean, I've been on mood stabilizers pretty much the entire time we've been together. Gary has enforced this. I have no choice — '

'So, if you had a choice, you wouldn't be on meds?' said Ben.

Lie! Lie! For the love of God, lie. 'If I had a choice, no I wouldn't be on meds,' said Ren. 'I'd be swinging from chandeliers nightly.'

'Well, I'd never stop you doing that,' said Ben.

What if I was swinging naked on a wrecking ball?

'Ben, maybe you don't know enough about the whole bipolar thing,' said Ren. 'Maybe you need to find out more . . . '

'Good idea!' said Ben. 'And I can buy a crystal ball, a deck of tarot cards, have my palm read, so that *all* the details of our future will be revealed, so that I can really *really* walk away with the full facts of how this nightmare of a life with you would have gone if I hadn't had such a lucky escape! Phew!'

Ren smiled. 'But I'm not sure you're really understanding — '

'You go crazy sometimes, you're miserable other times,' said Ben. 'Big deal. Aren't we all like that?'

Nooo. 'No,' said Ren. *Really. No. Not like this.*

'Ren, you be who you have to be; I'll be me, and we'll work out the rest when it shows up.'

The paranoia, the suspicion, the extra helpings of crazy . . .

'I'm good with this,' said Ben. 'Don't worry. This isn't a terminal illness diagnosis, this is manageable.'

Uh-oh.

'It *is* a nightmare of a life for the other person,' said Ren. 'I've been there.'

'Not with me you haven't,' said Ben. 'Not with me.'

* ★ *

Ren woke the next morning and looked at Ben, sleeping like he hadn't a worry in the world, as always.

I would love your gentle, untroubled-waters mind.

He rolled away from her.

If you have any sense, keep rolling.

She put her arms around him and kissed his back.

'That's nice,' he muttered.

'I better get to work . . . '

He turned around to her and opened his eyes. 'Come here,' he said, holding out his arms. Ren lay back down, warm and safe, until the alarm blasted again.

'I really better go,' said Ren, sitting up. 'See you next week?'

'Don't put a question mark at the end of that sentence,' said Ben. He pulled her back down and kissed her.

'OK,' said Ren. 'I won't.' She hugged him. 'Thanks . . . for being so wonderful.'

'No — you're wonderful,' he said. 'Just the way you are.'

I beg to differ.

★ ★ ★

The office was quiet when Ren arrived in. It was unchanged. The roof had not fallen in. There was paperwork to be done, phone calls to be made. Life would continue whether she had said something out loud the night before or not.

She bumped into Gary in the hallway. She was about to tell him about the visit to the ranch.

'Ren — go through everything on the robberies, OK? There might be something we missed.' He walked on.

Shit.

'Yes,' said Ren. 'OK.' She was calling out to his fast-departing back.

She went in to Cliff.

'Did you get security footage from the Littleton robbery?'

'We did,' he said.

'Can you email it to me?' she said.

'Sure. And, Ren — I spoke with the ME in Butte about the journalist OD. He says there was nothing there that gave him cause for concern. Heroin overdose in a shitty motel.'

'Really?' said Ren. 'Don't you think it's totally

227

weird he was about to run a damaging story about the Princes and he dies right beforehand? And he wasn't a known user?'

'It could just be a coincidence,' said Cliff.

'Hmm,' said Ren.

'Have you sunk your teeth into Robert Prince?' said Cliff.

'Maybe,' said Ren, 'but I haven't started shaking my head . . . '

'Yet,' said Cliff.

★　★　★

Ren sat back and watched the footage of the robbery. She studied the similar style, the customers dropping to the ground as the first robber jumped up on the counter and fired, the second guy going to the cashier, handing the note. Their faces were still completely concealed. There was something bothering her. She couldn't put her finger on it. She knew she was good with video. She could spot things.

She watched again.

She called up the Conifer video and watched that. There were six customers in the branch. One of them was wearing a large sun hat and sunglasses.

A disguise! Albeit a comedy disguise. A plant? Bring-Your-Mother-to-Work Day, concealed weapon in her muumuu?

Ren hit Pause. The woman was only barely in frame. But there was something about her . . .

Ren looked at the map; five strikes: Welton Street, Glendale, Englewood, Conifer, Littleton.

Conifer was an anomaly; they were still moving east/west as Gary had said, but Conifer was further into the mountains and Littleton was back to the flatlands.

Ren watched all the videos again. Then she looked at the still images taken. Something was strange. She looked at the Glendale photos. There was something off.

They're the wrong photos. They're not of the most recent robbery.

She searched in her computer. The photos she was looking at were of a 2010 robbery in Glendale. Someone had named the new set of photos too similarly. Problem solved.

She went back to her file on the Conifer robbery. She watched the video again. She did her first read-through of the witness statements. And she realized why that little old lady was familiar: it was Delores Ward. Cabin Lady.

Hmm . . . wasn't the abbey's money all controlled centrally by Eleanor Jensen?

33

Ren called Eleanor Jensen.

'Eleanor, you mentioned that you're in charge of the finances at the abbey, is that correct?' said Ren.

'Yes,' said Eleanor.

'And that your policy is, effectively, common ownership?' said Ren.

'In the most part, yes,' said Eleanor. 'For a lot of the women who come here, money, for different reasons, has become a problem for them: whether they needed it for drugs, stole it and got arrested; had a husband who controlled their finances; became corrupt in the pursuit of money . . . whatever the reason, to come here and have the worry of money taken away from them can be freeing. They have everything they need to eat and drink, to be comfortable. And they get real joy knowing that the money we make here is helping the underprivileged. And, here, everyone is in the same boat. Obviously, I'm in charge of the finances and they trust me with that. That's also important to me, because the women's ability to trust has been destroyed by their previous circumstances. They have a tentative start here, learning to trust again, whether that's me, the other women, anyone.'

'And Delores Ward, even though she lives out in that cabin . . . she is part of your community?' said Ren.

'Oh, absolutely,' said Eleanor.

'So, could she have her own bank account, for example?' said Ren.

'A bank account?' said Eleanor. She laughed. 'No. This is a woman who lives alone, has no internet access, no mode of transport. She doesn't even receive mail. She has no family. Some other members of the community may have bank accounts. It's not like we would stop them or monitor that.'

'Well, I'm looking down at a list of witnesses to the bank robbery in Conifer,' said Ren. 'On the same day as a murder. And her name is right here: Delores Ward. She told us she was in her cabin all day, apart from a trip to the chapel.'

'Yes — that's what I thought too,' said Eleanor. 'This is so strange. Honestly — Delores' day is a minimum twenty-one hours in that cabin with a few trips over and back to the chapel for prayer, but even that isn't a strict schedule. We deliver her meals to her, but she's always there to accept them, unless she's unwell. And if she's unwell, we take care of her in the abbey. The idea of her being off the property without my knowledge is . . . it would be a surprise.'

'The robbery was just before one p.m.,' said Ren, 'so she could have had time to get there and back.'

'But how?' said Eleanor.

'Well, could she have gotten one of the staff at the ranch to take her?' said Ren. 'Or one of the kids?'

'Maybe one of the staff, even though I don't

think she would,' said Eleanor. 'But certainly not one of the kids — I can't see her condoning that kind of behavior, even if it would benefit her.'

'I admit it does seem strange, but at the very least, she — and whoever was in the car with her — were likely to have driven by the scene of the shooting.'

'Oh my goodness, I didn't think of that,' said Eleanor.

'OK,' said Ren, 'well I need to speak with Delores again. It's important.'

'Yes, of course,' said Eleanor. 'She should be in her cabin . . .'

Ren put down the phone. Robbie had arrived while she had been talking to Eleanor.

'Cabin Lady was lie-telling!' she said. 'Everyone is lie-telling!'

'What?' said Robbie.

'Her name is on a list of witnesses in the Conifer robbery,' said Ren.

'I haven't even looked at those yet,' said Robbie.

'She was interviewed by one of Kohler's guys — she was one of the first to be interviewed — in an age-before-beauty kind of way — so she was gone before we arrived. And after that, we were all about the bandits.'

'Why would she lie about that?' said Robbie.

'And to your purty face,' said Ren.

'And yours!' said Robbie.

'We need to go and speak with her,' said Ren. 'She could have seen anything on that road home. And, apart from the audacious lying

— how the hell did she get to the bank and back?'

'Well, she sure suckered me,' said Robbie.

'And to think we were going to sleep on her sofa . . . '

★ ★ ★

Ren knocked on Delores' cabin door and held her badge up to the small window when her face appeared. Delores struggled with the latch before it opened.

'Come on in,' she said.

I wonder have you been tipped off by Eleanor.

'We're here about a different matter today,' said Robbie. 'We just read that you're on the witness list for the bank robbery in Conifer on May 14th. You never mentioned that.'

'Did you think that was important?' she said. Her voice sounded shaky.

'Well, it could be . . . ' said Robbie.

'But . . . you really only asked me about the car at the ranch,' said Delores. 'And I said that I heard voices some time between ten and noon, which is true.'

'And then you said you went to the chapel . . . ' said Ren.

'Yes, and I went to the bank after that,' said Delores. 'Were you interested in that timeframe too? You said midday . . . '

I cannot look at Robbie because I will see the same feelings of idiocy in his eyes.

'So, how long have you been banking in Wells Fargo in Conifer?' said Ren.

'Is this relevant?' said Delores.

Shit.

'Well, no,' said Ren.

'Because, I'm not your bandit,' she smiled. 'And you read my statement. I told the Jefferson County Sheriff's Office detective everything I saw, which was pretty much nothing, because I dropped straight to the floor . . . well, as straight as an eighty-year-old woman can.'

How come you have a bank account is what I want to ask you.

'How did you get to the bank that day?' said Ren.

'I hitched a ride with one of the gentlemen from the landscaping firm,' said Delores. 'I don't know his name, but Eleanor will have the details.'

'And did he bring you back from Conifer?' said Ren.

'No, I came back with Burt Kendall . . . he owns the Auto Sales and Auto Parts store. He's very good to us at the abbey.'

'And did you go all the way down Stoney Pass Road?' said Ren.

'No,' said Delores. 'We took the first right. From what I heard, the young lady's . . . death . . . would have happened further down the road.'

'That's correct,' said Ren. 'I forgot to ask — on the day of the shooting — did you pass any other cars on the road?'

'No,' said Delores.

Everyone turned as one of the postcards slid from the wall, landing picture-side down at

234

Delores' feet. Ren bent down and picked it up. Delores' arm shot out. Ren stalled, quickly glancing down, scanning it. It was addressed to Delores Ward at the abbey. All it said was *Having the time of our lives! Love, Teddy and Thomas.* Ren turned it over. It was a faded, dated image of Huntsville, Texas.

Fun and games and death row.

'Do you want me to pin it back up?' said Ren.

Delores nodded. 'Yes. Gee, that must be twenty years old now . . . sons of one of the women who used to stay here. Sweet, sweet boys.'

'It's nice that they thought of you,' said Ren.

'It sure is,' said Delores. 'I'm sorry for the confusion I seem to have caused about the day of the robbery. I do recall answering all your questions, but they were all focused on the burning car. On the subject of the robbery, because you said you were working with the Sheriff's Office, I assumed that all your records were together. And on a day like that, certainly, that it would be even more important that everything was linked in a way that would help you all carry out your investigation in the most convenient and practical way.'

BURN.

★ ★ ★

Ren and Robbie walked away from the cabin.

'Fail,' said Ren.

'Yes,' said Robbie.

'She was a little jumpy about the postcard,'

235

said Ren. 'Maybe some of them have contents of a 'personal' nature.'

'Doesn't bear thinking about,' said Robbie.

'What made me laugh,' said Ren, 'was her saying that Burt Kendall was good to them. I noticed a big fat Kendall's sticker along the windscreen of that fresh-from-the-box minibus that the abbey ladies were cruising around in. He had about fifty thousand reasons to be nice to them.' She paused. 'Though, they probably buy a bus about once every thirty years.'

Robbie smiled. Ren took out her phone. She had one bar. She Googled Kendall's. The company appeared across a range of auto and transport sites. She clicked on an article from the *Conifer Courier*. There was a photo of Evergreen Abbey's bus and, standing in front of it, Burt Kendall shaking hands with Eleanor Jensen.

'I stand corrected,' said Ren. 'Kendall donated the bus to the abbey. I am a bad person. I am not charitable.'

Her phone beeped with a text from Janine.

Update with Kohler at 3 if you're free . . .

Ren showed Robbie the text.

'Do we qualify as free while our bandits are still on the loose?' said Robbie.

'Like, what would Gary do?' said Ren.

'Let's face it — it's more a question of 'What would Ren do?' . . . despite what Gary would do . . . '

34

Janine was winding up a call when Robbie and Ren arrived into her office.

'Well, that wasn't great news,' she said. 'That was my guy in New York about the Viggi Leinster and Angelo Marianelli case. He says that the detectives who took the original statements were rookies . . . one of them was shot dead in the line of duty within six months, the other quit the force shortly afterwards. The sergeant in charge of the case was promoted a year later to lieutenant, but was eventually jailed for corruption a few months shy of his retirement.'

'Noo . . . that does not sound great,' said Ren.

'So, as to why there were not more statements from the fancy guests, it could be down to rookie errors, intimidation, bribes . . . the list is endless.'

'And if the Vescovis wanted less hassle with their business,' said Ren, 'they may have been very happy to go along with whoever was paying cash for silence.'

'So,' said Janine, 'we know Mr Vescovi is dead and his wife is still alive. One fresh piece of information is that they have a daughter. Her name is Carolina. She would have been eight in 1957. Apparently she went off the rails young, got into alcohol, drugs, disappeared off to Florida . . . she's been estranged from the family for years.'

'Any Laura Flynn link?' said Ren.

'No,' said Janine. 'I should have just opened with that . . . '

'Or kept it as a cliffhanger,' said Ren. 'I could ask Eli Baer to see if he can get anything on the daughter?'

'Sure, go ahead,' said Janine. 'I'll do the same. Many hands . . . '

★　★　★

Kohler's briefing kicked off at three fifteen.

'Gentleladies and gentlemen,' he said. 'Here is your lowdown on our most recent developments on the Laura Flynn investigation. Still no trace of the weapon. The phone dump from Laura Flynn's phone hasn't thrown up anything unusual. The same goes for the Princes. They both tried her cell phone on Sunday night and Monday morning, neither got through. There are no records of anyone being admitted to hospital on May 14th with gunshot wounds or with burns that might have come from either the vehicle used in the robbery or the one at the ranch. We tracked down Laura Flynn's ex-boyfriend, Johnny Lynch, who has been living in Argentina for the past year, so he's out of the picture.'

Ren put up her hand. 'Did you guys take a statement from Burt Kendall from Kendall's Auto Sales?'

'I did,' said Logan.

'Could you just double-check what he said about bringing Delores Ward back from Conifer

238

the day of the robbery?' said Ren.

'What are you thinking?' said Kohler.

'Nothing in particular — I just wanted confirmation and to make sure he didn't see anything on the road.'

Kohler nodded. 'Well, I can tell you one piece of news about Kendall, for what it's worth — he's just filed for bankruptcy.'

'What?' said Ren. 'I read this morning that he donated a bus to Evergreen Abbey only last month.'

'Really?' said Kohler. 'I'm not sure about that.'

'Check it out,' said Ren. 'It was in the *Conifer Courier*. Eleanor Jensen was right there in the photo shaking his hand. Who donates a fifty-thousand-dollar bus when their business is about to go under?'

'So maybe he did torch the car for insurance,' said Janine.

'He's got an alibi for that morning,' said Logan. 'He was in Conifer from ten a.m. until two p.m. — there are multiple witnesses.'

'And two p.m. was when he gave Delores Ward a ride back to her cabin at the abbey,' said Ren.

'Strange that he didn't mention that part to me,' said Logan.

'Well, regardless of where he was, he could have gotten someone else to take care of the arson job,' said Janine.

'Some employees, maybe,' said Logan. 'A little overtime . . . '

'He's certainly got no problem hiring a loser or two,' said Kohler, 'but nothing came up on any of them. Or on any of the construction crew at the site. His sales staff are also clear. We'll keep looking.'

★ ★ ★

Ren and Robbie arrived back at Safe Streets just before six and filled everyone in on the briefing. Ren grabbed a bottle of water and settled at her desk. Her phone beeped with a text.

Home safe. Can't wait to see you next week . . . x

She smiled.

Me too. Sorry you're doing all the traveling . . .

He texted back:

Physically. You get the Ramblin' Mind . . . ;-)

Nick Cave. The Jeffrey Lee Pierce Sessions Project. She loved his taste in music.
She texted back a smile.
'Just a thought,' said Cliff. 'Does Kendall supply any cars for use at the ranch? Like the bus to the rehab?'
'Oh, Lord no,' said Ren. 'They have a little fleet of executive vans. So strange, these cars — the promise of fancy on the outside, while inside lies the sad and shabby reality of kids on their way to rehab.'
'Where do they go?' said Cliff.
'Wellness Partners at the Denver Tech Center,' said Ren.

240

'Great location,' said Cliff. 'I guess these rich kids can fly into Centennial on their private jets, get hustled into rehab under cover of darkness . . . or driven to The Darned Heart. That's what — a forty-minute drive?'

Ren shifted forward in her seat. 'Hold up,' she said. 'Something is rollerskating around the edge of my consciousness. And it's picking up speed. What is it, what is it?' She paused. 'Robbie!' She turned to him. 'The day after the murder, when we came to the ranch to speak with Kristen Faule. Do you have the photos you took?'

'Yes,' said Robbie. He slid his iPad from the bottom drawer of his desk. 'Why?'

'Do you remember the jizz car?' said Ren.

'Jizz car . . . ' said Cliff. 'Do I want to know?'

Robbie opened his photo gallery.

'Look!' said Ren. 'There it is! That spatter across the car . . . ' She paused. 'Pale pink.'

'Now I'm totally disturbed,' said Cliff.

'What is it?' said Robbie.

'It's strawberry milkshake,' said Ren. 'Evangelists and strawberry milkshakes. Go to YouTube: Howard Coombes, Centennial Airport.'

They all watched the video of Howard Coombes' radio interview outside Centennial Airport. Ren paused when the milkshake struck. It spattered behind Coombes onto the car.

'I was wondering why Coombes didn't fly into Denver,' said Ren, 'and I was wondering what the hell he was doing butting into Colorado business. I think he was here for another reason, and he was using his various appearances as a cover.' She paused. 'Google Image his family.'

241

There were lots of individual shots of Howard Coombes, and some with him and his wife. There were many more photos of the second most famous member of the family — child evangelist Jesse Coombes in his early years, dressed in his perfect little suits, or shirts and ties, standing in front of crowds in the tens of thousands, holding a microphone the size of his head.

The most recent photos of the entire Coombes family together were three years old. Ren studied them carefully.

I knew that boy was familiar . . .

'Everyone, I believe — I beLIEVE! — we have a mini-me-vangelist in our dirty midst!' said Ren. 'Looks like Howard Coombes' son, Jesse, is a 'guest' at The Darned Heart Ranch. We met while I was pretending to be a smoker . . . and he was pretending to be a counselor.'

Cliff leaned back in his chair. 'Well, how the mighty . . . tween . . . has fallen . . . How old is he now?'

'Sixteen,' said Ren. 'But he'd stopped preaching at about twelve . . . right before his father's sex scandal blew up. Can you imagine? You get put into regular school for some attempt at a normal life and this shit hits the fan. There was definitely some other fucked-up story about the Coombes,' she said. 'I just can't remember what it was or where I heard it . . .'

'It needs to pick up speed in the roller derby,' said Cliff.

'You said it,' said Ren. She was typing as she spoke.

'Where do they live, the Coombes?' said Cliff.

'California now. Dallas, back then,' said Ren.

She called up Jesse Coombes' preaching videos on YouTube. She stuck in her earphones. She remembered a documentary she had seen on him and how the female interviewer had been kind to him, but whenever the opportunity arose, had asked him about his childhood, whether he felt he was missing out, and each time he deflected. It was an extraordinary display of wits for a child so young. Ren scrolled along to the final few minutes of the documentary.

'Do you think you have missed out on a 'normal' childhood?' the interviewer was saying.

'No, ma'am,' said Jesse, 'but I do believe that there are millions of children all across the world who are. They are missing out on the childhood that the Lord wants them to have because they have not become familiar with His word. I wake up every morning with God by my side, I go to sleep every night the same. Sometimes, if it's a hot night and the air is very still, but then, suddenly, I feel a soothing breeze at my ear, I know that that is the Lord's breath. The Lord is speaking to me. And He is speaking to everyone through the scriptures. I have a childhood that is better than 'normal'. I am never lonely. I am never without His wisdom. I can open my Bible on any page and I will receive answers to my problems.'

'And Jesse, you are six years old,' said the interviewer, 'would you mind telling the viewers what kind of problems you might seek guidance for . . . ?'

'Why, Lord Jesus, I might say, *why* are sinners so blind to your light? Why, when they can see all around them all that is good, all that you have created, how can they spite you with their adultery, their fornication?'

The interviewer looked almost frozen. She couldn't ask what she wanted to ask. Instead, she just said, 'Well, thank you, Jesse, for talking to us.'

Annd thank you for the ratings.

Ren pulled out the earphones.

She did another search and found one of Jesse's more popular videos: Jesse Coombes, Austin, pink dress girl.

'Gentlemen,' said Ren to everyone. 'Gather round for a flavor of the madness. This is Jesse Coombes at the height of his fame.'

She turned her computer screen to the rest of the office, shifted her seat so she could watch too and hit Play.

In the video, Jesse Coombes was no more than ten years old, dressed in neat navy-blue pants, a white shirt and a gold-and-blue striped neck-tie. This time he had a headworn microphone. In the audience stood a girl of a similar age, looking at him adoringly, entranced, doing everything he was asking the crowd to do — clap, cry out, turn to the person beside them. The video cut to the girl at the end, when Jesse was meeting people. Her mother was behind her, pushing her toward him, like she was offering her as a sacrifice. Jesse Coombes' eyes were glazed.

'He has fans,' said Ren. 'He has mothers wanting to marry off their daughters to him.

Mothers who are waiting until he grows up and is old enough to date. Creepsville.'

The comments below the video ran the full length of the spectrum.

'I was lucky enough to see Jesse Coombes . . .'

'Dude, that is some messed-up shit . . .'

'Everyone KNOWS you like the flames.'

'Creeeeepy . . .'

'So moving . . .'

'His message is true to this day . . .'

Lunacy is, indeed, in the eye of the beholder.

35

Gary leaned into the bullpen and called Ren out.

'OK — what the hell?' he said. 'You're on YouTube, when you should be — '

'It's not like I'm watching cat videos,' said Ren. 'It's Laura Flynn. Howard Coombes, the evangelist — his son is staying at The Darned Heart.'

'So?' said Gary.

'There's something weird about the kid,' said Ren. 'I remember hearing a story . . . oh . . . *now* I remember . . . from a cop at a conference in Austin. It was a late night . . . I can't remember the details . . . or the cop.'

Gary stared at her. 'Quick . . . get the AUSA on the line.'

Funny.

'The Laura Flynn case is not ours,' said Gary. 'And you know that no one is going to get near the son of Howard Coombes.'

'I know that we're not running the show,' said Ren. 'But — '

'Ren of the 'I know, buts'.'

'I know — ' *Stop.*

'You're too involved,' said Gary. 'Focus on the bandits. I want them shut down.'

And I want you to shut the fuck UP. 'OK,' said Ren.

'And don't forget your appointment next week with — '

Yes, trust me, Gary. Trust me to take care of the appointment . . . that I had completely forgotten about.

'I won't,' said Ren. She walked back into the bullpen, her blood pressure soaring.

She sat down at her desk and opened the bandits file. She spent two hours with it, stopping only to put in eye drops. She went back to it again for another hour.

Bullet/brain. Hot needles/eyes.

★ ★ ★

Ren watched the surveillance footage of the Conifer robbery again. And again. Everett brought her coffee and a custard Danish. She wanted to cry. She kept watching the screen.

Bingo.

She stood up from her desk. 'I've got it! I've got it!' *Ha, Gary!*

'Got what?' said Cliff.

Ren called Gary. 'Can you come in here?' she said.

'Is it urgent?'

'Yes.' *Thank you very much.*

'Based on my exhaustive research,' Ren announced, 'I can tell you with no small amount of authority that Conifer was not the Shark Bait Bandits. It was a copycat robbery.'

Cliff did one of his signature moves: forearms on the desk, chair wheeled closer.

'I'm provisionally suggesting the Copier Bandits,' said Ren. 'Though, we may never encounter them again . . . it was probably a one-off.'

'Go ahead,' said Gary. He had his hands on his hips.

'Exhibit A was an admin error on our part,' said Ren. 'Some of the Glendale photos on our site were from an old robbery in 2010. The photos had similar titles, so don't go killing whoever did this. It was an easy mistake to make. And, hey, if they hadn't made it, I wouldn't have been so enlightened.

'So, where you see this guy in the video clearly wearing one of those big green plastic watches, that was not part of our Shark Bait Bandits' kit. So, whoever did the Conifer robbery got a bum steer when they researched the Shark Bait Bandits. I get why they chose them — their masks almost completely obscure their faces, and they're easy to find in stores. One small detail, though, is that in the Aurora robbery, they're the original brand. Our Conifer bandits are wearing knock-offs; they're a fraction of the price.'

'So, the Shark Bait Bandits are slightly less desperate for cash . . . ' said Cliff.

Ren laughed. 'Exhibit B is that this dude's belly is fake.' She pointed to the guy in Conifer standing on the counter holding up the AK-47. 'Because I've had fake, folding baby bumps on my mind recently, I looked back over this. There's a moment here where the butt of the rifle sticks into his belly and it makes an indentation; a squishy-looking one. Our guy has a pillow up there, or padding of some kind, because he wants to look like our Shark Bait guy, who — you can see in the original videos — has a very real belly, because in one of them, it's peeping out from under his shirt. Also, when our fake guy jumps down from the counter, you can see the belly fold.

'My theory,' said Ren, 'is that the Conifer robbery was carried out by a couple of locals. Psychologically, they're choosing their comfort zone because they're amateurs, but they're also trying to attach it to an outside gang they hope will never be caught.'

'So we're throwing Conifer back to JeffCo,' said Gary.

'Yup,' said Ren.

'Good work,' said Gary. 'Now, all we need to do is catch the real Shark Bait Bandits . . . '

Silent scream.

Ren called Janine when Gary left. 'Hey there,' she said. 'I'm throwing a case in yo' face.'

'Have we moved on to rap?' said Janine.

'No, I'm staying country,' said Ren. 'But Safe Streets is passing the Conifer robbery back to you. We think it's a copycat.'

'Really?' said Janine.

'Yes,' said Ren. She explained the details.

'Well, done, lady,' said Janine.

'Now, gather round,' said Ren, 'and I'll tell you the tale of the evangelist and The Darned Heart . . . '

36

Days passed with no new information on bandits, genuine or tribute. The Flynn case hovered, waiting for direction. Ren arrived at Safe Streets on an empty, tight stomach after a poor night's sleep, filled with scattered, panicked thoughts.

Stand back, people. Do not approach the beast.

'Good morning, Ren!' said Everett.

She smiled. *OK, that helps. Enforced interaction with kind humans.*

'I can see it,' he said. 'The lack-of-caffeine-thousand-yard stare . . . '

'Visible only to those similarly afflicted,' said Ren.

'Allow me to take care of it.'

'God bless you, Everett.'

Everett dropped the coffee to Ren's desk within ten minutes. 'Is it safe?' he said.

'What do you mean?' said Ren. *Irritated. Why am I irritated?*

'To talk you through what I have before you've finished your coffee?'

'No — it's perilous,' said Ren. 'Give me fifteen minutes to find the way to my human side . . . or work out how to mimic yours.'

'OK,' said Everett.

'Thanks for asking, though.' *And not drowning me in information when I'm delicate.*

Everett came back when she was finished.

'OK,' he said. 'You were talking about the Denver Tech Center a few days ago. Well, Robert Prince has interests there.'

'No way,' said Ren.

'Two things,' said Everett. 'One is a charity called ACORA.'

'I know that name,' said Ren.

'Yes,' said Everett.

'Pause and reflect,' said Ren. 'It's Robert Prince's mother's name! Acora Prince.'

'Correct,' said Everett.

'Anyone else involved in this charity?' said Ren.

'Yes . . . all six of the board members attended the same private school as Robert Prince — Harmon's. This is some interesting network.'

'He likes networks,' said Ren. 'Why does he need a charity when that Catholic organization he's in is all about giving?'

'The OCBLA is not all about giving,' said Everett. 'They're all about earning billions and influencing the government.'

'You know what I mean,' said Ren.

'The second organization is an energy company called NOVA,' said Everett. 'It's very strange. Just to give you the background: when Robert Prince's mother, Acora, died in 2001, she left Robert, among other things, a tract of land in North Dakota: five hundred acres in the Williston Basin. Her father, Walter Prince, had bought this land back in '53.' He paused. 'What do you know about fracking?'

'That it wasn't invented in 1953 . . . ' said Ren.

Everett smiled. 'Exactly. Walter Prince either knew the people involved in the Bakken Shale discovery or he got a lucky break, but either way, he bought himself five hundred prime acres. Like you said, fracking wasn't invented; a few years passed, no one was any closer to extracting the oil, so Walter Prince leased the land to a rancher and got a steady income from it. Cut to 2004 and the technology's been developed to access the oil reserves. When the oil companies come in and start throwing money at North Dakota landowners, Robert Prince, owner of said five hundred acres, is very excited. He's already a wealthy man, but, as we know, the bulk of it was inherited. He is keen on making his own money by setting up his own energy company, but to his great embarrassment, he discovers that he doesn't own the mineral rights. He had just assumed he did; his father was in mining — why would he buy land without the mineral rights? Those mineral rights, instead, are owned by the federal government. So, basically, Robert Prince loses out on millions and millions of dollars . . . '

'Yeah . . . fuck his life . . . ' said Ren.

'I know, right?' said Everett.

'So, why did he set up his own energy company without owning the mineral rights to the land?' said Ren. 'I don't get it.'

'He could be planning to buy other people's mineral rights,' said Everett. 'Apparently the oil and natural reserves there were massively underrated. There's a lot of money to be made.'

'This DTC thing is weird,' said Ren. 'There's Wellness Partners — The Darned Heart's rehab facility, along with Robert Prince's energy company and charity. Could you check if there's some connection between Robert Prince and the ranch that we don't know about, something financial . . . nothing to do with Conor Gorman staying there. Isn't it all a little cozy? The Princes, the rehab, the ranch . . . could Laura Flynn have stumbled across something that everyone is happy to collude in covering up?' She paused. 'Does Robert Prince by any chance own that rehab facility?'

'No, he doesn't,' said Everett. 'I checked that. But sit tight. Don't approach him with this yet. There is more digging to be done.'

'Thank you for all this,' said Ren. *I like your style.*

Ren's phone rang. It was Janine. She listened as Ren went through what Everett had found on Robert Prince's finances.

'My bombshell is bigger than yours,' said Janine.

'No competitions,' said Ren. 'Ever. I told you . . . '

'I just got off the phone from Barry Tolman,' said Janine. 'He has the DNA results on million-dollar baby Flynn/Prince.'

'And?'

'In words borrowed from Maury Povich, Jerry Springer, and co.: 'Robert Prince, you are not the father.''

'What the what?' said Ren.

'He's not a match,' said Janine. 'It's Ingrid Prince plus A.N. Other.'

37

Ren slapped the desk. 'You are shitting me. What the fuck? How does that work? How could he just let me take a swab like that?'

'Mix-up at the fertility clinic?' said Janine. 'Maybe this will be news to him too.'

'In that case we may just have found our motive . . . ' said Ren. 'The baby was the target.'

'If the Princes found out that the lab had screwed up and the baby was not Robert's, they could have wanted to end the pregnancy.'

'They could have told Laura Flynn about the mistake, they could have asked her to have a termination . . . ' said Ren. 'Maybe that was why she was researching on the neighbor's computer.'

'And she could have run away if that's not what she wanted,' said Janine.

'There's another possibility here,' said Ren. 'What if there was a fertility problem with Robert Prince, but he didn't want to admit that to his wife? He pays off the lab, they take care of the rest.'

'Hmm,' said Janine. 'What if he wanted to leave his wife? If there's no pre-nup, the baby would be the only thing tying them together . . . '

'If he really is a staunch Catholic, he won't believe in divorce, so it's very likely he didn't have a pre-nup,' said Ren. 'Wow, if you really wanted to excel at gold-digging, make sure your target is anti-divorce.'

'He could have met someone new,' said Janine.

'If it's a straightforward case of the lab screwing up,' said Ren, 'could Laura Flynn have found out in some way without the Princes knowing?'

'Maybe,' said Janine. 'Could that happen?'

'What if the lab realized their mistake and approached Laura to cover it up, tried to pay her off, instead of having to face Robert Prince? Maybe she didn't agree. Maybe they were never going to tell anyone. Maybe someone was hired to drive her off the road, make it look like an accident. It didn't work, so they were forced to do something else.'

'If Laura Flynn had died in an accident, or even if she had survived, but lost the baby,' said Janine, 'the lab's mistake would never have come to light — it would have been unlikely that any testing would have been done on the fetus.'

'The fertility industry is big business,' said Ren. 'The clinic that did this would have had a lot to lose by this going public. Can you imagine? If they can't get it right for a high-profile couple like the Princes, how is a regular couple — who've used all their life savings or remortgaged their home — going to stand a chance?'

'What if Robert Prince *was* told, then he told Laura, but she wanted to keep the baby?' She paused. 'Then what about the internet search into abortion clinics? Unless that was him . . . but I'm not really feeling that.'

'How will we work this?' said Janine.

'I'm going to arm myself with some religious

research and give that lying man a call,' said Ren.

'Speaking of religion . . . I have an interesting one for you. You know I watched those Jesse Coombes videos. Remember the comment about the flames underneath one of them? Her username was *worriedmom354*.'

'I love the insight the numerics brings,' said Ren. 'We know that there is a minimum 354 worried moms out there. Who knows how many more? 'We are now boarding Worried Moms 294 through 327' . . . Yes, though, sorry . . . what about her?'

'I did a couple more searches and she's shown up on other sites,' said Janine. 'And commented on the Coombes again too; none of them favorable. She's from Texas. She seems to know them personally. There's nothing specific enough that will get our bosses to put us on a flight there, but I've emailed you her details — maybe you can get someone from the Dallas field office to go talk to her. Her name is Terry Ragland, she's a nurse, doesn't seem too crazy, but definitely has an issue with the Coombes. Her posts about them specifically start about two years ago. Her most recent one was last week. The stand-out phrase for me was 'deviant fire-starting sociopath'.'

Ren got off the phone and looked up the Dallas field office. She got an email address for one of the Assistant Special Agents in Charge and forwarded Terry Ragland's postings and contact details.

★ ★ ★

Ren spent the next half hour researching the Catholic Church's teachings on surrogacy, before she called Robert Prince.

Holy shit do I have some shocks for you, Robert Prince.

He picked up immediately. 'Agent Bryce,' he said.

'Hello, Mr Prince, I would like to set up a meeting.'

'I'm flying into Denver in the morning,' said Robert. 'We can meet then. But I don't want anyone else present. I presume this is about the results of the paternity test . . . '

38

Ren stood in front of the mirror in the ladies' room in Safe Streets, dressed in a fitted silvery gray cotton shirt, navy-blue pants and belt, and navy-blue patent high heels. She powdered her face.

There's only one way I plan on shining this morning.

By whupping Robert Prince.

She grabbed a fistful of hair and turned to the side.

Hair up or down? Up or down? What do misogynists take more seriously? When a woman spends an extra five minutes pinning her hair up to look less whorish? Or when a woman is too busy cleaning the house and baking cookies to even consider her appearance?

Ooh.

Be fair to this man . . .

. . . who is a dickhead.

Stop.

Be fair.

Ren twisted and pinned her hair into a tidy knot at the base of her neck and walked down the hallway to the conference room. She stopped dead when she saw Gary Dettling standing inside with Robert Prince, both of them laughing, neither of them aware of her presence.

WTF?

Ren stood, watching, as the laughter stopped

and they both turned serious. Gary was nodding intently. He shook Robert Prince's hand and left. Ren stepped back into the shadows before he had a chance to see her.

What was that all about?

Ren went to Gary's office and knocked on the door.

'Hi,' she said, sticking her head in. 'Just checking is there anything I need to know about Robert Prince before I go in there?'

Gary put down his pen and looked up at her. 'In what sense?'

'In the sense of you laughing and joking with him in the conference room just now . . . '

Gary looked at her with great patience. 'Don't hate the player . . . '

'So that's all that was . . . '

'Yes, Ren,' said Gary. 'You do remember that I got a call on day one to hover around this bullshit because he's an important man. But you and I both know that important men are behind some of life's shittier events. So though I'm laughing, and hand-shaking — '

'Deep inside you're blue?'

'Yes,' said Gary. 'If you set aside your suspicion of Robert Prince, and imagine him as a victim in all this, you would see him as someone who has lost his child, along with an employee/family friend, and it is perfectly reasonable for him to ask for an update on the investigation. My interaction with him was carried out with an open mind and a keen eye on what I have to do to keep my superiors happy.' He paused. 'You should try it . . . '

Ren smiled. 'Will do. Sorry.'

★ ★ ★

Robert Prince stood up as Ren walked in.

'Good morning, Mr Prince,' she said. She shook his hand and sat down.

'Good morning,' said Robert.

'Why didn't you come to me earlier about this?' said Ren. 'When I took the swabs.'

'Why would I do that?' said Robert.

Liars often reply to a question with a question.

'To assist right away with the investigation,' said Ren. 'This is a significant development.'

'It's not a 'development',' said Robert. 'It's a simple fact.'

'You're a smart man,' said Ren. 'You know it's not that simple. You have told an extraordinary lie to the surrogate who was carrying *your* baby — both now murder victims — and to the mother of that baby — *your* wife. That's no small lie. It's lying on a grand scale. These women made huge life decisions based on false information. How is it possible that you can't see the repercussions that could have?'

'I can see that,' said Robert. 'But I know that neither of them knew.'

'Really?' said Ren. 'You really think you can be absolutely sure that your wife hadn't found out about this?'

'What is the scenario you have in mind?' said Robert. 'That my wife became aware of this and . . . what? Killed her unborn child and the woman who was bearing it? Don't be ridiculous.

260

Ingrid wouldn't hurt a fly. You've met her. I'm sure that it's as obvious to you as it is to everyone else. Ingrid is gentle, she's kind, she's . . . '

Trusting? Easily manipulated? Malleable? Easy to lie to? Which is it?

'She's?' said Ren.

'She doesn't deserve any of this,' said Robert. 'She just doesn't deserve this pain. And I hope you're not going to make it any worse for her.'

'Me?' said Ren.

'The FBI, the Sheriff's Office . . . ' He leaned forward. 'Let me explain. Ten years ago, I had a vasectomy.'

'Were you trying to buy time by not telling us this right away?' said Ren.

'Excuse me?' said Robert.

'Were you trying to buy time?' said Ren. 'It's been — what — nearly two weeks since I took the swabs? Did you need that time for some reason?'

'Why would I need time?' said Robert.

'You knew we would find out,' said Ren.

'I'm telling you now, am I not?' said Robert. 'To get back to what I was saying . . . ten years ago was the height of the 'Robert Prince, what a catch' nonsense in the media. I was a wealthy man, the perfect target for a gold-digger. At that time, I chose to protect myself by having a vasectomy. It's a reversible operation, I knew that. Now, though, my fear is about the health of my child because of my age. It may be an irrational fear, but it's a very real one. I don't have any specific health problem, just fears.'

261

'Did you consider genetic testing?' said Ren.

'I did, but I rejected the idea,' said Robert. 'It may sound selfish, but I didn't want to know if there was a death sentence hanging over my head.'

'I understand that,' said Ren. 'Why did you not discuss your concerns with your wife?'

'I . . . I didn't want to appear weak to her,' said Robert. 'I love my wife, I want her to be happy, that's all I want. I didn't want her to pay the price for falling in love with an old guy.' He smiled.

'You're hardly old,' said Ren, smiling back. *Come on, open up to me. Please. It's clear you love this woman and you are lying about something so monumental.*

'So, what did you do?' said Ren.

Make this make sense to me.

'I talked to the fertility doctor, explained my situation,' said Prince. 'He and I went through lists of donors, we found someone who looked like me . . . he took care of the rest.'

'How is your wife?' said Ren.

'She's heartbroken,' said Robert. 'She's at our house in the country.'

'That would be the Hamptons,' said Ren.

He nodded. 'Yes.'

'Does she know about this now — that you're not the father of the baby?'

'No,' he said. 'She has no idea. Nor will she.'

'Were you not concerned we would tell her the results of the swabs?'

'I knew you'd have to talk to me first,' said Robert.

262

'Did Laura Flynn know that you were not the biological father?' said Ren.

'Laura? No,' said Robert. 'Absolutely not.'

'Is there any way she could have found out?' said Ren.

'No . . . there was no paperwork about this, it was all done in private with the doctor and his office. He's a personal friend.'

'Can I ask,' said Ren, 'isn't there a conflict between your religious views and your decision to use a surrogate?'

He hesitated. 'I don't see it that way.'

'I'm quoting here,' said Ren, looking down at her notebook. 'It's from a speech given by the Pope. There is an 'inseparable connection, willed by God, and unable to be broken by man on his own initiative, between the two meanings of the conjugal act: the unitive meaning and the procreative meaning'. IVF separates those two parts,' said Ren, 'so the Catholic Church is against it.'

'If I was opposed to surrogacy,' said Robert, 'then I wouldn't have agreed to it in the first place, which I clearly did.'

'Maybe it was a decision you went on to regret,' said Ren.

Robert shook his head. 'Not one bit. I respect life, all lives.'

'So, in your mind, because your sperm wasn't used in the surrogacy, you hadn't been part of something that was against your religious beliefs?' said Ren. 'Is that it?'

'I simply love my wife more than I love God,' said Robert. 'Yes, I've been Catholic all my life,

263

but I didn't know Ingrid all my life. When I met her, I saw the world a different way. She changed my life. And as time went on, I could see how clearly she wanted to be a mother, and what a good mother she would make.'

'Did you not think that she wanted to be a mother to *your* baby, because she loved *you*?' said Ren.

'It would still have been my baby,' said Robert. 'I would still have considered it that way.'

'Vasectomies are also against the Catholic Church's teaching . . . ' said Ren.

Robert Prince nodded. 'Yes.'

'And that's OK with you too,' said Ren.

Robert nodded. 'Yes. Can you see that I may just be guilty of not agreeing with every single tenet of the Catholic Church?'

Thereby guilty of being quite the hypocrite.

'This was a private decision,' said Robert. 'This was not something that Ingrid or I would ever publicly discuss.'

'So, it was all right to do this, if it was kept secret,' said Ren.

'I love my wife,' said Robert. 'I think anything I do that is born out of love for her is the right thing to do.'

What dark multitude could that cover?

39

'For goodness' sake,' said Robert, 'I'm a moral man — obviously I meant anything in the realm of what is good and moral.'

That tone of voice . . . the arrogance . . . the self-righteousness . . .

Hit him. Now. 'Mr Prince, I'd like to talk to you about the OCBLA,' said Ren.

Robert nodded. 'What would you like to know?'

'What your involvement is with them,' said Ren.

'I've been a member since 2002,' said Robert. 'Via charity work I had done post 9/11 to support the families of the firefighters, police, EMTs who lost loved ones in the attack. The OCBLA was pretty new, I met some of the members, I was impressed with what they were doing, I joined up.' He paused, studying Ren's reaction. 'I acknowledge it's an exclusive club of wealthy men — mainly men,' said Robert, 'but there's nothing sinister about it.'

Who said anything about sinister?

'We support each other, various causes, we meet for dinner every now and then, we have guest speakers, authors, Church figures, politicians . . .'

'When you failed in your leadership bid in 2005,' said Ren, 'did you feel it was because you weren't married?'

His eyes went wide. 'No, I did not. That's ludicrous.'

'You lost out to a married man with children,' said Ren. 'Did you feel in 2010 that maybe not being seen as a family man could have been a problem?'

'No,' said Robert. 'No. And I don't appreciate this line of questioning, Agent Bryce.'

'I have to ask,' said Ren.

'You're wasting time,' said Robert.

'Did the OCBLA contribute to a settlement for the victims of two Catholic pedophile priests in Denver?'

Robert paused. 'Yes.'

Ren waited.

'I see by your face that that doesn't impress you,' said Robert. 'You're presuming that this is something negative, that this was about me supporting pedophiles or about me paying to make a problem go away.' He leaned forward. 'Not so, Agent Bryce.'

Patronization rocks. Check later if that's a word: patronization. I'm not convinced.

'I'm not patroni . . . ' *shit,* 'presuming anything,' said Ren.

'I contributed so that victims were compensated,' said Robert. 'The diocese didn't have the funds to pay them. The priests are long dead, they are no longer a threat. I'm not supporting pedophiles, I'm supporting victims who otherwise either wouldn't have received a dime or would not have seen the money in their lifetimes.'

What do I do with that information?

'It's quite difficult to find one's honorable

266

deeds viewed in such an unfavorable light . . . '
said Robert.

'Well, I like victims to be compensated too,'
said Ren. 'In that, I like to bring their killer to
justice.'

'What are you trying to say?' said Robert.

'You're presuming that this is something
negative,' said Ren.

He stared at her. 'This conversation has taken
a juvenile turn.'

Ren stared through him. 'Do you think Laura
Flynn might have felt betrayed if she had
discovered that you had lied to her?'

'I don't know what Laura would have felt,'
said Robert, 'I don't quite know how the mind of
a surrogate works. And I'm a man, I don't expect
ever to understand maternity and all that goes
with it. I'm happy for that to remain an enigma.
I was concerned for my wife and I was
concerned for Laura, that they both had the very
best.' He paused. 'I haven't done very well . . . '

⋆ ⋆ ⋆

Ren went back to her desk and called Janine to
tell her about the interview.

'Ugh,' said Janine.

'And his explanation about not wanting to be
a father because he's 'so old' is ridiculous,' said
Ren. 'One hundred and twenty is old in my book
— not fifty-five.'

'It's weird, we've stumbled into this private
world of Robert Prince and it seems perfectly
normal to him, but it's just . . . bizarre.'

'Maybe Laura stumbled onto something private too . . . ' said Ren.

'Is it the religious militancy or . . . the wealth . . . ?'

'I don't know,' said Ren. 'All I know is it's an alien world.'

'Did you hear anything back about 'worried-mom'?' said Janine.

'Let me check my mail,' said Ren. 'Yes, I have a response. Blah, blah, blah . . . Terry Ragland . . . will talk to you herself . . . situation two years ago with her son and Jesse Coombes . . . Coombes assaulted him. The mother is working shifts, she can talk tomorrow morning, seven a.m., Denver time.'

'Intriguing,' said Janine.

'Early,' said Ren. 'Does she not realize Ben Rader is coming tonight? Does she not *know* how hot he is?' She heard beeps on the line. 'OK, gotta go — Robbie is calling me.'

'Hey Ren,' said Robbie, 'I need a big favor. Can you get something in the bottom drawer of my desk?'

'I can,' said Ren.

'I can't get back just now and I left my iPad in there. I need it later.'

'Sure. Do you need me to drop it by your place?' *That I haven't been in for so long.*

'No, just keep it safe,' said Robbie. 'I'll call by your place later to pick it up . . . if that's OK?'

'Of course it is. Will you stay for dinner?' said Ren. 'It's just me and Ben.'

'Oh, he's back?' said Robbie. 'Great.'

'Great,' said Ren, 'see you later.'

Let's see if we can't all be friends . . .

40

Ben had arrived at Ren's at six and she was there to meet him. She left him in the shower so she could start dinner. He came down with his hair still wet, wrapped his arms around her and kissed the back of her neck. 'I just want to make sure you're OK after everything we talked about the last time,' he said. 'I didn't want you to worry that I was freaking out while I was gone.'

'No . . . ' said Ren, 'I wasn't worried at all.'

He smiled. 'OK. That's good.

'I did a little research on the whole bipolar thing . . . ' he said.

'Or the two halves of the bipolar thing . . . ' *I am high-larious.*

He made the sound that people make when their attempt at serious conversation has been thwarted.

'Seriously, though, I wouldn't make a habit out of researching,' said Ren.

'It was very interesting . . . ' said Ben.

Yes: if you're feigning clinical objectivity and emotional detachment.

'You can't unknow some of the things, though,' said Ren. 'And not all of it will be me. Just so you know. Every bipolar person is a special kind of wonderful.' She smiled. 'Like, I will never buy a yacht. But that will be purely because I would not be able to secure the financing.'

'Who knows what the future holds?' said Ben.

'But, please promise me,' said Ren. 'Promise me that you won't get obsessed by it. Consider your research done.'

'OK, I just have one question,' said Ben. 'And it's because I did read a lot about this, like you said, and it does seem to be different from one person to the next . . . well, not different, but . . . it can be pretty bad . . . '

This is going to be a shit show.

'What do you want to know?' said Ren.

'What it's like being manic,' said Ben. 'For you . . . '

'Really?' said Ren. *Really?*

He nodded.

Lie, lie. For the love of God, lie. Ren turned around to him. 'OK . . . mania turns everything to magic, it turns everything you look at into a beautiful and wild eventual problem. It is a glorious thing. It is a psychological Midas touch. Everything is intoxicating.' *You look at a man and he is the most amazing man in the world.* 'You have to own the dress in the store window that has caught your eye. You have to own it right there.' *And if it's whorish, even better.* 'Your head feels like it's filled with air, a new kind of air and if everyone breathed it, it would make the world a better place.' *And when people around you are not breathing it, they seem really dull and unambitious.* 'You get so many ideas and they are good. You achieve a lot. You make links.' *Until everything starts to overwhelm you and you want it all to go away.*

Ben nodded. 'OK . . . '

'When it's good, it's very, very good and when it's bad, it's rotten . . . ' said Ren. *Sometimes you know that the result of your behavior will be a disaster of some kind. And it doesn't stop you. It is like being suddenly stupid. And the aftermath is like a slideshow. Like the end of The Hangover. But, it's not about after-the-fact photographs: even at the time, everything is like a beautiful pop and flash. Imagine knowing that the outcome of doing something will be a disaster. But you only get a tiny window in which to capture that knowledge — it only sticks its head up for a moment. If you don't grab it while you can . . . well . . . you're fucked. Imagine a grenade coming your way. The pin is out. You only have seconds to run. You should run. Instead, before you know it, you reach out and catch it. Pccchhhhh . . .*

'Does that answer your question?' said Ren.

Ben frowned. 'I guess so. What I read online was way worse. Phew.'

Ugh.

Ben wandered into the living room. Ren started to stir-fry strips of marinated chicken. She turned on the extractor fan.

'Hey,' said Ben, walking in with Robbie's iPad. 'When did you get this?' He stopped walking.

'I can't hear you,' Ren shouted. 'The fan.'

Ben didn't reply. Ren turned around to him. 'What?' she said. She turned off the fan. 'What is it?'

Ben was swiping his fingers across the screen.

'Hey,' said Ren. 'That's Robbie's. What are you doing?'

'Em, realizing it's not yours,' said Ben. He looked up. 'Unless you like Filthy Sluts Taking it Every Way or Cum Shots to Monster Tits or — '

'I do . . . ' said Ren, 'but that's not the point . . . '

Ren walked over as Ben kept going through screens.

'What the — ' Ren's eyes went wide. 'What? Oh my God. This is wow . . . porn on a . . . well, Utah scale.'

'He's been working the choirboy thing well.' Ben laughed.

'Shut it down,' said Ren. 'He told me to take it from the office, because he knew I wouldn't dream of turning it on. Jesus. He knew he could trust me.'

'And he was right to trust you,' said Ben. 'You didn't turn it on. It was me.'

'Can't unsee, can't unsee,' said Ren. 'Can't unknow, can't unknow. OK — turn it off now. He could be here any moment.'

'I'm turning it off, relax,' said Ben.

'Don't tell me to relax,' said Ren.

'Woo.'

'This is . . . ' said Ren, 'Robbie's . . . not like this.'

Ben was laughing at her.

'I'm serious,' said Ren. 'It's not funny. You don't know him. He can't be cool with this. Like, religion-wise.'

I knew it was more than his parents' divorce.

'He's not himself,' said Ren. 'He's been so strange with me over the past while. I thought it was because . . . ' *he liked me and I rejected him, then I went out with someone else.*

'Because what?' said Ben.

Ren shrugged. 'Just that I see less of him.'

'Because of me?' said Ben.

'Just in general,' said Ren. 'But it makes sense
. . . he was so weird a while back when I dissed
the concept of sex addiction — '

'Lack of self-awareness or boyfriend-awareness
there,' said Ben.

Ren smiled. 'I think this is a real problem for
Robbie.'

He goes to the bathroom in work a lot.

He's been late a lot too.

'He hasn't been to see his mother in so long,'
said Ren. 'He probably can't face her.'

'He probably can't recognize her because of
the blindness . . . ' said Ben.

Stop making fun of my Robbie. 'I know it
seems really funny,' said Ren, 'but I'm telling you
this whole thing will be agonizing for him. He's
my friend, Ben. I care about him a lot.'

The doorbell rang. Ben and Ren stared at each
other.

'He better not ask to use the bathroom,' said
Ben. He powered off the iPad, then glanced at it.
'I'll wipe this clean,' he said, winking.

'Rein it in, for the love of God,' said Ren.

'Don't mention reins in front of him . . . '

'Stop,' hissed Ren as she walked to the door.

'Hey,' said Robbie, walking in, hugging her
tight.

No hard feelings.

41

The next morning, Ren tore herself away from the hot body of Ben Rader. She threw on a pair of shorts and a tank and went downstairs. She made a pot of coffee and sat at the dining-room table.

She dialed Terry Ragland's number. She'd clearly been waiting by the phone.

'Before we start, I just want to say I'm really embarrassed by all this,' said Terry. 'I mean . . . writing posts like that. Hiding behind the . . . anonymity.'

'That's OK,' said Ren. 'I'd just like to hear what you have to say about Jesse Coombes. Your posts about him are the only time you use 'worriedmom' as your username . . . '

'I don't know how much detail you want,' said Terry. 'I'll just tell you the story as I see it. The agent in Dallas said you were a nice person, easy to talk to.'

'Well, I hope you think so too,' said Ren.

'To give you the short version first,' she said. 'Jesse Coombes beat the crap out of my son, pulled down his pants, took a photo on his cell phone and threatened to show it to everyone in school. And that's not the weird part. That's the most normal part of this whole story.'

Okaaay.

'It boils down to this friendship between Jesse Coombes and a boy called Dominic Fisher,' said

Terry. 'They both started high school the same year, they were both bullied — Dominic because he was, well . . . dirt poor, rough around the edges. He was one of the inner-city kids bussed in to the high school. He was into all kinds . . . breaking into places, stealing, and he had a thing for cars — he'd been hotwiring since he was eleven. Jesse Coombes, on the other hand — bad enough that he was a child evangelist, now his father's just been caught in a sex scandal. So when Dominic joined the school, Jesse and him struck up this friendship, they both loved cars, they were both outcasts. Apparently, Dominic taught him all he knew. Rumor has it, there were more than a few times that Dominic took the blame when they were caught, even though Jesse was the one acting out. Jesse had made his family a lot of money and his parents felt so guilty about everything, they gave him access to it, so this kind of dazzled Dominic and probably made him easy to manipulate. He didn't have a problem being associated with this family that was in the middle of a scandal. He didn't seem to care what Howard Coombes was up to. But the Coombes parents very much cared what Dominic Fisher was up to and how that could affect their son. Now to where it gets weird: the Coombes organized this big huge party in their house for Jesse's fourteenth birthday. You know — too amazing for the kids not to accept the invitation, my own son included. The Coombes invited Dominic too, because it would have been obvious otherwise, but he didn't stay long — he got ill and had to go home — '

Was poisoned by daddy Coombes more likely . . .

'I'm sure it was deliberate,' said Terry. 'The rest of the boys got to sleep over. My son came home on Sunday, went to bed, and woke me up in the middle of the night with stomach pains. He wouldn't let me go near him. I'm a nurse — of course, I insisted. He was bruised all over. His body, though, not his face. He swore blind that he fell, that it was nothing. I told him I'd send the police to Jesse Coombes' house if he wouldn't tell me what happened. So he did. It still makes my skin crawl.' She took in another deep breath.

'Karl — that's my son — said that he looked through Jesse's things during the sleepover when everyone was still downstairs, and he found a bunch of sermons — written by Jesse and dated from around that time . . . even though Jesse had come to the school telling everyone he was done with all that. Some of the sermons were about love and forgiveness. Others were ordering Satan to repent and to renounce his wicked ways — Bible quotes, the works. So all along, it seems Jesse was acting publicly like the whole evangelism thing was behind him, but clearly it wasn't. Then Karl found a journal and, inside, the title page says *The Rubyman*. It seems clear that The Rubyman represents the devil . . . until Karl realizes, because of some of the stories, that The Rubyman is actually Dominic Fisher. Jesse has written that The Rubyman is tempting him, and wants to destroy him, but it's real clear that, at the same time, Jesse loves this Rubyman. Karl was freaked out, but he kept snooping. He was real embarrassed telling me all this. That's not what my husband and I taught him . . . to snoop like that.'

'Of course not,' said Ren. *It never is.*

'Karl found photos of Dominic Fisher. Lots of them. A bunch tied up in red ribbon. Just regular photos. But, then he finds a few more that look like maybe Dominic didn't know they were being taken. Like Dominic asleep or a long shot of him cutting someone's lawn with his shirt off, that kind of thing. Then Karl found a cell phone . . . with an inbox that had a lot more photos, even more recent, sent from Dominic Fisher's number — photos of a more personal nature. Karl looked in the sent items and realized that Dominic Fisher thought he was sending these photos to a girl. There were even photos sent back from this imaginary girl . . . except she wasn't imaginary . . . Karl recognized her from YouTube. It was from one of Jesse Coombes' preaching things, whatever they call them. I don't know if you ever saw it. Austin: Pink Dress Girl. She had kept in touch with him over the years in a fangirl kind of way.'

Oh. My. God.

'This poor young girl was sending Jesse Coombes photos and he was using a throwaway phone to send them to Dominic Fisher and get naked ones of him back,' said Terry.

Holy. Shit. Unholy shit.

'That's when Jesse walked in,' said Terry. 'He found Karl going through his things and he went ballistic. He beat the crap out of him, took that photo of him, tied him to the radiator. The rest of the kids were out front at this time. Jesse gathered up the journal, the sermons, the letters, the phone, everything — went down to the barbecue and threw them all on. He doused them with lighter fluid and up they went. Then he came back in to Karl, told him if he breathed a word to anyone, he'd send the photo to the whole school first, then come back and 'torch' him too. Karl had already mentioned to me that there'd been two fires in the school since Jesse started there, and he was definitely seen close to one and with a burn on his hand after the other one. So, Karl believed the threats.'

'I'm not surprised.'

'I don't know whether Karl said anything to anyone about what happened at the party, I know he begged me not to, but rumors started to circulate around the school. Two weeks later, Dominic Fisher's family moved away. And by the end of the summer, the Coombes had also moved and Jesse started high school with a clean slate.'

'And do you know where Dominic Fisher is now?' said Ren.

'I heard the poor kid died last year,' said Terry, 'leukemia.'

'Did you ever tell the Coombes what Jesse did to Karl?' said Ren.

'No,' said Terry. 'I had promised Karl I wouldn't.'

'How's your son doing now?' said Ren.

'Oh, he's great,' said Terry. 'He's doing great.

Straight As. Doesn't give his mama an ounce of trouble.'

Seems like he fared a whole lot better than Jesse Coombes.

Ren thanked her for her help and went back upstairs, sliding in beside Ben Rader, careful to wake him up and send him off on a high.

Ren lay there afterwards with a heavy feeling in her stomach.

The terrible affliction of caring about someone who has to go.

'How am I expected to get up?' said Ren.

'Well, I certainly don't expect it,' said Ben.

Ren let out a breath.

'This is it . . . ' said Ben. He kissed her shoulder.

'The. End,' said Ren.

'Tune in next time!' said Ben.

'You'd be mad not to!'

'I'm so proud of you,' he said, squeezing her tight.

'Speaking of madness . . . ?' said Ren.

'I'm serious,' said Ben.

'There's no need to be proud,' said Ren. 'But, thank you.' She curled away from him, onto her side, tucked her back against his chest.

I want to stay here.

'You know what,' she said, 'this is the first time I've told a boyfriend about the bipolar thing before everything went to shit.'

'So that's a good sign,' said Ben. He put his arm around her, rolled her back so she was facing him. He looked her in the eye. 'Now, relax, OK? Everything is fine.' He held her cheeks and kissed her lips. 'I love you.'

He pulled back and smiled. She was caught, but she stayed. She allowed herself to breathe.

'I love you too,' she said.

Dun. Dun. DUN.

42

Ren arrived into Safe Streets, beaming.

'Hasn't your boyfriend gone home this morning?' said Cliff.

'Yes,' said Ren, 'he has.' She leaned in to Cliff and whispered, 'But not before I told him that I loved him . . . '

'And how much Valium have you taken as a direct result?' said Cliff.

'Collapsing in five, four, three . . . '

'Well, good for you,' said Cliff, patting her arm. His lip started to quiver.

'OK, I know that's not about me,' said Ren. She tilted her head. 'Did you have a fight with Brenda?'

He laughed. 'I did not,' he said. 'But I am very happy for you. Ben is a good guy.'

'With poor judgment.' Ren fired up her computer. 'Speaking of good guys, here comes Everett King!'

'Well, what a welcome,' said Everett. 'I might need to hear that every morning.'

'Do not expect consistency from Ren Bryce,' said Cliff.

Ren nodded. 'And that's one of my lines.' She looked around. 'Who's here?'

'Everyone,' said Cliff.

Ren waited until the team had gathered and Gary had arrived. She called Janine, put her on speaker and told them all Terry Ragland's story.

'So, Jesse Coombes is a violent evangelical car-torcher?' said Janine.

'Firestone and brimstone . . . ' said Cliff. 'So, we've got one kid in there who has a history of carjacking, hotwiring and beating the shit out of people . . . and we've got Conor Gorman, a kid with a history of beating the shit out of people . . . '

'Oh, and he crashed a Lotus, didn't he?' said Ren.

'And they're just the kids we know about,' said Janine.

'But there's a big difference between messing around with cars, beating kids up and shooting dead a pregnant woman . . . ' said Ren. 'I mean, it doesn't sound good for Jesse Coombes, but it could be just that he wanted to run away from the ranch, took Kendall's car, is driving down Stoney Pass Road, comes across Laura Flynn being shot at, panics, returns to the ranch with the car, lights it on fire, tells the Faules, they handle it, believing that he wasn't responsible for the murder and not wanting the murder to be in any way associated with the ranch — whether that's just the publicity in general or the fact that it's revealed that one of their teens was in a position to escape in the first place . . . or set a car on fire.' *Pheeew.*

'Option two,' said Cliff, 'is Jesse Coombes comes across Laura Flynn, tries to carjack her, kills her, panics — '

'Where does he get the gun, though?' said Ren.

'Maybe it was her gun,' said Cliff.

'If she had a gun, a young Irish girl like that . . . she must have really felt that her life was in danger,' said Ren. She paused. 'That's why she drove back from Chicago! She had a gun. She wouldn't have gotten through security at the airport . . . '

'You think she went all the way to Chicago for a gun?' said Gary.

'No,' said Ren, 'but it was part of the plan. Who else do we know she had contact with there?'

'I can check that here,' said Janine.

Ren sat forward. 'Hold on. Didn't Laura Flynn stay in the Ramada Bolingbrook during her trip there?'

'Yes,' said Janine.

Ren Googled it. 'That Ramada is not far from Stateville prison. Seven miles. I've even got hits here from a forum recommending it as a good place to stay if you're visiting someone there. Holy shit.' She stood up. 'Derrick Charles — the NFL buddy of Kenneth Faule who's supposed to have strangled his wife. Isn't he in Stateville? Could there be a connection that way?'

'Cue: me,' said Everett. 'Robert Prince donated fifty thousand dollars to Derrick Charles' appeal fund back in September.'

'No fucking way,' said Ren.

'*All* the fucking way,' said Everett.

Gary looked like he was regretting the union of Ren Bryce and Everett King.

'When did you find that out?' said Ren.

'First thing this morning, I just didn't get a chance to say it,' said Everett.

'Robert Prince is like some kind of stealth donor,' said Ren. 'If this didn't all happen before the murder, I would think he was paying everyone off . . . '

'Go talk to the Faules,' said Gary.

Woo-hoo!

★ ★ ★

Kristen Faule was in the stables when Janine and Ren arrived at The Darned Heart. She kept them waiting in reception, before taking them to her office when she arrived, her hair wet from the shower.

'Mrs Faule,' said Ren, 'did you know that Robert Prince had made a donation to Derrick Charles' appeal fund?'

Kristen Faule's eyes went wide.

Ooh. You did not know. You are shocked by this.

'No,' said Kristen. 'Kenneth deals with the appeal fund.'

'Were you aware of a connection between Robert Prince and Derrick Charles?' said Ren.

'No,' said Kristen. 'Let me call Kenneth in here.'

She pushed each button of her husband's extension number with ill-contained anger. 'Kenneth, can you come in here, please? The detectives are here again.'

Again.

Kenneth came in and sat down. 'How can I help you?' he said.

'Do you know why Robert Prince was

284

donating to Derrick Charles' appeal fund?' said Ren.

Ther's an irritating tapping sound.

He paused. 'How did you know about that?'

I choose the meaningful stare in response to your bold question. No words.

'Well, like anyone else,' said Kenneth, 'because he believes in his innocence.'

'Did he know Charles before the case that you're aware of?' said Ren.

'Not that I know,' said Kenneth. 'From what Mr Prince told me, he read about Charles' case in the newspaper, thought that it didn't ring true, and he decided to put some money toward the campaign to have him released.'

'So you spoke to Mr Prince personally?' said Ren.

'Yes,' said Kenneth.

I wonder why Robert Prince didn't donate totally anonymously?

'He wanted to keep this absolutely private,' said Kenneth. 'He was insistent, because of his position, that it may not look good to some people.'

Like the OCBLA.

He turned to his wife. 'I signed a confidentiality agreement,' he said. 'Sorry, but I couldn't say anything, even to you.'

'It's just that there are many people in the spotlight who've been found guilty of crimes, while protesting their innocence,' said Ren. 'Why do you think Derrick Charles' case caught Robert Prince's attention?'

'Maybe he was a Broncos fan?' said Kenneth.

'Maybe Derrick Charles had carried out charity work for one of the Princes' favorite charities? I really don't know. You should maybe ask him.'

He said it politely, but there was a tone.

Ren realized the irritating sound was Kristen Faule's fingers tapping on the table. She noticed Ren noticing and she stopped.

'Has Robert Prince gone to Stateville to meet with Derrick Charles?' said Ren.

'Not that I'm aware of,' said Kenneth. He turned to Kristen. 'You?'

'No,' said Kristen.

'Does that strike you as odd?' said Ren to Kenneth. 'That he donates money, but he hasn't even met the man?'

'No,' said Kenneth, 'should it?'

'It's just . . . ' said Ren, 'if I was handing over a large donation, because I believed in someone, I'd want to meet them, because . . . well, I would venture that, although the money is of a huge help to the accused, the fact that a stranger is standing before them, looking them in the eye and telling them that they believe in them would be what mattered.'

Kristen shrugged. 'I guess so.'

'Robert Prince is a busy man,' said Kenneth.

'Do you know anything about Laura Flynn and a visit to Stateville?' said Ren. *Could Robert Prince have sent her there?*

'Laura Flynn?' said Kristen. 'The murder victim? No.' She frowned. 'Kenneth?'

He shook his head. 'No. Certainly, Robert Prince never mentioned her.'

43

Ren and Janine walked down the steps into the parking lot.

'It's all so strange,' said Janine. 'I'll call Stateville when I get back to the office, see if they have a record of Laura Flynn visiting Derrick Charles.'

'And I will call my dear friend, the wildly generous Robert Prince,' said Ren.

'Hold off until we know more about whether she actually visited Stateville.'

'Well, I can ask about his donation,' said Ren, 'without getting into anything about Laura.'

Ren was driving behind Janine, not far from Conifer, when she called.

Ren picked up. 'I miss you too . . . these past ten minutes have been killing me.'

Janine laughed. 'I just got a call from Kohler . . . we got a breakthrough on our Copier Bandits. A couple of kids playing in Pine Gulch Cemetery found a little black 'toy'. One of them brought it home, showed it to his mom, but it wasn't a toy — it was a GPS signal jammer, perfect if the bait money at the bank had a GPS tracker. And, we have traced it to local fool, Morgan Greene. A real idiot; you know, the kind of guy goes into a bar, shoots his mouth off, brags about whatever he can. Smart enough not to mention a robbery, dumb enough to mention GPS signal jammers. He's twenty-nine, lives with his stoner buddies not far from here. He works for Burt Kendall or used to work for him; he lost his job last week because of the bankruptcy. Apparently the last pay check any Kendall employee got was at the end of March. We're going to bring him in this afternoon. Kohler and I are going to take him on.'

'Pincer movement,' said Ren.

'It'll be fun,' said Janine.

Ren hung up and dialed Robert Prince's number.

'Mr Prince, it's Ren Bryce here — do you have a minute?'

'I do,' said Robert. 'What can I help you with?'

'I was wondering about your donation to Derrick Charles' appeal fund . . . '

'Yes?' said Robert Prince.

'What led you to donate?' said Ren.

'I read a piece on him in the *Denver Post*, during one of my visits,' said Robert. 'I believed his defense's story of an intruder. Derrick had been in debt to many people. He had a lot of enemies. I just couldn't see that there was evidence that he killed his wife and children. He looked like a very happy family man.'

'Did you know him personally?' said Ren.

'No,' said Robert.

'Had you met him?' said Ren.

'No, never,' said Robert. 'I called Kenneth Faule because of what I read and I was very impressed with him. That was why I chose The Darned Heart for Conor. I believed it was a place that would straighten him out.'

'Did any of your contacts — friend, family,

otherwise — know Derrick Charles or his family personally?' said Ren.

'No,' said Robert. 'You have to understand, Agent Bryce, I'm a man of means and it's — I don't want to say 'easy' — but it is possible for me to see a cause I believe in and donate to that cause, without knowing more than I read in the article or the letter or whatever medium I come across a story of someone in need. It's why you hear all the time, an anonymous benefactor paid for the surgery of some poor two-year-old cancer victim that was featured in the newspaper, etc., etc. That's because of people like me.'

Oh, gooood for youuuu. In the tone of Christian Bale.

'Don't you ever question things any deeper?' said Ren. 'You're putting a lot of faith in journalists.'

'I trust that they have fact-checked, at the very least, on such important cases, and anything I'm not sure of, I follow up on.'

Could he be a little naïve? Or am I?

'Agent Bryce, is this relevant to what happened to Laura?'

'I need to make more inquiries,' said Ren.

'Do you think I have put her in danger in any way by making this donation?' said Robert.

I don't fucking know! 'I'll keep you informed,' said Ren. 'Thank you for your time.'

★ ★ ★

Ren arrived back in Safe Streets. Robbie was on a call. Everett got up and came over to her desk.

'You look overly excited,' said Ren. 'I see financials dancing in your eyes.'

'Well,' said Everett, 'I may have found our answer as to why Robert Prince set up the energy company. It turns out that, back in 1953, Walter Prince bought a second tract of land in Williston, North Dakota: a three-thousand-acre cattle ranch. For some reason, though, in January 1958, that land was transferred to a trust fund, managed by the Prince family's law firm in Butte, Montana. This land was *not* inherited by either Acora or Robert Prince. It's likely that they didn't even know it existed.'

'Oh my God,' said Ren. 'Back in November, Robert Prince was given letters from the Prince mansion that were to do with a Butte law firm.'

'Well, it mightn't have made good reading for him,' said Everett, 'because the second tract of land *does* come with mineral rights. The land he got is worthless, but the land the mystery benefactor got is worth anywhere up to fifty million dollars.'

'Ouch,' said Ren. 'But, I don't get it . . . there was obviously no bad blood between Walter and Acora and Robert. From what I read, she inherited everything when her father died . . . and then it went to Robert when she died.'

'Walter Prince either had someone else he was close to . . . '

' . . . or he was forced to sign over the deeds to someone for baaad reasons,' said Ren. 'If Robert Prince found this out, I can't imagine he would have taken that information lightly.'

'No,' said Everett.

'Could Robert Prince already know who owns this land?' said Ren.

'I don't know,' said Everett. 'It's possible.'

'Does he have any claim on it?' said Ren.

'If it was handed over because of a blackmail situation, yes, but only if the blackmail could be proven.'

'So many years have gone by — I'm wondering how easy it would be to prove . . . ' said Ren.

'Maybe he *was* able to prove it, hence the new company,' said Everett. 'What do you know about Walter Prince? Was he involved in shady dealings?'

'What I know is that he wasn't a nice man at all,' said Ren. 'When he was only a teenager, he rounded up a posse to beat a man to death. Albeit a suspected pedophile . . . the father of one of three young girls who disappeared slash were murdered — it was called the Orchard Girls case . . . '

'Did Walter Prince do time for it?' said Everett.

'Oh, no,' said Ren. 'The Princes were far too untouchable. And it was all rumor.'

'Well, if I can follow more of this trail, I could wend my way closer to the truth,' said Everett. 'What makes him blackmailable.'

'Go, Everett, go!'

★   ★   ★

Robbie had tuned into their conversation, after he had ended his phone call. He was listening to

291

them, but with a faraway look in his eye. When five o'clock came, he got up and gathered his things.

'See you tomorrow,' he said. He left, his head down.

I can't watch him suffer any more.

Stay out of it.

Don't.

He needs help.

Don't be so naïve. Maybe he loves this new life of pornography.

He is miserable.

Go.

Ren ran down the stairs after him.

'Hey,' she said.

Cold feet. Cold feet.

'Hi,' said Robbie.

'Can we chat for a second?' said Ren.

'Sure,' said Robbie. 'Everything OK?'

'Let's go sit in your car,' said Ren.

'OK . . . I'm getting nervous.'

She laughed. 'Don't be.'

I'll take care of that part.

44

Ren and Robbie got into his car. He turned on the air conditioning.

'Ooh, that's nice,' said Ren.

'So, what is it?' said Robbie. He had his hands on the steering wheel as if he was about to drive.

How do I do this? Why am I doing this? Am I helping? Am I making things worse? Will this destroy our friendship? I cannot tell him that Ben has also seen his iPad. Or would that bother him? Maybe not. But I don't want him to think I snooped. I didn't. I was thrust into this nightmare. Everything happens for a reason. Shut up. Maybe he left the iPad with you for a reason. Oh . . . maybe he did.

Ren looked at him.

'It's just,' said Ren, 'is everything OK?'

He shook his head, really slowly. Eventually, he said, 'No.'

'I thought not,' said Ren. 'Do you want to talk?'

'I don't know if I can,' he said.

'Please,' said Ren. 'There is nothing you can't say to me, you know that.'

'I know.'

'And it will go no further.'

'I know that too.'

Wait. Wait. Wait.

'I've . . . ' He paused. 'I've developed a problem . . . with pornography.'

Thank God I got my Home Alone *shocked face out of the way with Ben.*

Ren nodded. 'It's OK, Robbie. Really.'

'What?' said Robbie. 'It's not. You don't mean that.'

'I do,' said Ren. 'I know you. I know this is not what you want. I understand how it could happen.'

'Can you see how repelled I am by this?'

'I can feel it,' said Ren. *Radiating off you.* 'And my heart is breaking for you. Because I know who you are. I really do.'

'If you had told me that I ever, in a million years, would be this guy . . . ' said Robbie. 'I know what I want in life. I want to get married to a nice girl. I want her to be the one. The first one. Girls like that, nice girls . . . they're hard to meet.'

'Guys like you are hard to meet,' said Ren. 'Life's good guys.'

'You still think that?' said Robbie. Tears welled in his eyes.

'Of course I do,' said Ren. 'Nothing changes that.'

'But these women . . . they're so degraded and I'm . . . ' He paused. 'Enjoying that.'

'And you are not alone,' said Ren.

'Does that make it right?' said Robbie.

'It's not about right,' said Ren. 'It's about you suffering. I just don't want you to suffer. And I can see that you are. You're not the cheery Robbie I know and love. You're preoccupied. And it's affecting work now too. I just didn't guess it was this.'

'The choirboy . . . '

'Hey,' said Ren.

'You know what I mean,' said Robbie. 'I'm a virgin Mormon Boy Scout. I'm not stupid. I get it. But all it does is make me feel worse. Like if people really knew me, they'd think differently.'

'Listen, everyone thinks 'if people really knew me',' said Ren. 'You are not the first man to have done this. And definitely not the first Mormon. So, just stop.'

Robbie let out a breath.

'I don't know how much you want to tell me,' said Ren, 'but . . . has it gone any further?'

'I . . . went to a bar,' said Robbie. 'I picked up this one girl. She was beautiful. I took her home . . . but nothing happened . . . ' He paused.

'OK,' said Ren. 'Well, that's good, isn't it? Your dream is still intact.' She studied him for a moment. 'And, you know what, Robbie? Even if your dream wasn't still intact, things could be even better with the first woman you sleep with in a relationship. Or with your future wife, if they're not the same person. They don't have to be the same person, Robbie. You don't have to — '

'OK . . . I did sleep with her,' said Robbie. 'I slept with her, and more. Other women. And . . . ' He shrugged. 'I don't want to be that guy.'

'You're not that guy,' said Ren. 'But you can't be the beat-yourself-up-guy either.'

'Remember a few months back we were talking about sex addiction . . . '

Ooh. Ren nodded. 'Yes. You were very annoyed with me . . . '

295

'Not about that,' said Robbie. 'You were talking about sex and you said to me 'Who knows what might happen when you get a taste for it' . . . '

'And you said I was being insensitive.'

'Yup,' said Robbie. 'Because you were right. I had waved goodbye to my tenth one-night-stand that morning.'

'It was nice of you to wave,' said Ren. 'And there must be some kind of merit badge for ten.'

Robbie smiled.

'And — hello — you let her stay all night . . . ' said Ren. 'That's nice too.'

'I'm sure I'm the only loser hanging in there for hugs,' said Robbie.

'Well, I give free hugs . . . and they're free of guilt too, so you know where I am.'

'I am so ashamed of this,' said Robbie.

'Um, it's me, Robbie,' said Ren. 'Sexual shame — '

'Well, I wish I could be as breezy as you about it.'

'I'm not breezy! The rest of the sentence was: sexual shame is more common than you think.'

They sat in silence.

'I want you to know something,' said Robbie, eventually. 'When . . . when I told you how I felt about you . . . that wasn't about sex. It's . . . was . . . more than that. I don't want you to think that was where I was coming from. What I mean is, this whole problem of mine is only over the past six months or so.'

Thank God I didn't drive you into a world of one-night stands.

'I know that,' said Ren.

'I mean, not that I've never thought about — '

'OK, Robbie, OK — you should talk to someone about all this. You need to give yourself peace.' Ren paused. 'And about the other thing, don't worry, OK? You don't need to say anything more about it. We're friends. Nothing is going to change that.'

'Ben is a great guy,' said Robbie.

'Hey, I'm surrounded by them,' said Ren, smiling.

'You're being so kind,' said Robbie. 'But I still think I'm damned.'

'You know what they believe at The Darned Heart Ranch?' said Ren.

Robbie waited.

'That you can knit a problem away.'

'What?' He turned to her.

Ren was miming knitting. 'You know . . . idle hands . . . '

For the first time in months, she heard Robbie's wonderful laugh.

★ ★ ★

Ren drove home that night, thinking of the pain Robbie had been trying to hide and how heartbreaking it was that he had been suffering alone.

I hope you'll be all right, Robbie Truax. You deserve to be.

Her cell phone rang. *Yay, Janine!*

'Well,' said Janine, 'we got our guys for the Conifer robbery: it was, indeed, Morgan Greene with sidekick, another Kendall's employee, Reece Gill. I think we also have them for the car at the ranch. Looks like an insurance job, but we can't prove anything yet. That's the only explanation I have for Greene and Gill still working for Kendall after he stiffed them back in March: he told them to burn out the car during the ranch job and they'd get their money when his insurance kicked in.'

'Kendall was a little smarter, to give him his dues,' said Ren. 'He bypassed the insurance company hoops by having the Faules cover it. He probably persuaded them that the insurance company would go straight to the theory that one of the kids was responsible for the arson.' She paused. 'But the Faules must think someone was capable of this. Why else would they pay out all that money?'

'That's a good point,' said Janine.

'The Faules must have had proof,' said Ren. 'They must have either seen it happen or had proof that someone under their care did it. They *know*. They're lying to us.'

'The key is — are they lying because of something more sinister than just lighting a car on fire?' said Janine.

'I mean, if you just shot someone, you're going to have blood all over you,' said Ren. 'You get back into a car, that's going to have blood all over it.'

'Exactly.'

'If we're going to get to the bottom of it,' said Ren, 'it's Greene, Gill or Kendall who we're going to have to put the pressure on . . . '

'We can leave them stew a little while,' said Janine. 'Let them think about what's in their best interests . . . I've already scared Greene, that he could be tied in to a high-profile homicide.'

'What if it's a high-profile resident at the ranch that's the problem?' said Ren.

'You mean our firestarter, Jesse Coombes?'

Ren nodded. 'No God-fearing petty criminal would want to stir up the wrath of Howard Coombes.'

'That might explain why Greene went so weird about the whole thing,' said Janine. 'Jittery.'

'Like the Faules.'

'Greene is definitely sweating,' said Janine. 'Oh, and another piece of dramz — Burt Kendall didn't donate the bus to the abbey. Apparently, an anonymous donor sent him a letter with a cashier's check and told him to pretend he donated it. It would help the abbey, but it would also guarantee Burt Kendall the exposure in the newspaper and get him some goodwill. Win – win in his eyes. Except he was in so much crap, nothing would get him out of it.'

'Did you see the letter?' said Ren.

'No,' said Janine, 'he got rid of it, but he did say it was postmarked Cheyenne. It arrived in the mail on April 7th, so it was probably sent the day before. I spoke with the bank and the check he received was dated March 31st.'

'So, basically, whoever was paying for the bus was going to do it anyway, but was helping out Burt Kendall at the same time.'

'It appears so,' said Janine.

'So, can we assume that whoever it was is acquainted with the abbey and with Burt Kendall? Someone local?'

'Probably,' said Janine. 'But does any of this really matter to us? This anonymous donor is not a bad guy on the loose.'

'Janine Hooks, I am shocked,' said Ren. 'It matters, it all matters. It's Nancy Drew shit. It's about solving things. *Any* things. *All* things.'

'I've been getting it wrong all this time . . . ' said Janine.

'Hold on — where was the check from?' said Ren.

'Butte, Montana,' said Janine.

'That's where the Prince family is originally from . . . ' said Ren. 'Everett's been filling me in on Robert Prince's various holdings.'

'So . . . ' said Janine.

'What do you make of that?' said Ren.

'An origami swan.'

'Calming,' said Ren.

'Oh, and I spoke with Stateville,' said Janine. 'No visit from Laura Flynn to Derrick Charles. She's not on his visitation list, she hasn't put in a request to be on it.'

'Shit,' said Ren. 'So . . . she just chose the Ramada nearby for the holy hell of it? Or could she have been meeting someone there?'

'Kohler would have said if there was a known link between her and any of the other guests,' said Janine.

Aaaagh. My instincts are failing me.

Is it the meds?

45

The following morning, Ren awoke to an email in her personal account that sent a bolt of panic through her. She read it again.

No. Not now. Please. No.

She called her brother, Matt.

'I feel mean saying this,' said Ren. 'Really mean. But I just got an email from Annie. She's coming home next month. I am about to be homeless.'

'It'll be nice for you to see her again?' said Matt.

'I know — I'm horrible,' said Ren.

'I'm kidding, I'm preying on your guilt,' said Matt. 'Shit. That's a bummer. What are you going to do?'

Probably go off the rails . . .

'Bear in mind . . . moving house, Ren. It's a possible trigger for you . . .'

Triggers . . . the sparks that light the fuse that sends the bipolar person shooting into the atmosphere on a high or spiraling underground into darkness.

Ren leaned toward mania. She knew her triggers. Some were the things that affected everyone, sane or otherwise: stress, moving house, bereavement, the end of a relationship. Then there were triggers common to most bipolar people: travel, sleep deprivation, tension at work/home, junk food, excess caffeine. Then

301

there were the ones brought on specifically by her job: criminals and the high-energy pursuit thereof.

It was the best job in the world.

Adrenaline, adrenaline, adrenaline, mania.

Stress, stress, stress, mania.

Party on.

'Are you there?' said Matt.

Ren sighed. 'Trigger Watch with Matthew Bryce . . . '

'Shut it,' said Matt. 'And talk to Batman about these things.'

★ ★ ★

Dr Leonard Lone sat at his desk, part-framed by two leafy plants, one on each end of the window sill behind him. Outside, the sun was beating down and it seemed to be making him glow.

'You know, Ren, that triggers are not respecters of medication,' said Dr Lone. 'If you can think of them, maybe, as kryptonite.'

Woo-hoo! Superhero stuff!

'Triggers get through the net,' said Lone. 'They know where your weaknesses lie. As long as you know that you're not invincible by being on meds.'

'I'm too normal to feel invincible.' Ren laughed. 'You can't feel invincible if all you're doing is, like, washing the dishes.'

'Do you wash the dishes a lot?' said Lone.

'No,' said Ren. 'That was a bad example.'

'Do you feel ordinary on medication?' said Lone.

'I *know* I'm ordinary,' said Ren. *But sometimes I'm Ren Rader! Fearless delusionist!*

'You're not ordinary,' said Lone. 'Trust me — you're not someone I would ever file under the word 'ordinary'.'

'Am I extraordinary?' said Ren.

He laughed. 'Yes, Ren. You're extraordinary . . . '

'Thank you.'

'Your mood is stable, Ren. But you can't associate stability with 'ordinariness'.'

Ren thought of Conor Gorman sitting on the sofa of The Darned Heart. *Conor Gorman is like me. Uncomfortable in ordinariness. Likely to buck against whatever makes him feel that way . . . stable home, ranch with a bunch of teens he probably feels he has nothing in common with . . .*

Dr Lone continued. 'It's a dangerous thought to allow to take root.'

And Jesse Coombes believes God whispers in his ear. He can't possibly think he's ordinary.

'No one wants to feel ordinary,' said Lone. 'The problem is that, if you associate that with meds, your first step in trying to feel 'extraordinary' is to stop taking them.'

Ren nodded.

In forty-three residents of The Darned Heart, could Conor Gorman and Jesse Coombes have found each other? Who's going to tell me that? What about the abbey? Could either of the boys have been sent there to help out? As punishment? Would Eleanor Jensen tell me if they were?

'It's important to understand that,' said Lone. He sat back, his head tilted.

Shit. What?

'To really take it on board,' said Lone.

Yeah, yeah, yeah. 'I know,' said Ren. 'Keep taking the meds.'

'I'm hoping that some of these points will stay with you and help you when you're alone and faced with certain choices,' said Dr Lone.

'Yes,' said Ren. 'Thank you.' She stood up to leave. 'Just one thing . . . if triggers bypass meds . . . ' *Then what's the point of taking meds?*

Dr Lone waited.

'Aw, nothing,' said Ren.

'Nothing . . . ' said Dr Lone.

Ren walked to the door. 'Triggers are much easier to handle when they're part of a weapon — not when they're the weapon itself.'

When she turned back, she could see a stillness in Dr Lone's face. He just knew. They both did.

The previous hour had been a waste of time for both of them.

★ ★ ★

Eleanor Jensen welcomed Ren into the abbey library. Ren took out two photos and set them on the table in front of her: the first was Conor Gorman, the second was Jesse Coombes.

'Ooh,' said Eleanor.

Define that reaction . . .

'What do you want to know?' said Eleanor.

'Well, anything you might know about either of these boys,' said Ren.

Eleanor pointed to Jesse. 'He's done some work in the library, just in the last couple of weeks, seems like a nice, respectful young man.'

I bet he does.

'And I'm not familiar with the other young man,' said Eleanor.

'OK,' said Ren.

Eleanor waited a while before she spoke. 'There's something else. Something small. Well, I guess that's for you to decide . . . '

Ren nodded.

'There was a girl who came here from the ranch,' said Eleanor. 'She's gone now, this happened back before Christmas — she said that one of the boys over there was very dark, he read dark books, wore skull rings . . . '

So far, sounds like my boyfriend . . .

'I know lots of teenagers are like that,' said Eleanor, 'and I think this girl was a little princess type, so it probably seemed more dramatic to her. She said he showed her a bone one night and told her it was a real finger bone, that kind of thing. He gave her the creeps, but nothing more came of it.' Eleanor looked at the photos again. 'It may have been one of these boys, it may not, but I thought I'd let you know. There could be twenty more boys like that over there, it wouldn't be a great leap.'

'A bone?' said Ren. 'Could that have had anything to do with the cemetery?'

'No,' said Eleanor. 'I asked Detective Kohler had any of the ground been disturbed and he said no, thank God. You heard the cemetery was tidied . . . '

'Yes,' said Ren. 'Do you have any idea who did that?'

'No — certainly it wasn't any of the ladies of the abbey. And we really tried to keep that cemetery a secret from the kids. I don't know why graves are such a draw to them. They're the ones with their whole lives ahead of them — death should be the furthest thing from their minds. Not that we expected tidying to be part of what they might do there . . . '

'I'd like to get a copy of the map of the abbey, if that's OK,' said Ren.

'That's not a problem,' said Eleanor. She got up and went to a drawer underneath a table by the window.

Ren looked down at the photo of Jesse Coombes and thought about his journal, the fixations, the inability to bury his past.

Is that what happens when you're bombarded with religion from such an early age?

Jesse Coombes' first obsession was *The Lord*, so when his parents plucked him out of that world, it must have been a shock, he must have felt alone. And as soon as he went into the real world of high school, he had a new fixation — Dominic Fisher, an outcast, like himself. And maybe, when he was plucked out of his life again and sent to The Darned Heart, he found in Conor Gorman a similar soul.

Could he have developed a fixation on him? Could he have been desperate for Conor not to leave?

306

46

Eleanor spread out the map of the abbey on a glass-topped table by the window.

'Here you are,' she said. 'Do you want to take a look?'

Ren got up and joined her. It was the same map Kohler had. She looked at the building outlines on it again: chapel, school, schoolmaster's lodgings, theater, guest house for visitors. There was something familiar about the theater, about its design. She looked out the library window where she could see the outline of the theater being built on the grounds of the ranch.

'Is that the same design as the one here on the map?' said Ren.

Eleanor compared the two. 'Looks like it is,' she said. 'Well, how about that?'

'Did you give them the plans?' said Ren.

'No,' said Eleanor.

'Are they online anywhere?' said Ren.

'Not that I'm aware of,' said Eleanor.

'It's a little coincidental,' said Ren.

Eleanor looked like she was waiting for Ren to elaborate.

I have nothing.

'Anyway, I digress,' said Ren. 'There's another reason I'm here. Did you know that Burt Kendall didn't, in fact, pay for the bus that was donated to you?'

'Pardon me?' said Eleanor.

'I spoke with Detective Hooks from the Sheriff's Office . . . Burt Kendall was sent a cashier's check from an anonymous donor and asked to pretend the donation was from him.'

'That's bizarre,' said Eleanor. 'I had no idea. Why would he do that?'

'Publicity, goodwill,' said Ren. 'It was from a bank in Butte and it was postmarked Cheyenne. Do you know anyone in either place who might want to support the abbey?'

'No,' said Eleanor. 'I mean, Lord knows all the connections our residents have, but feel free to talk to everyone. I can send an email around. You just don't know if someone had a relative who was in poor health and wanted to pass on funds before inheritance tax became an issue . . . but, it's the Burt Kendall involvement that makes no sense.'

'I know,' said Ren.

'What date was on the check?' said Eleanor.

'March 31st.'

'And when was it sent?' said Eleanor.

'More than likely on April 6th,' said Ren.

'April 6th,' said Eleanor. 'Why is that date in my head?' She paused. 'Oh,' she said, 'because Delores Ward organized some protest and that was the day they were coming back.'

'Where was the protest?' said Ren.

'Williston, North Dakota,' said Eleanor.

'Williston?' said Ren. *WTF? Where Robert Prince owns land?* 'Was it an anti-fracking thing?'

Eleanor laughed. 'No — it was an anti-sins-of-the-flesh thing. There are two new strip clubs there to cater to all the oil workers with not a lot else to do with their money. She was joining a group of protesters outside.'

'But why those particular strip clubs?' said Ren. 'When we have some perfectly bad ones here. Is Delores from North Dakota?'

Eleanor paused. 'I have no idea where she's from. It's not something we talk about. People are free to be who they want to be here,' said Eleanor. 'We have a Clean Slate Rule. We even have a clean slate hanging in our hallway. It's our subtle way . . . '

Don't you get curious? 'Williston . . . that's a long drive,' said Ren.

'Yes — about eleven hours,' said Eleanor. 'And in the old bus, that can't have been pleasant.' She laughed. 'Some billionaire oil man could have spotted the bus and sent us a pity gift.'

Ren laughed. 'Do you mind if I just check my phone?' she said, taking it out. She opened Google Maps and put in Denver, Butte and Williston. If a bus was traveling from the abbey to Williston, the route went right through Cheyenne. Could it be possible that one of the ladies of the abbey mailed the check to Burt Kendall that day?

'Eleanor,' said Ren. 'Is Betty Locke here — did she drive the bus that day?'

'Yes,' said Eleanor. 'Let me call her in.' She reached over to an old-style phone on the table. 'Cute, isn't it?' she said.

'I think I'd like to move in here,' said Ren.

'The detective with the phone in the library . . . ' said Eleanor.

Ren laughed. *I like you, Eleanor Jensen.*

★ ★ ★

Betty sat down on the armchair beside Ren, her eyes bright with curiosity.

'I believe you and some of the other residents made a trip to Williston in April,' said Ren. 'Do you remember . . . did you stop off in Cheyenne on the way?'

Betty paused. 'Yes,' she said. 'Yes, we did. Why do you ask?'

'Just clearing up a few details,' said Ren. 'What happened in Williston?'

'I'm sorry — meaning what?' said Betty.

'I heard you were protesting against strip clubs,' said Ren.

'I have never seen anything like that place,' said Betty. 'There is this vast man camp outside the town and it holds — it must be — a thousand men working for the mining companies. There is nothing for them to do other than drink and fornicate. Honestly, we looked ridiculous. We did our best, but we looked ridiculous. We weren't even treated with any kind of respect by people walking past. Poor Delores took to her bed.'

'Wasn't it her suggestion that you go there?' said Ren.

'Oh, yes,' said Betty, 'we should have known better. She doesn't get out much these days, and I guess we were so happy to see her getting involved that we went along with it.'

'And when you stopped in Cheyenne, did

310

everyone stay together or did people go their separate ways?' said Ren.

'We all pretty much stayed together,' said Betty.

'Did Delores manage to make it out and about at all?' said Ren. *Trying to act casual* . . .

'Yes, I think so, but . . . I can't be sure,' said Betty.

'OK, thank you,' said Ren.

'Do you think Delores has done something?' said Betty.

'No,' said Ren. 'Not at all. Like I said — just clearing up a few things.'

All I'm hearing is Butte, Montana, Williston, North Dakota. And Robert Prince. And Delores Ward.

Have Robert Prince and Delores Ward got some kind of connection?

47

Delores Ward opened the door to the cabin and welcomed Ren in.

'Can I get you coffee?' said Delores.

'No, thank you,' said Ren. 'But water would be great.'

Delores went to her little refrigerator and brought Ren a bottle of Poland Spring.

'What can I do for you?' said Delores.

'I'd like to ask you about your trip to Williston in April,' said Ren.

'Oh,' said Delores.

'You stopped off in Cheyenne,' said Ren.

'Yes,' said Delores. 'I was feeling unwell. And I wanted to mail a check to Burt Kendall.'

'Oh,' said Ren. *Wind out of sails. Damn.*

'Why did you want to send Burt Kendall a check?' said Ren.

'We needed a new bus,' said Delores. She smiled. 'That journey was particularly bad, so it was quite ironic that I had planned to send the check during that trip.'

'But why anonymously?' said Ren. *And where did you get the money?*

'I didn't want to embarrass him, I didn't want the ladies of the abbey to know, and I wanted to help him because I was aware he was in financial difficulties. I wander around the grounds and I've spoken to him and some of his workers. I wanted to do a good deed and have him get some benefit too. I've always preferred to give quietly. I have family money. I can afford it.'

'The cashier's check came from Butte, Montana,' said Ren. 'Are you from Butte?'

She smiled. 'I'm from here.'

Why would you say otherwise?

'Why did you go all the way to Williston for your protest?' said Ren.

'Prostitution is wrong,' said Delores. 'The camps there are filled with men who traveled there to make their fortune, just like during the Gold Rush. It perpetuates the notion that women can be bought, and treated like dirt, and disease can be spread, and they put these women's lives and health at risk. It's an injustice and it's like a step back in time. I wanted to stop that terrible, damaging cycle.'

'What brought you to Evergreen Abbey?' said Ren. *Fleeing a life of prostitution?*

'It's an old and sorry tale,' said Delores. 'A man broke my heart . . . '

See, love is a nightmare.

'Not before he had taken my family away from me,' said Delores. 'Christmas Day. So I was left with no one.'

Yikes.

'You don't have to talk about this,' said Ren.

But, please, carry on.

She didn't.

'Sit down,' said Ren. 'Let me get you some water.'

'Thank you,' said Delores.

They sat in silence.

313

'Delores, do you know a man called Robert Prince?' said Ren.

Delores frowned. 'No. I can't say that I do. Who is he?'

'He's a very successful businessman,' said Ren. 'He's based in New York, he's got businesses here in Colorado, but his family are originally from Butte, Montana.'

'I have no family connections there,' said Delores.

Damn you! Little old lady . . .

'OK,' said Ren. 'Laura Flynn, the victim of the shooting . . . she was his housekeeper.'

Something flashed across Delores' face.

What was that?

'Would you know anything about that?' said Ren.

Delores shook her head. 'No.'

Silence descended once more.

'Are you OK?' said Ren, eventually.

'Yes,' said Delores. 'Yes.' She paused. 'If you need to be somewhere, you go ahead.'

'Are you sure you're OK?'

Delores nodded. She moved to stand up.

'Stay where you are,' said Ren.

'No, no,' said Delores. 'I can at least walk you to the door.'

Ren gave her a hug before she left. Delores flinched.

Ooh . . . I didn't think that through. Poor impulse control.

But Delores smiled. 'Thank you,' she said. 'Thank you.'

★ ★ ★

Ren sat in the Jeep and started the engine. Her phone rang. It was Janine.

Ren picked up. 'Hey, girl.'

Silence from Janine.

'Are you OK?' said Ren.

'Yes . . . I'm sorry,' said Janine. 'I'm . . .

Crying . . .

'What is it?' said Ren.

'I was right,' said Janine. 'About the unit . . . they're cutting the unit.'

'*What?*'

'They're cutting the cold case unit.'

'Oh my God, no,' said Ren. 'No way. How can they do that?'

'They can and they have and . . . '

'But, I don't get it,' said Ren. 'When did they say that? Have they given you notice?'

'They haven't said it officially,' said Janine. 'Logan, the sweetheart, had heard, and tipped me off.'

'Aw, bless his heart,' said Ren. 'But *fuck* . . . '

'I knew there was something up when they moved me from my office . . . '

'So, what's their plan?' said Ren.

'I don't know, I'll have to wait and see what the sarge says. Logan didn't know, but he figures I'll just be joining the other investigators.'

'Well, as scenarios go, there could be worse outcomes . . . '

'I know,' said Janine, 'but I don't want to lose my unit.'

'Of course you don't,' said Ren. 'It's just . . . well, thank God they're not throwing you out on the street.'

315

Silence. 'I . . . just can't believe it,' said Janine, eventually. 'I'm not saying I'm amazing or anything — '

'You *are* amazing,' said Ren. 'What are you talking about? Fuck this. Where are you now?'

'Where all the best cries happen . . . '

'Ryan Gosling's arms?'

Janine laughed and cried. 'I wish. I'm in the ladies' room . . . '

'What time are you finished up?'

'Five.'

'I'll be there,' said Ren.

'Don't be ridiculous,' said Janine. 'I'm fine.'

'Please,' said Ren. 'In my mind, I'm already gone. See you in Woody's at five forty-five p.m. Be there or be . . . '

'Fired.'

'Stop.'

Ren put down the phone.

Don't cry. Don't cry. This will work out. She is Janine Hooks. She is kick-ass. She is the best. And I have to do something to help. Rader and Hooks! Um . . . Bryce and Hooks! Oh my God. Where the hell did that come from?

48

Ren and Janine sat in Woody's. There had been no real food, just snacks and beer. Ren checked her watch. It was close to midnight.

'I have to call Ben, just give me two minutes.'

'Say hi from me,' said Janine.

'I will,' said Ren.

I am lucky to have a man like Ben. I am so lucky.

Ren went outside onto the sidewalk and dialed Ben's number.

'I will preface this by saying I have not been drinking at all,' said Ren.

'So, you're hammered,' said Ben.

'Exactly,' said Ren. 'Janine and I are drowning our sorrows.'

'What sorrows?' said Ben.

'Well, poor Janine has been tipped off that the cold case unit is about to be cut.'

'Not Janine, no way,' said Ben. 'Tell her I'm sorry, send her my love. Idiots.'

'I know,' said Ren. 'I will. And my sorrow is about becoming homeless. Annie Lowell's trip around Europe has come to an end. I have to hand my, slash, her home back . . .'

'What?' said Ben. 'No. When?'

'She'll be back in Denver next month,' said Ren. 'It'll be so lovely to see her, but I can't bear the idea of leaving the house.'

'You could move in with me,' said Ben.

Ren paused. 'Um . . . you live in D.C . . . '

'You know what I mean . . . ' said Ben. 'I could apply for a transfer to Denver . . . '

Can. Not. Breathe.

'What?' said Ben. 'What are you thinking?'

'Literally I had no thoughts on that,' said Ren. 'None.' *I was too busy trying not to pass out.*

'Could I ask you to have some?' said Ben.

Ren smiled. 'Yes. I'm . . . I will think about that.'

Aaagh.

'I meant to ask you,' said Ben, 'are you supposed to be drinking on those meds you're taking?'

Well, fuck you, Ben.

'Ren? Are you there?'

Fuck you.

'Ren?'

Fuck. You.

'What?' said Ren.

'I'm just asking . . . '

'Yeah, well don't ever ask me that again,' said Ren.

'Hey — '

Beep. Beep. Beep. Beep.

★ ★ ★

Janine had ordered more drinks.

Wonderful, unwise move. I love you.

'Ben sends his love, and was sorry to hear your news,' said Ren.

'He's a sweetheart,' said Janine.

Hmm.

318

'I got some good news on Jesse Coombes while you were outside,' said Janine, holding up her phone. 'Well, not for him, but for us. His cover's been blown at the ranch, a tabloid's gotten hold of the story. Now that it's in the public domain, we shouldn't have a problem gaining access to him.'

'Not if Howard Coombes can help it,' said Ren.

'Well, he's more than welcome to sit in,' said Janine.

'Won't that be fun?' said Ren.

Janine tried to smile.

'You'll get through all this, Janine Hooks,' said Ren. 'We will focus on, in the wise word of Charlie Sheen, 'winning'. You're a strong lady. It's what first attracted me to you.'

'I have a confession to make,' said Janine. 'Speaking of attraction. I might have a spot soft for someone . . . '

'Ooh,' said Ren. 'Who?'

'Robbie. Your Robbie.'

Oh, shit.

Janine stared at her. 'What?' she said. 'What? Define that reaction!'

I caaaan't.

'I say this with great heaviness of heart,' said Ren, 'but I wouldn't go there, if I were you.'

'What?' said Janine. 'Why?'

And now I'm the one sending wind from sails. 'He's just not in a great place,' said Ren. 'I don't want to betray a confidence, but . . . I don't think he's ready for a relationship. You're my best friends in the world, you know I adore you both,

319

but . . . I don't want you to be hurt in any way.'

'What?' said Janine. 'Robbie wouldn't hurt a fly.'

'I know,' said Ren, 'but, please, just trust me on this. He wouldn't mean to hurt you, obviously. He's just . . . he's got family stuff going on.' *Not porn stuff. Nothing to do with sex addiction.* 'He hasn't been himself,' said Ren, 'and I just don't want to see you get caught up in anything. That's the most I can say. And I mean it with no disrespect to either of you.'

'This sounds really serious,' said Janine. 'I'm thrown . . . '

'Look, I've been in your shoes, years ago — I was warned off someone . . . not that I mean I'm warning you off Robbie . . . but anyway, I ignored the advice. And I wish I hadn't. You're more sensible than me. I'm hoping this will work on you.' She smiled.

'I'm not bending my brain around Robbie hurting people,' said Janine. 'Sorry.'

'I know,' said Ren. 'It's . . . complicated.'

'Well, I'm surprised . . . I thought we'd really connected. Maybe I mistook his . . . ' She shrugged. 'Maybe I mistook some kind of vulnerability for openness. I thought it meant he liked me.'

'No — I'm not saying you didn't connect!' said Ren. 'I'm just saying . . . '

One month ago my reaction would have been the exact opposite. Go for it! Yay!

'What?' said Janine.

Oh, I am a destroyer of dreams.

'I just don't want you to be hurt. I mean, of

320

course he likes you . . . '

Can we please stop talking about this? Though, this is my fault. Who gives me the right to say anything or to stop anyone doing anything? If I had never been born and Robbie and Janine met in a bar, they could have gotten together, she would have to take on whatever issues he had, he may have told her, he may not —

'I guess,' said Janine, 'it's like — meeting a nice guy like Robbie . . . it doesn't happen to me every day. Every year . . . It's all right for you.'

'What?' said Ren.

'Well, you've got Ben,' said Janine, 'and possibly that cute guy over at the bar you've been smiling over at for the past half hour . . . '

Ouch. 'I'm not *smiling* smiling.'

'I don't think *he* sees it that way,' said Janine.

'I don't care what way he sees it,' said Ren. 'I don't even know the guy.'

Silence.

'It's just . . . you've got someone,' said Janine. 'So I just don't think it's particularly fair that you stop me from going near Robbie. I thought you'd be cheering me on.'

'I've got someone because I met him, just like this, at a bar, just like you could meet someone here tonight.'

'Yeah, if you weren't . . . '

Weren't what? 'I'm not stopping you going for it with Robbie,' said Ren. 'That's your decision. I'm sorry I said anything. I was trying to — '

'I'm sorry too,' said Janine. 'Let's agree to disagree.'

'I really was only — '

'It's OK,' said Janine. 'I can't just unlike him, though.'

Ren nodded. 'I know.'

'I'm going to the ladies'.' She left.

Shit. I totally screwed up.

The cute guy at the bar smiled over.

Well, hello, there. Yes, I'm quite the catch. I've just hung up on my boyfriend — yes, I have one! — I've pissed off my best friend, and I am nuts.

Ren buried her head in her phone until Janine came back.

'I guess we should be heading home,' said Janine.

'Yup,' said Ren. She got up and started putting on her coat.

The cute guy made a sad face.

Ren smiled at him.

Consider yourself lucky.

Like one of Aileen Wuornos' surviving johns . . .

49

Ren woke up the next morning, her head throbbing, her stomach hollowed out.

Where am I?

The drapes . . . the walls. Oh. Janine's. Oh . . . Robbie. Oh . . . Ben.

Shit.

Ren picked up her cell phone.

She texted Ben:

Sorry about last night. But please don't ask me about meds/alcohol.

Ben replied:

I forgive you for last night. But if you're doing anything that affects how you treat me, I am going to ask about it.

Ooh. You're right.

I'm sorry. Talk later. XX

You actually are right. Who the hell do I think I am? I need to stop speaking to everyone.

She texted Janine.

R u awake? Sorry about last night. Please ignore what I said about Robbie. I am not the relationship police. XX

Janine texted back.

And neither am I. Sorry too — smiling at cute
guys not a crime. Breakfast at Table Mountain
Inn x

Ren sat in front of a half-eaten plate of waffles,
bacon and blueberries, an almost-empty glass of
orange juice and a half-full mug of coffee. Janine
had a fruit salad and a black coffee.

'I need drugs,' said Ren.

'Your wish . . . ' said Janine. She handed her a
bottle of Advil.

'Thank you, thank you, thank you. I can't
believe I ran out.'

'Neither can I.'

Ren's phone started to ring. 'Ooh,' she said.
'Eli Baer, N.Y. — please let it be something
enlightening.'

She picked up. 'Hey, Ren, it's Eli — I've got
some interesting news for you. I've taken another
look at the phone records of the Princes' home
phone. There's a cell phone number on it that
we've traced to a Carolina Vescovi.'

'Oh my God,' said Ren. 'As in Vescovi's
restaurant? As in the last place Viggi Leinster was
seen alive?'

Janine's eyes went wide.

'Yes,' said Eli.

'So the case Laura Flynn wanted to talk to
Janine about was definitely that?' said Ren.

'Looks like it,' said Eli. 'I've mailed you her
number.'

'Thank you, Eli. We could use some good

324

news on this day of great suffering.'

'What happened?' said Eli.

'Drinking, Eli. Drinking happened.'

Ren hung up. 'Can you believe that?'

'Wow,' said Janine. 'A breakthrough over breakfast.'

The door to the inn opened, the bell rang. Ren turned around. 'Oh my God,' she said, turning back to Janine, leaning in. 'It's the guy from the bar.'

Janine looked past her. 'Don't look — I shit you not, he's coming our way.'

'Ladies,' he said.

'Hi,' said Ren and Janine.

'Did you enjoy your night?' he said.

'Yes, we did,' said Ren. 'But we're definitely regretting some of it. You?'

'Well,' he said, eyeballing her. 'It could have ended better . . . '

You baaad man. 'Well,' said Ren, 'maybe next time you'll have a happy ending.'

He laughed out loud. Janine did too.

Oh. Dear. God. That wasn't even on purpose. 'Well, enjoy your day!' said Ren.

He handed her his business card as he was leaving.

'You have to be kidding me,' said Ren when he was gone. 'Men are unbelievable.'

'That was high-larious,' said Janine. 'Don't you admire his courage?'

Ren held up the business card. It felt alive in her hand. 'Please let it say he's a clown. Or any kind of circus performer. Or a wedding planner.' She looked down at it, then turned it toward

Janine. The only thing printed on it was a phone number.

Janine raised her eyebrows. 'Serial killer it is, then . . . '

'Imagine sleeping with that guy,' said Ren.

Don't imagine that. Why would you do that?

'I mean, he looks normal,' said Ren. 'And he's gone in the morning and the only thing left behind is this! I'd be in the shower for a week.'

'That's why I don't do anonymous hook-ups,' said Janine.

'I'd love to say 'neither do I'. Well, I can say neither do I . . . any more.'

'It's just so dangerous,' said Janine.

Ren pointed a corner of the business card at her. 'So you're absolutely sure you don't want this . . . '

They finished breakfast laughing, and stepped out onto the street.

Ugh. Too hot. Too hot. Someone up there is actively trying to set me alight. A dark angel with a magnifying glass . . . Ben's guardian angel. Smile at another man: feel the wrath of a thousand suns sear your skanky soul.

Ren threw the card into the next garbage can.

I just smiled at the guy. Jesus.

Imagine if I had slept with him. Stop.

But imagine.

What is wrong with you?

Janine was staring at her phone. 'I've always wanted to say this,' she said, looking up.

'Say what?' said Ren.

'Well, well, well . . . '

Ren laughed. 'Well, well, well what?'

'I just got a text from Kohler,' said Janine. 'Sweating has taken place: Morgan Greene has decided to sell someone's soul to the devil to get a lighter sentence on the robbery.'

'Whose soul?' said Ren.

'Jesse Coombes',' said Janine.

'Praise the Lord.'

★ ★ ★

Kohler was waiting for them in an empty interview room at the Sheriff's Office. There was a paper evidence bag on the table.

'Greetings, ladies,' said Kohler. 'Take a look inside of this.'

'What is it?' said Ren.

'It's an offering from Morgan Greene,' said Kohler. 'Turns out we had the story of the car at the ranch all wrong. It seems Jesse Coombes was up to his old firestarting tricks. And more . . .'

Ren and Janine put on latex gloves. Janine reached into the bag and pulled out a journal: dark, once white-edged, now dirty, partially burnt.

She opened it. Ren leaned in to look. There was a photo clipped to the corner of the blank contents page. It was of Conor Gorman. There were more photos . . . Conor Gorman, sitting on one of the sofas at the ranch, smiling.

Handsome young man.

There were a few more underneath: Conor in the tack room, his back to the camera. Conor on the basketball court. Conor walking into the shower block. Conor . . .

Whoa.

WTF?

'That headless body shot,' said Ren. 'That's Conor. I know by the red bracelet.' She looked at the next one.

'Well, that's a fresh tattoo,' said Ren. 'Look at the scabs.'

Across the bottom of his back was a tattoo of a reclining black cat with its paw stretched up toward his right shoulder blade.

'He had to have gotten it while he was at the ranch,' said Ren. 'Ranch security is as high as ever. Is there a tattoo parlor in Conifer?'

'No,' said Janine. 'But there's Ink Corp in Golden.'

She flipped through the rest of the pages of the journal. Each was titled *Sermon*, followed by a colon, and the subject. *Sermon: Pain, Sermon: Ability, Sermon: Shame, Sermon: Penance.* The final one: *Sermon: Betrayal.* Betrayal. Betrayal.

'This belongs to Jesse Coombes,' said Janine.

She went through more of it. There was one last photo of Conor, a simple headshot, and all over it was scrawled in red ink:

Rubyman Rubyman Rubyman Rubyman Rubyman Rubyman.

50

Ren, Janine and Kohler all stared at each other.

Kohler raised his eyebrows.

'And how did Morgan Greene say he had this?' said Ren.

'He's saying nothing,' said Kohler. 'He wants promises.'

They laughed.

'I've left him to think further about it,' said Kohler.

'This is fucked up,' said Ren, taking the journal from Janine. 'Is Jesse Coombes completely insane? I mean, did anyone check behind his ear for a 666?'

'That's standard JeffCo procedure . . . ' said Kohler.

'He tried to burn the journal, though,' said Janine. 'Would that not show he's over this infatuation? And, it's not like he did anything extreme with the first 'Rubyman'.'

'If he was trying to burn it, it's because it's evidence of the crazy,' said Ren. 'Evidence of how obsessed he was. This could be an escalation.' She handed Janine one of the shirtless photos of Conor.

Janine turned to Kohler. 'I'll talk to the judge about this little journal development — that should hurry things along with the warrant.'

Kohler nodded. 'Oh, I think so.'

'I am going to kick Kristen Faule's Disney

ass,' said Ren. 'The lying — '

'You'll have to play nicey nicey until we get to speak with Jesse Coombes,' said Kohler. 'Not that I'm trying to tell you how to do your business . . . '

Ren smiled. 'Is this litter-warden vengeance?'

'Oh, you weren't there when he bawled them out of it,' said Janine. 'You did him a great service.'

'Do they all hate me now?' said Ren.

'I kept your name out of it,' said Kohler. He smiled.

'Janine made a major breakthrough on Viggi Leinster,' said Ren.

Janine flashed a look at her.

'Really?' said Kohler.

'Yes,' said Janine. 'Turns out that's the case Laura Flynn was calling me about the day she died. There's a call I can make while we're waiting to hear back about Jesse Coombes.'

★ ★ ★

Janine and Ren sat in front of Viggi Leinster's file. They had propped the photo up in front of them. It was an affecting image; Viggi Leinster was a beautiful, elegant innocent. Tousled blonde hair, huge blue eyes that weren't lost or vacant, but maybe a little sad.

'Ready to rock?' said Ren.

'I sure am,' said Janine. She dialed Carolina Vescovi's number. Ren listened in on the other line as Janine explained who she was and asked about the phone call from the Prince home.

'Oh,' said Carolina. 'Yes. A friend's daughter is working on a documentary for film school on my parents' restaurant. She wanted to use a montage of photos my mother had and the school told her she would need to get permission from anyone featured in them.'

'And one of the Princes was featured?' said Janine.

'Yes — Walter Prince. My mother recognized him. His only surviving relative is his grandson, Robert Prince.'

'And did he give you permission to use the photo?' said Janine.

'No,' said Carolina. 'I was *under no circumstances* to use the photo.'

'Really?' said Janine.

'Oh, yes,' said Carolina.

'Did he say why?' said Janine.

'No,' said Carolina, 'that was the strange part. You could barely even see the man's face. It was his big bulky shoulder, a sliver of a profile, nothing very identifiable. However, it still had to be done properly, according to the film school. There was a woman in the corner of the photo — again, you could barely make her out, kind of looking up at him a little starry-eyed.'

'Do you think they were together?' said Janine.

'Hard to say,' said Carolina.

'But your mom didn't say that it was his wife . . .'

'No,' said Carolina. 'It wasn't his wife. Not that it mattered who she was — when Robert Prince called me back, he said we couldn't use the photo, and he threatened legal action. Then

331

his wife called back, again, very nice and said was I sure that this was Walter Prince, that her husband had been quite upset and she couldn't understand why. I said 'Yes — I know my mother's elderly, but her memory is sharp.''

'Ms Vescovi, if I sent through a photo of a woman, could you take a look at it and see if you recognize her from any other photos in your mother's collection?'

'Absolutely,' said Carolina. She gave Janine her email address.

Janine emailed the photo of Viggi Leinster. She could hear the ping of Carolina's inbox, the click of her mouse. And, eventually, a gasp.

'Oh my gosh,' said Carolina.

Ren and Janine exchanged glances.

'That woman,' said Carolina. 'Her eyes. She's the same woman at the edge of the photo with Walter Prince. She was beautiful. She . . . she . . . who is she?'

'Her name was Viggi Leinster,' said Janine. 'She's been on the Missing Persons list since 1957. The last confirmed sighting of her was at your parents' restaurant.'

'Wow — I've never heard anything about that,' said Carolina. 'But, then, I was only a child . . . '

'There are no witness statements from your parents in the police report,' said Janine. 'We believe they had to have been in the restaurant that night. There was a party for the premiere of *Nights of Cabiria*. It was a big event.'

It sounded like Carolina Vescovi was crying.

Janine and Ren stared at each other.

'Ms Vescovi?' said Janine.

They could hear her struggle to control her breathing.

'Is everything OK?' said Janine.

'I . . . I . . . I'm going to have to call you back . . . '

'Please,' said Janine, 'if there's anything . . . '

'I . . . will call back . . . I promise.'

The line went dead.

Ren and Janine put down the phones.

'What are we supposed to do with that information?' said Ren.

'I have no idea,' said Janine.

'So, Walter Prince and Viggi Leinster knew each other,' said Ren.

'Walter Prince was one of the last people to see a missing woman alive,' said Janine.

'And there's no record of him in any of the police reports . . . ' said Ren.

'What has gotten her so upset?' said Janine. 'What's the rest of her story?'

'We'll leave her to compose herself,' said Ren. 'I'm sure she wouldn't hang up for no reason.'

Kohler was standing there as they looked up.

'Sadly, you can't hang around to find out,' said Kohler. 'Jesse Coombes awaits.'

51

Kristen Faule had arranged for Kohler and Ren to meet with Jesse Coombes in the art therapy room at the ranch. Ren turned to Kohler as they arrived at the door. 'OK, out of the two of us, I would venture that I look the most harmless . . . and this kid's father is a raving misogynist — '

'Can you believe he's letting the kid do this alone?' said Kohler.

'I absolutely can,' said Ren. 'And here's why . . . something's going on with Howard Coombes. Some shit is about to hit the fan and he is avoiding the law and he's avoiding facing his son. He has fucked up in some way. I know it.'

'These people don't deserve to have kids,' said Kohler.

'Nope,' said Ren. 'So, back to the misogyny. If Jesse Coombes is anything like his daddy, he may look at women as the weaker sex . . . You do the routine stuff and I'll come in with the hard questions . . . '

'Are you trying to avoid saying good cop/bad cop?' said Kohler.

'It cheapens us.'

★ ★ ★

The art therapy room was filled with light, in contrast to the emo presence sitting at the desk by the wall in front of rows of student paintings.

334

The images were almost entirely rich with color. Ren pictured a buoyant teacher with an overstretched smile, running around, taking all the black ink away, pausing at the red ink, tempted to do the same, but deciding — no! — it could also be used for lips or beach balls or prom dresses or hearts or roses! Not just blood!

Jesse Coombes was leaning forward, his fingertips pressed together, his hands making a circle in front of him that he kept opening and closing. As he looked up, Ren could see he still had traces of the youthful looks she had seen in his videos, but hadn't recognized in him the first time they met.

'Hello, Jesse,' said Kohler. 'I'm Detective Kohler, and this is Special Agent Ren Bryce, she's an FBI agent with Safe Streets in Denver.'

'Sir,' he said, nodding to Kohler, shaking his hand.

'Hello again,' said Ren. 'We met before . . . '

'Hello, ma'am,' said Jesse, standing up. He reached and clasped Ren's hand as he shook it. 'Of course I remember you. I'm sorry I lied that day.'

'As long as we agree on the truth from now on,' said Ren.

Jesse nodded.

'We'd like you to talk us through the morning of Monday, May 14th, please,' said Kohler.

'Well, I'll try,' said Jesse, 'but it seems like a long time ago. I know it isn't, but it just feels that way.' He paused. 'Breakfast is the same time every morning in the main lodge — eight a.m. I usually get up between seven and seven thirty, take a shower, head over then.'

'And is that what you did that morning?' said Kohler.

'Yes, sir,' said Jesse.

'What time was breakfast over at?' said Kohler.

'Eight forty-five,' said Jesse.

'Where did you go afterward?' said Kohler.

'Classes begin at nine,' said Jesse. 'I went to class — '

'We can get a copy of your timetable for that morning,' said Kohler. 'Your attendance records.'

Jesse swallowed. 'Sure,' he said. 'That's OK . . . '

Hmm. 'If they've been in any way tampered with,' said Ren, 'there will be consequences. This goes beyond the ranch, Jesse. And it's a homicide investigation . . . '

He stared down at the ground. 'I know, ma'am. But I don't know anything about the homicide. I swear on the Bible, I do not.'

Ren and Kohler glanced at each other.

'You believe in the truth, don't you?' said Ren. 'In being honest.'

'Yes, ma'am,' said Jesse. He looked up at her.

'Please, Jesse, for your own sake, for everyone's, tell us what happened that morning,' said Ren.

As she waited, her gaze traveled along the wall of artwork, some of which looked like it was painted by ten-year-olds . . . probably the last time these kids felt safe or loved or happy or cared for. There was one image of a back garden; green grass, a barbecue, a picket fence and birthday balloons — red! When Ren looked closer, the fence posts were graves with names on them. Lots of names. And the birthday balloons were created by the brush being flicked over the page. Spatter. And the barbecue tools were guns and knives and they were covered with birthday-balloon red.

Jesse Coombes' birthday barbecue . . .

Kohler said nothing to break the silence.

'Tell me about the car,' said Ren, turning to Jesse. *Tell me about the beautiful flames.*

Jesse's gaze jerked toward her. 'What about it?' He paused. 'The car that was burnt out?'

'Yes,' said Ren. *Patience.*

'I don't know,' he said. 'I just heard about it after . . . '

Ren leaned down to her satchel and took out the brown paper evidence bag. She set it in front of him. She slid out the journal. 'We found this, Jesse . . . '

He blushed.

I do not want to humiliate you.

'How?' he managed to say.

'A man called Morgan Greene had it,' said Ren. 'Do you know him?'

Jesse shook his head. 'Not really.' He paused. 'He told me he'd get rid of it.'

'He didn't,' said Ren. 'He kept it to use against you. He lied to you. What we need to know is your side of the story. All we have so far is this, and his promise to tell us the rest. He wants a lighter sentence.'

Jesse started to cry.

'When I was your age,' said Ren, 'I had a journal. I used to write down every single thought

337

I had. It wasn't a very happy time for me. I found that journal a few years back, and I read it. It was horrible. So little of it reflected who I am, or even how I saw those years looking back. Do you know what I did, Jesse? I burned it. I threw it in the fire in my mom's house when she wasn't looking and I was very happy to see it go up in flames. And the idea that anyone else would have read it, back then or even now . . . well, I couldn't bear it. Detective Kohler and I are not here to judge you or to judge what you've written. We're just here to get to the bottom of things. We are working on a very important investigation here and we need your help. We need your truthful answers. We have no interest in embarrassing you.'

Jesse nodded. 'Thank you . . . '

'So . . . ' said Ren. 'Take your time.'

'I . . . I got some bad news the night before . . . '

Ren waited.

'News about my father . . . ' said Jesse. He snorted. 'And I heard it from his publicist. Even though my father, apparently, had just flown into Centennial Airport. I found that out the next morning. Anyway, the publicist that I've never even spoken to before told me that a story could possibly break about my father, that it was not for definite that it would, but that if it did, I had to be 'prepared' . . . which meant prepared to lie about it, as opposed to being emotionally prepared. Nice.'

'What was that news?' said Ren.

'My father has gotten his secretary pregnant,' said Jesse. 'Newsflash: my father is an asshole.'

338

52

Ren looked at Jesse Coombes and the destruction wrought by the boy's own father, a man who chose to dictate to the world how they should live, while living an entirely different way himself.

I will never understand the mind of people like that. Live, let live. Or shut the fuck up.

'When you heard about your father, how did it make you feel?' said Ren.

Jesse smiled. 'Now you sound like a counselor.'

'OK,' said Ren. 'How about you tell me how you reacted . . . '

'Well . . . ' said Jesse. 'I couldn't sleep, thinking about it all . . . and at about five a.m., I'd had enough. I went outside, I walked and walked and I ended up in the grounds of the abbey. I didn't even know I had crossed over. But I was there and then I was past the chapel and then, then I came across this cemetery. It was all overgrown, all these people's memorials just covered in weeds and stuff, and I just thought of people's legacies being destroyed and it was all just so depressing. I thought of my time on earth, my father's, everyone's. I pulled away a few weeds to read the headstones and I see a little baby grave and it just . . . it just broke my heart. I thought of myself, how shitty my father is, how hard he's made things for me, all my life, and I felt ungrateful. I felt spiteful and unforgiving and unloving. I felt like I was judging, when I am not the one to judge. Only Our Lord shall judge. I looked at that little baby's name carved into that stone and I thought, she didn't stand a chance, she did not stand a chance in this world. Baby Ward. I cleared away the rest of the weeds and I kept on clearing and I kept on clearing. By then, it was breakfast time and I . . . I had to go. But when I was at breakfast, I realized that I had left this pile of scrub just there in the cemetery, and I thought about the wildfire that just happened and I thought about how hot it was and how stupid I'd been and then I decided that I couldn't leave everything there, but that if I set some kind of controlled fire in the cemetery, it would look like a hate crime or something. So I got one of Kendall's cars and picked up all the weeds and scrub and stuff, put them in the trunk, and drove it back to the fire pit. I threw all the weeds in there and lit it on fire, you know, so it could burn safely . . . As I was watching the flames, I started thinking about my father and his new baby and how he lies all the time, and I had horrible thoughts and I felt horrible that any part of me was like my father and . . . the journal . . . the journal was part of that. So I went to my room, I got it, and I came back. My plan was to throw it in there. That's when Morgan Greene showed up.'

'Did you know him?' said Ren.

'I knew him to say hello to, from him working at the ranch.'

'What did he say to you?' said Ren.

'He grabbed the journal from me, wanted to look at it,' said Jesse. 'We struggled, it dropped, I kicked it into the fire pit, but it didn't land in the flames. He reached down and grabbed it out, started looking at it.'

'That can't have been easy,' said Ren.

'No, ma'am,' said Jesse.

'What happened next?' said Ren.

'Well, he said that if I wanted it back, we could come to some arrangement.'

'And you really wanted it back,' said Ren.

'Yes, ma'am,' said Jesse. 'He said he would take care of the accelerant, set the car I'd used on fire. He'd do all that stuff. All I had to do was keep my mouth shut. He wouldn't say I did it, I wouldn't say he did it, but enough doubt would be cast that no one could really be sure. He was lying, though. Once he knew that the car was burnt out, he went straight to the Faules and told them he had seen me hanging around the fire pit. My clothes stank. It was obvious.'

'How did the Faules react?' said Ren.

'They were angry at first,' said Jesse. 'But then they were very understanding when they heard about the situation with my father. I had to take the hit. I couldn't tell them that Morgan Greene had forced me into it, because he still had the journal. Kristen scheduled extra therapy for me, and she and Kenneth agreed to pay for Mr Kendall's car.' He paused. 'What happened with Conor's aunt later that day . . . that was something no one expected. I'm sure the Faules didn't want to have to lie to you — they're good

Christian people — but I think they'd already gone so far.'

'How the Faules responded to all this was their choice, Jesse, and it's not something for you to worry about,' said Ren.

'But I — ' said Jesse.

'You made a bad judgment call,' said Ren, 'because of an emotional situation you found yourself in.'

'I should have known better,' said Jesse. 'I'd been getting help.'

'It takes time,' said Ren. 'You have to be patient.'

But you don't get off that lightly.

Ren shifted her seat a little forward. 'Jesse, could you tell me a little more about your feelings for Conor Gorman?'

Jesse reddened. He shook his head. 'Please don't . . . please don't ask me that. It's embarrassing.'

'I'm afraid these are the questions I need answers to,' said Ren.

'I tried to burn the journal for a reason,' said Jesse.

'And what was that reason?' said Ren.

'I'm not that person anymore,' said Jesse. 'It's like what you said about your journal.'

Ren nodded. 'What person is that?'

'I don't really know. Intense?'

Ren waited.

'Maybe I care about people a little too much,' said Jesse. 'I have a lot of love. I have all the Lord's love inside me, because I need to have enough to give to each and every person who does not believe that they have it, that they were born with it, that the Lord placed it right there for them, the same way as He placed their eyes and ears and their ten fingers and their ten toes. It's just you can't see it.'

Alrighty, then . . . You can only suppress the crazy for so long.

'So I have to show them that it's there,' said Jesse. 'But people often aren't open to that. They're afraid. So you have to hide it until a time comes when you can release it. Only then can I stand before them and let them know about that love and have them walk away with that love in their hearts. Can you imagine what storing all that love feels like? Maybe . . . I don't know . . . but maybe when I wasn't standing up in front of crowds any more, maybe when I wasn't sending all of that love out there, there was too much of it left inside me. And when only one or two people are getting all that love that I have to give . . . hundreds-and-thousands-of-people worth of love . . . maybe they won't ever understand.'

Or maybe some day, someone will.

'Did you ever consider that Conor's aunt wanted to take him away from the ranch?' said Ren.

'No,' said Jesse.

'Did he say anything like that?' said Ren.

'No,' said Jesse.

'What does 'Rubyman' mean, Jesse?' said Ren.

'It's one of my father's terms,' said Jesse. 'I am to invoke The Rubyman when faced with danger. He is my inner strength, The Rubyman. Rubies ward off evil, restrain lustful thoughts — '

'Who were you having lustful thoughts about?' said Ren. Again, Jesse reddened.

'OK, let's save that question,' said Ren. 'Let's get back to The Rubyman . . . so he's not the devil?'

Jesse looked horrified. 'No, no, no. The opposite. And The Rubyman is what's inside me — it's not someone else. It's not an external power.'

'Can you explain how The Rubyman related to Dominic Fisher?' said Ren.

Jesse's eyes went wide. 'How did you know about that?'

'That doesn't matter,' said Ren. 'But, please explain that to me.'

'He was guiding me into dark ways,' said Jesse. 'He got me stealing, hotwiring cars. He . . . I was taking the wrong path.'

'And the photos of Dominic Fisher that you had on that secret cell phone?' said Ren.

'I . . . I didn't want to send that girl photos of my body,' said Jesse. 'The girl in Austin. I . . . I . . . wasn't as buff as Dominic. I didn't work out. I'm so ashamed. So, I took photos of him, he had no clue, and I sent her those instead, like, with his head chopped out of them. I told her it was because of who I was . . . that I couldn't get caught with ones that had my face in them.'

'It was my understanding that you took those photos of Dominic Fisher for yourself,' said Ren.

'No, oh my gosh, no,' said Jesse. 'They were for her. Who told you that?'

Someone very eager to misinterpret the

344

actions of an evangelist.

Someone not unlike myself . . .

'And she sent you nude photos,' said Ren.

'Yes, but that wasn't what I wanted . . . I didn't ask for them.' He shrugged. 'But I probably shouldn't have kept them, I know.'

'In what way,' said Ren, 'did you believe that Conor Gorman was guiding you on the wrong path if you were also invoking The Rubyman because of him?'

Jesse frowned. 'Um . . . I . . . his anger. He kind of feeds in to anger, and I don't like that. I was worried that I was beginning to do the same. Anger scares me. I like Conor a lot, he's my friend, but . . . I'm not sure he's very good for me.'

'In what way?' said Ren.

'He's kind of aggressive,' said Jesse. 'That's all. He's cool, though. But . . . the things he's done, like running away, the bar fight, all that. I'm here at the ranch because I want help. I need it.'

'Tell me about the photos of Conor,' said Ren.

'He asked me to take them,' said Jesse.

What?! 'Why?'

'I have no idea,' said Conor. 'He wanted one of his tattoo, anyway.'

'What did you take them with?' said Ren.

He paused. 'The camera from the photography class. I borrowed it. I printed them out there when the teacher was out of the room.'

'And why did you still have them?' said Ren.

'Conor didn't want them any more, told me to get rid of them. I was just trying to kill two birds with the one stone.' He looked at Ren. 'I'm sorry about all this. I want to take responsibility for my actions. I don't want to be like my father. I don't want to ever hear the word Rubyman again.'

Me neither.

'My father looks outward for somewhere to lay the blame for his own actions,' said Jesse. 'He created this myth, so he could blame *that* for his wrongdoings. Like, if The Rubyman did not come forth when called, then it was his absence that was the issue. That way, my father can't lose. He has all kinds of people, real and imagined, to blame his actions on.'

'It sounds to me like your therapy is working,' said Ren.

'Thank you,' said Jesse, 'because if I end up like my father, the Lord's work will have been in vain.'

Still holding a torch for the crazy, bless your heart.

53

Ren and Kohler started down the hallway to Kristen Faule's office.

'I did not expect that,' said Ren.

'That's what's called a curveball,' said Kohler.

'I feel so sorry for him,' said Ren. 'Jesus. Howard Coombes is odious.'

'Kid didn't stand much of a chance,' said Kohler.

'He's been brainwashed,' said Ren. 'It's like his father is half-cult leader, half-showbiz dad. Have you ever watched *American Idol*?'

'My wife watches it,' said Kohler.

'I admit I watch it too much,' said Ren, 'I admit I love it. Though I am tiring of the same songs being sung over and over again — '

'That's what my wife says . . . '

'Anyway, if you've ever watched it — you know those teenage girls who sing a song and they smile during the whole thing, even though the song is not a happy song? It's like they've never really listened to the lyrics. Most of them have been performing since they were tiny little things, singing songs with adult lyrics that their parents didn't even want them to understand at that stage, anyway. Their job was just to sing and smile. Well, I think Jesse Coombes was a sing-and-smile kind of kid, smiling and not really understanding the words.' She paused. 'Now he does. And maybe he's going through audience

347

withdrawal. The poor kid is so used to performing that he's empty without an audience.'

'That art room was the same kind of thing,' said Kohler. 'Put on a happy face. Do you think they take the black away from them?'

'I do,' said Ren. 'That barbecue drawing . . . '

'I guess they have to give them creative control,' said Kohler. He paused. 'All the same, I'd like to know if that was my kid's idea of party planning . . . '

'Barbecue at our place! You'll be dying to come! D'oh — coming to die!'

'Are you buying it all?' said Kohler. 'That he didn't leave the ranch that day . . . ?'

'I don't know,' said Ren. 'It would be my worst possible nightmare to discover that he's only realizing the error of his ways now because of some monstrous wake-up call . . . '

'In the form of murdering a pregnant woman?' said Kohler. 'Well, however much of a screw-up his father is, however much a victim he might be, there's something about that kid I don't like.'

'I'm not sure what vibe I was getting from him,' said Ren, 'or if he was struggling too hard not to send out any vibe. Either way, there's a disturbance in the force . . . ' She paused. 'Can you do the talking, the accusing, the fingerpointing with Kristen Faule? I'm done. I'm done.'

'Are you avoiding saying good cop/bad cop?' said Kohler.

Ren laughed. 'This time it's bad cop/silent cop.'

Kristen Faule looked at Ren and Kohler with a weariness in her eyes to rival Jesse Coombes'.

What is this place doing to everyone? Shouldn't it be enriching them?

'Should I be worried about any of that artwork?' said Kohler.

'No,' said Kristen.

'Was there a reason you chose the art therapy room for our meeting with Jesse Coombes?' said Kohler.

'Yes — it's a comfortable setting for him.' Her tone was sharp. 'Was there a painting in particular that bothered you?'

'I didn't study them all,' said Kohler, 'but the barbecue . . . '

Kristen shook her head. 'It's a scene from a young adult novel. That was the subject last week.'

Kohler asked her about the car, the cover-up, the lying.

'Hand on my heart,' said Kristen, 'I know that Jesse Coombes had nothing to do with what happened to Laura Flynn. I hope you believe me. He is incapable of violence.'

'We know that Jesse Coombes badly beat a school kid not two years ago,' said Kohler.

'I am aware of that,' said Kristen. 'I am breaking confidentiality — in his defense — to tell you that he told his counselor all about that, he wrote it on his entry form, explaining that it was a changing moment in his life, a defining moment. It was reactionary, because of his father's original sex scandal. He came to the ranch and was taught that anger is a perfectly acceptable emotion, but that the key is to channel it into something productive. We were successful to that end, which is how he got into the terrible situation with the fire that morning. He had decided to do some good with his anger, to tidy the cemetery. But when it came to cleaning up after himself, again with the best of intentions, it all went wrong. That was why we 'covered' for him. Kenneth and I felt that he had learned a valuable lesson in anger management, and we couldn't see him punished for what was an accident.'

'Well, just to inform you,' said Kohler, 'that Morgan Greene and Burt Kendall appear to have scammed you. Morgan took a personal journal of Jesse's and told him to stay quiet about his presence there that morning. Morgan Greene threw on the accelerant. Jesse is innocent.'

'That's what I've always thought,' said Kristen. 'I believe in that boy. I just desperately want him to have a chance in life. I watched that documentary on him before I ever came in contact with him and it just about broke my heart. He was a lost boy even then. And, off the record, I think that Howard Coombes is one of the vilest men I have ever come into contact with. A man who is happy to keep throwing his family to the wolves, over and over, until they are picked clean. It's disgusting.'

Kristen looked to Ren, her eyes filled with pleading. 'I'm not a liar . . . I didn't want to lie. I was . . . trying to do the right thing.'

Ren said nothing.

I'm sorry. I'm just tired of people trying to do the right thing and sabotaging my investigation as they do it. I get you, I don't get you. I'm tired.

Kristen's office phone rang. Ren could hear the faint voice of the receptionist. 'Not right now,' said Kristen. 'Thank you.'

Ooh. Oh. Now, I've got it.

'Visitors' day here is Sunday, is that right?' said Ren.

'Yes,' said Kristen. 'Why do you ask?'

'Why Sunday?' said Ren.

'Because families are often free to travel,' said Kristen. 'And the kids begin their Monday morning fresh from those visits. They go to bed earlier on Sunday nights, they get that contact, so it's easier for them.'

'So does that mean that they're not allowed phone calls on Sunday nights?' said Ren.

'That's correct,' said Kristen.

Ren thought about it.

'Mrs Faule, after everything, after *everything* you just spoke to us about,' said Ren, 'you're still withholding?'

'Withholding?' said Kristen.

Ren leaned forward. 'Why don't you hand me that phone you confiscated from Jesse Coombes?'

Ren turned to Kohler. His eyebrow was raised.

Yeah: bad cop/worse cop.

351

After terse goodbyes, Kohler and Ren left Kristen Faule in her office.

'So, Jesse Coombes had a phone in the ranch,' said Kohler. 'How did you know?'

'How else would he have been able to hear about his father's impregnating ways the night before the murder? That was a Sunday,' said Ren. 'When Janine and I were here the last time, Kenneth Faule came in and handed her a confiscated phone. He put a sticker on it and wrote what I thought was a number on it — 96226. I was reading it from the reflection of the silver frame on her desk. If you look at 96226 a different way, it reads JESSE. It's Kenneth Faule's writing: *J* like a nine, *E*s like sixes, *S*s like twos. It's how Jesse took the photos of Conor . . . I couldn't see him getting away with sneaking off with a proper photography-class camera.'

'I'll drop this into the lab for processing,' said Kohler. 'I'll take care of Morgan Greene, and send Janine your way, so you can check out the cemetery, confirm the kid's story.'

'Thanks,' said Ren.

Ren hovered in the foyer of The Darned Heart, rummaging through her purse for her keys. She could hear footsteps behind her, quickening footsteps. She turned around. Kristen Faule was coming down the hallway toward her. When she reached her, she grabbed Ren's arm. Hard.

What the fuck?

'Please,' said Kristen. 'I know what I did was wrong, but . . . ' She took a deep breath. 'It's just . . . '

Ren gently pulled her arm away.

'Agent Bryce, can you please do something for me?' Her face looked suddenly haunted.

What the — 'Yes . . . ' said Ren.

Kristen locked eyes with her. 'Can you make sure that Derrick Charles doesn't ever see daylight?'

54

Ren couldn't tear her eyes away from Kristen Faule. She struggled to process the shift from Jesse Coombes to Derrick Charles. But Kristen was plowing on.

'I'm worried that, because of Robert Prince's donation, Kenneth's campaign for Derrick's release will work,' said Kristen, 'and that can't happen.'

'Why not?' said Ren.

'Can I tell you something without my husband finding out?' said Kristen.

'I can't guarantee that,' said Ren. 'No.'

Kristen looked away. 'This is all a mess,' she said. 'This campaign . . . '

'The campaign?' said Ren.

Kristen looked down. 'No . . . not the campaign . . . well, yes . . . but . . . '

Who is this version of Kristen Faule I see before me?

'Is there anywhere we can sit down?' said Ren.

Kristen nodded. 'Yes.' She glanced at her watch. 'The meditation room should be free.'

Please don't make me sit on a mat . . . or one of those weird stools . . .

Kristen opened the door into a small room off reception. She nodded at the receptionist to let her know that's where they were going. There were some regular chairs inside. Kristen took two out and set them opposite each other.

She held her head in her hands, then swept

her fingers through her hair.

Hurry up! Jesus!

'It's just . . . it doesn't matter . . . ' Tears welled in Kristen's eyes.

Oh, no. I'm sorry. You can't back out now.

This is something personal. Very personal.

'Derrick Charles has met someone new while he's been in prison.' *I lied.* 'She is twenty-six years old, she has two young girls, aged seven and four, so if there's anything you know . . . '

Result.

Kristen swallowed hard. 'All I can do is tell you my experience with Derrick Charles. First of all, what you don't know about my husband is that he genuinely believes that he is not racist . . . '

What? Where is this going?

'So,' said Kristen, 'he has African-American friends, African-American teens at the ranch, all that. However, what he is against is inter-racial relationships. Weird, right? I didn't even realize until after we were married. I mean, he had all these African-American teammates, friends . . . we were already married when he made a comment one day about an inter-racial couple we saw out in a restaurant. Then I realized we were only friends with the players who had African-American wives.'

Annd . . .

'Anyway, Kenneth was away . . . his father had taken ill. I was home, Derrick called over to see how everything was . . . '

Oh. Dear. God. You slept with Derrick Charles.

355

'We had a few drinks, one thing led to another . . . I had always found Derrick attractive . . . We ended up in bed.' She was staring down at her hands.

Silence.

'He beat me black and blue.' She turned to Ren.

'Afterwards?' said Ren.

'During it, afterwards . . . I know that at first, at the very beginning, he was sweet, but it was all a game. Not even a game. He had already won. He destroyed me that night. He destroyed me. And how he looked at me when he was walking out the bedroom door. The smirk. It is seared into my brain. It was a smirk that said 'I know you can't tell your husband this, I know you can't tell anyone this.''

Why in God's name are you telling me?

'You seem like a strong woman,' said Kristen. 'You look like you don't take any shit from anyone. I wish I was like you.'

Ren shook her head. 'No. What happened to you could have happened to anyone. How were you to know? I've looked into Derrick Charles. He had no history. That's why his appeal is progressing. He is saying that he never laid a finger on a woman.'

Kristen snorted. 'A finger — no. He likes the full force of his fist. And I mean that in all kinds of ways. He is insane. And . . . he . . . bit me. It was a deep bite. Do you know what I had to do? I had to take a kitchen knife to my own shoulder. I had to cut out around the teeth marks and pretend to my husband that I had a skin cancer

356

scare. I had to tell him that I had a biopsy while he was away.'

Oh my God, you poor woman.

'Kenneth has been rubbing SPF 50 into me ever since,' said Kristen. 'And every time his hand goes over that hideous scar . . . ' She started to cry. 'He's so gentle . . . '

I have heard some grim things in my time . . .

'I am so sorry,' said Ren. 'What a terrible thing to have to go through. And alone for all these years.'

'Derrick Charles is an animal,' said Kristen.

How can you let your husband campaign for his release?

'Yet he managed to convince Kenneth to support him,' said Kristen. 'Can you imagine how sick that man's mind is? How twisted he is? He gets off on every part of this. How does someone end up like that?'

He has definitely done this to other women.

'How long before his wife and children were murdered did this happen?' said Ren.

'It was two years beforehand,' said Kristen. She nodded. 'I know — he has to have done this to other women in the meantime.'

And before that. And after that. And we will get him.

'I can't have children because of Derrick Charles,' said Kristen. 'So, I'm sorry if I come across to you like some defensive, lying . . . witch. Or that I don't care about Laura Flynn. I absolutely do. I'm not that kind of person. I'm just . . . I'm fighting for the ranch. I'm fighting for the only baby I have . . . '

'I'm so sorry,' said Ren. 'So terribly sorry for what you've gone through. I can't imagine what it's been like for you.'

'I just wanted you to understand,' said Kristen.

'I do,' said Ren. 'But you can't bring your fight into my investigation. I understand why you did what you did. But it's wrong to have withheld evidence. It was wrong for the ranch and for Laura Flynn's memory and for Conor. I don't mean to sound harsh. I will get you all the help you need. And I will do everything I can about Derrick Charles — '

'I hope so,' said Kristen.

'But not without you going on the record,' said Ren. 'I'm sorry that there's no other way.'

Kristen looked down. 'Maybe, the time has come.'

55

Janine was getting out of her car at the parking lot of the abbey when Ren arrived.

'Kohler filled me in,' said Janine.

'Well, I got more for you,' said Ren. She told her about Kristen Faule and Derrick Charles.

'Holy shit,' said Janine. She paused. 'Howard Coombes . . . what he's done to his family. Ren . . . what if Jesse Coombes came across Laura Flynn and she represented everything he hated at that moment? A pregnant woman who was about to take someone away from him?'

'Oh, God,' said Ren.

★ ★ ★

They took Ren's Jeep to the cemetery. As Kohler had said, it was on a small plot of land that was recently tended. There was a mix of headstones and metal crosses standing over no more than twenty graves. The gate was padlocked shut and rusted. Instead, they walked around the side until they could find the missing fence posts that gave access.

'It's just so poignant that Jesse Coombes would think to tidy this place,' said Ren. 'It's like . . . fuck. He's a teenage boy, he should be out having fun with his buddies, instead of creeping around here in the middle of the night to keep his anger problems under control because his father is a dickhead.'

They stopped at the grave with the most prominent headstone and read the inscription.

Fr Daniel O'Sullivan
1st Chaplain of Evergreen Abbey
b. 1877 d. 1959
I am at peace.

'He has to be Irish,' said Ren. 'Not to buy into clichés, of course.'

'Of course . . . ' said Janine.

'I once dated an Irish guy,' said Ren. 'It was all liquor and sex.'

'We're in a cemetery . . . '

'He was a total depressive, though,' said Ren. 'And I couldn't compete with his mom. He called her mammy. It freaked me out. I broke it off with him before she came to visit. He'd see us side by side and know she was The One.'

Janine laughed.

They walked to the back of the cemetery. 'Oh,' said Janine, pointing. 'Maybe Jesse Coombes didn't quite succeed in fully taming that anger of his.'

Close to the corner, a gravestone had been broken, parts of it scattered about.

'Surely he knew we were going to come check out his story,' said Ren.

'It might not have happened on the same night,' said Janine. 'Because Kohler would have mentioned if he saw a desecrated grave during the search.'

'Good point,' said Ren.

They both put on gloves and picked up the pieces of the gravestone.

'Jigsaw time,' said Ren.

'Finally, work and play have collided.'

'Every time I'm around work and play collide,' said Ren.

'What was I thinking?' said Janine.

They laid out the pieces of stone on the ground behind the grave.

'We're missing bits,' said Ren.

'Well spotted,' said Janine. Deadpan.

'OK, we've got an *E, L, E* and a *b. 1940*,' said Ren. 'And an *R, D*. And a *d. 1957*.'

'And a *BA* and a *b. 1957*.'

The rest of the inscription was impossible to read or gone. Ren stopped.

'Oh my God,' she said. She turned to Janine. 'Jesse Coombes talked about a baby's grave. Baby Ward. Look — there's a *b. 1957* and a *d. 1957*. A baby who died at birth? And . . . the mother . . . the letters . . . '

Ren pulled out her phone.

'What is it?' said Janine.

'I need to call Eleanor Jensen,' said Ren. 'Hi, Eleanor, it's Ren Bryce — do you have access to the admission records of the abbey? Like, when it was an abbey, originally?'

'There's an old file cabinet here,' said Eleanor. 'I've never really poked around in it too much.'

'Could you look up Delores Ward's details?' said Ren.

'Is there some kind of problem?' said Eleanor.

'No,' said Ren, 'it's just something I need to find out. I'm putting you on speaker with Janine

Hooks from the Sheriff's Office.'

'OK, hello,' said Eleanor.

'Delores Ward wasn't very forthcoming when we spoke about where she came from,' said Ren. 'Nothing untoward. I just really need to know if she's from Butte, Montana.'

Ren could hear the rattle and scrape of a filing cabinet being opened and the clacking plastic of the tops of the file folders.

'OK, I've got Ward,' said Eleanor. 'I've got it . . . ' She paused. 'Oh,' she said. 'Delores Ward, born in 1940, doesn't say where. Came here to the abbey in 1957 . . . used to be one of 'Ma's girls' . . . Ma was one of the madams, the brothel keepers on Colfax. Oh. Well, that can't be right . . . '

'What?' said Ren.

'There are medical files here,' said Eleanor. 'Oh . . . ' Her voice had plunged an octave. 'Oh . . . it says here Delores Ward died in 1957 in childbirth. Daughter, Baby Ward, stillborn on the same day.'

Ren and Janine stared at each other.

'Thank you,' said Ren. 'Please keep this confidential, Eleanor. I'll get back to you.'

She hung up.

'Oh my God,' said Ren. 'Whoever is in that cabin, stole the identity of some poor lady-of-the-night who died in childbirth. Why?' *Why? Why?*

Ren and Janine jumped back into the Jeep.

'But what's Delores Ward got to do with Jesse Coombes?' said Ren.

'Only one way to find out,' said Janine.

★ ★ ★

As they drove, the sky darkened, as if a switch had been flicked. Ren sped up the driveway to The Darned Heart. Outside the main building, groups of kids and adults were standing around. Two security men were in a huddle with Kristen Faule.

'What the hell is going on here?' said Janine.

They ran up to Kristen Faule. 'What happened?' said Ren.

'They got into a fight,' said Kristen. 'Conor and Jesse. Conor's gone.'

Janine called the report in to Kohler.

A boy in a ranch staffer T-shirt appeared in the doorway with Jesse Coombes beside him, holding a bloodied towel to his head. Jesse looked over at Ren and Janine.

He pushed the staffer to the ground . . . and ran.

56

Ren and Janine sprinted after Jesse, following him down the hallway toward Kristen's office.

'Jesse!' said Ren. 'Stop! Put your hands where I can see them!'

He kept running.

'Jesse!' said Ren. 'You don't want to do this. You really don't want to do this. You'll be in bigger trouble.'

He started to slow.

Do the right thing, Jesse. Do the right thing.

Jesse stopped. He turned around. 'I'm sorry,' he said.

Rinse, repeat.

★   ★   ★

Jesse Coombes did not have the physique for fighting, nor the face, nor the demeanor. Nothing about the cuts and bruises looked right. He didn't even seem to know how to hold himself as an injured person. He was almost hovering on the chair.

'Jesse, where is Conor?' said Ren.

'I don't know,' said Jesse. He was tilting his head up, so his good eye was facing her. The other was swollen shut.

Ren slammed her hands on the table. 'Where is he, Jesse?'

'I told you, I don't know.'

They both looked up as rain began to pour down on the skylight above them.

'How was he when he left?' said Ren. 'What was his state of mind?'

'He was angry,' said Jesse. He looked away. 'I told you. Conor's always angry.'

'About what?' said Ren.

Jesse wouldn't shift his gaze from the floor.

Ren turned to Janine. 'We're not getting a lot here, Detective Hooks. Would you mind staying with Jesse, while I go talk to Mrs Faule?'

'No problem,' said Janine. 'Go ahead.'

★ ★ ★

Kristen Faule was standing outside the room with one of the young residents beside her, another boy of around Jesse's age.

She turned to him. 'Could you give us a moment, please?'

He walked a little way down the hallway.

'What's going on?' said Ren.

Kristen leaned in. 'Conor Gorman's in a lot of trouble. Even more so, now, after what he did to Jesse. We found out three days ago that Conor desecrated a grave in the abbey's cemetery — '

'That was him . . . ' said Ren.

Kristen nodded.

'How do you know that?' said Ren.

'He didn't do too great a job of washing the dust out of his hair, off his sneakers . . . washing the hammer he used, putting it back properly in the tool shed . . . '

Isn't that Covering Your Tracks 101?

'We tried to contact Robert Prince,' said Kristen, 'but we couldn't get hold of him because he's away on business and isn't taking calls. We did get in touch with Ingrid Prince who said she would fly in from New York yesterday afternoon and pick Conor up last night. We decided to terminate his stay here.'

Wow.

'Did she come?' said Ren.

'She called last night to say that she was delayed,' said Kristen. 'She was packing up the house in Golden and said that she would come by in the morning instead. This morning. She still hasn't showed.'

'Do you think Conor was happy or reluctant to leave?' said Ren.

'I . . . don't know,' said Kristen. 'He seemed neutral on the topic. Apathetic.'

'He's a smart kid,' said Ren. 'Don't you think it's strange that he didn't make more of an effort to hide what he had done?'

'I hadn't thought about it,' said Kristen. 'I put it down to an angry outburst — hot-headed lack of thinking, more than anything.'

'So, what happened between him and Jesse?' said Ren.

'That's why I brought Kyle. Kyle, can you please come speak with Agent Bryce? Thank you.'

The boy walked over.

'Nice to meet you,' said Ren. 'Can you tell me what you saw?'

'Conor and Jesse got into a fight in the men's room,' said Kyle.

'Do you know why?' said Ren.

'It was, like, different things. Conor was giving out to Jesse about what he did to the cemetery — '

'What Jesse did?' said Ren.

'Yes,' said Kyle.

Ren and Kristen glanced at each other. *Shouldn't it have been Jesse giving out to Conor?*

'Then Jesse was calling Conor a liar,' said Kyle. 'He pushed Conor, he told him he had betrayed him again, he said that's all anyone does. He told Conor that he was fucked up, that he lied to him, he'd used him, and he'd promised he wouldn't leave. Conor said it was none of Jesse's damn business what he did with his life.' He paused. 'They were talking about a phone. Conor was going crazy about that.'

The confiscated cell phone.

'Is there anything else you can think of?' said Ren.

'No,' said Kyle. 'I'm sorry.'

'Do you know where Conor might have gone?' said Ren.

'No,' said Kyle. 'I don't really know Conor.'

'OK,' said Ren. 'Thank you.'

'Please wait down the hallway, Kyle,' said Kristen.

'I'm going to go back in to talk to Jesse,' said Ren. 'If you hear anything, please report to me immediately.'

'I will,' said Kristen.

Ren stuck her head into the interview room and called Janine to the door to quietly fill her in.

They went back in to Jesse and sat down opposite him.

'Can I get a drink?' he said.

'No,' said Ren. 'OK, Jesse — you were overheard saying to Conor earlier that he betrayed you 'again' — what did you mean by that?'

'Just that he was leaving the ranch,' said Jesse. 'He's my only friend. I need a friend right now . . . with my dad and everything . . .'

'Were you trying to stop Conor from leaving today?' said Ren.

'*He* attacked *me*,' said Jesse. 'Anyone who was there saw that.'

'And why did he do that?' said Ren.

'Just because I asked him about leaving,' said Jesse. 'He's been acting really weird. Since you interviewed him . . . it was like you'd given him a really hard time or something — I don't know. He came out of there mad.'

'We did not give him a hard time,' said Ren. 'I can promise you that. Quite the opposite. We offered our condolences about his Aunt Laura. We were respectful. We were trying to gather information for our investigation, and he thanked us at the end. I'm having a hard time believing that he could have walked away from that interview angry.'

Jesse shrugged. 'I'm just telling you what I saw. He didn't say that you had given him a hard time — that was just my understanding of it.'

'From now on, I need you to stick to the facts,' said Ren. 'Your understanding of events might not reflect the reality, OK?'

368

Jesse nodded.

'Why was Conor talking about the cell phone?' said Ren. 'I'm presuming that was the one we got today from Kristen Faule.'

Jesse went very still. 'Yes. He wanted to use it, but I told him I didn't have it any more. I had let him borrow it a few times before. The Saturday before his aunt was killed, I heard him talking to her about Robert Prince, about fraud, about Robert probably going to jail, about how it was Conor's chance to leave the ranch, to start a new life . . . '

'So you did think he was planning to leave,' said Ren.

'Yes,' said Jesse, 'but I swear to God, I didn't do anything . . . '

'Did you see his Aunt Laura as the person who would take him away from you?' said Ren.

Jesse frowned. 'No. It sounded like Conor wanted to leave. It didn't sound like anyone was forcing him.'

'You burned the journal two days later, you burned the photos of Conor — are you sure that wasn't because you were mad at him?' said Ren.

'No — he was leaving, he said he didn't need the photos any more,' said Jesse.

'Why did Conor run away today?' said Ren.

Jesse shrugged. 'Because of what he did to me, how he would be in trouble because of the grave . . . and I guess he doesn't want to go back to the Princes.'

57

Janine's phone started to vibrate. She took it out.
She leaned in to Ren and whispered. 'It's a New
York number . . . I think it's Carolina Vescovi.
I'm going to step outside.'

'Sure, go ahead,' said Ren.

She took out her phone and texted Everett.

Boy at ranch lent phone to Conor Gorman, says
he heard him talking about Robert Prince and
fraud — Kohler processing phone records. Any
updates? Also, where is RP? Anything on flight
records?

Ren turned back to Jesse. 'I need you to think
where Conor might have gone.'

'Conor could go anywhere,' said Jesse. 'He
doesn't give a . . . he doesn't care.'

'OK,' said Ren, 'tell me the rest. You fought in
the restroom . . .'

'Yes,' said Jesse. 'And then we were out in the
hallway . . . and out by the stables.'

'And then what happened?' said Ren.

Her phone beeped with a text from Everett.

On the case. Will call pleasantly.

'We shouted at each other a little more,' said
Jesse, 'and that's when he punched me in the
face. He split the skin. He stormed off. I

couldn't see. There was blood pouring into my eye.'

'Jesse — did Conor say he was annoyed at you for tidying the cemetery?' said Ren.

'Yes, but I don't know what it had to do with him. I mean, he trashed it — he's the one people should be mad at. I don't get it.'

Then it hit her. *Tidying it up was the issue. When Jesse tidied up, he uncovered the headstones, including the one that revealed Delores Ward's secret. For Conor to have gone and broken that exact headstone is a little too coincidental, meaning that Conor knows Delores Ward . . . and perhaps he owed her a favor or was expecting one in return. But why? What could a woman like Delores Ward have done for Conor Gorman?*

★ ★ ★

Outside in the hallway, Janine picked up the call from Carolina Vescovi.

'I'm sorry for getting off the phone so abruptly,' said Carolina.

'That's OK,' said Janine. 'Is everything all right?'

'I . . . I . . . guess I never believed that people could bury a memory like this,' said Carolina. 'But . . . but I had,' she said. 'That woman in the photograph. She was . . . I was eight years old. I remember I was in the restaurant, we used to live above it. I was supposed to be in my room, but I had snuck down and I was playing in the coat check. I was sitting on the

371

floor underneath where the coats were hanging down from the rail. And . . . a man came over to me and he started talking to me. He crouched down, told me how pretty I was. I remember him reaching out, rubbing my cheek. It was horrible. I was terrified. And then, this beautiful face appeared. This face right here in front of me. Viggi Leinster. But she looked as terrified as I was. And she put a hand on his shoulder and squeezed it. I remember her beautiful red nails and how her knuckles turned white. She said to him, 'Come on, now, honey. Our table is ready.' He looked really angry. When he was out of the way, this woman reached out, took my hand and pulled me up to standing.

'She said, 'Sweetheart, you run along up to your house and never, ever, come down here on your own again. And if you see that man again, you make sure you don't talk to him.'' Carolina paused. 'A couple of nights later, I saw him again. I was looking out the window in the back courtyard. And I saw my father roaring and shouting at him. It was Walter Prince. It was only when I saw her face that I connected the two.'

Janine's heart was pounding.

'I spoke with my mother about that time,' said Carolina. 'She said that Viggi Leinster kind of burst onto the scene on the arm of Walter Prince. There was a huge age gap that no one spoke of, but Mom reckons that Viggi couldn't have been more than sixteen or seventeen years old. I couldn't believe it, but you know . . . when you're young, you think everyone is so much older than they are. Apparently, she used to tell people she was going to be an actress. Silver screen or no silver screen, this girl shone, my mother said.

'No one had heard of Walter Prince in New York and, at first, they passed themselves off, not as husband and wife, but as father and daughter. How creepy is that? They lived in a beautiful apartment, they led a glamorous social life, they hosted parties. They were popular people. Anyway, eventually, their secret came out. But all it seemed to do was make them even more exotic. And then? She was gone, and he was gone. I'm saving the worst till last. The reason there are no statements from my parents in the police report is because they were paid off by Walter Prince. Everyone in the restaurant that night was paid off.'

'Even the kitchen staff, busboys?' said Janine.

'Yes,' said Carolina.

'One of them said that Viggi was having an affair with a man called Angelo Marianelli,' said Janine.

'I can tell you for sure that was not true,' said Carolina. 'Angelo Marianelli was gay. Closeted, but I know my parents knew.'

'Did you know he disappeared six weeks after Viggi?' said Janine.

'No, I did not,' said Carolina, 'but it all sounds very strange . . .'

'Thank you so much for finding all this out for me,' said Janine.

'I want to tell you, though, my mother is very, very sorry,' said Carolina. 'She's lived with this for so long.' She paused. 'And that poor woman's family . . . what must it have been like? God help them.'

Janine didn't tell her that she had never known a thing about Viggi Leinster's family. It was as if she was beamed down from above, a falling starlet with a blank-slate past.

★ ★ ★

Janine was reeling. Walter Prince had been a pedophile. He had abandoned his family in Butte, traveled to New York with a girl young enough to be his daughter. He had preyed on an eight-year-old girl under her parents' noses. It seemed like the only thing that stopped it going any further was the intervention of Viggi Leinster . . . who disappeared shortly afterwards. Poor, dear Viggi Leinster. And a paid-off kitchen porter sent the rumor out that Viggi Leinster had run away with another man and they had lived happily ever after, location unknown. So what happened? Did Walter Prince follow them and have them both killed? Or had Viggi been killed the night of the film premiere and the sighting in Denver was a hoax? Had Marianelli been sent to look for her? Had he found her? Had he killed her? Did Walter Prince worry that she would reveal his secret? Was it a secret?

Then it hit her. *The Orchard Girls*. The vigilante attack. Walter Prince led the posse of men, not because he was honorable, not because he wanted justice, but so he could lay the blame

374

at a dead man's feet, so he could play the hero. It was pedophile Walter Prince who murdered those three little girls when he was only sixteen years old.

58

Janine walked back into the interview room. She locked eyes with Ren.

What have you got?

'We'll be right with you, Jesse,' said Ren. She and Janine went out into the hallway.

Janine talked her through the conversation with Carolina Vescovi.

'Let me call that woman from the Prince mansion,' said Ren. 'See if she can shed more light on Walter Prince.'

Ren went through her phone and found 'Prince Mansion Lady'. She called her office number. A woman answered.

'I'd like to speak with Barbara Hynes,' said Ren.

'Mrs Hynes no longer works here,' said the woman. Curt, clipped.

'Oh,' said Ren. 'Do you know how I could get a hold of her?'

The woman hesitated. 'No,' she said. 'I'm afraid not.' She hung up.

Ren stared at her phone. 'Well, someone's been acrimoniously terminated . . . '

Ren and Janine searched online and Janine eventually came up with a cell phone number for Barbara Hynes.

'Hello, Mrs Hynes?' said Ren. 'This is Special Agent Ren Bryce from Safe Streets in Denver. We spoke a while back about Walter Prince . . . '

'Yes,' said Barbara, 'and it cost me my job.'

'Your job?' said Ren.

'Yes,' said Barbara. 'I didn't get the memo. Once the story about the murder of Robert Prince's housekeeper hit the media, all staff were instructed not to speak about the family to anyone, and to refer all questions to their legal team.'

'I'm sorry to hear that,' said Ren.

'Not as sorry as I am,' said Barbara.

'Is there anything else you can tell me about Walter Prince?' said Ren. 'Anything else you knew about the vigilante attack on the Orchard Girls father?'

Barbara didn't reply.

'Were there any rumors about Walter Prince?' said Ren. 'Anything you mightn't have mentioned to me before. This is really important.'

'Well,' said Barbara, 'isn't it interesting that, before the year was out, Patrick Prince — Walter's father — had bought a site to build his mansion on and he moved the family lock, stock and barrel out of town? The orchard is part of that site.' She paused. 'All I can tell you is that, when my father was a boy, he was told to never touch an apple from that orchard, that he'd probably end up choking on bones.'

★ ★ ★

Ren repeated the conversation to Janine.

'I was thinking about Viggi Leinster,' said Janine. 'If she arrived in New York with Walter Prince, then do you think she might have traveled with him from Butte? If she was sixteen/seventeen in 1957, that makes her having been born 1940, '41.'

Ren Googled Viggi Leinster, Butte, 1941, 1957.

'Oh God, said Ren. 'I've got a news story: Christmas Day tragedy, 1955, at the home of the Leinster family in Butte, Montana: Father, Bruce; Mother, Lynda; Sons, Teddy and Thomas. All their years of birth are included, the youngest being their daughter, Virginia . . . b. 1941.'

'Virginia . . . Viggi,' said Janine.

'The names Teddy and Thomas were signed on the postcard that fell from Delores Ward's wall,' said Ren. 'She told me about the man who broke her heart. She said it was '*not before he had taken my family away from me*'. Delores Ward is Viggi Leinster.'

Christmas Day, the day after their annual ball, Walter Prince burned her family's house down, so he would have no resistance, so they couldn't fight him, so everyone would think she had died along with them.

So 'he could take her away'.

So she could become Viggi, and she could be his . . . for as long as he wanted her.

Janine paused. 'The headstone! The chaplain in Evergreen Abbey. Didn't you tell me that the Princes were originally O'Sullivans? Patrick 'Prince' O'Sullivan was one of the first of the family to emigrate to Butte. If the chaplain here was born in the 1870s, then he could have been Patrick Prince's brother . . . he may not have traveled as far west as Montana. And he may just have been persuaded to give Viggi Leinster shelter after what she went through at the hands of his nephew, Walter Prince.'

'That last sighting in Denver was real,' said Ren.

★ ★ ★

Ren called Eleanor Jensen.

'I'm sorry for leaving you hanging,' said Ren. 'We're just looking into a few things. I wanted to ask you about Fr Daniel O'Sullivan. What do you know about him?'

'Not a lot,' said Eleanor. 'Just that he was the first chaplain here, he lived at the abbey, he said mass here every day of his life. He welcomed every nationality, he turned no one away. He accepted alcoholics, down-and-outs, ladies of the night — the kind of people who wouldn't be welcome elsewhere. He was a hero around here.'

'Was he Irish?' said Ren. She could hear Janine's cell phone ringing behind her.

'Yes,' said Eleanor. 'A Cork man, from what I gather.'

'Thank you,' said Ren. She was nodding at Janine, but Janine was engrossed in her call.

'Agent Bryce,' said Eleanor. 'What about Delores Ward?'

'I can't get into that right now,' said Ren, 'but you have nothing to be concerned about.'

'Are you sure?' said Eleanor.

'Yes,' said Ren.

'Because she's here at the abbey right now.'

379

'Oh,' said Ren. 'She's not in her cabin?'

'No,' said Eleanor. 'We finally persuaded her to move in here. They're dismantling the cabin today. Delores came to an arrangement with Burt Kendall. Can you hear that rain? Honestly. I don't think that cabin could survive that kind of downpour.'

'We need to find out some more details,' said Ren, 'and we will be coming by to speak with Delores later on.'

'Who *is* she?' said Eleanor.

'Someone we believe had a terribly tragic life,' said Ren. 'Until she came to Evergreen Abbey.'

★ ★ ★

Janine finished her call, then stared at her screen intently. She walked over to Ren.

'OK, I just got a call from a case manager at Stateville,' said Janine. 'She heard about the inquiry about Laura Flynn and Derrick Charles. She says that the name Laura Flynn came up in connection with a totally different inmate. They had a mail watch on him. Laura Flynn sent him a letter.'

'Who is he?' said Ren.

'A man called Frankie Gorman, currently serving an eighteen-year sentence for aggravated sexual assault and burglary.'

'Oh my God,' said Ren.

'Conor Gorman's deadbeat dad.' They both said it at the same time.

'Holy shit,' said Ren. 'Ho. Lee. Shit. What did the letter say?'

'She emailed me a PDF,' said Janine. 'It says: 'Dear Frankie, Conor and I are in trouble. I know it probably seems unfair getting in touch after all these years, but I couldn't think of anyone else who would care enough to help. I will be in Chicago on May 12th. I'm staying at the same hotel as my sister. I don't know if there is time to put me on your visitor list, but, Janey Mac, you know how much I'd love to see you. Regards, Laura (Flynn).''

'And did he try to get her on his visitor list?' said Ren.

'No,' said Janine. 'This was only sent a week before she died. She probably didn't know she'd have had to be background checked, she would have needed more time. But why would she go to Chicago if there was no guarantee of meeting with him?'

'Did the case manager ask Gorman about all this?' said Ren.

'Yup — he said he got the letter, big deal, he hadn't seen her in ten years, since right before he went to prison.' She paused. 'What does Janey Mac mean?'

Ren laughed. 'That, I learned, is the Irish way of saying Jesus Christ . . . if you don't want to piss your 'mammy' off.'

'That guy taught you a lot,' said Janine. 'Why is Laura Flynn saying she'd love to see Frankie Gorman, when we know that the family thought he was a loser?'

'Looking for money?' said Ren. 'Like, support for Conor if she was about to take him out of the country? Letting his father know in person that they were leaving the United States? But, again, I can't see her doing that, because of his loserdom.'

'She says 'I'm staying in the same hotel as my sister.' Why would she say that? Why would he care where she stays?'

'Hmm,' said Ren. 'I do not know.' She told Janine about Delores' move from the cabin. 'I mean, it wasn't long ago that she didn't want to budge. She was adamant she was going nowhere. Now, this turnaround. Conflicting behaviors all round . . .'

'That's for sure . . .'

'The headstone was revealed by Jesse several weeks ago, were anyone to have noticed the cemetery,' said Ren. 'But Delores must have only realized that a few days ago . . . otherwise she would have gotten Conor to take care of it as soon as she knew. Maybe she's planning to leave. She could hardly say that to Eleanor. She would go along with whatever new accommodation she had set up for her in the abbey.'

'She's been hiding something in that cabin,' said Janine.

They both considered it.

'Angelo Marianelli,' said Ren. 'What if Angelo Marianelli tracked her down . . . and she . . . took care of him?'

'I think you've got it,' said Janine.

Ren's phone started ringing. 'It's Everett,' she said. She put him on speaker.

'OK, I have updates,' said Everett. 'Burt Kendall has set up a new company. It's called ETS, Energy Transport Services. And they've just been awarded a one-million-dollar contract from NOVA. From Robert Prince. The company is registered in Williston, North Dakota. Do you know how many trucks are going back and forth there every day? Water, chemicals, drilling equipment, pipes . . . this is a one-million-dollar contract, but it's worth a hell of a lot more than that.'

'That has to be through Delores Ward's recommendation,' said Ren.

'And yes, flight records confirm Robert Prince has taken several trips there . . . ' said Everett.

'Were any of them around the beginning of April?' said Ren.

'Yup,' said Everett. 'He was there April 4th through 7th.'

'That was the same time as Delores Ward,' said Ren. 'I think we've just found out who owns the second tract of land with the energy rights.'

59

Rain poured down the library windows of Evergreen Abbey. It had started without warning; instant gray skies quickly turned black, the rain fell, aggressive, relentless. Through the blurred glass, Delores Ward had been watching the tracks of the green digger move through the thick mud, Burt Kendall at the wheel. The bucket rose and struck the walls of the cabin, gouging out chunks. He was gone now, driven away by the downpour.

She hurt. For six decades, she hurt. She had prayed and prayed and prayed. She had sought forgiveness, but she hadn't found it, not in her heart, not where it mattered.

There was a knock on the library door. Conor Gorman walked in, drenched, his boots covered with mud, his jeans spattered. He slumped into one of the chairs at an old mahogany table. Delores sat down opposite him. He slid a battered metal box toward her. 'I think they're all there.'

'Thank you,' said Delores. 'God may just be on my side after all.'

'Whose bones are they?' said Conor.

'A bad man,' said Delores. 'Sent by an even badder one.'

'Badder — I like that,' said Conor. He smiled. 'Who was the badder one? Seeing that you killed this one.' He pointed to the box.

Delores frowned. 'It's not a joke. The other man, I recently discovered, you have a connection to. Robert Prince is your guardian? Well, it was his . . . grandfather, Walter, who sent this gangster after me.'

'Why?' said Conor.

'It's all in the past now. Robert Prince has turned out to be nothing like him.'

Conor snorted.

'Really?' said Delores. 'I've found Robert Prince to be nothing other than charming and generous.'

Conor stared at the ground.

'You don't seem to like him,' said Delores.

Conor shrugged.

'Let me return your things,' said Delores. She reached behind a line of books at the bottom of one of the bookcases. She took out a military-style bag and handed it to him. It was limp, mainly empty, with just a few objects gathered at the bottom.

'Thank you for looking after this for me,' said Conor, setting it on the table in front of him.

'Well, you kept my little secret for me, all these months,' said Delores. 'And you helped with the gravestone.'

Conor shrugged.

'So, what's in the bag that's so important?' said Delores.

'Nothing,' said Conor. 'Just . . . it's hard to keep anything private over there at the ranch.'

Delores let out a breath. 'So you're leaving . . . '

'Yes,' said Conor.

'I'm sorry I got you in trouble because of the cemetery.'

'It was a pleasure,' said Conor.

Delores shifted in her seat. 'Are you running away?' she said. 'Or have you been expelled into the care of the Princes?'

'I'm running,' said Conor. He looked around. 'But not so I end up somewhere like here. How can you live here? And for so long?'

'This place was the only good thing that came out of my time with Walter Prince,' said Delores. 'Walter was sent here by his father when he was seventeen. That was a long, long time before I knew him. His uncle Daniel used to be the chaplain here. Fr Dan was still here when I arrived. I confessed my sins to him. And the sins of his own nephew, but they didn't seem to come as any surprise to him. He was an incredible man. The abbess here was an incredible woman. They took me in, they saved my life. They gave me a new identity. Later, when the abbess was dying, she told me about Walter, that he had been sent there that summer by his father, Patrick, 'to be straightened out'. But she said there was something 'very wrong' with Walter Prince. She caught him, she said, 'interfering' with one of the girls, the daughter of one of the workers at the abbey. And do you know what the abbess did? One night, she took a shotgun, marched down to the barn where Walter was working and she pointed the barrel right between his eyebrows, told him to leave and never come back. The whole debacle caused a family feud. Patrick Prince and Fr Daniel never again laid eyes on each other. Patrick Prince wiped him out of the family history.'

'Sounds horrible,' said Conor.

'That's one word for it,' said Delores.

'Well, I gotta get out of here,' said Conor. 'You won't tell anyone?'

'No,' said Delores. 'I'm setting your young soul free.' She smiled. 'Just promise me, Conor, that you will fill your life with goodness. Help people. This is your chance.'

They heard footsteps down the hallway, voices getting louder. Instinctively, Conor reached for his bag, sliding his hand into it, pulling out the bloodstained gun inside.

Delores' eyes went wide. 'No,' she said. 'No. A gun? You? But . . . oh my goodness. You . . . but that was your aunt. That was your family and you . . . ' She held a shaking hand to her mouth. 'Oh my . . . oh my . . . '

'Shhh,' said Conor. 'Shhh.'

'And I had it here all along?' said Delores. 'How could you? You told me — '

Conor pointed the gun at her.

'What are you doing?' she said. 'Conor!'

'I said shut up,' said Conor.

The voices and footsteps became more distant. The only sound was the rain.

'Laura was taking me away,' said Conor. 'I didn't want to go, OK? I didn't want to. I have my reasons. She was going to ruin my life. And do you want to know what else? See this gun? I know where she got it. From my father. He's alive and she never told me. So, do you think that's someone I can trust? Fuck her, coming to 'save my life'. She didn't know shit about my life. She had no clue what mattered to me.'

'But surely *she* mattered to you,' said Delores. 'You have to turn yourself in.'

Conor laughed. 'No,' he said. 'I'm going take my inspiration from . . . you.'

He pulled the trigger. He pulled it a second time.

As the rain poured down the windows, and the blood seeped from her body onto the white tiled floor, Delores Ward felt washed away. In her dying moments, she was Virginia Leinster again, Virginia before Viggi. She had buried Viggi the night she buried the corpse of Angelo Marianelli.

She thought back to the last night that she saw her best friend, Acora Prince. They were both just seventeen years old, standing on the balcony above the foyer of the Princes' magnificent home. Acora's mother stood between them. They were all dressed in exquisite ball gowns. Acora's mother brought the room to silence with a delicate clap of her hands.

'On my right,' she said, 'is my baby girl, Acora, and on my left, her dearest friend, Virginia, such beauties, both. Sisters, really.' She paused. 'Though Virginia may be something quite different to my husband, Walter?' she said. 'Maybe whore . . . or harlot . . . '

Virginia Leinster shivered at the memory of the awful hysteria that was creeping into the woman's voice, at the gasps and shrieks that had broken out in the crowd. She remembered Walter rushing toward them — to rescue who, she was not sure. But before he made it to the balcony, his wife had taken Virginia by the hair and was pulling her backwards until she was lying, face up, watching the rage, the mental breakdown of her best friend's mother. She began to drag Virginia by the ankle down the stairs. Virginia remembered the bump of each step against her spine, how her dress began to hike up around her thighs, how she desperately clawed at it to keep it down. She was crying, trying to cover herself and Acora's mother snapped, 'I would think you've been looking for these,' and held up a pair of red satin panties. She threw them at Virginia, leaned in, and stuffed them down the front of her dress. And she started to drag Virginia down again, her head now banging off each step.

Virginia felt it as if she was there all over again. Her spine ached, the back of her head, her heart. It was a piercing pain that she rarely allowed in. And it brought with it a shame of extraordinary depth, a shame that had blossomed inside, filled every space it could. She had never wanted to accept who those red panties belonged to. She accepted it only on the day that Walter Prince told her he was leaving New York to go back to his family. But she had always known . . . Acora had stumbled in church one day; they must have been no more than thirteen years old. Her dress had caught on the pew and Virginia had rushed to protect her friend's modesty. Though she had spared her blushes, she caught sight of what that man had forced her to wear.

It was the scarlet under the white that he liked.

60

Janine ran down the steps of The Darned Heart and grabbed one of the Sheriff's Office investigators.

'Could you please come with me? I just need you to look after a young man we've been interviewing.'

'Yes, ma'am,' he said.

'Any sign of Conor Gorman?' said Janine.

'No, ma'am.'

'Walk with me,' she said.

As they got to the top of the steps, Ren was running toward them.

'I just got a call from Eleanor Jensen,' she said. 'There's been a shooting at the abbey. Delores Ward is dead.'

Janine turned to the investigator. 'Third door on the left!' She pointed him down to where Jesse Coombes was waiting, Kristen Faule standing guard outside.

Ren and Janine pulled up outside the abbey, abandoned the Jeep, ran up the steps and through the open door. Eleanor Jensen stood at the top of the stairs in the open doorway of the library, white-faced and covered with blood.

'Are you injured?' said Ren, running up to her, two steps at a time.

'No,' said Eleanor. 'No . . . '

'Who's in there?' said Ren.

'Just Delores,' said Eleanor. 'She's been shot.

She's dead. She's dead.'

Janine went past Eleanor into the library.

'Did you see who did this?' said Ren.

'No,' said Eleanor. 'I just heard the gunshot, I came running. Then I could hear a car being driven away.' Her legs buckled under her.

Ren crouched down and helped to move her to a sitting position against the wall. 'Wait there, I'll get you a chair.' She went into the library . . . where the lifeless body of Delores Ward lay.

'One to the head, one to the chest,' said Janine. 'No sign of the weapon.'

'That poor woman,' said Ren.

Not far from the body was an open metal tin and dark bones scattered across the floor. Janine walked over to it.

'Looks like we've got a partial jaw bone, femur, tibia . . . ' she said.

'The broken pipe must have washed them out from under the cabin,' said Ren. 'My guess is that the bone the girl saw someone waving about was real. And it was Conor Gorman who found it. If Delores saw him looking around, or if he called to the cabin . . . he might just have agreed to keep her secret. And later, she would keep one for him. Was it just that he was making sure he could get away from the ranch? Was he getting rides with Kendall's crew or something? Was that how he got into Golden the night of the bar fight?'

Janine looked down at the body. 'The pull of a trigger . . . and the whole world is changed.'

Ren was staring out the window at the rain, at the broken-down cabin.

Triggers. Oh my God. Triggers.

'Triggers!' said Ren. She turned to Janine. 'You said there was a tattoo place in Golden . . . '

'Yes,' said Janine.

'Can you find out when Conor Gorman got his tattoo?' said Ren.

'Sure.'

'I need to make another call,' said Ren. She walked a few feet away and Googled the number for the Southampton Police Department in New York.

'My name is SA Ren Bryce. I'm calling from Safe Streets in Denver. I need to speak with whoever handled an MVC on New Year's Eve last,' she said. 'Driver's name was Conor Gorman.'

'Let me put you through to Detective Lin,' said the operator.

Ren introduced herself and repeated her request.

'Yes, Conor Gorman,' said Detective Lin. 'Do you want to know what he did — he crashed a Lotus Series 2 Super Seven into a tree on Tuckahoe Lane. I died a little inside. It was like watching *Ferris Bueller*, only they trash the car before they make it home.'

Ren laughed. 'Was he alone at the time?'

'He was,' said Lin. 'Thrown right from it, without a scratch. Unbelievable. Lucky little shit. He had the arrogance to take that baby out — no clue how to handle it. That car has evil manners . . . '

Evil manners. I love it.

'I heard later from a neighbor that before he took it, there was a disturbance outside his home about a half hour earlier,' said Lin.

'Outside the Princes'?' said Ren.

'Yes,' said Lin.

'He had a fight with Robert Prince, then took his car?' said Ren.

'No — with the wife,' said Lin. 'She probably asked him to take the garbage out. The kid's a brat.'

'Did she come pick him up?' said Ren.

'In the end, yes — he had been on a bender for a couple days before we picked him up,' said Lin. 'She showed up, spared him Robert Prince killing him, I'd say.'

'OK,' said Ren. 'Well, thanks for filling me in.'

So, Conor Gorman fights with Ingrid, implodes, then realizes: act out, and Ingrid will come my way. Rinse, repeat.

She turned to Janine. 'Conor Gorman fought with Ingrid Prince New Year's Eve — right before he crashed Robert Prince's Lotus,' said Ren.

'Conor Gorman got that tattoo late May,' said Janine.

Ren checked her calendar. 'That was after I interviewed him. I told him that Ingrid Prince was the one who said he should stay at the ranch. Robert Prince said she was creating distance, she didn't want Conor to see her as a mother figure. She must have been getting vibes from him. Every time Conor Gorman has acted out . . . it was connected to Ingrid Prince. She's his trigger.'

'He's obsessed with Ingrid Prince.' They both said it at the same time.

'Oh my God,' said Ren. 'She abandoned him today, too. She was supposed to pick him up. She didn't show.' Then something hit her. She could feel herself go cold. 'Janine . . . Laura Flynn wanted to take him away from Ingrid Prince . . . and he didn't want to go. He didn't want to leave Ingrid. He killed Laura. It was Conor Gorman.'

61

Ren called Kohler and explained her theory.

'We'll put the ranch and the abbey on lockdown, and issue an alert. Any idea where he's headed?'

'We don't know yet which car he's taken,' said Ren. 'We've got someone here trying to work that out. We think he could be headed to the Princes' rental in Golden.'

'We'll send someone there,' said Kohler.

'We'll meet you there,' said Ren.

Ren called Kristen Faule. 'Did you hear back from Ingrid Prince?'

'No,' said Kristen. 'I also tried Robert Prince, and had no luck.'

Shit. 'If Ingrid arrives at the ranch or if she makes contact with you in any way, please go directly to one of the Sheriff's Office investigators at the ranch. Do not try to contact the Princes yourself.'

'OK,' said Kristen. 'OK.'

The panic in your voice. Your baby is under attack.

Janine's phone started to ring. She picked up.

'Detective Hooks? This is Casey from Ink Corp tattoo shop. That kid you were asking about that came in for the cat tattoo? He's just been here. He wanted another tattoo — lettering this time. I told him the guy he needed for that wasn't here, he wouldn't be back for another half hour. He was so pissed.'

'What lettering did he want?' said Janine.

'Uh . . . 'Angry cats get scratched skin' . . . but in Swedish. Weird.'

'Did you see where he went?' said Janine.

'No,' said Casey. 'But he was mad as hell.'

'When did he leave?' said Janine.

'Right before I called you,' said Casey. 'I'm not sure about his mental state. And I thought I might have seen, like, blood on his neck. Like he had tried to wipe it away . . . '

'Thank you for letting me know,' said Janine. She ended the call.

★ ★ ★

Ren and Janine sped toward the Princes' rental.

'His father abandoned him,' said Ren, 'his mother died, Laura's gone. He's been pushed over the edge.'

Ren phoned Ingrid Prince. She picked up. *Hallelujah*. 'Mrs Prince, have you seen Conor today?'

'No,' said Ingrid. 'I was to pick him up at the ranch this morning, but I've been tied up here at the house. Robert is going tomorrow instead when he gets back.'

'We believe that you might be in danger,' said Ren. 'We're on our way. Do not open the door to Conor Gorman. Lock yourself in.'

'To Conor?' said Ingrid. 'Why not? Why isn't he at the ranch?'

'We think he's very angry with you for not

showing up today, Mrs Prince,' said Ren. 'We think he's fixated on you. We believe that he killed Laura Flynn because she wanted to take him away from you. And we think you upset him too by not showing up today. Please, stay safe. We're on our way.'

'I don't want to stay here, if he's coming this way,' said Ingrid. 'What if he's able to get in? I should go somewhere.'

'It's a secure property,' said Ren. 'Have the security gates been breached?'

'No,' said Ingrid.

'Is there any other way onto the property?' said Ren.

'No,' said Ingrid. 'No.'

'Then stay right where you are,' said Ren. 'Lock your doors. The Sheriff's Office should be there right away.'

'I'm afraid to stay here — ' said Ingrid.

'It's the safest place to be,' said Ren. 'Trust me.'

★　★　★

Twenty minutes later, Ren and Janine were pulling up to the gates of the rental. They were wide open. Cars from the Sheriff's Office were abandoned out the front, lights flashing.

Fuck.

Ren and Janine jumped out of the Jeep. The first thing they saw was a stream of blood snaking down the driveway. It was coming from under a black tarp, the shape of a body clear.

Oh God.

The driver's door to Ingrid Prince's Range Rover was open.

Kohler started walking toward them.

Ren could vaguely hear crying. They looked beyond the body, beyond the driveway into the house where Ingrid Prince was rocking back and forth, an investigator beside her, her arm around her.

'What happened?' said Ren.

'He must have gotten the code,' said Kohler. 'He got in the back door. She heard the noise. She came out the front, tried to leave, he ran after her, he raised the gun. She says she barely remembers. She panicked. She reversed. She knocked him down. She's distraught in there. She's covered in blood. She won't see a doctor, says she's fine. She just wants her husband. She said she tried to help him . . . but it was too late. She said he said sorry, though. He said sorry about Laura.'

Ren looked past Kohler to the lump under the tarp. 'What the fuck is all I have to say. What the fuck . . . '

'Better him than her, I guess . . . ' said Kohler.

62

A week later, Ren, Janine and Robbie managed to have the same evening off. They sat in Woody's having pizza.

'Can anyone call this a celebration?' said Ren.

'Definitely not,' said Janine. 'This is called simply: sustenance.'

Bare sustenance for you, my beautiful, delicate friend.

'Do you want to hear something beyond fucked-up?' said Ren.

'Coming from you?' said Janine.

'It's about Walter Prince,' said Ren. 'I realized how he stalked two of those little Orchard Girls — it was the letters the Irish immigrants dictated to him. They weren't just telling their families back home what was going on with their children — they were giving him information he could use to find them or gain their trust. Like 'Little Mary is eleven now, getting so big, walks home every day by the creek . . . ' Walter Prince didn't mail those letters, not out of spite, but because they could have been used as evidence against him . . . What a sick fuck.'

'That just gives me shivers,' said Janine.

'People will visit the Prince mansion for the Christmas Eve ball or pay for the guided tour . . . ' said Ren. 'When really, I think it should only be open for Hallowe'en.'

'I think we should go,' said Janine.

'Sign me up,' said Ren. She turned to Robbie. 'Do you have your iPad?'

'Yup,' said Robbie.

'Can I take a look?' she said. *Please tell me you've cleared your History.*

'Sure, go ahead,' said Robbie, handing it to her.

'I just want to see if the grand event's still going ahead after the entire Prince family shitstorm,' she said.

'I doubt it,' said Janine.

She Googled the Princes, put in the timeframe of the previous week. 'Ooh,' she said. 'Stalker shots.'

There was a picture of Ingrid Prince, taken on the beach in the Hamptons the previous weekend. She was dressed in a blue floaty cover-up and a floppy hat.

'That woman is so stunning,' said Ren. She showed the others.

Janine pointed to the caption: *After some time away from the spotlight following the tragic death of her friend, Laura Flynn, ex-model Ingrid Prince, five months pregnant, debuts her baby bump on the beach at her Hamptons' hideaway.*

'Debuts her Moonbump,' said Ren. 'But, yikes. She hasn't announced the fake miscarriage yet.' She raised her eyebrows. 'The longer the delay, the greater the empathetic outpourings, I guess.'

'Celebrity is so weird,' said Janine.

Ren scrolled down to the next photo of Ingrid Prince in a beautiful mismatched bikini: red bottoms, blue-and-white stripes on top. And sandwiched in between, a very clear, very real baby bump.

Janine, Ren and Robbie all stared at each other.

Oh. My. God.

'Looks like Conor Gorman's obsession with Ingrid wasn't a one-way street,' said Ren.

63

Ingrid Prince was waiting for her driver at the rental in Golden. She had returned from New York for the last time to finally pack her things. She sat now on a high stool, elbow bent, leaning with her forearm on the kitchen island, scrolling through texts. They had been popping up on her cell phone all morning, since the Hamptons photo appeared online.

Hey, hot mama!
Looking good! x
Suits you!
Ah, the secret hideaway . . . B-)
Must check has hell frozen over: it appears your belly is bigger than mine . . . ;-)

Ingrid held a hand to her belly. Twenty-two weeks gone; her baby conceived on an icy January night in Golden in front of the fire with a handsome boy, fresh from a bar fight. This was her golden child, her golden ticket. And quite by accident! Fate had been kind! And Robert wouldn't know the difference. Whether the baby would have dark Irish looks from a line of rich Princes, or common Gormans; no one would be able to tell. And if there was ever a reason for her husband to look closer, she was the keeper of the secret he would never want revealed, a secret even the tabloids wouldn't want to publish. It still turned her stomach to think of it.

She had burned the Special Forces badge. When the package arrived from the Prince mansion, she just thought it would be some more interesting stuff; Robert had shown her some of the things from the first package. She thought it would be jewelry or tattered love letters or something old and exciting. But it wasn't. It was a badge that meant Desmond Lamb could not possibly have been Robert's father: he was gone for almost the entire year of 1957; the timing was all wrong. But it was worse than that. And when she had found out, it was too late. Laura Flynn was already pregnant. She had told Laura, she had confided in her in the way that one confides in a dependant; you can tell a true dependant anything. They can't leave. They have no home, no money without you. She had begged Laura to have an abortion. She would still get paid. Ingrid would pay her. She had done the groundwork — she had researched clinics on Simone's laptop. Yet, still, Laura had wanted to keep the baby. Who wants to keep a baby that isn't even theirs; when the mother herself doesn't want it? It wasn't a baby, anyway. It was some kind of monster.

She was surprised that Laura had told Conor the day she came to take him away. She was surprised at someone as vulnerable as Laura deciding to run. Laura Flynn was braver than she thought. And Conor, more volatile, more dangerous, and more in love. Didn't men want no ties? Didn't sixteen-year-old boys? Why was sex not enough? It was bizarre.

404

Conor's phone call to her the night before Laura died: 'Laura knows something about Robert. She's on her way here. I have to meet her tomorrow. She wants me to leave with her. But I won't. She can't make me. Now's our chance, Ingrid. She said she was in Chicago, talking to some guy who could get us into Canada and back to Ireland. But now's *our* chance. To start a new life. If Robert's been doing something wrong, if he's, like, going to go to prison for fraud or something . . . we can be together . . . '

That was another thing that turned her stomach. 'Start a new life' with Conor Gorman. How ridiculous. What did he think was going to happen? She would do a spread in *Harper's* announcing her love for the just-turned-seventeen-years-old nephew of her dead immigrant housekeeper?

She laughed out loud. And at the idea of Robert Prince and fraud. People assume so much about the wealthy. There was no fraud in Robert Prince's world. There was no taking — only giving; money and love and second chances.

She loved to hear Laura's stories about the Irish underworld in New York. Particularly the one about Janey Mac — Nicky McMullen — from the dive bar in Yonkers who had fled to Chicago and became Janey Mach III. She had given Laura a new purse when she got pregnant. It had a GPS tag in the lining, expertly stitched. She was carrying her baby, after all. It was not difficult to trace Laura from a throwaway phone. It was not difficult to hire someone to follow her in Chicago, and to pay Janey Mac off — he didn't give a shit about Frankie Gorman or his delinquent son.

Unfortunately, Nicky McMullen got cold feet when he saw Laura's bump. Chickenshit.

But for Conor to get rid of her problem was the biggest revelation, though Laura had brought some of it on herself; she had told him too much. He had thought Laura was lying when she said that the Princes were trying for a baby. Conor had believed that all those appointments the Princes were going to was because they were divorcing. Laura must have wondered how Conor could have had a clue what was going on in the Princes' marriage and why he seemed to care so much. And when his aunt mentioned his father, told him where the deadbeat was, was forced to admit that she had known all along, he had grabbed the gun and told the woman who had saved his life that she was messing up his life. And the impulse, the fear, the love, the hormones, the pain, the everything that had been poured into this one handsome boy exploded. Loser. The panic, the tears, when he called her from his creepy little friend's cell phone . . .

At least Conor had proved coachable: rip the tag from the purse, make Robert, anyone, look bad, make me look good. Create just enough suspicion to send people off in different directions. They would be a team; she and Conor would create a little tornado that would throw dust in everyone's eyes, blind them just a little until a better suspect emerged. Whoever

406

... Robert ... the creepy little friend ... any-one.

Everyone had secrets. And even the most harmless ones could look sinister through a prism of suspicion.

She thought of the women in the tabloids who had their multi-millionaire husbands by their balls and bank accounts. Incongruous couples, with public declarations of love so effusive they couldn't possibly be real. Relationships that bloomed in this microclimate of extreme wealth were not about feelings held in hearts, but secrets held over heads. She knew how it worked. When you are invited into the inner circle, you look very carefully around you, you observe. And you look for hiding places, for what lies twisted in silken sheets or behind lifted eyes, what words pass collagen lips, or are bitten back by ultra-white veneers.

With these secrets, I thee wed.

For better and better, for richer and richer.

In her case, the secrets she had uncovered came along after the wedding. Robert had fallen so clearly, so desperately in love she didn't need secrets for diamonds and golden bands to slide up her ring finger. Secrets were her eternity ring.

⋆　⋆　⋆

Ingrid heard a noise at the front door. Light on her feet, she walked out into the long polished hallway. Her suitcases were at the end by the door: a set of five, olive green, edged in brown leather with accents of gold.

Now, there was banging at the door, hammering. Ingrid froze. The door burst open. She felt a rush of adrenaline.

This is not how it ends. This is not how it ends. This is not how it ends.

She backed into the kitchen, then turned, set to run for the French doors, but she could make out two dark figures standing there. Ingrid was briefly blindsided by her reflection in the glass.

She knew what she looked like to others. She knew what her husband looked like.

A Swedish proverb came to mind: *Alla kánner apan, men apan kánner ingen.*

Everyone knows the monkey, but the monkey knows no one.

The back door burst open. She wasn't expecting women. It was the agent. And the detective.

'Ingrid Prince,' said the agent. 'You are under arrest for Solicitation to Commit Murder in the First Degree.'

Ingrid Prince closed her eyes.

I am innocent. I am innocent. I am innocent.

64

Janine and Ren walked into the interview room. Ingrid Prince sat at the table, washed-out, beautiful, erect, even after waiting for three hours. Her hands, chained and cuffed, were on the table in front of her. Ren blinked and got a flash of the sunny Hamptons beach, the casual beauty of the expectant mother. She refocused. Ingrid was staring at her. Ren could feel herself go cold.

How did I not see this before?

Was I blinded by beauty ... maternity ... wealth?

I have never been blinded by beauty or maternity or wealth; we are all equal.

Ren blinked. Ingrid did not.

But I was blinded.

Ren thought of the orange bottle of mood stabilizers in her bathroom cabinet.

Not blinded ... numbed.

Ren was suddenly acutely aware of Janine beside her. They turned to each other. A slight frown came and went on Janine's face, as if she had been reading Ren's mind.

Unlike the previous interview with Ingrid Prince, there was a lawyer seated beside Ingrid; she no longer needed to pretend that she had nothing to hide. The veneer had cracked.

The lawyer looked to be in her late fifties, a plain, heavy, jowly woman, no doubt as groomed as she could be without caving in to society's expectations of how a woman should present herself: neat bun, tidy but thick eyebrows, smooth skin, no facial hair, but no makeup, no adornments, nothing to draw the attention away from the fierce set of her face, the just-try-me eyes. Ingrid Prince's message was clear: there is no beauty in this, this is serious. My serious, non-frivolous, law-loving lawyer believes in me — shouldn't you?

Ingrid Prince, your downfall will be your belief that the surface can make things right.

Janine talked everyone through the formalities. Ingrid refused to answer every question put to her. Her lawyer was dazzling.

As if we expected anything less.

Ren and Janine stood up. 'We're going to take a short break.'

★ ★ ★

Ren and Janine returned to the interview room fifteen minutes later. Ren set down the records to Jesse Coombes' cell phone. The phone number of the rental in Golden was highlighted.

Janine began. 'We have confirmed that Conor Gorman made calls from Jesse Coombes' cell phone to you at the following times: Saturday, May 12th, nine p.m. . . . after Laura Flynn called Conor Gorman to arrange to meet him; Monday, May 14th, one p.m. . . . after Conor Gorman shot the only person who ever truly loved him, your 'dear friend', Laura Flynn.'

'Here, also,' said Ren, 'are the admission

records for The Darned Heart Ranch: Conor Gorman ran away on January 8th — the night he was picked up for fighting at the Ace-Hi Tavern in Golden. It appears from these records that he didn't show up at the ranch until the following morning. Romantic night?'

Baby-making night?

Not a flicker.

'And here,' said Janine, 'is the sworn testimony of a man called Nicky McMullen, aka Janey Mac. We discovered that Laura Flynn reached out to Frankie Gorman in Stateville, sent him a letter we now realize was a coded way of getting Frankie to send Janey Mac to meet her at her hotel. You found this out too. And Janey Mac says you paid him twenty-five thousand dollars to kill Laura Flynn before she got back to Colorado. But when he met poor Laura, who looked so like her sister, Saoirse, who Janey Mac once loved so dearly, he was a little spooked. He didn't do it. But he followed her. And he couldn't stop thinking that she was pregnant and that he shouldn't be doing this. But he kept going. And . . . well, when it came to the crunch, he just didn't have the heart. He fired a few shots, pretended to you that she sped away before he had a chance to fire again. Detective Hooks here works with a marvelous lab in the UK that got his print from the shell casing that flew into Laura's car.'

Ingrid almost smirked.

Goosebumps.

Ren could sense Janine stiffen.

'This just in,' said Ren, 'an account from one

411

of your neighbors of an altercation outside your apartment in SoHo between you and a former model by the name of Sunny Soto. We spoke with Sunny Soto. You were weeks away from signing a joint cosmetics campaign back in the Nineties. It was the first time a company had chosen two models to feature in each shot. That contract was worth many, many millions. But, Sunny Soto got pregnant. Yes, she was only nineteen, but she was very happy about the pregnancy, the father was her high-school boyfriend, she loved him, he's now her husband. But you, apparently, were not happy. You wouldn't have been hired . . . '

Nothing.

'You spiked her food with an abortion drug,' said Ren. 'She lost her baby. She found out years later when Sandro Cera, the photographer — in a drugged-up stupor — told her. And you retaliated, selling stories about him and his drug use to destroy him. You promised you'd do the same to her, so she kept quiet. I was wondering why Laura Flynn was so desperate to run when she did. Sunny Soto showed up on your doorstep that week. She had read the gossip piece that you were pregnant and it pushed her over the edge; you who hated children, thought she was pathetic for ever wanting a child, that she was ruining her life, but when it suited you with your multi-millionaire husband, you want one. She showed up roaring and screaming and you fought. What you didn't know was that Laura Flynn ran down the steps after Sunny Soto when you went back inside. She heard the story. She

412

told Sunny Soto to find the courage to report it, but she didn't . . . until now. Laura Flynn knew what you were capable of, didn't she? She knew you would stop at nothing. Laura had said no to the abortion already, but she realized you would never give up until you got your own way.'

'What do you think of Robert Prince?' said Ingrid.

What the fuck?

'My husband,' said Ingrid, drawing the word out long enough to turn it into something grotesque. Her lawyer laid her hand on Ingrid's forearm. Ingrid brushed her away.

'Do you think he's a catch?' said Ingrid. 'Do you?'

Ren and Janine stayed silent.

'I bet you do!' said Ingrid. 'I bet you do!'

Still, Ren and Janine remained silent.

'Robert Prince, handsome millionaire, great catch, lucky me, lucky all the beautiful women,' said Ingrid. She leaned forward in her seat. 'He's a monster!'

'You tried to convince us of that before,' said Ren. 'We know that your husband is not a monster. He is a kind and a charitable man.' *I was wrong, wrong, wrong.*

'He's a monster!' said Ingrid, her voice rising into a shriek. 'He is! Do you want to know who his father is? A horrible man, a creep, a liar, a coward, a — '

'Desmond Lamb was a war hero,' said Ren.

Ingrid laughed, mocking and cruel. 'I got the badge, you idiots! I got the army badge. Don't you get it? Desmond Lamb was gone in 1957, the entire year Robert was conceived. It's impossible Desmond Lamb was his father.'

Ren's stomach tightened.

'You get it now!' said Ingrid. 'You get it now.' Her face was contorted, making her more ugly than anyone would ever have believed possible. 'Walter Prince is his father! I got a DNA test, plucked a hair from Robert's head in the throes of passion! Know what I heard from the lab? 'Evidence of consanguinity.'' She leaned in again, her eyes wild. 'His grandfather fucked his own daughter and out came Robert Prince! What kind of catch is *he*? The kind you throw back in the ocean. The kind that is weak and damaged and obscene. Why else would I want the baby dead? I was expecting genetic gold.'

Ingrid Prince closed her eyes.

Click flash click flash click flash.

I am a victim. I am a victim. I am a victim.

65

Ren and Janine sat in the Sheriff's Office canteen.

'I need a shower after that,' said Ren, 'a scalding hot one. That was like being in a crypt. How could I not have seen that? Or felt it? It's freaking me out.'

'I didn't see it either,' said Janine. 'But it's not freaking me out. She's a talented woman. It's her job to transform, she's been doing it all her life. Her job is to conjure emotions and have whoever's watching her believe them. I'm guessing that tears, grief and trauma are the most dramatic, therefore the easiest to mimic. Feigning love may be a lot harder. However freaked out you might be, can you imagine how Robert Prince feels?'

'Poor man,' said Ren. 'I'm presuming that he knows his own dark secret, that that's why he had the vasectomy in the first place.'

'Incest is one step beyond even tabloid acceptance,' said Janine.

'He barely wanted to go public with the pregnancy,' said Ren. 'Now, there's all this . . . ' She paused. 'You know, I'm not sure if 'child of two killer parents' has a better genetic ring to it . . . '

'Yikes,' said Janine. She studied Ren. 'You look miserable.'

'I am,' said Ren. 'I am.'

'We got her in the end,' said Janine.

'I'm not a fan of ends,' said Ren. 'I like starts and middles.'

'Don't you like happy endings?' said Janine. 'And wishing them on strange men at breakfast.'

They laughed loud.

'When will *his* victims show up, I wonder . . . ' said Ren.

'Can you imagine?' said Janine.

'I've been trying not to,' said Ren. 'So . . . Viggi Leinster and Angelo Marianelli — solved.'

'And not Girl Scout Peggy Beck,' said Janine.

'Ah — not yet,' said Ren. 'Maybe all the attention drawn to the area might help. Everything happens for a reason. I presume you still get to follow through if anything shows up . . . '

'Yes,' said Janine.

'We haven't caught our Shark Bait Bandits,' said Ren. 'Though I do not give a shit about them.'

'Not all crimes are created equal,' said Janine.

'How are you holding up about the unit?' said Ren. 'Are you OK?'

'I'm OK,' said Janine. 'Tomorrow is another day.'

'Tomorrow Never Dies,' said Ren.

'If Tomorrow Comes,' said Janine.

'Oh my God,' said Ren. 'I remember that! The mini-series. It was Sidney Sheldon.'

'Starring — wait for it — Liam Neeson . . . '

'No way!' said Ren. 'I do not remember that. I will have to re-evaluate that.'

'It's on YouTube,' said Janine. 'It's sad that I know that.'

'Well, we can reminisce further ... if tomorrow comes ... ' said Ren.

'That's appalling,' said Janine. She went to YouTube, called up the video.

Ren laughed as they watched. 'The music! I remember the music. *DNN dnn dnn dnn DNN dnn dnn dnn DNN*. I will get sucked in,' she said. 'I have to stop this.'

'We're delaying the inevitable.'

'To the duped husband ... '

★ ★ ★

Robert Prince looked ghostly, with lines that looked deeper, eyes that looked darker. The top two buttons on his crumpled shirt were open and, for a man of his poise, it was all wrong.

Ren and Janine walked into the room.

'Can I get you a coffee, Mr Prince?' said Janine.

'No,' said Robert. 'No, thanks. I've already had too much ... when, really, all I want to do is sleep.'

You're reaching out. You have no one.

'Your wife is refusing to speak with us,' said Ren.

'It's not in her interest to,' said Robert. 'And we all know now that Ingrid Frank does nothing that is not in her interest.'

'We're very sorry,' said Ren. *For focusing on you.* 'For your loss.' *Losses. Multiple losses.*

Janine nodded her support.

'Thank you, both,' said Robert. 'I appreciate it. Because the rest of the world is going to think 'He still has his millions, what has he got to worry about?' As if you can only be wealthy if you trade your humanity for it.'

'It's been a very difficult time for you,' said Ren.

'And will continue to be,' said Robert. 'At least with the land and the charity, I can do something. I can focus on that. What's your favorite charity, Agent Bryce, Detective Hooks?'

Oh, no. Please don't do this to me. I thought you were a killer.

'I'm serious,' said Robert. He smiled. 'Please, allow me to make a small donation. I would never have . . . I . . . you saved me.'

I suspected you. I suspected you. I thought you were the controlling sociopath and your beautiful wife was the victim. Jesus Christ. You owe me nothing. I owe you.

'People will benefit from this,' said Robert. 'I know you had to look into me as a suspect. I understand that . . . if that's what's worrying you.'

'Thank you,' said Ren. *It is. It is. It is.* 'We can discuss that later.'

'OK,' said Robert. 'I will hold you to that.'

'Now, can you tell us about Delores Ward?' said Ren.

'Well, back in November, I found a letter from my grandfather to his law firm, requesting that they transfer a tract of land to the woman whose details they had previously been apprised of; those details were not included in the letter I

418

found. I called the law firm, they said that they could not, by law, speak to me, that it was a private matter between this woman and my grandfather. They wouldn't tell me what their relationship was, nothing. I put a private investigator on the case. He tracked the deeds to Delores Ward of Evergreen Abbey, but said that she had died in childbirth in 1957, a year before the transfer was made. So I knew there was some form of identity theft at play. I called the abbey to ask them what they knew about Delores Ward, and they asked me would I like to speak with her. You can imagine my surprise that Delores Ward was 'alive'. Of course, I hung up the phone. The following day, I was on a flight to Denver and I arrived at the abbey asking to meet her.'

'So, you got to speak with her?' said Ren.

'I did,' said Robert. 'I heard her whole sorry tale. You know, Evergreen Abbey was the only shelter she had heard of for women. Walter had spoken highly of it, and of his uncle . . . but then he had hinted that his own time there had come to an abrupt end. Delores wondered was that because of his uncle realizing there was something not quite right with Walter. After all, she grew up in Butte, she had heard the rumors about the Orchard Girls. She chose to go to the abbey, to tell Fr Dan her story. He was a priest — she figured that she could confide in him, and, of course, she was right. But Angelo Marianelli managed to track her down, and she was forced to kill him in self-defense. Once Delores knew that Walter had stooped to this

419

new low of ordering her murder, she returned to Butte one last time and that's how she got him to sign over the land. She said if anything came of her terrible ordeal, it would be her ability to carry out charitable works.' He put his head in his hands. 'I can't begin to tell you how ashamed I am of what my grandfather did. But we agreed to make it right in the only way we could at this stage, which was to set up ACORA in honor of my mother and of Virginia Leinster.' He looked up at them. 'Did you see the postcards on Delores Ward's wall?'

Ren nodded.

'They're 'from' her family,' said Robert. 'The family who died in the fire. Any time she went on one of her trips, she wrote postcards to herself and signed their names.'

66

The next day, Ren arrived into Safe Streets and threw her bag onto her chair. It missed and landed on the floor. She heard a clatter of plastic.

'Please let that not be my new compact,' she said.

Cliff was smiling up at her, but there was something sad in it. 'Coffee?' he said.

'You know I love you,' said Ren, 'but you know you favor a weaker format.'

Cliff walked over to her and put a hand on her shoulder. 'You can make your own. You're coming with me.'

'Out?' said Ren.

'Well . . . to the conference room.'

'Okaaay,' said Ren. 'Have you got a stripper lined up for me, balloons, high-school friends I haven't seen for years?'

They made coffee and went into the conference room and sat down.

Ren pointed to Cliff's mug. 'See, I worry when I see a translucent rim around the edge of coffee. I detect weakness.'

Cliff looked down. 'I could do with some strength.'

'Hey,' said Ren. 'How are you doing?' *You look shattered.*

'Ren, we got some bad news a couple weeks ago,' said Cliff. 'Brenda's cancer is back . . . '

'No,' said Ren. 'No. But . . . ' *I thought she got the all-clear.*

'I know,' said Cliff. 'Nine years . . . we thought she was out of the woods.'

'And . . . what have they said?' said Ren. *How can this be happening to you wonderful people?*

'Aw, sweetheart,' said Cliff. 'Don't you set me off . . .'

He patted her hand. She grasped his hands across the table.

'I am so sorry,' she said. 'How is Brenda holding up? How are you? How are the girls?'

'The doctors are saying six months,' said Cliff. 'We've had a little time to bend our brains around it but, to be honest, I can only say this to you . . . it hasn't made one bit of difference. I'm a mess.' He broke down. 'I'm sorry.'

'Don't be,' said Ren. 'It's me, here.'

'I'm lying to her,' said Cliff. 'I'm telling her I'm fine, we're going to be fine, and I'm not . . . and we're not . . .'

What can I possibly say to that? 'If there's anything you need . . .'

'I'm going to take time out,' said Cliff. 'I'm going to go back to the Sheriff's Office in JeffCo. I need to be more available for Brenda and the girls, I need to have a shorter commute.'

'You'll be working with Janine,' said Ren. 'She'll keep an eye on you.' She squeezed his hand. 'I'm glad to hear that you were able to make arrangements that will hopefully make things a little easier.' She paused. 'I'm going to miss you so much. The office won't be the same. You are such a huge part of why I look forward to coming in in the morning.'

'Thank you, Renald. You too.'

Ren started to cry. She got up and hugged him. 'I love you, Clifford James,' she said. 'This isn't right.'

Everything's changing.

No. No. No.

Trigger.

★   ★   ★

When Ren got back to her desk, there was an email from Gary to ask the team to gather in the bullpen at two thirty p.m. Ren had re-read the mail several times looking for clues as to subject matter.

To know whether I should feel nervous.

Zero clues. Damn you, Dettling.

Her phone rang. 'Ren — it's Gary — can I see you for five minutes before the meeting?'

Nooooooooooooooooooo! 'Sure, no problem.'

★   ★   ★

At two twenty p.m., Ren sat down in Gary's office.

Minimalist, mahogany, monument to control.

I have spent less time here in the last five months than I have . . . Too much math.

Gary was sitting back in his chair looking unnaturally relaxed.

Almost like he has no words of censure in mind.

'You know,' said Gary, 'this is the first time at

423

the end of a big case that I haven't almost fired you.'

Do not mention meds.

'I just wanted to say well done,' said Gary. 'How you've handled your treatment has been very impressive. I respect you a lot for that, Ren. I know it's not easy. And I'm sure it seems like everyone is trying to spoil your fun, but, this is how it should be. You seem . . . content.'

Content: possibly the most depressing word in the English language.

Death. Knell.

'Well, I'm glad you're pleased with my progress,' said Ren.

I'm glad you're pleased.

Gary narrowed his eyes.

Fuck you, Gary, for your freakish powers of reading me.

67

Ren left Gary in his office and went into the bullpen. Robbie was on the phone. Everett was sitting on the edge of his own desk.

'Where's Clifford?' said Ren, looking around.

Robbie finished his call. 'Cliff's taken the afternoon off.'

'I hope everything's OK,' said Ren.

'I think so,' said Robbie. 'He didn't say.'

Ren walked over to Everett. 'Come on, you have to find this more interesting than numbers: rich woman sleeps with sixteen-year-old boy, tries and fails to have her surrogate killed, then gets handed that surrogate's death on a plate by said boy who now thinks he can run off into the sunset with her . . . '

'Nope,' said Everett. 'It was the idea of the financial dealings. That's where my heart lies.'

'You mean that,' said Ren.

'I do, sadly. It's why I'm single.'

'Single?' said Ren. 'You?'

'Yes, shock of the whole investigation, I know,' said Everett. He smiled.

'Maybe your girlfriends would worry that you'd analyze their credit card spending . . . '

'Nope,' said Everett. 'I leave that for the bad guys . . . and agents whose cases I help out with. You have a serious shoe issue.'

'I call a serious shoe issue having to wear low heels,' Ren said, looking down at her boots.

'Well, I'm guessing Jimmy Choos aren't helpful for all that running around . . . ' said Everett.

'From that reference, I have deduced that at some point in the Nineties — or early 2000s? — you dated someone who watched *Sex and the City*.'

'Yes, I did.'

'And you're, perhaps, left scarred by how much money she poured into shoes. Was it your money, I wonder . . . '

'Uncanny,' said Everett.

'Anyway — you'd stay single if you met Ingrid Prince,' said Ren. 'At the very least, you'd stay away from beautiful blondes. She was ice-cold. Yet I had my sights set on Robert Prince.' She shook her head.

'No happily ever after for that Prince and Princess,' said Everett.

Ren laughed. 'God . . . literally no one has been left happy after this. Anyway, I wanted to thank you for all your help.'

Everett nodded. 'You're too kind. And you're ignoring that my help guided you in the wrong direction . . . '

'That's not how it works,' said Ren, 'you didn't. You did some masterful digging.'

Everett reached back to the desk behind him. 'Did you see this?' He handed her the *Denver Post*, folded open on page four.

There was a huge photo of Howard Coombes, weeping like a baby at a press conference.

'Is he for real?' said Ren.

'I know,' said Everett. 'He screws his kid up,

426

then shows up in his beloved spotlight crying like a . . . person who gives a damn.'

'At least they put a photo of his pregnant mistress underneath to remind readers what a shit he really is,' said Ren. 'The level of denial . . . '

'I know,' said Everett.

Ren started reading some of the article. 'He's actually still trying to focus on Jesse being at the ranch — what a sick fuck. He says Jesse fell in with the wrong crowd — hello?'

'Men like Howard Coombes?' said Everett. 'Well, there's a special place — '

'On television for them,' said Ren.

Everett laughed.

Hey, I can talk to Everett King. I can judge people in front of him and psycho-analyze them. Unlike with Grabien.

'OK,' said Gary, walking into the bullpen, raising his voice. 'Everyone listen up.'

He waited for quiet.

'As you know,' he said, 'the process of replacing Colin Grabien on a permanent basis has taken longer than expected. And this is a formality more than anything . . . but I'd like you to give an official Safe Streets welcome to Everett King.'

Yaaaay! You sly one.

'Official Safe Streets welcomes take place in bars, just so you know,' said Ren.

'Bon voyages do too,' said Gary, faux deadpan.

Well, if he hasn't fired me yet . . .

The team gave Everett a round of applause. He stood up and gave a curt little bow. 'Thank you very much, thank you,' he said, raising his hand in the air, election-style. He swept his hand through the air. 'The flourish was for Ren.'

'Thank you, thank you,' said Ren. *Everett King ROCKS.*

He sat down.

'OK,' said Gary, 'as some of you already know, we've heard some very sad news this week about Brenda James. Cliff has decided that it's best for all the family if he returns to JeffCo while Brenda is undergoing treatment. Reluctant as I am to let him go, I know that it can't be avoided. But, here in Safe Streets, we've always benefited from having a JeffCo member of the team. So, we'll be carrying on with that tradition with our newest team member, who is set to join us within the month.'

'Who?' said Ren. 'Who?'

Gary smiled. 'Detective Janine Hooks.'

Tomorrow, tomorrow, I love ya, tomorrow.

68

Dr Leonard Lone's office was filled with beautiful classical music as Ren walked in.

'What is that?' said Ren.

'*The Cider House Rules* soundtrack,' said Dr Lone.

'Can we leave it on?' said Ren.

'Absolutely,' said Lone.

Ren nodded. 'Thanks.' She sat down.

'So, Ren, how are you?'

'Well, I've made my boss happy. Can you believe it?'

'Of course I can,' said Lone.

'It goes against everything I stand for . . . '

'I happen to know you have a very good relationship with Gary Dettling.'

'I do,' said Ren, 'I know. I'm lucky to have him. But it's just weird not having him on my case . . . ' She paused. 'Usually, he's sniffing around a little more.'

'Well, I guess he feels he has less to worry about when he sees you working steadily and not making too many . . . hasty . . . decisions.'

My favorite!

'How are things with Ben?' said Lone.

'Well . . . in no particular order, we had a fight about lying, I told him I was bipolar, he asked me about meds and alcohol, I wished he would fuck off but didn't say it out loud, *emotions: under control*, we had a fight, I said it wasn't his

429

business, he said it was, I have to move out of my house, he suggested he move to Denver, I said I'd think about it . . . and then this old woman tells me she has destroyed her entire life because she fell in love with this horrific pedophile murderer.'

Ooh.

Dr Lone leaned forward. 'Ren — '

'No, I know,' said Ren. 'I know that last bit wasn't about Ben. I mean that was just another thing that happened. Separately.'

'Remember we spoke before about catastrophic thinking . . . ' said Dr Lone.

'Yes,' said Ren. 'I'm venturing that, even though I wasn't connecting Ben and that old lady or the murdering guy, somewhere in that sentence you were getting a catastrophic thinking vibe.'

'It's about connecting love and bad things,' said Lone.

'I know,' said Ren. 'I don't mean to. I might need to start listening to different songs. I listen to a lot of break-up songs.'

'So, on the work front,' said Dr Lone. 'You solved the murder of that poor pregnant woman.'

Ren nodded. 'Yes.'

'And did you engage in any risky behavior while doing that?' said Lone.

'I did not,' said Ren.

'Good for you,' said Lone.

Emotions: under control.

'But one of my best friends — his wife has terminal cancer, which is heartbreaking,' said Ren. 'They're an amazing couple. They've been married forever. They've got these wonderful children . . . '

'Love is a wonderful thing,' said Lone. There was a hopeful look in his eye.

Silence. Bird song. Cicadas.

'But she has cancer,' said Ren. 'He's losing her. I'm not sure how wonderful love is.'

69

Ren was lying in bed beside a sleeping Ben Rader. He had arrived that night. They had gone to Gaffney's, Everett was there, Janine was there. Everyone was welcoming, everyone partied.

Ren lay on her back, staring at the ceiling, her head still swimming a little.

This was the best night I've had in I can't remember. I love this beautiful man lying beside me. And he loves me.

How did I get so lucky?

She took a deep breath.

I should have worked out Ingrid Prince sooner. I could have been sharper.

Ren looked down at Ben and wondered if she could wake up beside him every morning. She hadn't lived with anyone in almost two years . . . since Vincent. She didn't particularly like living alone, but then, if she was living with someone . . . if she was living with Ben . . . what if he was a total nightmare?

I like things the way they are. I don't like change.

Trigger.

But Ben is easy. He's laid back. Nothing upsets him. I don't think I've ever heard him complain.

That's weird.

He doesn't get stressed out about anything.

That's even weirder.

He's such a brilliant cook.

He tidies up after himself!

He's so organized.

Oh my God.

I am the nightmare to live with.

He is the one who needs to give all this some serious consideration.

She looked down at him.

Conor Gorman reminded me of you; the darkness, the edge, the magnetism. Maybe loving you blinded me to that. If I didn't love you, maybe I would have looked closer at him. I wouldn't have believed he was good, like you are.

Maybe I can't do this job and love. Maybe love and work are incompatible. That's depressing. Why am I having sad thoughts? I'm a happy person. My default setting is happy. This was a great night. Do I just believe that goodness is wrong?

She stroked Ben's face.

I'd keep sleeping if I were you. Things are easier with me when you're asleep.

She stared at the ceiling a little more, waited for her body to relax, her mind to quiet. An hour passed. Finally, she got up and went into the bathroom.

Ooh . . . looking good.

I would have worked out Ingrid Prince sooner . . . if I wasn't . . . repressed.

If my thoughts weren't . . .

Inhibited.

Reined in.

Ren opened the medicine cabinet and took

out her bottle of pills. She shook one onto her palm.

Yes. I feel good.

But not amazing.

Still, though . . . stable is good.

She leaned on the sink.

And ordinary.

Remember: you can't associate stability with 'ordinariness'.

I feel good.

She sucked in a huge breath.

But not amazing.

She looked into the mirror.

I want to see giant pupils and sharper cheekbones. I want to feel hollowness in my lungs. I want my head to feel like it's a vast hangar waiting to be filled with magical magic things. I want my heart to surge. I want to drink and fuck and laugh all night, every night.

She studied the pill . . .

Stabilizer, stabilize thyself!

She tipped her hand.

Ha!

The small white pill slid down the plughole.

Ren looked back up at the mirror and smiled.

Come on, Mr Mania, take me back.

Supersize Me.

Acknowledgements

To Darley Anderson and all the team at the Darley Anderson Literary, TV and Film Agency, thank you so much for everything you do.

To my dear editor, Sarah Hodgson, respect and thanks for your wise words, trusted judgment, and support in ways too numerous to mention.

Thank you to Kate Stephenson for her excellence, positivity and calm.

Many thanks to Kate Elton and to everyone at HarperCollins who makes this happen.

To Rhian McKay, thank you for the copy-editing skills I am tempted to spell 'skillz'.

To the powerhouse that is Moira Reilly, thank you, thank you, thank you for being a wonderful friend, supporter, and prophet of joy.

A big thank you to the kind and diligent Tony Purdue.

Thank you to the following experts and their generous research assistance — any errors are author-generated. Tell your friends.

A huge thank you goes to Jefferson County cold

case detective, Cheryl Moore, for her generous awarding of time, enlightenment, advice, and late-night laughs.

To SSA Phil Niedringhaus, Man Most Likely to Fire Ren Bryce, thank you, as always, for your help and support, and for the seminar on multi-agency critical response.

To Becky Farr Seidel, thank you so much for answering my questions on charitable donations.

For insight into the fascinating science of genetics, thank you to Dr Arthur L. Beaudet, professor and chair of molecular and human genetics at Baylor College of Medicine.

To Michael Dobersen, MD, Forensic Pathologist, thank you for all your help on the corporeal aftermath of violent acts.

To Thomas J. Ragonetti, thank you for your lawyerly instruction on wills and trusts, for your interest and support, and for introductions to helpful friends.

To Ryan Kopseng, thank you for sharing your knowledge of the North Dakota oil business.

The revelation of writing this book has been the discovery of a real Pat Prince with astonishing echoes of the fictional one . . . minus the family skeletons. Pat Prince, you are the original and the best. Your emails are always an inspiration.

Thank you for sharing your race car expertise, and thank you for 'evil manners'.

To Sue Booth-Forbes, you are instrumental in all my tales coming to life. Thank you for the beautiful world of Anam Cara, expertly helmed, selflessly shared.

To Mary-Jane Robinson, gifted ghostwriter and anti-spectre; when you're around, the room goes warm.

To Arthur Beesley, thank you for taking a machete to the undergrowth of financial shenanigans.

To all the readers who get in touch, and all who come to crime events, it is always a pleasure.

To my amazing family, thank you for being exactly that. Love you all to bittts.

To my wonderful friends — I don't know how I got so lucky. But I do know I'm eternally grateful.

A defiant thank you to Paul Kelly, deflector of much-deserved thank yous.

We do hope that you have enjoyed reading this large print book.

Did you know that all of our titles are available for purchase?

We publish a wide range of high quality large print books including:
Romances, Mysteries, Classics
General Fiction
Non Fiction and Westerns

Special interest titles available in large print are:
The Little Oxford Dictionary
Music Book
Song Book
Hymn Book
Service Book

Also available from us courtesy of Oxford University Press:
Young Readers' Dictionary
(large print edition)
Young Readers' Thesaurus
(large print edition)

For further information or a free brochure, please contact us at:
Ulverscroft Large Print Books Ltd.,
The Green, Bradgate Road, Anstey,
Leicester, LE7 7FU, England.
Tel: (00 44) 0116 236 4325
Fax: (00 44) 0116 234 0205

BLOOD LOSS

Alex Barclay

When a teenage girl is beaten and raped, in the grounds of a derelict asylum, FBI agent Ren Bryce is called in to assist. But she is soon diverted to a missing persons' case when an eleven-year-old girl and her teenage babysitter vanish without a trace from their hotel room. Faced with conflicting evidence and inconsistent witnesses, Ren works obsessively to unravel the dark family secrets at the heart of the case, before it's too late . . . Determined to uncover the truth, Ren's behaviour becomes increasingly reckless. Putting her own safety at risk, she enters a world where innocent lives are ruined for profit . . . and kidnap, rape and murder are all part of the deal.

BLOOD RUNS COLD

Alex Barclay

When an FBI agent is found dead on the white slopes of Quandary Peak in Colorado, a brilliant but volatile agent is drafted in from Denver to lead the investigation. As she fights personal demons, pressure from Washington and dwindling leads, the case stalls and a career falters. But as summer comes, Quandary Peak has disturbing new secrets to give up. And as one agent fights failure and hopelessness, another has left behind a trail that leads to a man with a dark past and even darker intentions . . .